FAULT LINES

ALSO BY D.J. McCUNE

Death & Co.
The Mortal Knife

D.J. McCUNE

DEATH &Co.

FAULT LINES

All rights reserved. Typeset in 10.5 Berling LT Std on 15.5 Ariane Goudy.

Printed and bound by CPI Group (UK) Ltd, Croydon

www.hotkeybooks.com

HOT
KEY
BOOKS

First published in Great Britain in 2015 by Hot Key Books
Northburgh House, 10 Northburgh Street, London EC1V 0AT

Text copyright © D.J. McCune 2015

The moral rights of the author have been asserted.

A CIP catalogue record for this book is available from the British Library.

ISBN: 978-1-4714-0271-5

Hot Key Books is part of the Bonnier Publishing Group
www.bonnierpublishing.com

For my family, with love

Chapter 1

dam Mortson stretched luxuriously, basking in a unique sensation of calm, and feeling the sheets rub along his bare skin. It had been a long, hot summer in London and typically it was getting hotter, just as he was about to go back to school. Tomorrow he'd be going into fifth form – but that still left him with one final day of freedom.

Usually his day began with one of two things – his alarm clock blaring, or someone telling him to get dressed and get ready to guide a dead person's soul into the afterlife. But mercifully, today that hadn't happened. Not yet at least.

Throwing the sheets aside, Adam hopped out of bed and stood in front of the long mirror, staring at his reflection. His blue eyes looked brighter beneath sandy hair lightened by the sun. His pale Mortson skin was never going to turn bronzed but a few lazy days in the park with Melissa had tanned it a little, freckles dusting his nose. Thinking about Melissa made his heart jump, then glow warm. He had one more precious day ahead with her and unless some global catastrophe struck, he wanted to make the most of it.

Most guys his age didn't need to worry about global disasters – but then Adam wasn't exactly a normal teenager. His family were Britain's leading fast-response Lumen – guardians and guides of the dead – and like all the Mortson men, Adam was expected to be available 24/7 to step into the Hinterland, the place of souls, and guide the dead through their Lights; whispering directions for their journey onto the Unknown Roads.

The Mortsons were used to dealing with the trickiest souls, those who had died suddenly or unexpectedly. Sometimes even violently. Adam had never been any good at being a Luman, in spite of his impressive pedigree. Still, the last few months had marked a step in the right direction. The nerves hadn't gone completely but it was beginning to get easier.

As he showered and dressed, he tried to push the Luman world out of his head and focus on the day ahead. It would be his last chance to spend some quality time with Melissa for a while. Once they were back at school she would be working at weekends and he would be trying to squeeze his Luman life and his school work into twenty-four measly hours. Not for the first time he contemplated this juggling act without enthusiasm.

Still, at least they had today. As he buttered his toast and poured a glass of orange juice he tried to think of everything he wanted to do. It was the last proper day of summer and he wanted to make it perfect. They were going to hang out in the park and he knew there was a funfair on. He was thinking lunch, ice cream, buying Melissa a present and hopefully some alone time, if they got lucky.

As he finished the last bite of breakfast, his father Nathanial walked into the kitchen, humming under his breath. 'Good morning, Adam.'

'Morning,' Adam said. 'Quiet night.'

'Yes, thankfully it was. It's always nice to get a full night's sleep.'

'Nice for everyone,' Adam muttered. No overnight call-outs meant no sudden deaths in the Kingdom of Britain. It was a rare event.

'So, back to school tomorrow.' It was a statement, not a question and while Nathanial didn't exactly look happy about it he wasn't frowning either.

'Yes.' Adam hesitated. 'Big exams this year. I have to do well if I want to stay on for sixth form.'

Nathanial paused, then changed the subject. 'Well, at least you won't have to miss your first day back for our trip tomorrow.'

'Yeah, thanks,' Adam said. Most of his friends would have been delighted to miss a day of school to go away for the weekend – but then he wasn't most people. Arranging to go after he finished school was a big gesture on his family's part. 'What do I need to bring?'

'Oh don't worry about that. Your mother and Chloe will pack for you.'

Adam grimaced. Another thing that made him uneasy about the Luman world: there was always a doting woman waiting to take care of you. Women weren't allowed to be practising Lumen – so their only chance to shine was in the home. The best that Chloe could hope for was a good marriage. That was part of the reason behind the trip. They were going to Ireland

3

to visit 'Uncle' Paddy. The McVeys weren't technically related to the Mortsons but they were old family friends.

He sneaked a glance at his father, who was humming under his breath, looking unusually happy and relaxed. It seemed a shame to spoil Nathanial's good mood but he had to broach a tricky subject. 'So . . . I know we're swooping tomorrow . . . but there's my other trip to think about. The one with school.'

Nathanial froze, jug of juice poised in mid-air over his glass. 'Yes. Still thinking about that one.'

Adam tried to keep his voice level. 'It's just . . . obviously I'm not swooping there. So I need a passport. And they can take a while to process so the form would really need to get sent away. You know, and then you can always decide later if I can go or not.' *Please let me go. PLEASE.* He sent up a silent prayer to whatever gods watched over teenagers wanting to go on their first ever holiday abroad.

'Applying for a passport involves identifications, Adam. It involves us putting ourselves on the radar.' Nathanial was – as Adam feared – frowning. 'It means putting us all at risk.'

'But you have a cover. The business thing.'

Nathanial poured his juice and raised it in a silent toast. 'I prefer not to have to use it.' He took a long sip and studied Adam. 'Let me think about it. We'll get one trip out of the way before we start worrying about another.'

Adam nodded, trying to hide his frustration. There was no point pressing the issue. His father was High Luman of Britain. On cue, his death sense flared. He could feel that it was only one soul but it seemed politic to be polite. 'Would you like me to go with you?'

Nathanial set down his glass and shook his head. 'No it's OK, Adam. Enjoy your time off. We have a busy few days ahead.' He hesitated. 'I know your trip to Japan means a lot to you but I have to think about all of us. I need a little more time to consider it. I know you understand.'

There was nothing more Adam could say. All he could do was hope his father would decide to take the chance.

On the bus a couple of hours later, Adam stared out of the window and thought about how his life had changed over the last few months. From the outside things probably seemed to be exactly the same but *he* knew things were different.

One thing that had helped was learning a little more about his family's past. Adam had always felt out of place in his family; the odd one out. Maybe it was because everyone else seemed to *get it*. They seemed to be Lumen to the core and know instinctively what to do, especially his father. Nathanial seemed like a natural-born High Luman – calm, compassionate and under control.

But after learning about a dark chapter in the Mortsons' history, Adam knew that his father had never intended to be High Luman. He'd been forced to step up and take on the role after a scandal had almost destroyed the whole family. Adam could still see the photo which had unlocked his family's secret past – and the Nathanial in the picture had been a carefree boy, not knowing that his life was about to change forever.

Adam knew that his father could have crumbled. He could have wailed that it wasn't fair and let the Mortsons lose their honoured place and sink into obscurity – but he hadn't. Instead he had worked harder than should have been humanly possible and brought the family back from the brink of ruin. He had married the woman he loved, Adam's French mother Elise, and had three sons and a daughter. Aron, the eldest, had already been Marked and become a full Luman. Seventeen-year-old Luc was nearly ready to follow and Chloe had betrothal on the horizon. Nathanial had even given a home to his sister Jo, whose prospects had been destroyed by the tragedy and who had been shunned by the family she was supposed to marry into.

Adam had always respected his father but somehow knowing what his father had done had inspired him. Nathanial had stepped up when he had to and maybe that meant that Adam could too.

He was getting better at it. His nose still bled sometimes when he swooped to death scenes and his stomach still churned when he spoke to the souls and guided them into their Lights, but he had discovered that taking some slow breaths often managed to keep his nausea at bay until he got home. Adam knew that Nathanial was pleased with his progress and his mother had softened her disapproval. Even Luc didn't make fun of him as often.

The downside of this was that it was putting Adam's time at school in jeopardy. Adam knew that he had only been allowed to stay at school until he found his feet as a Luman. Now that he was improving there was increasing pressure for him to leave and devote himself to the Luman world. After all, most Lumen left school at the end of primary school, having learned the basics of reading and writing.

But for Adam that wasn't enough. He was determined to

stay on at school, even in the face of his family's resistance. Not just because he wanted to pass the exams he needed to go to university and train to be a doctor. There were other things he liked about school, like hanging out with his friends. And of course hanging out with Melissa.

Still, today they had one precious afternoon together. Adam pushed the Luman world from his thoughts. The sun was shining and he was determined to make the most of it.

When Adam finally reached the park, Melissa was already there. He paused and just watched her for a moment. She was lying on her stomach on the grass and chewing on the end of her pen, her bare legs bent up behind her. She had a fine, beaded chain around one ankle. As he watched she switched to chewing her lip and the pen moved, skimming over the sketchpad in front of her.

She was so beautiful. Maybe not to everyone but for him there was no one he wanted to look at more in the world. Even now, he sometimes couldn't believe that she was there to meet up with him. He still got excited about seeing her.

As if feeling his scrutiny, she looked up suddenly, a tiny frown of concentration on her face – which turned into a smile when she saw him. He grinned back, feeling the warmth in his chest expand in a little bubble. 'Hey.'

She rolled over onto her back and grinned at him upside down. 'Why are you still standing?'

Adam flung himself down beside her. She had brought an old, stripy beach towel with her. The colours had faded but it was just about big enough for both of them to lie on if they were very close together. Adam had no objections to that at all.

Melissa rolled onto her side and kissed him, propping herself up with one elbow. 'So, stranger, what have you been doing?'

Adam shrugged. 'Nothing much. I've just been at home. Helping my father a bit.'

'At home in the prison house?' Melissa traced one finger along his jawline and down his neck, softening her words.

Adam didn't answer and not just because his skin was sparking everywhere her finger brushed against him. It was impossible to make Melissa understand about his family without revealing the Luman world – and that was totally forbidden. His life was all about limiting information to both Melissa and his family. Any other guy his age could just say, 'I'm going to meet Melissa. My girlfriend. I've been seeing her for six months now. We're going to hang out in the park.' But Adam wasn't supposed to have a girlfriend. In due course his family would help him find a Luman wife. They would have Luman children and the whole cycle would repeat.

It depressed him and he was determined to enjoy today. He reached for her hand before his skin caught fire. 'What have you been doing?'

Melissa shrugged. 'The usual. I've been working most days. And then I've been looking after Mum. She's just finished her chemo.' She stopped, pressing her lips together. It took a minute for her to speak again. 'Anyway, she's tired, so she wanted me to go out today so she can sleep. She told me to enjoy the sunshine before school starts.'

Adam squeezed her fingers. 'So that's what we'll do.'

'Yeah. There's stuff on today. There's a funfair and they've built a big stage for a concert. We could have a look around.'

At the mention of the stage and a concert Adam's stomach clenched. Last time Adam had been at an outdoor concert bad things had happened. Things that were still haunting him at night, in his dreams. He cleared his throat. 'Yeah, that sounds good. But let's just stay here a while.'

Melissa raised an eyebrow. 'And why do you want to stay here?'

Adam grinned. 'Why do you think?'

She smiled and kissed him again – and this time he didn't care about his skin catching fire.

This time he just lay down, pulled her in close and made the most of it.

A long time later they finally pulled away from one another. Adam brushed the hair off her cheek and kissed her cheekbone, letting Melissa nuzzle in close to him. He loved her. He loved her and ached for her and never had enough of her. Just occasionally they managed to go somewhere and be completely alone, but not enough. It was never enough.

A couple of times he had been to her flat. Her mum's illness meant that she wasn't working and spent more time at home but twice they had managed to get the place to themselves. The flat was small and crammed with pictures and knick-knacks, but it was cosy and clean. Melissa's room was tiny but she had covered every inch of the walls with paintings and posters and her bed had a patchwork throw. Adam had felt like he was in a cocoon with her, just them at the centre of a rainbow.

He had avoided meeting her mum. There were lots of secrets

he had kept from Melissa – but only one that felt like a betrayal. He had known that her mum was ill, before anyone had, even Melissa. It was a mystery he still couldn't explain. He didn't want to shake her hand – the same thin, wasted hand he had seen in his dreams, before he had ever met her. He couldn't bear lying to her – or lying yet again to Melissa.

Now Melissa was lying on the towel and looking up at him. He stroked the warm, bare skin on her stomach, just above the waistband on her shorts, and she made a soft noise in her throat and pulled him down beside her again. It felt weird, coming up for air minutes later and realising that the rest of the world was still moving around them. People were walking dogs and riding bikes and throwing frisbees. In the distance they could hear music.

They sat up and moved apart, trying to get their breath back. Melissa looked around and sighed. 'Why does summer have to be over? I can't be bothered going back to school.'

Adam stroked the back of her hand. 'At least we can see each other every day.'

'I guess.' Melissa paused. 'But I want to see you outside school as well.'

'It's hard.' Adam bit his lip.

'I could always come round to your place, you know.'

'My parents don't let us have friends round.'

Melissa frowned. 'They don't like you going out but they don't let you have people round? They sound great.'

'No, they're . . . It's not like that.' Adam could feel the conversation heading in a direction he really didn't want it to. 'They just worry about me. They want me to do well.'

'Yeah, well, so does my mum. She's always going on about my exams but she still lets me go out!'

It's not the exams they're worried about, Adam thought. 'I'll try and get out more, I promise. We can go back to Petrograd. It was cool.'

'Yeah, it is. I won't even try and make you drink coffee this time.' Melissa smiled.

Adam relaxed a little. One thing about Melissa: no one could say she wasn't patient. She didn't push and push at him for answers, just as he never pushed too much about her family. He didn't know where her dad was; she rarely spoke about him. He sat up and felt something slide beneath his T-shirt.

'What *is* that?' Melissa slipped her finger under the fine chain round Adam's neck. 'I keep forgetting to ask you about it.'

He pulled away and sat up. 'Nothing. It's just . . . nothing.' *It's the keystone I wear; the keystone that helps me into the Hinterland, where I guide the souls of the dead into the afterlife.* Adam tried to imagine her face if he told her the truth. He would probably get away with it; she'd assume he was joking.

'If it's nothing why do you always wear it?'

'I don't *always* wear it,' Adam said.

Melissa smiled and kissed his neck. 'You don't wear it when you have your top off. But you wear it the rest of the time, even in school. I saw it down your shirt.'

Adam raised an eyebrow. 'This is what happens when you look down people's shirts.'

'I thought it was one of those medical disc things. You know, like those ones that say there's something wrong with your heart.'

Adam pretended to clutch his chest. 'Only when I'm with you!'

Melissa shrieked and pushed him away. '*Ew!* You're going to make me throw up in a minute. That is *sooooo* cheesy!'

Adam grinned. 'Sorry. Do you want to go over to the fair? They have one of those upside-down things if you really want to throw up.' He stood up and took her hand, pulling her to her feet, delighted to have changed the subject. They rolled up the towel and Adam slung it over one shoulder, trying to be gallant. As they wandered towards the sound of music the path grew busy with people of all ages. Some of them were eating ice creams; others were clutching stuffed toys won at stalls. There was a buzz of happiness in the air.

Somehow the happy atmosphere made it harder to bear it when his doom sense flared.

Chapter 2

dam's stomach was his usual early warning sign but this time the pain lodged at the side of his neck. It was intense and burning, radiating down through his chest. He grabbed the sore spot and groaned.

Melissa stopped and looked at him, alarmed. 'Are you OK?'

Adam nodded but it took a moment before he could make his mouth work. 'I'm OK. Just pulled a muscle.' His jaw felt numb, like it wasn't working properly. What the hell was he going to do?

Like all Lumen, Adam had a death sense – a feeling that told him when someone had died so he could go and guide their soul into their Light. However, Adam had another ability, one that was rare even by Luman standards. He was a Seer – a Luman who could sometimes feel deaths before they actually happened. He had spent most of his life blocking his premonitions, trying to keep his ability secret from his family (who thought he had lost his ability as he grew up). Usually he kept his doom sense at bay but just occasionally it forced its way through – and often it was because the victim was close by.

For a while Adam had tried to use this ability for good. He had deliberately tuned into his doom sense and gone to save the people who should have died. This was totally against Luman law and Adam had almost been caught a few months earlier, risking not only his own life but his father's too. Since then he had forced himself to tune out his premonitions and leave the victims to their intended Fate.

But it was much easier to ignore someone who was going to die far away from you. Judging by the strength of his doom sense the next victim was close by. Maybe he or she was actually here in the park.

Melissa was still watching him, concerned. 'Do you want me to get someone?'

Adam shook his head. 'No!' He drew in a deep breath and counted to five, the way he did when he was in the Hinterland. As he breathed out the pain receded and he could begin to think clearly again. 'Sorry. I'm OK. I must have just moved my neck funny.'

He took Melissa's hand and set off along the path, weaving in and out of the crowd, half pulling her behind him. After a minute she pulled her hand away. 'Slow down! What's the matter?'

'Nothing! I just need to . . . see something. I'll meet you in a minute.' Before she could protest Adam jogged off, running along the grass to avoid getting stuck. His heart was hammering in his chest, adrenalin making him feel sick. The path ahead was jammed and he had to slow down and wait to pass between two high hedges, emerging into the open space by the funfair.

Ahead of him the park was packed. Immediately around him were dozens of colourful stalls, selling sweets and candyfloss and tempting people to have a go at shooting ducks or catching plastic fish in a whirlpool. Beyond the stalls garish machinery rose up into the air, lights flashing everywhere. The people on board screamed joyfully, as they were whirled around and flung upside down.

His first thought was that maybe something dramatic was going to happen – a rollercoaster carriage plunging off the track or someone falling from their safety harness. But when no mental image appeared he frowned and began to push through the crowd, ignoring a few pointed complaints, totally focused on finding the next victim.

As he passed the first row of stalls the pain in his neck returned with a vengeance. He clapped a hand on it, trying to massage it away, but if anything it was growing stronger until he could barely breathe. Desperately, he searched the crowd, knowing that the only way to make it ease was to see what his doom sense wanted him to see.

He was into the second row of stalls, stretching up on tiptoe as the pain intensified again. He retched in the back of his throat and spun, feeling dizzy from all the quick, painful breaths. He was going to faint. He could feel it. There was a pulsing light and then blackness behind his eyes. He couldn't breathe. He was going to fall. He was going to die.

And then, as his knees gave way, he saw the van just a few metres from him. A man in a striped apron was smiling and handing out ice creams. Adam's eyes ran dully over the queue and locked on a man near the front. A man who was standing with a woman and two small boys, waiting patiently for ice cream. And as Adam watched he saw it – saw it unfold right in front of his eyes, a glimpse of a very near future.

The man holding the ice creams, giving them out, then collapsing. The ice cream lying on the ground beside him and the wasp crawling onto it – the same wasp which had just stung the man, triggering a fatal allergic shock.

The pressure lifted from Adam almost immediately. The premonition had passed; he had seen what his doom sense wanted him to see. The world came back into focus. Adam was on his knees on the ground. Two women stopped beside him, one of them clasping his shoulder. 'Are you all right, love?'

Adam nodded. 'Yeah. Thanks. I just tripped.' His voice sounded weak but he cleared his throat and tried to sound convincing. 'Really, I'm fine. But thanks.'

He watched the women walk away, then turned back to the ice-cream van, his stomach knotting with anxiety. The man was still at the front of the queue, tickling the smaller of the two boys and laughing. The older child was whining and the woman spoke to him sharply. They were just a normal family having a nice day out but everything was about to go wrong.

Adam could stop the awful thing that was about to happen – but he couldn't move. He didn't *dare* to move. Because all he had ever meant to do was save people so they could enjoy their physical life a little bit longer. That was how it had all started. So what if it was cheating the Fates out of a soul? There were plenty more to choose from.

Except the Fates hadn't seen it that way, especially the

thread-cutter. In his mind's eye Adam could still see Morta, the last thread-cutter, beautiful and blazing with anger as she had pointed the Mortal Knife at the Kingdom of Britain and threatened everyone he loved. Messing with the Fates didn't end well – especially when they were being helped by a Luman with a grudge against the Mortsons.

Adam had been trying to save lives but more people had died than he could ever have imagined. The guilt of that would stay with him forever. He had learned his lesson. His own actions might seem small but they had consequences beyond anything he could ever have imagined. It was too great a risk intervening. It was too risky breaking Luman law – not just for his own sake but for the sake of everyone he cared about.

The man was at the front of the queue now, taking ice-cream orders from his family. He looked cheerful, laughing and joking with the ice-cream man, who was grinning back. He didn't have any idea that he was about to die. There would be no time for him to kiss his wife or hug his sons or say goodbye to his physical life. And Adam was going to stand here and let it happen.

Except suddenly Adam found his feet moving. His brain caught up a second after his legs. *Don't be stupid! Of course you can save him! You can just get into the queue and pretend it was luck! No one needs to know you're a Seer! How could anyone ever prove that you knew what was going to happen? You're just a responsible citizen in the right place at the right time, brushing a wasp away from a man in a queue, just like you'd want someone to do for you!*

The man was holding four cones between his cupped hands.

He was bending down to hand a strawberry cone to the younger boy, who was dancing about delightedly. The wasp was hovering behind the woman, buzzing against her blonde hair. The man was handing her a chocolate cone and giving the older boy a vanilla ice cream. The wasp moved from the woman's hair to the man's shoulder. It was crawling up his T-shirt and he was blissfully unaware, licking round his cone as pink ice cream melted along the edges.

Adam pushed into the crowd, almost knocking one of the children over. He took a deep breath, raised his hand and swiped the wasp downwards, away from the man's neck. It was a direct hit and the wasp fell to the ground stunned. Adam promptly stood on it.

The man turned round startled. He glared at Adam and was just about to say something when an elderly woman piped up from behind, 'Oh, well done, dear!' Adam and the man turned in unison. She was beaming at Adam. 'This young man just saved you from that nasty brute!' She pointed at the ground and the man followed her finger. 'Flaming wasps! They're terrible this time of year. Vicious things, I do hate them!'

The man's eyes were wide. He turned to Adam and nodded. 'Thanks, mate. Bloody wasps. I'm allergic to the buggers. I have to carry an adrenalin pen.' He fumbled in his pocket with his free hand, then frowned and handed his ice cream to his wife, searching the other pocket.

His wife looked furious. 'Have you forgotten your Epipen again? How on earth can you forget it at a place like this when you know it'll be swarming with wasps? What would you have done if it had stung you?'

'Oh, give over, it wouldn't have stung me,' the man said but he looked worried. 'We're going home now anyway.' He nodded at Adam again and said, 'Cheers.'

'No problem,' Adam said.

'Would you like an ice cream, dear?' The old lady was still beaming at him.

Adam tried to smile but his heart was still thumping. He'd saved the man. Job done. Time to get out of there. 'No thanks.'

He slipped out of the queue. Now he had to find Melissa. She was going to be so annoyed. How was he going to explain his sudden disappearance? He stood on tiptoe, trying to see over the heads of the throng but there were just too many people packed into the hot, airless space between the stalls. Great. She could be anywhere – and the longer he was away the more annoyed she was going to be.

He swept his eyes over the crowd again and they snagged on a figure in the shadow of a stall selling toy weapons. The man was tall and very still. He was wearing a black hooded sweatshirt and the hood was up, even on this hot day. Adam felt a strange prickle down his spine. There was something familiar about the man but his face was hidden.

Adam hesitated, unsure whether to go towards the man or whether to run away – but the man made the decision for him. In the time it took Adam to think the man turned away and disappeared.

It took several minutes to find Melissa and when Adam finally stumbled upon her she was every bit as annoyed as he'd predicted. She was perched on the edge of a fountain, letting the spray mist over her. Adam couldn't help smiling when he saw her. The mist was catching the sunlight and turning into rainbows all around her, making her look like a fairy.

She was frowning. 'Where did you go? I was looking everywhere for you!'

Adam took her hand appeasingly. 'Sorry. I just thought it would be nice to go and win you one of those things from the stalls. I wanted to surprise you.' She was staring pointedly at his empty hands so he babbled, 'It was too busy. I couldn't get to the stalls but we could go over now?'

Melissa sighed and checked the time on her phone. 'No, it's OK. To be honest, I better go home. Mum will wake up soon. She usually has a nap in the afternoon and then we have some tea. And I want to call in to Alter-Eden to see if I can get some extra shifts.'

Adam nodded. Melissa had been working in Alter-Eden for a couple of years. It wasn't his kind of place at all – it was full of vintage and alternative clothing – but Melissa loved it. Plus, now that her mum was so ill, she was the one who was helping to pay the bills. He thought about the money lying in his bank account and cringed inwardly. He would have given her money in a heartbeat but two things stopped him. First of all, she wouldn't take it. He had tried to give her some money before, when her mum first got her diagnosis, but Melissa had refused.

Worse than that, she had asked him questions about how he could afford to hand over a month's rent to a girl he barely knew. When he explained that his parents would never know, she had looked tense. 'Your parents must be loaded if you can give away that much money without them even noticing.' Things had been awkward for several days afterwards and now they never mentioned money at all. He knew they were from different worlds. It didn't matter that his family had made that money a long time ago. He could never explain how they had done it.

They walked through the park towards the exit and the bus stops beyond. Melissa said almost casually, 'You won't believe who I saw in the park? Michael Bulber was there with his mates.'

Adam groaned inwardly. Michael 'the Beast' Bulber was the official bully of Bonehill Charitable School. His father was Mr Bulber the head teacher, known as The Bulb by his pupils because of his squat build and shiny, bald dome. The Bulb was a former professional wrestler who had been forced to leave the sport after allegedly paralysing an opponent in a dirty fight. He had passed on his vicious nature to his son, who was just about to go into the upper sixth. The Beast was generally a democratic tyrant – he dished out terror on an equal opportunities basis – but having briefly dated Melissa he held a special hatred in his heart for Adam.

'Did he say anything?'

Melissa shook her head. 'He didn't see me. I think he's finally given up on me anyway. He had some new girlfriend at Easter. She was Italian. Bella somebody.'

Adam bit his lip to stop himself sniggering. 'Oh yeah, I heard about that.'

They had reached Adam's bus stop. He kissed Melissa briefly. 'Do you want me to walk round to the shop with you?'

'No it's OK. I won't be there long. But are you around tomorrow night?'

Adam shook his head. 'I'm away this weekend.'

'Let me guess. It's a family thing.'

Adam shrugged. 'Kind of. I just have a really big family.'

Melissa looked at him seriously. 'You always say it like that's bad but you're lucky. You're really lucky.'

'I guess.'

'I wish I had a big family. It would make things . . . easier. With the way Mum is. People could help out.'

Adam wanted to say something heroic, like *Everything will be OK* or *I'll help you!* But what was the point? It would be a lie. His good feelings turned down a notch. Instead, he took her hand and squeezed it and kissed her again as hard as he could.

He watched her walk away, wishing they could go home together.

The bus was stifling and crowded until it got closer to Adam's area. It dropped him off further from his house than his usual bus did but he didn't mind. It was still hot and summery and the air smelled like flowers and barbecue smoke. Adam sighed. Just once he would have loved to go home and find his father turning burgers and sausages on an outdoor grill but his mother would never allow it. Women weren't allowed to guide souls but they were expected to cook, clean and run a perfect household. In spite of the hot weather Elise would be immaculately dressed and serving something complicated for dinner.

Still, as he turned into his street Adam grinned. An unlikely figure was jogging towards him, wearing a lime green vest and very tight running shorts. Her black hair was pushed back from her shiny forehead by a purple headband and she had gigantic silver headphones clamped over her ears. She reached the electronic gate at the same time as Adam and folded in half, gasping for breath and checking a timer. 'This heat is killing me. Open the gate, will you? My hands are too sweaty.'

Adam grinned and placed his palm on the electronic scanner pad. It recognised his palm print and the high iron gates slid open without a sound. He waved at the gap. 'After you.'

Auntie Jo straightened up and groaned. 'I swear all this healthy living will be the end of me.' She hobbled into the garden.

Adam followed her, still smiling. Of all the many changes in his life over the last six months, the strangest thing of all had been Auntie Jo's metamorphosis. Back in March she had been the same Auntie Jo he had known all his life: a whiskey-swigging, toast-munching, horror film fanatic. But after a particularly difficult period for the Mortsons, Auntie Jo's drinking had begun to spiral out of control.

Nathanial had promised Adam that he would intervene. Adam had no idea what his father had said or done but Auntie Jo had begun something of a transformation. She had ditched the whiskey for a start, followed soon after by her equally addictive toast habit. She ate three meals a day and had a solitary slice of toast at bedtime. But after a few weeks she had taken things further. Adam arrived home from school to find that Auntie Jo was out walking. Over time the walking became faster walking and finally running.

Now a considerably smaller Auntie Jo spent her afternoons pounding the pavements while Adam was at school. Elise had

23

never made any comment but Adam knew that his father was relieved. Aron kept threatening to take their aunt along to the gym with him although Adam thought that might be a step too far.

'So where have you been this afternoon?' They had reached the end of the long gravel drive and paused in front of the grey stone house with its graceful, leaded windows. Auntie Jo stood beside one of the yew trees, doing a series of complicated stretches.

Adam shugged. 'Just out.'

Auntie Jo raised an eyebrow. 'Don't *you* start with the "just out" business! It's bad enough that I never get a straight answer out of Luc without you getting evasive too.' She frowned slightly. 'Although he still isn't out and about the way he used to be.'

Adam's mood nose-dived further. Luc had been through a lot, not that he could remember. Adam was partly to blame for his brother's ordeal but there was no way he could confess to anyone, least of all Luc. 'He's fine. He's been out loads more the last couple of weeks.'

Auntie Jo nodded. 'Yes, he has. I used to worry about him when he was sneaking out at all hours but I have to say I worried more when he stopped going out. Still, knowing Luc he had good reason to lie low. He probably had some girl's father after him with a shotgun.' She rolled her eyes and set off round the side of the house, heading for the kitchen. The family rarely used the front door.

Adam followed her more slowly. Sam and Morty, the family's Irish wolfhounds, came bounding to greet him. They were working dogs, a gift from Uncle Paddy in Ireland. They would be going home for a visit the following day. Adam hadn't been lying to Melissa when he said he had a family thing. 'Uncle' Paddy wasn't technically his uncle, just as his children weren't Adam's cousins – but they would soon be family by marriage, when Adam's sister Chloe got betrothed to Ciaron, Uncle Paddy's eldest son.

Adam paused at the back door, reluctant to enter the house. As soon as he stepped inside, his summer day with Melissa would be over. Life would be back to the usual never-ending grind of homework and Luman life. He turned and watched the sun slant across the garden, taking one last appreciative sniff of the barbecue-filled air.

Then, sighing, he opened the kitchen door and went inside.

Chapter 3

he following morning Adam was sitting on the bus before most of the family were even awake. It had been another quiet night with only a couple of call-outs, which meant that for once Adam was bright-eyed, not bleary-eyed, as he made his way up the long driveway of Bonehill Charitable School.

Bonehill had been founded by a philanthropist many years earlier and maintained by a trust. Places were awarded by lottery which drew a huge variety of pupils from all over London, regardless of their family's background or income. It was generally considered a good school although the appointment of a former wrestler as a head teacher had certainly raised eyebrows in some quarters. Still, although The Bulb was terrifying he hadn't actually wrestled anyone to the ground – although had he known the various ways in which Adam and his friends had humiliated him, he would have been sorely tempted.

Adam grinned as he made his way to his form class. His friends weren't exactly cool but they did have a rather unique set of skills that put them squarely at the top of The Bulb's hit list. Archie could draw anything, including the perfect woman. Dan had occasional flashes of genius in between irritating everyone around him and Spike would probably end up on *Wanted* lists around the globe thanks to his computer wizardry.

They had used those skills to good effect when The Bulb had cancelled their planned school trip to Japan and they had managed to get it reinstated. His whole year group would be heading away in just a few weeks. Now all Adam had to do was persuade his family to allow him to get a passport and go on the trip. As soon as they got back from Ireland his campaign could begin in earnest.

He smiled as he reached his form room. Melissa was standing outside waiting for him, texting one of her friends. It was strange seeing her looking so formal in her uniform, when yesterday he had been lying beside her in the park. The memory sent his blood rushing off in various directions round his body and he had to think hard about The Bulb's orc-like face to calm down.

There was time for a quick kiss before their form teacher Mr Fenton came out into the corridor threatening stragglers with various atrocities if they didn't hurry up. Once inside they were treated to one of Mr Fenton's meandering rants, involving them being fifth formers and expected to work as they had never worked before unless they wanted to trigger a series of events culminating in the earth being thrown off course and smashing into the sun. As a thwarted astronaut Mr Fenton's diatribes often took an astronomical turn.

It was break time before Adam finally managed to go in search of his friends. He didn't even have to think about where they would be; his feet set off on their usual path to the library. He grinned as he walked. He had barely seen his friends over the summer, pretending that he was away for most of the break. He let them assume that he was on holiday, rather than revealing that his trips around the globe had involved mopping up souls after a series of natural disasters.

His friends were at their usual table near the back of the library, doing their usual things. Dan was laying out walnut pieces to spell out a series of rude words. Archie was flicking through a manga book and offering helpful suggestions for new words to spell out. And Spike . . . well, as ever Spike was hovering behind his laptop. Adam's smile faded a little. Things with Spike had been awkward for a chunk of last year. Would the summer have been enough to calm his friend down?

Dan looked up and grinned. 'All right, Adam?' He gestured at the word on the table. 'Is there a "k" in knobhead or not?'

Adam blinked. 'I've never really thought about it.' He sat down in his usual place and nodded at the other two.

'I've decided she's the one I'm going to look for in Japan.' Archie held out his manga novel and pointed to a character with enormous eyes and very small items of clothing. 'Without the cat ears and the tail obviously. That would just be weird.'

'You do realise she isn't real, don't you?' Spike didn't bother looking up from the screen. 'I mean, sorry to disappoint you, but you're not going to find her strolling round Tokyo.'

'You might if you come to the World Role-playing Game Exhibition.' Dan's eyes were shining with anticipation. 'I mean,

28

people take the costumes really seriously. There will probably be people there who've gone to South Korea and had tails and stuff grafted on!'

Archie looked queasy. 'People actually do that?' At Dan's nod he shuddered. 'You lot are far too literal. I don't mean she has to be exactly like Super Catnami. She just has to have similar . . . assets.'

Spike rolled his eyes and turned to Adam. 'So, good summer?'

'Yeah. What about you?'

'Yeah, it was all right. I went and worked in my mum's office, updating all their virus protection stuff. She's friends with the boss there. It was easy money. I got a new computer.'

'Cool.' Adam didn't know what to say. Spike seemed standard Spike but things had been very different last term. He wished he could just blurt out his thoughts. *Tell me, Spike, did you ever get anywhere with hunting down the mystery guy at the bombing in Trafalgar Square? And did you know – you were right? I was something to do with it. And I did delete the photo you found that might have linked my family to the whole thing. So even though I told the other two you were being crazy and paranoid, you weren't. You were right.*

'I got my new passport through.' Dan broke the awkward silence. 'I had about ten different photos taken before I got one I liked. We have two weeks to get them in.'

Adam's good feelings plummeted. 'Two weeks?' He'd known it would be soon but not *that* soon.

Spike nodded. 'There's loads of paperwork for the visas. I heard Lumpton talking about it.'

'She's not coming is she?' Archie made vomiting noises in

his throat. 'Trust The Bulb to turn our trip into some kind of dirty week away with Lumpton.'

There were groans of protest at the various mental images this conjured up. 'Bleach. I need bleach for my brain,' Dan whimpered. He turned to Adam. 'Is Melissa going?'

Adam shrugged. 'I think so. I mean it's not like we're having to pay much for it.' The trip was being sponsored by a former pupil at the school who had returned to Japan and built up an electronics empire. Because he was funding it their whole year group had been offered a chance to go, for only a token admin fee.

Archie was leering at him. 'Lucky we're sharing a room with you. You can tell Melissa's friends we'll keep them company.'

Adam snorted. Melissa's friends had only just thawed out with him. Of course that might have had something to do with him standing her up, disappearing mid-evening and throwing up on her on their first few dates. Still, he doubted Archie's perving would endear Adam to them.

There was a disturbance over by the door. Michael Bulber was walking into the library and like a shark swimming into a pond full of guppies a ripple of fear permeated through the room. Mrs Nostel, the teacher who ran the library, put down her mug of herbal tea. 'What are you doing?' Her voice was sharp. Adam felt a warm wave of gratitude. Mrs Nostel might be a bit of a hippy but she was one of the few teachers who wouldn't take any nonsense from the Beast. The library was her domain and she was protective of her usual inhabitants.

But Michael Bulber wasn't alone. 'Just showing some visitors around, miss.' He gave the librarian his most charming smile.

'Lucy might be coming to Bonehill so I'm just showing her and her dad around.'

Adam watched his nemesis sourly. He was acting so *normal* with the visitors, probably because Lucy was pretty and smiley and didn't know that her tour guide was evil incarnate. Adam had a feeling that very few people knew how vicious Michael Bulber really was. He was bad enough at school but out in the real world with no one to stop him the Beast had managed to find friends who were even worse than he was. Adam had encountered them once and hoped never to do so again.

Dan shuddered. 'Look at him pretending to be nice. We should warn her that he's horrible.'

'We should stay out of it and not say anything because we don't want to die screaming,' Spike muttered.

'He must be looking for a replacement for Bella the Wonderfish,' Archie said cheerfully – and far too loudly. The Beast was standing just across from them, showing the visitors the banks of computers, but Archie's voice had carried and he turned sharply. His eyes roamed across the group. Archie's mouth was hanging open, dumb-struck with terror – but the Beast moved on until his eyes locked with Adam's.

Lucy asked him a question, forcing the Beast to turn away and answer but the damage was done. Adam's friends fell silent, pretending to be absorbed in their own activities. Adam glared at Archie, who wasn't daring to lift his head from his sketchbook. Great. This was all he needed. Operation Wonderfish had been one of their more successful schemes, designed to distract the Beast from Melissa so Adam could go out with her in peace. It had worked too – worked better than

31

Adam could have dared to hope. He had been off the Beast's radar for ages as he moved on to fresh victims.

Still, a new year brought new opportunities. Michael Bulber had finished his tour and as he ushered the visitors towards the door, he made a detour past Adam, batting him swiftly round the back of the head, and said softly, 'I'll be having a word with you later, you little prick.'

Adam's stomach dropped. He watched the Beast laughing and joking with Lucy as they left the library and turned ferociously on Archie. '*Seriously*? What the hell was that?'

Archie was scowling but his guilt was all over his face. 'I was only messing! I didn't know he was going to hear me!'

'Nice one,' Spike said. 'Why not just gut Adam like a fish right now? Cut out the middle man.'

'She was *my* drawing!' Archie was glaring at them. 'The Wonderfish. I made her up. He would never have left you alone in the first place if I hadn't drawn her! You should be grateful the plan worked at all.'

'Yeah, but why ruin it when it worked?' Dan crunched gloomily through his walnut pile, although not before using the remnants to spell out D-E-A-D.

Archie swore, grabbed his bag and sketchpad and stormed off before anyone could say anything. Adam sighed and stared at the table top. Great. Just as things were off to a good start everything had to go down the toilet. It had been brilliant not having to worry about the Beast, especially because school hours were pretty much the only time he got to see Melissa. Now he was going to have to watch his back again. He groaned. 'Why did he have to say that?'

'He didn't mean anything by it.' Dan threw the last handful of nuts into his mouth, spraying them lightly with walnut shrapnel as he talked. 'Anyway, it doesn't mean anything really. The Beast was telling everyone about Bella. We just pretend that we heard about it from other people and then heard she wasn't coming here after all. It's not like the Beast can prove anything.'

Spike looked at him like he was mad. 'Since when has the Beast ever *needed* proof of anything? He's not exactly going to hold a fair trial. He's jury, judge and executioner rolled into one.'

Adam was trying to think things through but he didn't especially want to rake over his row with Spike last term. He picked his words carefully. 'How did you leave things with the Beast? You know, after we came back after Easter?' And silently he added, *You know, when you wouldn't speak to me for a month because you thought I had sabotaged your computer. And then after a while you gradually went back to normal but I know you haven't forgotten. Because you never forget about ANYTHING.*

Spike played it cool as usual. 'I didn't do anything for a while.' He stared at Adam, daring him to say something about their fight, then shrugged. 'But Bulber kept emailing and sending pictures so in the end I dragged it out a bit until he was doing exams and then Bella emailed to say she wouldn't be moving to England after all.'

'And what did he say?'

'He wasn't very happy so he called her a lot of names. Then Bella reminded him about all the pictures he had sent her. He shut up after that.' There was a gleam of triumph in Spike's eyes.

Adam didn't share his happiness. 'So what am I going to do now? What if he starts going after Melissa again?'

Spike looked up and for just a second Adam saw him smirk. 'Dunno. But you didn't like my last plan. So, unless you've got your own idea I guess you better stick to the art rooms if you don't want to be slaughtered.'

After a promising start Adam's day had gone downhill rapidly. He had managed to persuade Melissa to stay in the art room at lunchtime but it had been difficult on such a lovely, sunny day. He couldn't explain why because Melissa had never known anything about Operation Wonderfish. She thought the Beast had just given up on her. The last thing Adam needed was an indignant Melissa telling Bulber to back off.

Adam was filled with gloom, not just because he was back in the Beast's sights but because Spike's reaction had confirmed what he already suspected: his interference with Spike's computer search had been neither forgiven nor forgotten. By an extraordinary piece of bad luck, Adam had been caught on camera when he had used his doom sense to thwart a suicide bomber in London six months earlier. Spike had made it his mission to track down the bomber and his mystery companion. Adam's one piece of *good* luck had been that he was wearing a baseball cap and sunglasses and had been turned slightly away from the camera which had captured him.

However, Spike had managed to modify an ingenious piece of facial recognition software, which hadn't identified Adam but which *had* found a picture of some of his family. Adam had managed to delete the photo but not without Spike realising. Spike had guessed that Adam was hiding something in relation to the bomber. Adam knew that he wasn't a suspect himself as far as Spike was concerned – but his interference had encouraged Spike to start digging into Adam's life. After all, they had been friends for four years but Spike had never once been to Adam's house and they rarely met up outside school. Anyone would get suspicious at that, never mind a bloodhound like Spike.

All in all, it hadn't been the spectacular start to the new school year that Adam had hoped for. Now he had the prospect of a family weekend in Ireland to look forward to, complete with hiding his various breaches of Luman Law. He was feeling like a bit of a pariah these days, both at home and in school.

It was almost a relief when the final bell sounded. Adam had been given a special dispensation to swoop home after school, rather than hold the family up any more. He was glad none of his friends got his bus as he lurked in a quiet corner, waiting for the after-school rush to pass. Once the corridors were quiet he scuttled towards the toilets, planning to step into an empty cubicle and make a speedy exit.

'Oi, dickhead!' Adam turned and to his dismay saw the all too familiar face of Michael Bulber and his gang of minions. He didn't know why they were so late leaving but they didn't seem to be in a hurry. They always made time for a bit of entertainment, aka tormenting younger pupils. Adam took a quick glance along the corridor, confirming what he already knew – there was no one around to help him. He was on his own.

He also knew that he didn't have time for the Beast – and that he wasn't turning up at a Luman house party with black eyes and missing teeth. He turned and kept walking, quickening his pace. If he could just get round the corner he could disappear.

'Did you hear me, you little prick? I'm talking to you.'

Behind him Adam heard a lot of footsteps. He didn't want to run but he could hear that the Beast and his friends were speeding up. A couple of them were laughing and someone (probably Weasel, the Beast's most trusted minion) said, 'I don't think he heard you, Michael. We'll get a bit closer and then he'll hear us.'

Adam gritted his teeth. Someday he was going to think of something bad enough to do to Michael Bulber and his group. It was going to be painful or humiliating – or even better, both. He was going to make them sorry that they had spent so much time picking on people. They would think twice before they did it in future.

But today was not that day. Adam tried to look casual until the last minute but someone stamped hard behind him and he threw caution to the winds. He took off like a hare along the corridor, gaining a couple of seconds of surprise element before the pack recovered and started chasing him. As he ran Adam reached inside his shirt collar, groping for his keystone – and closed his fingers on thin air.

His keystone wasn't there. If he'd lost it Nathanial would kill him – assuming he survived the next twenty seconds. There was no time to think. He hurtled round the corner and ducked into the girls' toilets to buy himself time. Thankfully no one was inside. He ran straight into one of the cubicles, loosening his tie and fiddling to get his top buttons undone.

He could hear jeering outside as someone kicked open the door into the boys' toilets. There were lots of footsteps and cubicle doors slammed before some bright spark called out, 'He's gone into the girls'!' The laughter bought him another few seconds.

But the buttons on the new shirt were still tight. It was taking too long. Instead he pulled the bottom of his shirt out of his trouser waistband – and something dark and shiny slithered out, falling straight into the toilet bowl. Adam was just about to seize the keystone when he had one flash of inspiration. He stepped up onto the toilet seat and opened the high window. It would look like he had climbed onto the cistern and dropped outside.

Adam gritted his teeth and reached into the water, just as the door to the toilets was kicked open. 'At least you picked the right toilets, you little shit. Shall we cut your balls off and then you can come in here all the time, with all the other girls?' The Beast's friends laughed but Adam didn't care. He clenched his fist around the keystone and took a single step forward, willing himself into the Hinterland. The cubicle door slammed towards him and he flinched – but it passed harmlessly through the place where he had been standing a second before. Adam backed away through the toilet as the Beast grinned into the cubicle – only for his face to fall as he found it empty.

Adam breathed in slowly, trying not to make any sound, knowing he was being ridiculous. Yes, he could still see the physical world but he was no longer there, thanks in part to his keystone. The Hinterland, the place of souls, was another realm altogether. It lay on top of the physical world, like clear film over a map. Adam could see everything, including the Beast's snarling face, but he could no longer be seen himself. It was like standing behind a one-way mirror.

The Beast's friends had already searched the other stalls.

37

Weasel came up behind Bulber and pointed up at the window. 'How did he climb out so fast? Little prick.'

Michael Bulber didn't answer for a moment. From the safety of the Hinterland Adam watched him, knowing that Bulber was remembering another time when Adam had made a miraculous escape right beneath his nose. The Beast wasn't going to admit that to his friends of course. He was glaring up at the window, as if he were trying to imagine Adam's escape through it. Maybe he was trying to convince himself. At last he scowled. 'Yeah, he got lucky. He won't get lucky next time. Chicken shit.'

Adam didn't wait around to hear any more. He walked through the wall, emerging on a grassy strip between the school and the car park. He had never been so glad to be swooping for home.

Chapter 4

 few minutes later Adam was outside the back door of his house, clutching a small suitcase and a suit in a long bag. His mother had been pacing about the kitchen like a caged tiger when he got home, curtly informing him that everyone else had been ready for hours and arriving any later would be an insult to their hosts. Adam had managed to apologise through gritted teeth, although he longed to pour out his tale of woe. Not that Elise would have any sympathy of course. She would be happy about anything that could put Adam off school.

Now they were all standing around Nathanial, who was checking that the dogs had their keystones on. Sam and Morty were working dogs as well as family pets – herding souls in the Hinterland – but for this weekend they were on holiday, just like the rest of the family.

Chloe was standing silently beside the largest suitcase Adam had ever seen. She was chewing on her lip and staring into space. Adam knew it was probably better staying quiet but some devilish part of him couldn't resist winding her up. 'We're only going for two nights, you know. You're not going to live there.'

'Yet. Not going to live there *yet*.' Luc grinned. 'At least it's only September. That time we went to visit in January and they made us go for a walk on the beach . . . I thought I was going to die.'

'Don't be such a wimp,' Auntie Jo said. 'It's a beautiful place. Clears the gunk from your lungs. I'll be going for a run on the beach tomorrow. And if you've enough energy to wind people up, you've enough energy to come with me.'

Luc rolled his eyes. 'You know, I liked you better back when you only loved whiskey and zombies.'

Elise came out of the back door holding an armful of clothing. 'Take your coats.'

Aron blinked. 'But these are winter coats!'

Elise's lips tightened further than should have been humanly possible. 'The weather is unseasonable in Ireland.'

'Right, I think that's us.' Nathanial patted Sam's ears and the huge dog rested his head adoringly against his master's hip. 'So Patrick has placed our Keystone in the garden. We'll have no problems getting there. Everyone ready?'

Adam gulped and nodded. Swooping had a way of making him feel like he'd been turned inside out. The family stepped into the Hinterland.

'Let us arrive at the same moment,' Elise said, always conscious of putting on a good show – even if no one would see them in the Hinterland. '*Un, deux, trois!*'

Adam closed his eyes and clutched his keystone, letting it do what it had to do. There was a rush of sensations – being squeezed until his breath disappeared; falling into a bottomless

40

pit; being plunged into icy water – and finally a flare of pins and needles prickling across every bit of his skin. When he opened his eyes London was gone, replaced by a different view and a different house. Adam turned his back on the building and instead looked at what lay beyond: the sea.

Portstruaine was a village on the very northernmost tip of Ireland. Uncle Paddy's house was on the very tip of Portstruaine and standing in the sloping garden revealed the Atlantic in all its angry glory. The water was grey and endless, broken only by roaring white surges that swept up to the coastal path snaking along beneath the bottom of the garden. The wind was howling; Adam could feel it, even here in the Hinterland. Somehow it always crossed the veil between the physical world and the place of souls.

'We'll go to the side of the house. Remember, people walk along the coastal path so moving in and out of the Hinterland needs to be kept out of sight,' Nathanial said.

Luc was staring down at the water with barely concealed horror. 'You'd have to be a maniac to walk along there with that coming towards you.' He pointed at an enormous wave bearing towards the shore, then crashing and foaming on the rocks beside the path.

Auntie Jo grinned. 'Living in London is making you soft. A few days with your cousins will harden you up. They're made of sterner stuff.'

One advantage of being in the Hinterland was that the luggage was light. They trooped up the lawn past the front of the house, grey and pebble-dashed with large windows for appreciating the view. It was built on a low cliff with views of the ocean in three directions. To the right lay the cliff path; and half a mile away to the left lay a long, golden beach, the village just visible beyond.

As they reached the side of the house a stable-style door opened and 'Uncle' Paddy came out. 'I'm feeling something moving in the Hinterland.'

Nathanial nodded at them all and they stepped back into the physical world. 'Hello, Patrick. Thanks for having us.'

'Any time! Sure you're long overdue a holiday!' Uncle Paddy grinned around and waved them into the house. 'We'll do the greetings inside. Get in out of the wind. Hello you pair!' He petted Sam and Morty's heads, took Chloe's luggage and ushered them all towards the door. Nathanial took Elise's case and Aron made an awkward movement towards Auntie Jo, who smirked and said, 'I can manage, thanks.'

Adam slipped through the door into a long, warm kitchen. Luggage was dropped on the kitchen floor and various chairs. 'The boys can take your bags upstairs in a minute,' Uncle Paddy said, rubbing his hands together.

Auntie Jo looked round. 'It's still summer, you know. Did nobody tell the weather here?'

'The weather here makes its own rules.' They turned and saw Aunt Orla smiling at them from a doorway, drying her hands on a tea towel. 'Don't worry, it's just a storm. It'll pass and by tomorrow you'll think you're in heaven.' She turned back and bellowed into the hall. 'Would yis ever hurry up? Our guests are here!'

There was a flurry of movement and the thunder of footsteps on the stairs. A moment later six people burst into the kitchen – a small boy, four girls ranging in age from tiny to teenage and finally Ciaron, their real reason for being here. He was smiling but his eyes locked on Chloe and his cheeks flushed. Chloe's flushed in sympathy.

'It's been far too long since we had you all here.' Aunt Orla beamed at them. 'The boys are that tall! It's as well we've plenty of food in.'

Finally there was the inevitable round of hugs, handshakes and kisses. The air buzzed with laughter and voices and Adam felt himself relax. He loved coming to Ireland. His mother was so formal when they had visitors but Aunt Orla was laid-back to the point of being horizontal. As a hostess, she provided a bed, a good fire, a hearty meal and as much tea and whiskey as you could drink. Other than that, you were free to get on with things and entertain yourself. He grinned at his 'cousins' and felt a fleeting pang, wishing that Melissa was there. She would love it. But Melissa would never get to be there. It was a fantasy.

He'd managed to burst his own bubble and deflate.

Uncle Paddy was looking round the kitchen and frowning. 'Where's Caitlyn?'

Ciaron shrugged. 'She said she was going to feed the dogs.' Uncle Paddy bred Irish wolfhounds. Some were sold as pets and breeding dogs but the best were reserved as working dogs for the Luman world. He always said he didn't want any show winners bringing people to his door.

Uncle Paddy's frown deepened. 'She should have been here.'

'Leave her alone, Patrick,' Orla said easily. 'She'll be in better form when she's been outside for a while.'

Auntie Jo raised an eyebrow. 'Is Caitlyn still a wild thing?'

Ciaron grinned. 'Mum used to say she was a changeling and that the fairies had left her.'

'There's nothing wrong with a bit of spirit in a girl,' Aunt Orla said.

'Never did me any harm,' Auntie Jo said, while Elise nodded and made a poor effort to agree.

'Do you want the dogs over in the barn, Patrick?' Nathanial winced as he watched Sam and Morty frolicking round the kitchen, loving the noise and bustle and hunting for food.

'I'll take them,' Adam said quickly. He liked seeing all the other wolfhounds.

'Do you remember where the barn is?' At Adam's nod Uncle Paddy smiled. 'Good man. You can put them in the pen at the far end, beside the other Luman dogs. Caitlyn'll show you.' His smile faded. 'And tell her to get herself back over here when she's finished.'

Adam nodded again and clicked his tongue at the dogs. They followed him as he flung open the door, braced himself and stepped back outside. The 'barn' was at the end of a small field. Away from the shelter of the house the force of the wind took Adam by surprise. Yesterday in London he'd been lying in the park in a T-shirt but here it was a different world. What had Aunt Orla said? *The weather here makes its own rules.* He turned and squinted back at the Atlantic, watching it rage against the rocks, eyes tearing in the wind. It was like living beside a moody weather god.

The dogs barked as the gale hit them, then bounded joyfully across the grass. Adam bent against the wind and jogged over to the double doors. They were closed but not bolted and he could see the gleam of light inside. As he opened them a thunder of barking rose up from the pens and seconds later Adam heard a ferocious growl. A huge wolfhound was standing in front of him, so big it made Sam and Morty look like whippets. It was easily the size of a pony. It stood eyeing him and the growl faded but it didn't make any friendly signs.

'Caitlyn?' Adam called. He wasn't scared – the wolfhound was a Luman dog and it would never attack a Luman. Even so, it was disconcerting facing something big enough to eat you.

'Och, get out of it, Storm.' The dog turned towards the voice, transforming into a welcome party as a black-haired girl appeared from one side. 'How are you, Adam?'

'Caitlyn?' Adam was stammering which was ridiculous because he'd known Caitlyn forever – only in the six months since he'd last seen her something had happened. She'd turned into a rock star.

She raised an eyebrow over a piercing green eye. 'Who do you think it is? I suppose Da sent you to get me.'

'Well, I brought the dogs over.' In the face of another raised eyebrow Adam felt his cheeks flush. 'But they're out in the field.'

Caitlyn walked past him and peered out of the door. 'Running mad, more like.' She put two fingers to her lips and gave a long whistle, the pitch rising and falling. The dogs stopped as though a lightning bolt had hit them, then bounded towards the barn. They leapt up at Caitlyn but she pushed them down and gave a sharp command in Gaelic. *'Suígí!'* The dogs sat immediately and gazed up at her adoringly. At last she petted them. 'You two are spoiled, so you are.'

'They're not!' Adam protested – then saw a mental image of Sam and Morty sprawled on the floor in the den in front of the fire. 'Well, maybe they are a bit. But it hasn't done them any harm.'

Caitlyn shrugged. 'They'll be all right unless they have to do a lot of jobs. That's when you'll notice it. Not wanting to get out of their beds in the night.'

There was an awkward pause while Adam tried to think what to say. 'So how are you?'

'I'm grand. And you?'

'Yeah, good.' Adam hesitated. 'You seem . . . different. Since the ball.' The last time he'd seen Caitlyn had been at Aron's Marking ball back in March. Back then she'd been like all the other Luman girls – beautifully dressed and draped in jewellery. Something had happened, changing her; giving her this air of wildness. Maybe it was just being here. Adam could feel it, that untamed energy in the air. It made him want to sing. It made him want to jump off a cliff and fly.

Caitlyn's lip curled. 'Yeah, the ball. It was all right but I just looked around and realised I was like one of the pups. Waiting to be picked to go to a good home. And I realised I don't want to be picked. I want to do the picking but only when I'm good and ready. I suppose I got tired of being a good wee Luman girl.'

Adam nodded. 'I can understand that.'

'Oh, you can, can you?' Caitlyn smiled, softening her words, looking more like the old Caitlyn. 'And since when are you such an expert on girls?'

Adam shrugged. 'I'm not really.'

'Tell us something we don't know,' a familiar voice drawled behind Adam. He groaned inwardly and turned to find Luc

46

giving Caitlyn one of his trademark thousand-watt smiles. 'How are you, "cous"?'

Caitlyn seemed totally unimpressed. 'Oh look, it's God's gift, come to join us mere mortals here on earth.'

'Kind of you to say so. Your father sent me to get you. He seemed to think Adam might have trouble getting you back to the house.'

Adam scowled. 'We were just talking.'

'Yeah, we were,' Caitlyn said. 'But, you know, three's a crowd and all that. I better go and face the music. Sam and Morty are in the pen down at the end. It's good to see you, Adam.' She smiled at him and walked out of the barn.

'What about me?' Luc protested.

In response, Caitlyn tossed a few words of Gaelic over her shoulder. Storm, the giant wolfhound, stalked over to Luc and jumped up, putting his paws on Luc's shoulders and knocking him to the ground. Luc stared up wide-eyed from the stone floor as the huge dog bent his head and licked Luc's face from chin to forehead. Caitlyn clicked her tongue and the wolfhound bounded off after her. They could hear her laughing even over the roar of the wind.

Luc wiped his face disgustedly. 'What the hell was that? Some kind of *werewolf*? It's the size of a horse!'

Adam grinned and took the dogs to their pen.

It was a nice evening in spite of the awful weather. Auntie Orla had made a huge stew and cauliflower cheese. They all ate together, squeezed around the large kitchen table. The din was incredible as seven Mortsons and nine McVeys talked and laughed. A very flushed Chloe was sitting beside an equally flushed Ciaron. They alternated between joining in with the general hubbub and talking quietly to one another.

After dinner they headed up to the drawing room. Enormous windows ran from the ceiling to floor, looking out across the gardens onto the sea. Uncle Paddy lit the fire as dusk fell and Auntie Orla drew the curtains against the thrashing sea. 'Don't worry. The forecast is good for tomorrow. This'll blow itself out overnight. You won't know the place in the morning.'

Privately Adam had his doubts that the forecasters knew anything about the mad weather here but he was happy to just go with the flow. He sat back and listened to his cousins chatting and laughing. Only Caitlyn stayed quiet. Adam didn't know what Uncle Paddy had said on her return to the house but whatever it was it hadn't improved her mood. She had been silent and sulky all through dinner and now she seemed happy lurking in a corner of the room behind a magazine. It was only at bedtime that she slipped over beside Adam. 'I'm going to walk the dogs on the beach tomorrow. I'll be up early. If you want to come, meet me at the back door at seven.'

Adam nodded. He wondered if it would be a quiet night. Uncle Paddy and Ciaron had taken it in turns to do the handful of jobs that had come in – mainly fallen trees and tiles landing on unsuspecting drivers and pedestrians. Nathanial had volunteered to help but Uncle Paddy had gallantly declined his offer. 'Take a night off, will you man!'

Adam was crammed into a tiny room with his brothers and two sets of bunk beds. He didn't even bother protesting but took the bottom bunk while his brothers climbed into the top bunks. Aron was asleep in seconds while Luc lay playing a game on his phone, pausing now and again to message people.

It was weird sharing a room when he was used to having his own space. Still, Adam thought, it would be good practice for Japan – assuming he was allowed to go. *Please, please let me go*, he thought fervently. Once they were back home he would start begging in earnest. What would it be like, sharing with his friends? Dan would demand the top bunk and lie dropping peanut shells on whoever had the misfortune to be below. Spike and Archie would both be on their laptops, although probably looking at very different things . . .

Best of all though, Melissa would be there. Not in the same room (he could but dream) but definitely in a room nearby. He would be able to spend a whole week with her, just hanging out and chatting and maybe getting some time to sneak off together. Time on their own, away from everyone else. Why was it so hard? He lay thinking about her until he felt hot and uncomfortable, trapped beneath his brothers. All he had to do was *get there*.

Adam pillowed his head in his hands and stared blankly at the bunk above. He knew why his father was so reluctant to apply for a passport. The Luman world was secretive for obvious reasons. The Mortsons were an old family and wealthy, mainly because they had amassed a huge number of Keystones over the centuries. These stones were part of what gave their Luman owners power and speed but at one time they had been sold between families for vast sums of money and the proceeds locked away in Swiss deposit boxes. The keystone Adam wore around his neck was a fragment of one of these larger Keystones.

In the past it had been much easier to conceal the Luman world. Lumen had hidden in plain sight, keeping their fortunes hidden or pretending to be landowners. But in the last hundred years the world had changed. Proper records had been kept. Birth and death certificates were needed to do anything and everything. The Mortsons' home and expenses had to be routed through a convoluted series of companies and bank accounts. A handful of 'normal' people – mainly doctors, lawyers and bankers – knew enough about the Luman world to understand the need for secrecy but any contact with the authorities put the Mortsons on the radar. Adam could understand his father's reluctance to apply for a passport when the family could simply swoop anywhere in the world.

He knew it was selfish – but somehow he couldn't give up on his dream of going to Japan. He didn't want to put his family at risk but just for once, he wanted to be like everyone else in his class and just do the things that everyone else took for granted. And the thought of spending a whole week with Melissa was too much to let go of. He would have to be more persuasive than he had ever been in his life.

He fell asleep, dreaming heavy, happy dreams.

Adam awoke to a different world. He lay on the bottom bunk, blinking at the shaft of sunlight slipping between the faded curtains. A cautious peek revealed his brothers sleeping and the ceiling still over their heads, proving that the roof had miraculously stayed on through the hurricane. He gathered his phone, clothes and trainers and slipped out into the hall.

A few minutes later he was hovering outside the back door,

staring in wonder at an incredible view. The sea had transformed from a snarling grey beast into a blue mirror, reflecting the early morning sun and lapping the rocks. Walking past the end of the kitchen he could look left along the beach and in the distance just see the white gleam of houses. Adam sighed and swung his arms, feeling some of the tension of school and life drain away. You couldn't look at this and feel uptight. It was too big and empty. It made him feel small and his problems even smaller.

'Looks like it goes on forever, doesn't it?' Caitlyn said behind him. He turned to see her wearing short, denim cut-offs and flip-flops, flanked by six wolfhounds, including Storm the werewolf. None of them were on the lead but they were perfectly calm, probably because Sam and Morty weren't with them. Caitlyn pointed straight out to sea. 'If you sailed due north you would run into some of the Scottish islands. But after that, it's just the Atlantic for a very long way.'

'It's amazing,' Adam said. His voice sounded quiet. He *felt* quiet, in a happy sort of way. Peaceful somehow. Maybe this was why Uncle Paddy and Aunt Orla always seemed so chilled out. Looking out of your window at this every day probably put everything else into perspective.

He followed Caitlyn across the grass and down some steps at the bottom of the garden. They passed through a tall gate onto a treacherous little path above the water. The dogs walked sedately behind for a few minutes until they reached high, rocky steps leading down to the beach. At the bottom Caitlyn kicked off her flip-flops. 'You can leave your shoes here, if you want to paddle.'

Adam hesitated. The water looked lovely but it also looked

freezing. He remembered Luc dragging him in when they were younger and his skin burned a little at the memory . . . Still, Caitlyn had smirked in a challenging sort of way and he didn't want to look like a wimp. He kicked his trainers off, shoving his socks inside in a ball and hurried to catch up with her.

The beach was almost deserted. They could see a few runners in the distance and a man walking his dog but otherwise it was all theirs. 'I always come down early with the Luman dogs,' Caitlyn said. 'It gets busy later on and in the summer it's madness with the tourists but it's always quiet at this time. Means they can have a good run off the lead.' She gave a low, piercing whistle and the dogs transformed from well-trained, working dogs into pony-sized puppies, charging off along the beach, throwing up flurries of sand behind them.

Adam glanced at her. She seemed less sullen today, more like the Caitlyn he remembered, although there was still something wild and twitchy about her. She walked fast, stopping now and again to curl her toes into the sand or grin and kick water at him. He splashed back until his jeans were soaked and clinging to his thighs. The water was cold but not horribly so; just the kind of cold that made his whole body feel wide awake. He waited until she was laughing at two of the dogs as they chased each other through the water. 'You seem happier today.'

She stopped and stared at him, surprised. After a moment she shrugged. 'Yeah, I s'pose. I just hate all the sitting round being polite when we have people here. Everything has to be tidy and it's all, "Caitlyn, brush your hair!" Or "Caitlyn, would you ever crack a smile once in a while?" I wish people would just leave me alone.'

Adam snorted. 'You think that's bad? If we have any Lumen coming to the house my mother has a complete meltdown. It's new clothes, fancy food, candles everywhere. Chloe has to practise on the piano for hours, just on the off chance someone might want to hear her play. And if the Concilium are coming, then it's all black tie and green soup.'

Caitlyn grinned. 'Yeah, I get the impression that your ma likes everything done just so. We'll have to dress up a bit tonight because the stupid Concilium are coming. Not all of them, just a few of the Curators, but it's still a pain.'

Adam stared at her, dismayed. The thirteen Curators of the Concilium were responsible for upholding law in the Luman world. Most of them were decent and honourable – but not all. He didn't mind seeing Heinrich but there was one Curator who he really *didn't* want to see. He tried to keep his voice neutral. 'Which ones are coming?'

'Dunno. Does it matter?' Caitlyn's face had darkened. 'I have to be on my best behaviour whoever it is. You know, in case one of them wants to marry me off to his *son* or something. Because it would just be such a total *honour* and all that.' She rolled her eyes.

The penny was dropping for Adam. So *that* was why she was being like this. He tried to make a joke of it. 'Well, you could always get betrothed to Luc. At least life would be . . . interesting.'

She gave him an arch look. 'Yeah, thanks but there's good interesting and then there's spending-the-rest-of-your-life-in-jail-for-murder interesting. Anyway, I don't want to get betrothed to anyone. Not yet.'

'Yeah, but that's what Chloe said too,' Adam said, without really thinking about it until he registered the shock on Caitlyn's face. He backtracked frantically. 'Well, that's what she used to say! You know, before she started seeing more of Ciaron and all. Like obviously, she'd be really happy to get married to him. She really likes him.' *Great, Adam. Way to start an international incident.*

Caitlyn nodded but her expression became guarded. She changed the subject, pointing at the dogs and telling him a potted history of each of them. An hour later when they pulled their shoes on to return to the house she was still talking about inconsequential things. Adam smiled and nodded but he had a horrible feeling he had messed up big time.

And now he had to look forward to a whole evening of not messing up in front of the Concilium.

Chapter 5

he day passed pleasantly but too quickly for Adam. By early evening he was standing in the bedroom, gritting his teeth as he tried to get dressed alongside his brothers. His mother, ever prepared, had packed their evening wear and as he pulled on a bow tie he thought wistfully of the relaxed meal the night before.

Like all Luman homes Uncle Paddy's house had several formal reception rooms, ready for entertaining. Half an hour later Adam was in a candlelit sun room, looking out as the sun fell low over the Atlantic. The sky seemed to go on forever. His family were there too with the exception of Nathanial and Aron, who were waiting respectfully in the hall with Uncle Paddy's family, ready to greet the Concilium.

Auntie Jo joined him by the window, holding a glass of sparkling water and pointedly ignoring the wine and whiskey on the low tables. 'These things were always more fun when I could have a drink.' She looked tired but not unhappy.

Adam glanced at her, feeling awkward. No one had drawn

attention to her transformation, with the exception of Luc, who couldn't resist stirring when the opportunity arose. There was nothing personal in this; winding people up without making them hate him was one of Luc's special talents. Still, Adam thought the change in his aunt had been pretty spectacular. 'I think you're doing really well,' he said quietly.

To his horror Auntie Jo pursed her lips and her eyes glistened but she cleared her throat and murmured, 'Thanks.' To his relief she asked him about school the day before.

There was a thunderous knocking sound from the hallway beyond. Having leapt half a foot in the air Adam scowled. He could never get used to the Concilium's ceremonial arrival. Auntie Jo was talking and he tried to listen but his stomach was churning. Which of the Curators would be here tonight? There was one he couldn't bear to see.

Too soon Adam's worst fears were realised. A smiling Uncle Paddy entered the sun room and presented five of the thirteen Curators of the Concilium. Heinrich, the Chief Curator, was leading the way, smiling broadly and seeming genuinely pleased to see the Mortsons. The other Curators were greeting them politely.

But all Adam's attention was on the man who had slipped into the room last. Darian was the youngest Curator. He was a tall, handsome French man with blond hair and sharp green eyes. He greeted everyone around him courteously, lingering as he embraced Elise until she pulled away, as close to bad manners as she would ever come.

Adam hardly even registered the Darian who was physically with them in the room. All he could think of was Darian back in the Realm of the Fates, conspiring to bring the Mortsons to their downfall. To their deaths.

Even more chilling was the knowledge that no one else in the room had any idea who Darian really was. Adam alone watched in horror as the man smiled and shook hands with the very people he had plotted to destroy. As the Frenchman approached him Adam's throat went dry. He stood petrified, torn between rage and terror as he remembered the man's words: *The High Luman must bear his share of the blame*. How many people had died needlessly as Darian stood by, hoping to ruin the Mortsons and pluck Elise from the wreckage?

And then Darian was in front of Adam, who silently offered a clammy hand, staring helplessly. Darian was smiling but his green eyes were sharp and cold. '*Bonsoir*, Adam. I trust you are well?'

Adam nodded, not trusting himself to speak. He let go of Darian's hand, expecting him to move on as usual but the Frenchman stayed where he was, holding Adam's stare. What did he want? He had never shown the slightest interest in Adam before, which had suited Adam just fine.

Darian was studying him. 'We so rarely get a chance to talk, Adam. Tell me a little more about yourself. Are you still attending your school?'

Adam glared at him. Was he really going to have to do this? Stand there and make small talk with the man who had tried to have them all killed? 'Yeah.' It was the only word he allowed himself to say. It took all his effort not to shriek to the whole room, '*This man wants my family dead!*'

'How unusual at your age.' Darian was quiet. 'And why might this be?'

'Because I want to be a doctor.' Who the hell did Darian think he was, quizzing him like this? Darian wasn't his friend; he was his enemy, even if the Frenchman didn't know that Adam knew. He clenched his fists. 'I stay at school because I want to be a doctor.'

'But you will be a Luman.'

'Maybe.' Anger was making Adam reckless.

'There is no maybe, my young friend. A Luman is born to our work. To do anything less would be to bring shame and dishonour on your *noble* family.' Darian had a particular knack for saying one thing and conveying the opposite. The way he said 'noble' managed to drag up all the shame and degradation the Mortsons had experienced when another of their number had been unable to be a Luman in the past – not that Adam was supposed to know anything about old scandals.

Adam sucked in his breath. 'There's no shame in being the person you're meant to be. And I want to be a doctor.'

'And why is that?'

'Because I want to save people's lives.'

He knew immediately that he had said too much. Darian's eyes narrowed. 'Really?' The Curator's voice was quiet. 'An unusual aspiration for a Luman. Do you have any *experience* of saving lives?'

'Of course not,' Adam lied. 'But I will have. Some day I'll know exactly how to help people. Especially when other people have tried to hurt them.' He looked at Darian hard, trying to stare him out, but the Frenchman was smirking.

There was something about that smirk that almost made him throw caution to the winds and blurt out everything. It was Uncle Paddy who saved him. He joined them and nodded at Darian. 'Well, Curator, are you ready for some food?' He smiled at Adam. 'I'd say you're hungry Adam, if you're anything like Ciaron.'

Adam nodded and gladly followed him out of the sun room but he could feel the Frenchman watching him as he walked.

The meal should have been delicious but Adam was too much on edge to enjoy it. Uncle Paddy and Aunt Orla had so many daughters that for once Adam found himself at the middle of the table instead of stuck at the far end. Male Lumen always took precedence over females, which disgusted Adam but didn't seem to bother most Lumen a jot. He tried to enjoy his food but his stomach was a tight, sick ball.

He was forced to go upstairs for an after-dinner drink in the drawing room while the women and girls cleared up. Adam was tense and determined to stay with his father to avoid being caught unguarded again. He was still kicking himself for telling Darian about his plans to be a doctor. Darian was a Seer – like Adam he could often feel deaths before they actually happened. It was because of this that he had known someone was preventing deaths and cheating the Fates out of souls. So why on earth had Adam blabbered about saving lives? It wasn't a typical Luman aspiration. All he had done was make himself conspicuous, in some kind of petty bid to antagonise Darian.

Adam tried to listen to his father and brothers as they talked with Ciaron and his young brother but he couldn't help watching over his shoulder the whole time. There was no sign of Darian or Heinrich but Uncle Paddy was talking to the other Curators, making them laugh. Ciaron kept glancing at the door, probably waiting for Chloe to appear. Adam warmed to him. All right, he was sickeningly perfect but he *did* seem to like Chloe. Looking around, Adam knew that she would be happy here.

A few minutes later the women appeared and the room became three times as animated. Chloe was invited to play the piano in the corner and she managed to put on a faultless performance. Ciaron was beaming at her. Elise was smiling tight-lipped, torn between pride in her only daughter and disappointment that she was going to waste her accomplishments on such a small and insignificant Kingdom. The fact that her own family had felt the same way about her marriage to Nathanial didn't seem to register with Elise. History had a way of repeating itself.

It was a few minutes later before Heinrich and Darian rejoined them. Darian was smiling but there was something smug about it that unsettled Adam. The feeling that something was amiss grew stronger as he looked at Heinrich. His normal joviality seemed forced and he was looking from Nathanial to Uncle Paddy with barely concealed distress. Darian joined the group around the piano, applauding loudly as Chloe finished playing, and murmured something in Elise's ear. She nodded but took a step away.

Suddenly Adam couldn't bear it all any longer. He waited for Aunt Orla to begin singing and playing something faster than was considered ladylike and took advantage of the distraction. He crept out of the drawing room and made his way down the stairs, without any clear sense of purpose, until he walked through the silent kitchen and slipped out of the back door.

The last light was fading from the sky, bar the clean, silvery moonlight illuminating the waves beyond the garden. The day had stayed fine and dry and the sky was clear and starry. Adam walked away from the house, desperate for fresh air, and without really noticing he found himself at the barn.

There was a cacophony of barking but he'd heard Caitlyn enough to know what to say. *'Bígí ciúin!'* he said as commandingly as he could and the wolfhounds fell silent. He made his way to the far end of the barn and found Sam and Morty standing in their pen, wagging their plumy tails in greeting.

The dogs were always happy to see him and out here, away from the formality and pretence, he felt like he could breathe again. His mind was full of dark thoughts about Darian. Part of him could understand the man's hatred of Nathanial. After all, Nathanial had managed to win Elise's heart – and keep it in spite of tragedy and scandal. For Darian, who had always envisaged Elise at his own side, it must have been an awful blow.

But to go to the lengths he had – to be prepared to sacrifice the Mortson men, just so he would finally have a chance with Elise ... Adam swore so ferociously that Sam whined and tilted his head to one side and had to be petted reassuringly. Darian wasn't just ruthless; he was a psychopath. This campaign wasn't about love, whatever the man told himself – it was about his need to win. Elise was no longer the teenager he had fallen in love with, just as he was no longer her friend. They *could* have been friends if he hadn't been so tirelessly hostile to Nathanial all these years.

Adam's thoughts were interrupted by a fresh wave of barking. He jumped up and peered round the corner of the stall, just in time to see the barn doors open. He was about to call out a greeting, when to his horror he realised that it wasn't Caitlyn as he had hoped.

Three men were trooping into the barn – and none of them were going to be happy to see him.

Adam groaned inwardly and slunk back behind the stall end. Great. Now he was going to be in trouble. Slinking off from any Luman event was a big no-no, at least until the Chief Curator had left the party. Nathanial would be annoyed but Elise would be furious. His mother was especially sensitive to any breaches of etiquette.

The obvious thing to do was lie low. Adam eased away from the pen door and flattened his back to the stall wall. 'Sssssh!' he mouthed at Sam and Morty and for once they obeyed him and lay down at his feet. Maybe being back in Ireland and under Caitlyn's watchful eye was doing them good.

Adam had hoped that the men were just getting a chance to admire the wolfhounds. But his hopes were dashed when he heard their voices coming closer to the end stall. This wasn't a general tour for the benefit of the Concilium; this was three senior Lumen sneaking away from a party to have a private chat. Based on previous conversations Adam had overheard, he had a feeling they weren't going to welcome an audience.

He had a moment of indecision, torn between walking out before he could be discovered or staying still and hoping for the best. But as the voices drew closer another feeling kicked in:

curiosity. Why had they slipped away from the party when they could arrange a meeting at another time? Clearly something urgent had come up and Adam had learned that sometimes the things most worth hearing had to be overheard by stealth.

His legs were moving before his brain caught up with the decision. He crept across the stall and squirmed in behind the straw bales at the back of the pen. Morty tried to follow him but Adam hissed and gestured the big dog away. He whined but turned obediently and moved to the gate, wagging his tail in greeting as Nathanial, Uncle Paddy and Heinrich came into view. Adam lay absolutely still, his eye pressed against the gap between the bales.

Uncle Paddy was talking. 'And of course you know these two.'

Heinrich leaned over the gate and patted Sam and Morty's heads in turn. 'Of course. Both excellent animals.'

Nathanial nodded. 'They're good dogs. Agreeable and obedient.'

'Well, you know yourself, I keep the best as working dogs. There's a lot of demand for the Luman pups. If you think you'll be needing another one, Heinrich, you'd be as well to let me know and I'll keep you one aside.'

'I will do.' Heinrich fell silent. He was still petting Morty but absently.

'So you said you needed a word, Heinrich.' When there was no answer Uncle Paddy glanced at Nathanial.

'Is it about the Marking? Have you decided on a date?'

'Oh, the Marking. Yes, it will be soon.' Heinrich blinked and seemed to come back to the present. 'I hope just a few weeks away. I must discuss the date with the Lady Fates. I would like to have as many High Lumen there as possible.'

'You'll be glad to have an extra pair of hands. Alexander is young to be Marked but he's a good boy. Steady and kind. He's good with the souls, especially the children.'

'Aye, he's a fine lad. A credit to you both.' Uncle Paddy nodded in agreement.

'Yes. He is. We are most proud of him. More proud than you could know.' Heinrich didn't look proud. He looked tense and unhappy.

Uncle Paddy was never one for beating round the bush. 'Heinrich, you've a face like a wet Sunday in July. We see a lot of them so I know the signs. I have a feeling that it isn't the Marking that you want to be talking about. Do you want to tell us why we're really here?'

Heinrich gave a sharp bark of laughter. 'I do not *want* to tell you but I'm afraid I must.'

Nathanial put a reassuring hand on the older man's shoulder. 'Heinrich, whatever it is, you know we'll do whatever we can to help.'

Heinrich sighed. 'It is I who wish to help you, my friend. Believe me when I tell you I am trying to help although it may not seem like it.'

'Help me how?' Nathanial's face was calm but his hand dropped back to his side.

'By warning you. Darian has convinced the Concilium that there is still a rogue Luman at work in the Kingdom of Britain. He has gained the necessary votes to launch an investigation. He will be staying in your Kingdom to oversee your work.'

Chapter 6

or Adam, the silence that followed Heinrich's statement seemed to go on forever. He lay concealed, thankfully too stunned to even squeak with disbelief. It seemed he wasn't the only one.

Heinrich was the first to speak. 'I know this has come as something of a shock.'

'Yes. A shock indeed.' Nathanial gave a short, barking laugh. 'It's always a shock when you realise that another human being hates you enough to keep their loathing burning for decades.'

Uncle Paddy was less restrained. 'What in the name of the Fates is the man playing at? A rogue Luman at work? In *Britain*? Is he out of his mind?'

Heinrich sighed. 'Darian has made these accusations before, Patrick. This isn't a new allegation.'

Lying concealed, Adam could feel his heart beating faster. He had overheard this conversation once before. He had ignored it then, stupid enough and arrogant enough to think that he would get away with it. Because of this he had almost given Darian his heart's desire. Darian wanted to destroy Adam's

65

family; wanted it so badly he had been prepared to stand by and watch humans being killed to get rid of Nathanial. Only two people with this knowledge had survived – Adam and Darian himself. If he had realised that Adam knew, Adam would more than likely be dead himself by now.

But the investigation – why now? Adam hadn't saved a soul for six months. Six long months, feeling the horrible ache when his doom sense flared, ignoring it, knowing that he was condemning a soul he could have saved. He had kept his head down for six months – well, until a couple of days ago. He felt a prickle of unease. But what were the odds really that Darian would have found out about that? And even if he had, there was no proof that Adam had *known* the man should have died. He had been careful to keep the fact that he was a Seer well hidden from his family and the Luman community. What happened in the park was just good luck as far as any observer knew – a casual act of kindness, saving a stranger from a wasp sting.

Nathanial was talking. 'He made these accusations before and I found no evidence. If anything *my* Kingdom was under attack by . . . the previous thread-cutter. But to seek permission from the Concilium to investigate us is another level. What is this really about?'

'I don't know.'

'Of course you know!' Uncle Paddy was angry now and Adam could understand why. 'It's been twenty years! Will he hold a grudge against Nathanial forever? He can't bear to see Elise happy with someone else, the vengeful bastard!'

'His hatred cannot run this deep. Can it?' Nathanial sounded bewildered. Adam closed his eyes and answered the question silently. *Yes, Father, he hates you enough to see you dead and I nearly gave him the opportunity he needed.*

'Listen, enough of this.' Uncle Paddy had run out of patience. 'The whole thing's a farce. How that gobshite ever got himself on the Concilium I will never know but that's not our problem. Nathanial does not give consent to his presence in his Kingdom and there's the end of it.'

'No, Patrick. That is not the end.' Heinrich was calm but there was something taut in his voice that alarmed Adam. 'I wish it was the end of the matter but it is not. Darian is a Curator and as Curator he is entitled to certain . . . privileges.'

The silence that followed this pronouncement made Adam feel sick. He was waiting for laughter or anger or *anything* at all from his father; anything apart from this quiet. What *privileges* did they mean?

As if Heinrich had read Adam's mind he continued. 'I know the old ways are not always followed but the Laws remain unchanged. Darian is a Curator. He has asked to monitor Luman activity in your Kingdom and he has support to do this. He has also expressed his wish to spend time beneath your roof. He expects your hospitality. I spoke with him at length but he did not seem dissuaded.'

Nathanial was silent. Adam clasped his hand across his mouth, trying to stifle his protests. The thought of that monster in their house, like a snake in the grass . . . He tried to imagine Darian sitting at their table night after night. Adam wouldn't give him any reason to point blame at Nathanial – but what about the other Lumen in the Kingdom of Britain? Mistakes were sometimes made. Lumen were still human. Nathanial smoothed over disputes and guided his workforce calmly and fairly but how would the other Lumen cope with the constant scrutiny from a Curator?

More than that though, Darian would be living in their *home*, spending time with Elise. They had been close once; just one of the reasons that she had been expected to marry him. They barely saw their French relatives; they had never forgiven Elise for her 'betrayal'. Adam wanted to believe that his mother wouldn't give a hoot about their opinion – but they were powerful and wealthy and very persistent. If Darian did manage to find something and bring Nathanial down, would they pressure her to disown her husband and remarry? And would she go along with their plans, to save her family from complete ruin? Adam closed his eyes and shook his head. He was being crazy and paranoid. There was no way any of it would happen. Nathanial wouldn't put a foot wrong – and neither would Adam.

'There is another way.' Heinrich hesitated. 'If a place were to arise on the Concilium. If you were to become a Curator . . . then you could veto the visit. The Kingdom of Britain would no longer be your direct responsibility.'

'I don't want to be a Curator. I don't see enough of my family as it is, Heinrich.'

'Aron has come of age.'

'But Luc and Adam haven't. Both of them need me at home. They need support.'

'It's a fine opportunity, Nathanial. I would second you, you know that.' There was a pause as Uncle Paddy looked at Heinrich. 'Is it your own place you're talking about?' At

68

Heinrich's nod he grimaced. 'I'm sorry to hear that.'

Heinrich smiled. For just a second his shoulders drooped and Adam caught a glimpse of the burden he carried. Millions of people died every year and every single one of them had to be guided safely through their Lights. Heinrich had the ultimate responsibility for this. 'It has been a privilege but I confess that I grow weary.'

'How long?'

'Months. A year perhaps.' Heinrich shrugged. 'It is difficult to tell. There is much to do before then.'

'Including getting Darian to turn his attentions elsewhere,' Nathanial said. 'Let him come. Let him sleep beneath our roof and break bread with us. He will find our Kingdom beyond reproach.'

Heinrich sighed. 'I have no doubt of that, old friend.' He glanced at his watch. 'We should return before we are missed.'

'I'm sorry, Heinrich. That your time is short, I mean.' Uncle Paddy held his hand out and the Chief Curator shook it. 'I wish every Chief Curator followed your lead.'

Heinrich smiled. 'Let's see if you're still saying that in a month or two, Patrick.' He laughed. 'I am not stepping onto the Unknown Roads just yet. There is still time for me to do something outrageous.'

Nathanial smiled. 'There's still a Marking to look forward to.'

'Oh, to have more sons,' Uncle Paddy grumbled. 'They're straightforward, the boys. Get them Marked and get them to work. The girls are the tricky ones and I have five daughters to worry about. In fact, let's say I have six. Caitlyn alone will give me all the bother of two.'

The men laughed and followed him back towards the barn doors while Adam lay blinking at the ceiling and wondering what the hell he was going to do.

A few minutes later, Adam was sneaking back into the house, brushing off dust and instructing himself to stay calm. It was hard. The way he felt at that moment, calm was a pretty distant concept.

Upstairs, the party was in full swing. Music was playing and he could hear laughter and the clink of glasses. Just another Luman party. Just another freaky night in his freaky world; the world that he could never bring Melissa or his friends into. The world he wouldn't *want* to bring them into.

Adam looked in the mirror above the hall table, smoothing his hair and checking his back for stray specks of straw; breathing in slowly. What was the point in getting upset? He couldn't stop Darian coming to Britain. He couldn't even keep him out of their home. As long as Adam lay low and didn't save another soul there was no way for Darian to attack Nathanial. One thing was for sure: there was always a plan with the Frenchman. He didn't do anything unless he thought he would gain something from it.

Adam climbed the stairs back to the drawing room, trying to paste a smile on his face. He would be polite and normal and not let Darian or anyone else have the faintest idea what he was up to.

Of course, as ever, his plan didn't work out the way it was supposed to. As he was stepping into the drawing room a figure crashed into him, almost knocking him flying. He scowled and found himself facing an equally unhappy Chloe. 'What are you doing?'

'Just going downstairs for a while.' Chloe's face was flushed with something between excitement and annoyance.

'Why?'

She put her hands on her hips and glared at him. 'What's it to you?'

'I just want to make sure you're OK.'

Chloe rolled her eyes. 'Don't worry. I have plenty of *chaperons*. No danger of anything exciting happening here.'

Adam stepped aside but a twinge of unease made him hesitate by the door. He'd thought she was trying to sneak off to get some quiet time with Ciaron but he could see Ciaron on the other side of the room, laughing with Aron and Auntie Jo. Adam frowned and slipped into the alcove by the fire, pretending to look at the pictures on the wall but surreptitiously watching the door. An awful suspicion was forming in his mind.

Sure enough, a minute later a tall, blond-haired figure excused himself from his group and slipped out through the door, holding two glasses. The knot in Adam's stomach returned with force, beating a pulse in time with his heart. He counted to ten and sneaked out into the landing. He peeked over the banister, just as Darian reached the bottom of the stairs, glanced around and slipped through a door.

His heart in his throat, Adam crept downstairs. Darian hadn't dared to close the door fully behind him – that would be breaching protocol even for a Curator. Through the gap Adam could see his sister standing by a small piano. The room was lamp-lit and warm light sparkled on her earrings. She was holding a champagne glass and looking up at Darian, half confused and half pleased. Adam watched the older man smile at her and felt his stomach contract.

They were talking in French. Adam was competent but Chloe spoke the language like a native, thanks to Elise's determined tutoring. Standing just outside the door, Adam tried to follow the conversation. It all seemed fairly innocent – comments about the party, the food and the weather – the basic social chit-chat every Luman was trained in from birth. Still, if it really was as innocent as it seemed, why had Darian lured Chloe down into another room?

A minute later Adam's suspicions were confirmed. Darian raised his glass in a toast. 'You look very beautiful tonight. A young woman, not a girl.'

'Thank you.' Chloe smiled at him, not looking at all uneasy. After all, Darian was a Curator. Adam felt his fists clench. She would have no idea where this was going or what it was leading up to.

Darian adopted the tone of a teasing uncle. 'And who was all this effort for? Was there someone in particular you were trying to impress?'

Chloe's cheeks flushed. 'No . . . not really. Maybe . . .'

Adam could understand her discomfort. Betrothals were deeply private affairs and weren't supposed to be discussed outside those involved and their guardians. They were serious commitments that were rarely broken but when they did go wrong enormous hurt and humiliation was inflicted, not just on those involved but their whole families. Darian knew this better than anyone. Elise's family were still angry with her after all these years.

72

Darian smiled and feigned ignorance. 'Well, I don't know who he is but I'm sure he was impressed. More importantly, I was impressed.' He took Chloe's hand and raised it to his lips. 'I hope we will soon be spending more time together. It is my intention to visit your family soon. I look forward to getting to know you better . . . and your brothers of course.'

Suddenly, without knowing how, Adam was standing in the room with them. Chloe was staring at him horrified while Darian had drawn back a pace but was watching him with a hint of a smirk.

'What are you doing here?' he asked his sister.

'Nothing!' Chloe was glaring at him but Adam couldn't help noticing how she had edged away from Darian. 'Just talking! What are *you* doing more like?'

'I came to find you. You shouldn't be down here. Not with *him*.' Adam spat the last word out with more force than he had intended.

Darian's mouth was a tight line but it twisted into a cold smile. 'I assure you your sister's *honour* is safe with me.'

'I doubt that,' Adam said. He stepped towards the older man, anger making him reckless. 'I'm not sure you know much about honour.'

'Adam!' Chloe was looking at him with a mixture of awe and terror. She flicked her eyes sideways at Darian and then back to him. Adam could see the unspoken plea. *He's a Curator! You can't speak to him like that! You'll get into trouble!*

'Father wanted to talk to you.' When Chloe hesitated, Adam exploded, 'Just go!'

Darian made no protest as she left but watched Adam closely.

'How dare you?' The Frenchman was looking at him with more curiosity than anger and Adam realised he was asking a genuine question.

'I know what you are.' A tidal wave of memories came back, flooding through Adam's mind, threatening to make him lose all composure. 'I know what you want to do. Don't pretend to like her. You hate us. You hate all of us.'

'What dramatic assertions . . .'

'I know! I know about your Marking ball! I know my mother rejected you and what you want to do to my family!'

The shock on Darian's face gave Adam the briefest moment of satisfaction – until the Frenchman strode across the room, seized his throat and pinned him to the wall. 'What did you say?'

'You want my father out of the way so you can have my mother. She doesn't want you! She HATES you!' Adam's voice was a strangled croak. He tried to bend Darian's fingers away but the Luman was too strong. 'Let . . . me . . . go!'

The pressure on his throat eased but Darian didn't let go. 'Be careful, Adam. You are talking about things beyond your understanding. Remember who you are speaking to.'

'You think you're so important, don't you?' Adam grabbed Darian's fingers and jerked them off his throat, darting sideways and backing away from the Luman. 'Morta was important but she's gone now. You could be gone too.'

Darian's face tensed. 'I have no idea what you're talking about.'

'Yes you do.' Adam was shaking with something between fear and rage and exhilaration. He had spent six months imagining this moment; imagining getting to tell Darian exactly what he

74

thought of him. 'Stay away from my family or I'll tell everyone what you really want and what you'll do to get it.'

Darian blinked. Then, unbelievably, he smiled. He stepped towards Adam. 'You do not know me at all, Adam. You seem to think I have some dark secret when my reputation is spotless. Perhaps there is a guilty conscience at work. You have a secret of your own, *non*?'

'No, I don't! Just stay away from my sister!'

'What's going on here?' Nathanial was standing in the doorway, Uncle Paddy at his shoulder. His father stepped into the room and looked from Darian to his son. 'I said what's going on here?'

'Your son was speaking in a disrespectful manner. That is all you need to be concerned about.' Darian was icy calm. 'Of course discourtesy and deception are not uncommon in your family, as I myself know only too well.'

'Adam, go into the other room.' Nathanial gestured to what seemed to be a bookcase but Uncle Paddy stepped forward and turned something. A moment later the shelf swung back, revealing a doorway into the room next door. 'Wait for me there.'

'He was with Chloe,' Adam protested. 'He was down here on his own with Chloe. Asking her stuff about our family. About *betrothals*!'

'That's enough, Adam. I'll deal with it.' Nathanial wasn't looking at his son; he was looking at the Frenchman with the closest thing to hate that Adam had ever seen on his father's normally composed face. 'Leave us.'

Uncle Paddy nodded and gestured to the door. Adam had

no choice but to give Darian one last glare and step into the other room. Uncle Paddy swung the door closed behind him and Adam was confronted once again with a bookshelf. He tried to press his ear to the door but he couldn't hear a thing.

Frustrated, he turned away and tried to get his bearings. He was in the reading room, a large room at the far end of the house. It overlooked the Atlantic although it was too dark outside to see. A fire burned in the grate in spite of the pleasant day and Adam hurried towards it, desperate for some comforting warmth. As he reached it, something moved behind him and he gave a yelp of shock.

'*Sssssssssssh!* It's all right, it's me!'

Caitlyn was lying on the sofa, wearing a silky dress the colour of slate. She had kicked off her shoes, revealing bare toes, the nails painted a shimmering dark grey the same colour as the dress. She was holding her phone and as she ripped out her headphones Adam could hear something dark and angry blaring out tinnily.

He scowled at her. 'Thanks a bunch. You scared the crap out of me.'

'What are you doing?'

Adam paced back over to the bookcase, struggling to hear what was going on in the other room. '*Ssssssh!* I can't hear.'

'Are you seriously telling me to shut up in my own house?' When Adam didn't respond there was a click and the angry music roared out of the speaker on her phone.

Adam glared at her. 'How can I hear what's going on next door?'

Caitlyn arched one eyebrow. 'Why do you *want* to hear what's going on next door? Who's there?'

'My father. And Darian, the . . . ' Adam tailed off, not able to find a bad enough word to describe Darian. Unfortunately, Adam was the only one who knew just how evil the Luman really was. The only other 'people' who had known what he was capable of had gone into their Lights, leaving him behind to deal with the mess.

'Darian's hot. Dunno why he never got married,' Caitlyn mused.

'Well, if he's so hot, let him come and stay with you instead of us,' Adam muttered, then immediately regretted it.

Luckily Caitlyn's music had reached a thrashing crescendo. She turned it down. 'Look, if you really want to hear what's going on, take the books off the shelf just by the door handle. There's a gap there. Not that I've ever listened in on anything.' She stood up and stretched like a cat. The grey dress rippled and tautened as she moved, robbing Adam's capacity for rational thought.

He turned away, feeling his cheeks flush, and busied himself finding the handle. But even as he slid the books out of their place on the bookcase he heard a door slamming in the next room. As he turned, Caitlyn moved up in front of him and pressed a finger to his lips. 'Ssssh,' she whispered, took his hand and pulled him away, back towards the sofa. 'Whatever's happened you've missed it. And I'm not supposed to be here. I'm supposed to be upstairs playing nice wee songs on the piano. So you can wait here and face the music but I need to move before I get busted.'

She was still holding his hand. Adam stared at her. Her eyes were dark and challenging. 'I thought you were a good boy, always doing what you're told. Maybe I was wrong.' She smiled at him and pulled his hand onto her hip. The fabric felt cool and silky in Adam's palm. 'You could always come with me.'

She was looking at him expectantly and Adam knew that look now and knew what she wanted him to do. Six months ago, before he had kissed Melissa, he wouldn't have had a clue. Now, instead of panicking, his mouth felt tingly, like it was expectant too. Only no matter how nice she looked and smelled and how soft her dress felt beneath his fingers, she wasn't Melissa. And he couldn't kiss her. He just wished his brain would hurry up and let his lips know because they were burning. But he *wasn't* going to kiss her.

The second Adam realised this, Caitlyn seemed to realise it too. Something passed fleetingly across her face but by the time she lifted his hand off her hip it was gone. She bent and picked up her shoes. 'I'll be walking the dogs again in the morning. Maybe see you then.' She smiled and slipped through the patio doors, disappearing into the darkness.

For a moment Adam wanted to follow her. Then, as the reading-room door opened, all thoughts of Caitlyn were lost as Nathanial's furious face loomed into view.

Chapter 7

wenty-four hours later, Adam was back in London, lying on his bed and feeling moody. School started properly the next day and from his form teacher's ranting on Friday he knew they were going to have about ten hours of homework a night. Still, anything was better than being at home and in the doghouse.

After Caitlyn had escaped into the darkness the previous night, Adam had been left wishing that he had followed her. He had been on the receiving end of what could only be described as 'the bollocking of the century'. Nathanial had paced round the reading room, berating Adam in low, angry tones while Uncle Paddy provided stony-faced, folded-arm back-up. He was told repeatedly that he had no right to speak to a Curator in such a manner, regardless of what he knew about the past. In fact, Darian would soon be their guest in Britain and it was therefore imperative that Adam went upstairs and apologised for his rudeness.

When Adam tried to offer a stuttering defence, he realised

that he couldn't actually say anything about what he knew. He couldn't *say* that Darian wanted them all dead or at the very least ousted, just as he couldn't mention the Frenchman's conspiracy with Morta. He couldn't even admit that he knew Darian was coming to Britain to spy on them because that would mean admitting *he* had been spying himself in the barn. All he could do was bleat unconvincingly about trying to defend Chloe's honour because he thought that Darian might fancy her. Remembering the incredulous expressions on Nathanial and Uncle Paddy's faces made his cheeks flush with humiliation all over again. They had looked at him like he was mad.

The worst bit had been actually apologising to Darian. No matter what harsh words Nathanial had exchanged with his nemesis behind closed doors he wasn't going to let his son insult a Curator. Adam had been frogmarched upstairs, where he had been led into a small study and been forced into a mumbled apology and a sweaty handshake with the Frenchman. Every word had felt like a stone in his mouth. Darian had given him a cold nod and swept from the room with an air of injured pride.

He'd been too despondent to get up early that morning for a walk with Caitlyn. And, if he was honest, he'd been uneasy about it too. He hadn't forgotten his treacherous lips the night before, tingling and telling him they would quite like to get acquainted with Caitlyn's lips. Was it possible for your lips to cheat without the rest of you following? Adam pillowed his head in his hands and scowled at the ceiling. He'd been going out with Melissa for six months now. He couldn't pretend he hadn't looked at any other girl in all that time (his eyes took that decision away from his brain most of the time) but this was the first time he had been tempted to do something more than look. It hadn't helped that Caitlyn had known he was tempted. When he hadn't turned up for the walk she had sent him a text, a single word: *Chicken!* She hadn't returned by the time a tense Nathanial had led them into the Hinterland to swoop home much earlier than planned.

Adam sat up abruptly. Enough thinking. He needed a distraction. He had one last blissful evening without homework so that wasn't going to work. He decided to go downstairs and forage for food and company. The den was empty although the fire was lit and a DVD was paused, a contorted face frozen on the screen. In the past it would have been a horror film but now it was something much more terrifying – one of Auntie Jo's excitable, American fitness gurus. Adam sighed inwardly and went in search of the health convert.

Auntie Jo was in the kitchen, sitting at the scarred wooden table, leafing through a Sunday newspaper and swirling a large glass of something green and glutinous. Her face was shiny and her mop of black hair was pulled back off her face by a lurid green sweatband. She glanced up and did an exaggerated double take. 'Cheer up. No one has died. Well, no one we know anyway.'

Adam rolled his eyes and grabbed the juice jug from the fridge. 'Ha-ha. Hilarious.'

'I thought so.' Auntie Jo's expression became glum as she contemplated the glass in her hand.

'What *is* that?' Whatever was in there looked almost . . . *alive*.

'Super-bionic veggie-charged slime. I mean juice.' Auntie Jo raised the glass to eye level. 'Try some?'

'No thanks,' Adam muttered. 'It looks too much like the last thing you made. The broccoli and banana stuff.'

'Yes, the only thing that tastes worse than broccoli and banana soup is burnt broccoli and banana soup. Maybe if your mother had made it I could have stomached it. Anyway, bottoms up.' Auntie Jo held her nose and took a deep gulp. A chunk of the green stuff slithered out of the glass and down her throat.

Adam turned away, feeling faint. It was still hard to believe he was looking at Auntie Jo sometimes. It wasn't just the weight loss and the running. It was *everything*. The old Auntie Jo would have been snarfing down toast and whiskey at this time of the night, not drinking mushed-up veggies. She would have been mocking the stupidity of horror movie heroines, not jumping about in trainers. Now she seemed to have traded one addiction for another. At least the green stuff was hopefully better for her than the whiskey had been – although it probably wasn't as appetising.

Auntie Jo sprang up from the chair, making a horrible yacking gargling sound and shaking her head vigorously. 'It's all right. You can look now. All gone. Well, most of it anyway. It doesn't taste that bad as long as you can't smell it. Not as bad as those Chinese herbs I had to boil up over the summer. Looked like someone had been out in their garden with a rake.'

'Is it hard not drinking?' As so often happened, Adam asked the question and immediately regretted it.

Auntie Jo didn't seem concerned. 'Sometimes. Social occasions seem to last a lot longer these days. That's not always a bad thing though.'

'You must have found it hard in Ireland though. When you saw Uncle Paddy's whiskey collection.'

'It wasn't as much fun as I hoped it would be. Nothing to do with the whiskey though.'

Adam put on his most innocent expression. 'Yeah, Father seemed to be in a really bad mood. He was downstairs with Darian for a while.'

Auntie Jo raised an eyebrow. 'You'll have to do better than that, Adam. You were downstairs with Darian yourself for a period if I recall correctly.'

Adam scowled. It had been much easier to lure Auntie Jo into confession mode when she had still been drinking. 'Want some toast?'

Auntie Jo held up an imperious hand. 'I am immune to bribery. Whatever was going on, your father will tell us when he's good and ready. You probably know as much as I do. Maybe more if you were foolish enough to start a shouting match with a Curator.'

'I thought he was after Chloe,' Adam protested, knowing how weak it sounded.

'I wouldn't put it past Darian,' Auntie Jo muttered, shuddering slightly. 'Anyway, I'm sure everything will become clear. Whatever he's up to isn't worth worrying about. He's a fool.'

Auntie Jo was so wrong about Darian that Adam felt like shrieking a warning. Darian was many things but he wasn't a fool. The problem was that Adam's family insisted on seeing him as some kind of spiteful, lovesick puppy dog – faintly ridiculous and easy to push away. Maybe Nathanial was beginning to realise what a relentless opponent he was but the rest of the family were still blissfully unaware. Not for long though. He took his juice over to the table and sat down facing Auntie Jo.

'There's a big feature about Japan in the magazine section. New technology, economic recovery, that sort of thing.' Auntie Jo passed the newspaper across the table and Adam stared at a glossy picture. A smiling geisha in clogs was talking on a tiny mobile phone while neon skyscrapers rose up behind her. Adam stared at the picture, imagining being there with his friends and Melissa. The longing inside him was so strong it was painful.

'You really want to go, don't you?' Auntie Jo was quiet. When Adam nodded she sighed. 'Your father isn't trying to be unkind. You know we need to stay off the radar as much as we can.'

'I know.' He *did* know – only knowing didn't make it any easier.

Auntie Jo sighed. 'Look, I probably shouldn't say this but I will. I think your father is going to agree to this. I think he wants you to have this chance and I think he will get you a passport. Your little outburst to Darian last night probably didn't do you any favours but I think you'll be OK.'

Adam stared at her, feeling his heart beat faster. Had he heard that right? Was she serious? 'He's going to let me go?'

Auntie Jo nodded. 'I think so.'

Adam leapt up, pushing the chair back so fast that it screeched horribly on the flagstone floor. 'Yesssssssssss! That's brilliant! I can't wait to tell Mel— mates. My mates! I'm going to tell my mates!' He turned away quickly, pretending to get more juice, cursing his own stupidity. *Seriously, genius?! You actually just nearly told her about Melissa?! Well, watch that passport you're getting go up in smoke – literally!*

'Adam.'

Something in Auntie Jo's voice cut through his excitement and confusion. It was only one word but it was the way she was saying it. He pivoted on the spot and her expression made Adam's blood run cold. It was a mixture of fondness and regret. 'What? What is it?'

Auntie Jo bit her lip. 'I shouldn't be telling you this either. But . . . I think you have a right to know. I think your father is going to get you a passport and I think he's going to let you go on your trip. But I also think he's going to ask you to leave school.'

'When?' There was a strange, icy feeling down the back of his head. Everything seemed very clear and bright. 'When is he going to ask me to leave?'

'Soon, Adam. I don't know for sure but I think it will be soon. He wants you to have your trip but I think you should try and see it the way he wants you to. A chance to spend some time with your friends – and a chance to say goodbye.'

Adam blinked at her. 'But why?'

'Because you're getting better, Adam. We've all seen it. You're becoming a better Luman all the time. You're finding your feet. School was never going to be forever.' Auntie Jo sighed. 'Try not to see it as a bad thing. It's a sign that you're ready to be a Luman. Your father wants you and Luc to come of age sooner rather than later.'

'When did he decide this?'

'He was talking about it today. I was surprised he seemed to be in such a rush but he obviously has his reasons.'

Adam glared at her – or rather glared through her. He knew why Nathanial was in such a rush. He wanted his sons to come of age and get Marked so they would be full Lumen. He wanted to get this out of the way while he was still High Luman, before Darian brought him down – or before he was forced to become a Curator just to keep the Frenchman at bay.

'Don't shoot the messenger!' Auntie Jo looked startled and Adam realised that his expression was murderous. 'You should be proud. It's a compliment.'

'Yeah, of course it is,' Adam muttered. He grabbed his juice and headed for the door, gritting his teeth to stop himself blurting out anything incriminating.

As the door swung closed behind him, he heard Auntie Jo's parting words. 'You're a victim of your own success, Adam. Try to be happy about it, will you?'

Chapter 8

oing into school the next morning, Adam was keenly aware of what he might lose. He sat on the bus, head tilted against the window, gently stroking the cuff of his blazer. He was probably the only fifteen-year-old in London who got up every day happy to be putting on his school uniform. Every time he pulled on his blazer and knotted his tie it was a statement to the world. *I am normal. I get on a bus and I go to school and I hang out with my friends and do my homework. No weirdness here.*

Now he already had a feeling of nostalgia as he crunched up the stony driveway leading into the school. As the main building loomed ahead of him Adam's throat tightened. Yes, he'd had to lie and yes, he'd had to cover up a lot but somehow he had managed to forge a life of his own here, away from his family and the Luman world. In all the years he had felt lost and useless at home, he had never felt that way here. He had told his friends so many lies but strangely this was still the place where he had been most truly himself.

There was no sign of Melissa in registration and somewhere beneath his concern Adam felt a guilty twinge of relief. He needed some time to put the weekend behind him. Plus Melissa wasn't easy to lie to, even by omission. Nothing had happened with Caitlyn but he had to admit: part of him had *wanted* something to happen. Melissa's eyes sometimes seemed almost supernatural, like lasers, able to see straight through him. Luckily she was a private kind of person and didn't pry too much, even though she thought his family sounded weird.

Thinking this gave Adam a pang of loneliness. His family *were* weird by normal standards but not in a bad way. They were good people. Melissa would like them, he was sure of that – but she could never meet them all. (She had encountered Luc before but had somehow managed to resist his charms – a fact that only made her more lovable.) What was he going to do when he had to leave school? How would he keep seeing her then? His heart scrunched up in his chest, a small, unhappy ball.

He could try and make it work. After all, Luc managed to have a fairly active social life in spite of working full-time as a Luman. His encounter with Morta had kept him closer to home for a while but he had slipped out the night before after his phone had beeped frantically all afternoon. If he could pull it off maybe Adam could too. He could pretend he was going to visit other Lumen families in Britain. Maybe there was a daughter he could pretend to like . . . for a week or two, until he got rumbled and ended up betrothed to a stranger to avoid a scandal. Adam scowled. Luc made it all seem easy but that was just the Luc effect. Adam usually managed to make things harder than they needed to be, not easier.

As he trudged towards the library at break he tried to think positively. Auntie Jo hadn't said he would definitely have to leave. Maybe she had misunderstood. And even if he *did* have to leave he would still get to go to Japan first. He would have a whole week with his friends and Melissa. Maybe they could come up with a plan. He could run away with her. Spike could probably hook them up with some fake ID so they could start all over again. It would be brilliant and they could dance off into some kind of Hollywood sunset . . .

Adam snorted and opened the library door, smiling at Mrs Nostel, the librarian. She raised her cup of herbal tea in salute as she talked on the cordless phone, her sparkly skirt twinkling under the library lights. He made his way to his usual table, looking forward to a bit of banter with his friends, but they were sitting round the table with funereal expressions. Archie was colouring something in with savage concentration while Dan had suspended his nut consumption, choosing instead to poke his almonds listlessly into a heap. Even Spike was glowering.

'What's wrong?' Adam's voice was shrill with alarm. He tried to imagine what could have reduced his friends to such despair and came up with the worst thing he could think of. 'Have they cancelled the Japan trip again?'

'Worse,' Archie said, tearing a page out of his sketchpad and flinging it across the table at Adam.

Adam stared at the page in incomprehension. It showed some kind of monstrous troll rampaging past skyscrapers Godzilla-style. Only there was something familiar about the troll . . .

Dan gave a quivering sigh. 'We're still going to Japan. But the Beast is going too.'

Adam stared at them for a long moment, praying that it was all an elaborate hoax. Six eyes stared mournfully back at him. 'But he can't. He's not in our year. It's only people in our year going!' There was an edge of hysteria in his voice that he didn't like. 'The guy who's paying for the trip said it's only for fifth year! He said it was too late for the sixth form because they'd already picked all their subjects for next year. Just fifth years!'

Spike sighed and gave him a disgusted look. 'The Beast is The Bulb's son. He's getting to go as a special treat. He's even allowed to bring one of his ickle friends to keep him company.'

'Weasel,' Dan said, his face the picture of gloom. 'He's bringing Weasel with him.'

Adam groaned and put his head in his hands. So much for the Hollywood sunset. A new film was playing out in his head and it was less romance, more dodgy horror . . . He tried to see a silver lining. 'Well, at least The Bulb is going. I mean, he won't let the Beast do anything too mental.'

'Yeah but Lumpton's coming. The Bulb'll be too busy having a love-in with her to even notice what the Beast is up to.'

'Yeah, it'll be all John Lennon and Yoko Ono in the bed for days and days,' Dan said, then shrieked resentfully when Archie flung his pencil at him. 'What was that for?!'

'OK, when you're a "visual learner" there are some pictures you can NEVER get out of your head!' Archie glowered.

Adam tried to erase the mental image of The Bulb and Lumpton tucked up together and restore some sanity to proceedings. 'Yeah, but even if Bulber is busy I doubt the Japanese police will let the Beast go round maiming people. I think they're pretty strict.'

Dan looked more hopeful. 'Yeah, maybe they'll see he's pure evil and go all Samurai on him.'

'How do you even know he's going?'

Spike raised an eyebrow. 'How do you think?' He turned his laptop towards Adam, revealing The Bulb's inbox. 'The Bulb has been a busy boy. He's been emailing the Sensai non-stop. It's sickening. Plus he's got most of the passports scanned in already and added to the confirmed list. *You* still need to give your passport to Fenton. Has to be in for next week. And if you're planning your own week-long love-in with Melissa she'll need to get hers in too. Neither of you are on the final list.'

Adam frowned. He would need to get to work on persuading Nathanial – but why hadn't Melissa handed her stuff in? 'Yeah, I'll say to her.'

'And if you're planning some precious moments together, make sure one of you brings *protection*.' Spike was smirking. 'You know, like a bazooka or a big stick with nails in it. Because somehow I don't think the Beast is going to sit back and let you two have your happy ending.'

Adam could hardly wait for lunchtime so he could phone Melissa. He had just enough credit left for a quick call. There was still no sign of her in school so he guessed she was at home with her mum. He slipped up to the art block, safe in the knowledge that he could hide in the store away from the Beast and that even if Ms Havens caught him she probably wouldn't confiscate his mobile. She was pretty cool for a teacher.

Melissa answered on the second ring. She didn't say hello but hissed, 'Sssssssh! Wait a second.' Adam stood and waited, hearing a door closing quietly on the other end of the line. A TV was on in the background but she must have turned it off because it cut off mid-sentence.

'Sorry,' Melissa said, still speaking quietly. 'Mum's asleep and I didn't want to wake her.'

'How is she?' Adam said. He wished he could forget the dreams he'd had months earlier, before Melissa's mum had been diagnosed. He still didn't *understand* the dreams or why he'd had them but he really hoped they didn't mean that Melissa's mum was facing a death sentence.

'She's OK, I think. But she has a cold so I stayed home with her. She has to be really careful after chemo because her immunity is low and she picks up loads of stuff. I told her to stay in bed after lunch.'

'She's really lucky to have you.' Adam's throat felt lumpy. Sometimes he felt so sad for Melissa. She hadn't seen her dad in years and the only other family she seemed to have was her aunt.

'Yeah but I'm lucky to have *her* too.'

'Yeah.' Adam sighed. He wanted to offer to call round and help her, like a normal boyfriend would – but he couldn't. He might get away with it a couple of times but his family would start asking questions and then he would either have to lie or get caught. Then he thought about Caitlyn's text the day before. *Chicken.* Maybe Caitlyn was right.

'So how was your weekend?'

'Yeah, it was good. Just a big family thing. Lots of food. What about yours?'

'It was OK. I got an extra shift yesterday and then my aunt came round for tea. It was nice.'

There was a pause. Why did it feel awkward? It wasn't normally awkward talking to Melissa. Adam tried to think of something interesting to say but nothing felt quite right. Instead he blurted out the important stuff. 'So you weren't in this morning but I think we have to get our passports in. For the Japan trip. We have to hand them in next week.'

'Oh right.' Silence on the end of the line. Then Melissa cleared her throat. 'Yeah, I need to see about that.'

Adam held the phone to his ear, waiting for her to say something else. When she didn't he tried to keep his voice light and jokey. 'What's to see about? It's a nearly free trip to Japan! Pack your bags!'

Melissa sighed. 'I don't know if I can go, Adam.'

Adam stared straight ahead, not seeing anything. 'What do you mean? They're paying for the whole thing! The guy in Japan? The one that used to go to school here? He's paying for everything. Seriously, *everything*. We don't have to buy a thing unless we want to.'

'I know that. It's not the money. It's . . . my mum.'

'But your mum wants you to go. She *told* you she wants you to go.'

'Yes, she does. But what if something happens to her when I'm away?' There was something unfamiliar in Melissa's voice; something he hadn't heard before. Anger. Proper, burning anger, bubbling just below the surface of her words. 'Who's going to look after her? Who's going to get food or clean stuff or make dinner if I'm in Japan? Who's going to make sure she hasn't fallen in the shower? Who's going to pick up her medicine from the chemist?'

'But your aunt is there . . . Couldn't she –'

'My aunt lives an hour away. She works shifts. She's already used up all her holidays looking after Mum so I could work over the summer. She can't just drop everything! Between the two of us we can manage but I can't go off to Japan and leave them. Maybe if she was feeling a bit better. But she's always so tired. She keeps picking stuff up – stupid stuff like colds and bugs.'

He knew he should stop talking. He knew he needed to nod and agree and say it was up to her because *it was*. So why wasn't his mouth listening to his brain? 'But you'll never get a chance like this again!'

Another silence, this one somehow harder edged. 'Yeah, well . . . maybe I'll never get a chance to spend a week helping my mum again. I won't be going to Japan, Adam. Not unless there's some kind of miracle. And after the last few months, I don't *believe* in miracles.'

The line went dead and Adam's phone screen lit up. *Call ended*. He stared at it, appalled. Had he really just done that? Had he really just had a go at Melissa because she wouldn't leave her mum and come to Japan with him? Leave her mum with *cancer* when she didn't want to?

He felt sick. What was the matter with him? Why had he tried to persuade her? *Because I want to see her. I want to hang out with her for a whole week, before I have to leave school and NEVER SEE HER AGAIN!*

'It's not up to you!' he hissed out loud at the voice, knowing it was crazy; knowing he was fighting a war with himself. 'It's up to her.'

The voice at the back of his head shut up. It couldn't argue, not really. But just because it was quiet didn't mean it agreed with him. He could practically hear it folding its arms and sulking.

Adam sighed. He should have realised by now. Every time he thought something was going to go right, he was virtually guaranteeing it would all go wrong.

Chapter 9

s the week went by, there was no sign for Adam that things were going to get better. His teachers, apparently furious that the pupils had enjoyed their summer holiday, were piling the work on at a rate never previously witnessed by him and his friends. Even Spike, who had a virtually photographic memory, complained that he was having to work in the evening, thus taking him away from his hacking community and plots for world domination.

Melissa was back in school on Tuesday morning. Adam had gambled that she would be and deliberately got the earliest possible bus so he could be waiting for her at the bottom of the school drive. When she saw Adam, instead of smiling and falling into his arms as hoped, she frowned. Adam could understand why she was angry.

He blurted his apology out straight away. 'I'm sorry. I was a total moron yesterday. I know why you don't want to go to Japan. I'm an idiot.'

Melissa blinked at his machine-gun style delivery but her

expression softened. 'It's not that I don't *want* to go. I just don't think I should go.'

'I know.' Adam took her bag and slung it on his own shoulder so he could put his arm around her. She rested her head against him for a moment before they started walking up the drive. This close he could see the dark shadows beneath her eyes. Her face was even paler than usual. He bent his cheek, feeling her hair rub against it as they walked.

'I thought she'd be better by now.' Melissa's voice caught and she tailed off. 'It's the chemo. It kills the cancer but sometimes it seems like it's half killing Mum too.'

'But she'll get better.' Adam felt like a fraud. He would never admit to Melissa how many hours he had spent online, searching for every scrap of information he could find about her mum's cancer, the treatments, the prognosis . . . There was every logical reason to think she *would* get better too – except for his dreams. They weren't like the premonitions he got when his doom sense flared into life. They were just weird and sad and he didn't know why he'd had them.

'I know. I know she will.' Melissa tipped her face back and kissed him but she seemed distracted.

Adam tightened his arm around her and wished they could run away somewhere to continue uninterrupted. He tried not to think about all the kissing he was going to miss out on in Japan. He would just have to cram it into school time instead.

One thing would make that easier. Since escaping from the Beast the previous week Adam had been keeping a careful eye out for his old foe. Every time he saw Michael Bulber his heart started beating faster, getting ready for fight or flight.

Twice, though, the Beast had seen him and merely smirked in his direction. By Friday the strain of waiting for reprisals was getting unbearable. Adam sat in the library with his friends, gnawing on the corner of his thumbnail, trying to figure out the Beast's nefarious scheme.

Eventually he couldn't contain himself any longer. 'OK. I didn't tell you but last Friday after school the Beast came after me with his mates. I got away but I've been waiting for him to catch up with me ever since. Only he hasn't. It's been a whole week and he hasn't done anything worse than give me a dirty look.'

Archie glanced up from his sketchpad. With the Japan trip looming he'd become even more obsessed with manga than before, a feat Adam would have previously maintained was impossible. 'How did you get away from him last week?'

'I legged it,' Adam said without shame. He *did* leave out the bit about hiding in the girls' toilets. He had a feeling his friends would take the mick rather than admire his ingenuity.

'Maybe he's just waiting till he has time to enjoy it.' Spike spoke from behind his laptop. 'Waiting to get you in some dark corner, where no one will hear your screams.' There was an edge of relish in his voice that made Adam wince.

'That's the thing, he's seen me already. He saw me on my own yesterday in the corridor. He could have jumped me then. He just looked at me and kind of *sneered* at me but he hasn't come after me again.'

'It's the Japan trip,' Dan piped up. 'He's keeping his head down because he wants to go on the Japan trip. The Bulb made a big deal about it in assembly. Anyone who gets detention between now and then will get pulled from the trip.'

'But The Bulb is hardly going to ban his own son from the trip, is he?'

'Yeah, but it's the board of governors who have to sign off the list,' Dan said, nodding sagely. 'Our form tutor was going on about it. It's not up to The Bulb. One of the governors is related to the guy paying for the trip and he's the one who'll pass on the final list. The Beast wasn't supposed to be on the list so they're already doing The Bulb a favour letting him go along.'

Adam felt a weight lift from his shoulders. 'Does that mean I'm safe?' He grinned. 'He can't get me. He can't *get* me!'

'He can't get you *yet*,' Spike muttered.

'Yeah, that's true.' Archie put his pencil down. 'Maybe he's going to wait till you're in Japan and get you then. That way he can do it when Melissa's watching too.'

Adam stayed quiet. He'd barely seen Melissa all week because she had been working on a special project for art. He hadn't told his friends that she wouldn't be going to Japan. He was still hoping for that miracle she didn't believe in.

It was a warm, sunny afternoon when Adam left school. As he walked from the bus stop to the house he loosened his tie and slung his blazer over one shoulder. Opening the back door he was greeted by a hubbub of familiar voices. To his surprise Uncle Paddy was sitting at the kitchen table, with Ciaron on one side – and Caitlyn on the other.

'There he is! The man in uniform! Give us a twirl, Adam.' Uncle Paddy was grinning at him.

Adam grimaced and did a mock curtsy. He was cringing

inside. Was it because of the teasing? Or was it because Caitlyn's bright eyes were fixed boldly on his?

'Stop teasing him, you old rogue,' Auntie Jo scolded. 'Or I'll give you some of my bionic wheatgrass and kale smoothie.' She shook her glass threateningly at him.

Uncle Paddy shuddered. 'I'll give that a miss, Jo, if it's all the same with you. You look grand, Adam. If you're going to wear a uniform, at least wear it well.'

Nathanial was sitting at the table with his shirtsleeves rolled up. This was most definitely his off-duty look. 'Our visitors are staying for dinner, Adam. We'll be eating early tonight, if that's OK?'

Adam nodded and threw his schoolbag under the table. 'Anyone want some juice?'

'Caitlyn, get some juice for him, love,' Uncle Paddy said.

Adam stopped and stared. The worst thing was that no one else even batted an eyelid. Why would they? A girl was a girl, even when she was a visitor in someone else's house. What else would she do, other than fetch food and drink for the men? He felt blood running into his cheeks, bathing them with heat. 'No, it's fine. I can get it myself.'

It was hard to even look at Caitlyn but when he finally dared her own cheeks had two high spots of colour. Her hands were hidden under the table but Adam had a feeling that they were clenched into fists. She cleared her throat. 'Can I go and see the dogs?' She met Adam's eye, with something as close to appeal as she would ever show.

'Yeah, they're outside,' Adam said quietly. He slipped over to the fridge and grabbed two cold cans of lemonade. Caitlyn was already at the back door.

'Don't go too far,' Elise said. She looked at Adam and nodded meaningfully at Caitlyn. His cheeks flamed hotter again but he managed to nod and get outside before anyone else could humiliate him.

Caitlyn followed him out with a look of sardonic pleasure on her face. 'Now Adam, don't be taking me too far away. I've my honour to be thinking of. You might find me so irresistible you'll ruin my prospects forever.'

'She didn't mean it like that,' Adam protested – then tailed off. They both knew that was *exactly* what Elise had meant. He handed her a drink by way of apology and she took it with a sidelong smirk.

Sam and Morty were in their pen, lying in the shaded end, panting beneath their shaggy coats. At the sight of Caitlyn they went mad with excitement until she rebuked them sharply in Gaelic. She ruined the effect by patting their heads and kissing their noses lovingly.

They let the wolfhounds loose and followed them towards the paddock in companionable silence. Adam took a swig from his can and pressed it against his cheek, grateful for the coolness. He glanced at Caitlyn as she walked. She was wearing long boots, tights and a printed skirt that skimmed her knees. Obviously it was colder in Ireland than it was here. She was already shrugging off her thin jumper, revealing a black vest top underneath. As soon as they stepped off the gravel onto the grass she stopped and kicked off her boots. 'Turn your back,' she commanded and when she allowed him to look again she had rolled off her tights and was standing barefoot and bare legged in the long grass.

'You get proper summer here,' she said. 'Pity you've no beach.'

Adam smiled. 'I can't imagine my father running round in shorts.'

'Never mind shorts. If we got weather like this I'd be wearing a bikini every day.'

Adam had to put a lot of effort into *not* thinking about Caitlyn in her bikini. 'Why are you here?' It sounded more abrupt than he had meant it to.

Caitlyn shrugged. 'Da said we'll be coming over a bit more. Probably so Ciaron can hang out with your sister. They were allowed into the parlour *on their own* today! Your mum was in and out about two hundred times though.'

'Yeah, but why are *you* here?' All his words were coming out wrong. There was something about Caitlyn; some edge that made him half pleased to see her and half nervous, like he might fall flat on his face at any minute.

Caitlyn raised an eyebrow. 'Well, I thought I'd be welcome.'

'You are. Sorry. I didn't mean it like that. It's good seeing you.'

She seemed mollified. 'Da says I'm spending too much time with the dogs at home. I have to start seeing more people.'

Adam looked at her curiously. 'You sound as if you like the dogs more than you like people.'

'I like them more than I like *some* people.' She smiled. 'You're all right though.'

Now it was Adam raising an eyebrow. 'Thanks. It's good to know I'm better company than a wolfhound.'

'I didn't say you were *better* company,' she retorted and laughed at his expression.

Sam and Morty bounded over, triumphantly bearing their favourite flat footballs. Adam threw one ball, Caitlyn threw another. Within a couple of minutes any awkwardness had gone. He was too busy laughing. Caitlyn grabbed the nearest ball and took off barefoot across the grass, holding the ball above her head to keep the dogs at bay, shrieking with laughter as they pursued her. Adam grinned and chased after her.

She reached the hedge just before him and turned so he almost ran straight into her. Her cheeks were flushed and her eyes were very bright. She was still holding the ball above her head and the sunlight turned her bare arms a pale, golden colour. She was looking at Adam with that same knowing, challenging look she'd had in the reading room and he looked back at her, half hypnotised, the dark green leaves framing her face so she looked like something wild from a fairy story.

Adam's lips were tingling and his hands were tingling and most of his body was tingling. He wanted to kiss her. *But she's not Melissa*, some shrieking, spoilsport voice called from the back of his head, but Melissa wasn't there and never would be. Caitlyn opened one hand and let the ball fall to the grass beside her. The dogs took it and ran but Adam barely noticed because with the same hand she was reaching out and touching his face. Her fingers trailed from his cheekbone down to the corner of his mouth and they smelled like grass and salt and lemonade.

She was still looking at him and he knew she wouldn't do anything else. She was waiting to see what he would do. He wanted to grab her hand and pull it round his back and put his fingers in her hair and kiss her but that voice was still wailing, *Melissa, Melissa, Melissa*, like a siren and suddenly it was getting louder, loud enough that he could hear it over his lips and his hands and the rush of his blood. He took a step back, away from her.

Caitlyn bit her lip and dropped her hand. Her eyes never left his. 'Chicken,' she said softly, without any anger.

There was a strange, pocking, gravelly sound behind the hedge. '*A-daaaaaaaaam? Où es-tu?*'

'Shit!' Caitlyn squeaked – and the moment was broken.

'It's my mother!' Adam lunged away from her while Caitlyn scrabbled for her boots and jumper. She thrust something into his hand and disappeared behind the yew trees.

Adam stared at his hand. It took a few seconds for his eyes to understand that he was looking at her bunched-up tights. 'What the hell am I supposed to do with these?' he hissed after her, then balled them up as small as he could and shoved them into his trouser pocket.

A second later a furious Elise wobbled round the corner on tiptoes, trying to keep her heels from sinking into the grass. 'What are you doing? I told you to stay close to the house! Where is Caitlyn?'

'I'm here, Mrs Mortson,' Caitlyn said cheerfully. Adam hardly dared to look, but she had pulled on her boots and slung her jumper round her shoulders, knotting the sleeves modestly across her chest. She was holding up an old tennis ball. 'Sam couldn't get his ball out but I was small enough to reach it. It was all tangled up.'

Elise's eyes narrowed. She glanced from her visitor to her youngest son but obviously couldn't find anything to reproach them for. At last she forced a smile. 'Dinner is ready. Come, we must eat before the food becomes cold.'

They followed her meekly back to the kitchen.

104

Chapter 10

inner passed off without any further misadventures. Elise allowed them to eat at the kitchen table, which was probably as much admission as she would ever give that Ciaron would soon become part of the family. There was one awkward moment when everyone had finished eating and goodbyes were being exchanged. Caitlyn stood beside Adam and held her bag against his hip, whispering from the corner of her mouth, 'Put my tights in the bag.' Adam glared at her but she nodded down insistently and after a cautious glance around he stuffed them inside as though he were disposing of a live grenade.

It was only after they had waved their visitors off and a grinning Luc slid up beside Adam and whispered, 'Didn't know you had it in you, bro,' that a horror-stricken Adam realised their handover had been spotted. But before Luc could say any more, Nathanial cleared his throat. 'I'd like to speak to you all for a moment.'

Adam glanced quickly at Chloe but seeing that she looked as mystified as his brothers he knew it wasn't going to be a betrothal announcement. With a sinking feeling in his stomach Adam realised it was time for the bad news to be broken to the rest of the family – the news he already knew. He tried to feign the same idle curiosity that Luc was showing. Elise's lips were pursed into a tight line and he guessed that her bad mood earlier hadn't just been because of his and Caitlyn's disappearance.

In the event, Nathanial had obviously decided to play down the significance of what was happening. 'I wanted to let you know that we'll be having a visitor. As you know, the Concilium are charged with overseeing all the work that we as Lumen do. Because of this they sometimes choose to spend some time in individual Kingdoms. I'm delighted to say that we are to have the honour of one of these visits and we will be joined by a Curator in the coming days.'

'Which one? Is it Rashid?' Aron asked. Adam knew that his brother got on well with the Indian Luman, who was one of the younger Curators.

Nathanial tried to smile. 'No, I'm afraid not. It's actually an old friend of your mother's. Darian.'

Auntie Jo put her hands on her hips and stared from Nathanial to Elise and back. 'You're not serious? Tell me you're not suggesting what I think you're suggesting? Tell me I'm hallucinating!'

Nathanial cleared his throat. 'As I said it's an honour to host any Cura—'

'He's not actually staying here, is he? He is, isn't he? Well of all the . . . ' Auntie Jo swore and for once Elise didn't even rebuke her. In fact, as Adam watched, his mother's lips were pursing so tightly they were disappearing into her face, possibly never to be seen again.

'Darian is a member of the Concilium and is entitled to our hospitality,' Nathanial said firmly. Only a slight pulse in his cheek betrayed his true feelings. 'I have been informed that he has made his own arrangements for accommodation but will be spending some time beneath our roof as and when is convenient for him. He wishes to get a chance to speak with us all.'

Luc was grinning. 'He's still looking for a wife, Auntie Jo. Just when you thought you'd been left on the shelf!'

Nathanial frowned. 'That's enough, Luc. Apologise to your aunt.'

'I was only joking,' Luc protested but seeing Nathanial's furrowed brow, he sighed and muttered, 'Whatever, sorry, I was only messing.'

Far from seeming offended Auntie Jo was looking thoughtful. She gave a small, strange smile and said nothing.

'We must be careful,' Elise said suddenly, making everyone jump. 'Darian is a friend of the family – but my family in France. He is no friend of *this* family.'

'Elise, there's no need for that,' Nathanial protested.

But Elise was shaking her head. She looked at each of her children in turn. 'Darian is not here as a *family friend*. He is here as a Curator. Everything must be done correctly. Yes?' She looked at Aron and waited until he nodded. 'No joking. No little stories. No slipping off to meet your friends.' This time it was Luc she was eyeballing and he nodded guiltily. She turned to Adam. 'If you *must* go to your school return immediately and say nothing.' To Chloe, she simply said, 'I know I can trust you, my darling. But if Ciaron visits, there

107

will be a *chaperon* at all times, *oui*?' She waited for a sign of agreement, then exhaled slowly. '*Bien*. He will find our home in order. Our Kingdom in order.'

'Does he think we're doing something wrong?' Aron looked puzzled – and worried. He was the Luman who had most recently come of age in the Kingdom of Britain. 'Does he think I don't know what I'm doing?'

'It's nothing to do with you, Aron,' Nathanial reassured him.

Adam wanted to nod in guilty agreement. *It's nothing to do with you, Aron. This is all on me. As usual.*

'Let him come,' Auntie Jo said suddenly. There was a half-smile playing around her lips. 'He'll find us very hospitable. *Most* welcoming.'

'Jo . . . ' Nathanial began.

'I mean it,' Auntie Jo protested. 'I'll make sure he knows how delighted I am to see him. In fact, if you'll excuse me, I'm going to go and begin my preparations now.' They watched her purposeful exit, Nathanial and Elise exchanging frowns.

'This could be a laugh,' Luc said. 'Anyway, Darian is like the youngest Curator ever. He must be doing something right. I'm going to watch and learn.'

Adam managed to restrain a snort. There was nothing Luc could learn from Darian unless he wanted a masterclass in murderous duplicity.

There was a shift in the room as Mortson death senses flared. Chloe winced and rubbed her stomach. It always seemed ridiculously unfair that women could feel deaths but unlike the men weren't allowed to be Lumen. It was especially unfortunate for Chloe, who was hair-trigger sensitive to any sudden deaths.

Nathanial sighed. 'A car accident. We were finished here anyway.'

'Do you want me to do this one, Father?'

'If you could please, Aron.' Nathanial put a grateful hand on his eldest son's shoulder. 'You'll do your usual excellent work.'

Aron slipped out of the room, looking pleased. The others followed until Nathanial cleared his throat. 'Adam, I wonder if I might have a word? In my study?'

Adam nodded, his stomach clenching. He watched Auntie Jo, Chloe and Luc head for the den, while his mother's heels pocked angrily out of the kitchen. He took a deep breath and followed his father into the study.

It was a cosy, pleasant room in winter, although the afternoon sun had made it too hot for comfort. The heat amplified the smells in the room – old paper, beeswax polish and Nathanial's understated aftershave. The walls were lined with books, including the most important book of all for Lumen: *The Book of the Unknown Roads*. It was a book – and a room – that Adam was much more familiar with than his father knew. Adam had sneaked in here on several occasions, trying to get information he wasn't meant to have.

Not that his father knew about that, of course. Adam watched him open the sash window, letting cool evening air flood in, bringing with it the smell of hot gravel and roses. Nathanial sank into the leather chair at his desk and gestured for Adam to sit down on the low reading chair near the door. It was all so familiar, even the hard edge of the seat base digging into the back of his thighs. How ironic that it should be in this room that Nathanial was going to make one dream come true and destroy another.

Suddenly Adam couldn't bear to hear what his father was going to say, even the good bit. He wanted to stall as long as possible. 'Why is Darian coming?'

Nathanial blinked at him. 'I've already explained that, Adam. Darian is a Curator. He has the right to observe the comings and goings of any Kingdom.'

'Yeah, but just because he *can* doesn't mean he has to. So why is he really coming?'

Nathanial studied him for a moment, then looked away, out towards the garden and the gathering dusk. 'He has concerns.'

'Concerns about what?'

'Concerns about me, Adam.' Nathanial turned back and fixed Adam with a level gaze. 'He has concerns about how I run this Kingdom.'

Guilt threatened to choke Adam. It was the injustice of it. Nathanial couldn't have been a better High Luman but he was being punished because of his son – and of course his wife. It was easier to think about the past than his own role in all this. 'Is this because of Mother? Because she married you instead of *him*?'

'Perhaps a little.' Nathanial smiled faintly. 'I think that may have influenced Darian somewhat. But, rightly or wrongly, he has concerns about how I do things and has decided to reassure himself. And that is exactly what we will do. We will reassure him that all is well and as it should be. That our family is a typical Luman family.' He paused, looking at his youngest son, and then sighed. 'And you must play your part in this, Adam, as we all must.'

'You mean by being a Luman and not going to school.' Hearing the words didn't make them any more real for Adam. Maybe it was the way his voice sounded, like it had been flattened.

'You know why you were allowed to go to school, Adam. To give you a grounding until you were able to become a Luman. I have watched you over the recent months and you have come on so well. The change is remarkable. I'm proud of you, you know. So is your mother, even if she doesn't say it.'

There was a tight lump at the back of Adam's throat. He thought it was something to do with the way his father was looking at him; the pride and affection on his face. There was a time when Adam would have given anything to get that look from either of his parents. Now, to his shock, he realised he didn't want it. He didn't want the weight of expectation it carried. 'But I can still go to school. I can keep doing call-outs as well. As soon as I get home I can be on duty.'

'No, Adam.' Nathanial was shaking his head.

'I can share the jobs with Luc,' Adam said, trying to pretend it wasn't happening. It wasn't that he hadn't *believed* Auntie Jo; it was just that it was different imagining something from actually hearing the words said out loud. 'He can do the jobs when I'm at school and I can do them once I get home. And next year, when I'm in sixth form, I get study periods so I can do all my homework in school and at the weekend. I can work all night if I have to on call-outs.'

'*No*, Adam.' Nathanial was shaking his head and his jaw was rigid. Adam might have felt sorry for him if he hadn't been too busy feeling sorry for himself. Nathanial looked, for just a moment, old and tired. 'We have given you as much time as we could. Maybe we were wrong to let you stay in school this long but given the mistakes of the past –'

'The *mistakes*?' Adam stared at his father, feeling any sympathy evaporate. 'Is that what Uncle Lucian was? A *mistake*?' And there it was, the spectre at the feast; the shadow on the family name. Lucian – Nathanial and Auntie Jo's older brother. The man who should have inherited the keys to the Kingdom and been the High Luman of Britain, but who instead had taken his own life so he could walk through his Light and be free of a Luman world he wanted no part in. It was only Auntie Jo's fear that Adam might walk the same terrible road that had persuaded Nathanial to let him stay in school this long. And now that he wasn't throwing up every time he guided a soul or getting a nosebleed every time he swooped, they thought he was ready to leave his sanctuary behind and become the Luman he was meant to be.

'That's not fair, Adam!' Nathanial looked angry – and hurt.

He was right. It wasn't fair. 'I'm sorry,' Adam said.

His father sighed. 'For what's it worth, I'm sorry too. You won't have to leave immediately; we don't want to create any suspicion. Your mother and I were thinking that when you have your holiday in December, that would be a good time. You have a few months yet. You can explain to your friends that we are moving and you have to change schools. Maybe you can say we're leaving the country.' Nathanial passed a weary hand over his face. 'I'm sure you can think of something more convincing than that. We've never had to do this before. It was much easier with the other three. They just finished primary school and we told their teachers that we would be homeschooling.'

Adam was only half listening. December. It sounded ages away. It usually *felt* like ages away, when Adam was standing at the cold, dark bus stop in the mornings and his friends were bewailing their homework and looking forward to the Christmas holidays. But the days and weeks would blur together and then one morning Adam would wake up and realise that this was it. The last day of school. The last day with his friends. The last day with Melissa. The last day of his own life, the life he would have freely chosen.

Nathanial opened the top drawer in his desk and pulled out a slim, white envelope. He held it out for Adam. 'I hope this might go some way towards softening the blow.'

Adam took it, opened it and silently reached inside. He studied the deep maroon cover, tracing his finger across the ornate golden crest. He turned to the laminated page at the front, studying the clipped capital letters: his name, his date and place of birth. His photo stared unsmiling from beneath his messy, sandy hair. His passport. He'd thought it was all he had ever wanted. He was wrong. It wasn't enough. It wasn't *nearly* enough. 'When did you get it?'

'Just this morning. You were rather heartfelt in your appeals last week. I had already passed on the paperwork to our friends in the relevant places. Once I gave them the go-ahead they were more efficient than I had predicted.'

Adam tried to imagine the 'friends' that Nathanial was speaking of; an invisible network of discreet bureaucrats, routing payments and paperwork through overseas bank accounts and front companies, making sure taxes were paid and updating records while keeping the Mortsons and their assets in the shadows. 'You told me it was too risky.'

'I was assured that when you've finished with it your passport will be "lost", cancelled and disappear without a trace.'

'OK.' So that was that. He didn't know why he was bothering but he couldn't help himself. 'I thought you wanted me to lie low when Darian's here. What's he going to think about a trip overseas?'

Nathanial pressed his fingertips together. 'I've been thinking about that. Before you go to Japan with your school you're going to go there with me. I want you to meet Hikaru, the High Luman of Japan. I know you've come across him before on call-outs but you've never met him properly. The fast-response Lumen in Japan have a long and honourable history because of their unfortunate geological positioning. I think you can learn from them. So, I will say that we have found a way for you to attend your school trip and get to know more about Japanese culture. Hikaru has daughters.'

Adam blinked. 'You're going to pretend I'll be getting betrothed?'

'Of course not, Adam.' Nathanial looked faintly irritated. 'These matters are far too sensitive to be used as some kind of cover. But there's nothing wrong with wanting to learn more about other Luman societies, even if you're doing it in a rather more unorthodox fashion.'

Adam was sceptical but there was no way he was going to talk himself out of the Japan trip. He stood up. 'Thanks for the passport.'

'You're welcome, Adam.' Nathanial looked like he wanted to say something more but stopped himself.

Adam was reaching for the door handle when he found himself turning back. 'Is this *all* because of Darian? Making me leave school now? Because I thought you would let me finish and then be a Luman. So making me leave now . . . Is it because of Darian? Because he's watching us?'

Nathanial sighed. 'No, Adam. It's not as simple as that.' He stood up and walked over to the window, looking out into the dusk. Surveying his castle in his very own Kingdom; the Kingdom Adam knew his father had never wanted but had taken on to save the family from complete ruin. Nathanial rested his head on the window pane for a moment, before turning back to face his son. 'Our world is changing, Adam. The friends we've had . . . people who watched over us. They won't be here forever. And I won't be High Luman forever. So now it's time for you and Luc to work hard and come of age. I want you both to be Marked as soon as possible. Once that's done it doesn't matter what I do. Your futures will be more secure.'

Adam tried to make his face puzzled but he knew more than his father thought. Nathanial was talking about Heinrich. Heinrich wouldn't be there to protect them forever and if Darian found evidence of a rogue in the Kingdom of Britain, Nathanial could lose everything. They all could, unless they played their roles to perfection. 'OK.'

Nathanial came over and opened the door for him. He rested his hand on Adam's shoulder and squeezed it briefly. 'Give the Luman world a chance, Adam. In time, I believe you will grow to love it the way I do.'

After the drama of the day, Adam felt exhausted as he dragged himself up the stairs. It was one of those days when he felt as though all his worlds were colliding together. School, home, Caitlyn, the Luman world . . . Everything was conspiring together to make his life more complicated than ever. He was looking forward to flinging himself onto his bed and just having some quiet relaxation time.

He was therefore dismayed to find his bed already occupied. Luc was lying back comfortably, head resting on every pillow and cushion in the room while he leafed through Adam's chemistry textbook. 'What is this stuff? Is it even in English?'

Adam glared at him. 'What are you doing?'

Luc lowered the book and pretended to study him. 'I'm trying to figure you out. Because most of the time you're just running about going to school and doing your homework and being a dweeb. And we're all looking at you thinking you're kind of stupid but cute, like one of those dancing cat videos online.' He sat up suddenly and swung his feet off the bed. 'Only then *today* you go for a little walk with our "cousin" and when you come back you're handing her back her *tights*. So now you're more like one of those videos with a talking dog and I'm thinking, *What's he up to?*'

Adam scowled. 'It wasn't like that.'

'What *was* it like?' Luc tilted his head and put on his best agony uncle face. 'Tell me all about it.'

'There's nothing to tell.' It wasn't often that Adam managed to get one over on Luc but he had a feeling that this was one of those golden moments. He intended to make the most of it. 'Get off my bed.'

Luc didn't move but studied him through narrowed eyes. 'Nothing happened, did it? Like you actually *didn't* do anything, did you?' He gave a sudden hoot of laughter. 'You are such a *loser!*'

'I didn't want to do anything,' Adam said, ignoring the

116

irritating voice at the back of his head calling him a liar.

Luc sighed and spread his hands in a despairing gesture. 'Look, here's the thing. Don't ask me how, don't ask me why, but Caitlyn has turned into a smokin' hot fox. And again – don't ask me why – she *likes* you. And just in case you hadn't noticed you're going to have to get betrothed – and you are *never* going to do better than that. So whatever she's offering, you'll want to be taking it.'

'Why are you so interested?' Adam sat down at his desk, eyes flicking across his textbooks, wondering which one he should tackle first. 'If you like her so much, why don't *you* get betrothed to her?'

'Maybe I will,' Luc said carelessly. He smirked at Adam's startled look. 'Things are changing round here, in case you hadn't noticed.' His smile turned into a frown. 'Seriously? All that stuff about Darian just coming for a lovely visit. Do you think a *Curator* just comes and stays with a High Luman for the *fun* of it? The Concilium are watching Father. Watching all of us. And if someone has screwed up in the Kingdom of Britain we won't be able to take our pick any longer. So I say again: if anyone half decent is on offer, take her. While you still can.'

He sauntered to the door. 'Oh . . . and I have a feeling I know why you didn't go for Caitlyn. You're still seeing that girl, aren't you? The one from Cryptique? What's she called again?'

'Melissa,' Adam said without thinking, then cursed himself as Luc gave him a knowing grin. 'She's just a friend. I'm not seeing her.'

'Yeah, of course you're not Adam. And of course you weren't sneaking off to meet her over your holidays or anything.' Luc rolled his eyes. 'Seriously, you think *I* wouldn't notice something like that? But you know what – let's just pretend you're telling the truth and you're just *friends*. Well, that's great, little brother. That's brilliant. Because you have exactly *no* future with her.' Luc studied him, not unkindly. 'You know that, right? And you know then that you would be a complete mentalist to turn down Caitlyn, yeah? Have a little think about it.'

Adam watched speechlessly as Luc sidled out of the room, easing the door closed behind him.

Chapter 11

hings settled down at school the way they always did: as though no one had ever been away. Over the next two weeks the weather stayed hot and most people couldn't wait for the last bell to ring. As Adam walked through the Bonehill corridors, he overheard cheerful plans for barbecues and outdoor gigs. There was a buzz of good humour in the air, in spite of the mountains of homework his year were being given.

And he had one reason to smile at least. He had finally handed in his passport and consent forms for Japan. As he gave the envelope to Fenton he imagined choirs of angels dancing gospel-style in the sky above. The fact that his form tutor took the passport with barely a grunt made him scowl. Fenton had no idea of the amazing strings that had been pulled to get it!

So, Adam was definitely going to Japan. He wanted to be happy about it but he had so many other things weighing on his mind, each of them a potential catastrophe in the making.

First of all was the constant worry about Darian. There had been no sign of the Frenchman in the Kingdom of Britain – or if he *had* been lurking, Nathanial wasn't telling anyone. Adam was determinedly ignoring the few whispering premonitions he received. He knew how to block them out; he'd been doing it for years and school was always a welcome distraction. He tried not to think about the people he was condemning to death.

One premonition was still troubling him – the image of Melissa's mum. Usually his doom sense flared because someone was about to die, fairly close to where he was. The more people were going to die, the further away he could feel them. But this one was completely different. He'd known about it months ago, before he was even going out with Melissa. But her mum seemed to be responding well to her treatment, apart from the setbacks when she caught infections. There was no reason to think that she was going to die.

Adam gave up trying to figure it out. It was a mystery but it wasn't something he could solve. His other premonitions had given him a chance to *do* something – change things in some way. But what could he do about cancer? Not unless – and here he felt inspired – it was some kind of weird sign from the universe that he was supposed to stay on at school and become a doctor. Maybe he would be an oncologist.

The more pressing issue was worrying about his own potential death. Yes, he was going on the Japan trip – but so were both The Bulb and the Beast. There still hadn't been any moves by his nemesis but Adam had no doubt that he was planning something terrible. The fact that the Beast was showing so much self-control was more of a worry than anything else. He was obviously saving himself for something horrendous.

Dan was becoming obsessed with it too. 'We need another

Wonderfish. Something to distract him.' It was break on Friday and the weather was scorching. Most people were outside lapping up the sun so the library was cool and quiet. He turned to Archie. 'Can't you send him some of your pictures? Then he'll think there's a Japanese Wonderfish waiting for him. He'll be too busy taking more photos of himself to worry about torturing us.'

'He's not getting any more of my pictures.' Archie's voice was flat.

'He wouldn't fall for it anyway,' Spike muttered. 'Thanks to big mouth practically telling him the whole thing was a fake.'

Archie scowled and coloured his picture hard enough to dent the page. 'Well, why don't *you* do something about it?'

'Too busy,' Spike mumbled. He closed his laptop and yawned. 'There's this group I found out about. They're like mega-hackers. Ultra-hackers. And I want in. But I've got to pull off something major. Plus I'm having to waste way too much time stringing The Bulb along.'

'String along how?' Adam didn't want to think about The Bulb. It was bad enough worrying about The Bulb's psycho son.

'He's driving me mad emailing the Sensai. I ignored him for months – I pretended the Sensai was on some ninja retreat in the mountains – but he's getting pretty crazy now. Emailing all the time, begging to know when they'll meet up. So I've had to start emailing some crap to keep him happy. It's all right though. I told him I'll leave him a clue at the Supercomputer Convention so we'll definitely be going there.'

'Genius.' Dan nodded admiringly. 'Can you tell him there'll be another clue at the RPG Exhibition?'

Spike shook his head. 'No, can't do it. But it's all right. I've seen the itinerary and they've kept a free day for us to go to all these different places. Turns out Fenton is into the whole cos-con comic thing.' He looked at Adam. 'That's probably why he looks so rough on Monday mornings. Spends his weekends LARPing. Pretending to be a knight and drinking mead.'

Adam grinned. 'More like pretending to be a cosmonaut and drinking vodka.'

Dan was beaming. 'This is going to be the best trip ever.' His face fell. 'Assuming the Beast lets us live long enough to enjoy it.'

Archie spoke up. 'Who is this Murai guy? Why's he being so nice to us? I mean, he's paying for pretty much the whole trip. How can he afford it?'

Spike snorted. 'He's got so much money he could send us to the moon and back. He owns the airline we're flying on. He owns a train company and a coach company. He owns computer companies and nuclear power plants and department stores and hotels. He pretty much owns a big chunk of Japan.' At their raised eyebrows he rolled his eyes. 'You didn't think I wouldn't find out *everything* about him? Seriously? I wanted to make sure we weren't going to be sold into slavery or something. Anyway, turns out he probably wants us for our minds, not our bodies. He likes having foreign workers. Thinks it makes his teams more creative.'

'We're going to have to get creative ourselves,' Dan said, looking gloomy. 'Otherwise the Beast is going to ruin everything.'

No inspiration came to Adam over the weekend. He'd been dreading Darian popping in for a cup of tea and a bit of murderous conspiracy but the Frenchman stayed away. In some ways it was good but everyone was on edge, especially his mother. Adam tried to keep out of her way as much as possible. He spent most of his days off up in his bedroom, catching up on his homework and trying to make some revision notes.

Japan was still the one, big thing he had to look forward to – although it was in danger of being contaminated by the Luman world. During lunch on Sunday Nathanial brought it up quickly, while Elise was distracted. 'Adam, I've been in touch with Hikaru to try and arrange a meeting. He's a busy man so we'll have to go whenever is convenient for him. I'm just warning you now in case you have to miss some time at school.'

Adam nodded. There was no point arguing about it. It wasn't like he would have any choice. But as he made his way to Bonehill the next day, he found himself resenting the meeting all the same. He didn't know Hikaru. He had a vague sense that he had seen him before, on a job somewhere. He knew that the Japanese Luman had two sons, one of whom had already come of age. Nathanial had attended the Marking although the rest of the family hadn't.

The good weather was still holding. He wished he could spend his lunchtimes walking round with Melissa but for once it wasn't the Beast stopping them. Melissa was fanatical about her art work and wanted to spend every lunchtime she could in the art rooms. Adam could understand this – at home she didn't have the time, space or money to get any work done.

At least they got some quiet time together. The art store was pretty much their only chance of privacy. After a very long and hungry kiss, Melissa pulled away from him. 'Look, I can't do this every lunchtime. I want to but I really need to get ahead with my coursework. Everyone else is doing loads at home and I just can't. I'm trying to do some extra things for Luna Kazuna's gallery show.'

'It's OK,' Adam said. He knew how much it meant to her. In fact, it was one of the things he liked best about her – she didn't need him around all the time. She had her own life beyond him. It was just as well really; she would have found him a big disappointment otherwise. 'When is the show again?'

'November. I'm putting in the painting I did last year but she's letting us submit two more pieces. If she likes them they'll go into the show too.' She hugged him suddenly and laughed. 'I can't believe my stuff is going into a real gallery! And Luna is so brilliant!'

Adam grinned against her hair. 'Yeah, she's really . . . unique.' He could still remember the eccentric artist's visit to Bonehill the previous year. It had involved a werewolf-sized bodyguard, too many cigarette butts and some seriously revealing clothing. He had a feeling it would stay with people for a long time to come . . .

Melissa pulled back and made a face. 'I know you think she's weird but she's really not. Anyway, that's why I have to work so much. But you could come up here on Thursday. And I'm going out on Friday night, with some of my friends.' She hesitated. 'It would be really great if you could come. They want to meet you. Ben has been torturing me. He keeps saying I have an imaginary boyfriend.'

Adam grimaced. He'd been avoiding meeting anyone

involved with Melissa. If they were like Melissa they would be normal and nice and friendly – which meant they would ask questions and want to know all about him. Which meant more lies to more people. It was a depressing thought but when he saw her hopeful face he couldn't bear disappointing her again. 'Yeah, it sounds really good. I mean, I need to check at home. But it should be cool.'

'Brilliant!' She kissed him, smiling as she did it.

'Yay,' Adam murmured. At that particular moment, he would have promised her exactly *anything*.

Adam was still smiling on the bus home. Now that the decision was made he felt nervous but happy about meeting Melissa's friends. Some of them were people she knew from work – and working in Alter Eden and hanging out on Flip Street all the time meant that Adam was guaranteed to be the least cool person there. He didn't care though. The only person he wanted to impress was Melissa – and happily he could do that just by showing up.

But on Wednesday evening his hopes were dashed. After dinner, when he was up in his room working, there was a hesitant knock on the door. A moment later Nathanial poked his head around the frame. 'Sorry to disturb you, Adam.'

'It's OK. Is everything all right?' Adam put his pen down, wondering what had prompted the visit. He couldn't remember the last time his father had come up to the top floor.

'Yes, everything's fine, thank you. In fact, I have some good news. I've just heard back from Hikaru and he's given us a time to call. He's very busy so it's good of him to fit us in at such short notice. We'll be going there on Saturday morning.'

Adam nodded. 'OK. At least I won't miss school.' He hoped Hikaru wasn't an early riser.

Nathanial smiled. 'Well of course you won't miss school! It will be late in the evening.'

Adam stared at him first with puzzlement and then dismay. 'You mean we're meeting him . . .'

'On Saturday morning, Japanese time. In our time it will be Friday evening. We'll be joining the family for breakfast so we'll just have a light evening meal here.'

'But . . .' Adam began – then tailed off. What was the point in saying anything? *Sorry, I can't go and meet the High Luman of Japan, who's graciously fitting us into his busy schedule, because I want to go and hang out with the girlfriend I'm not allowed to have.* It was a lost cause. He gritted his teeth and sighed. 'OK.'

Nathanial frowned, looking disappointed. 'I thought you'd be happy about the visit, Adam. It's a great honour to be invited to Hikaru's home. And of course it adds credibility to your trip to Japan, should any of the Concilium express . . . doubts about its appropriateness.'

Adam scowled. He had no need to ask who his father was talking about. 'When's he coming? Darian?'

'We haven't heard anything yet. I believe he's been talking with some of the other British Lumen. And if his investigations don't uncover anything untoward, he may well realise his mistake and leave the Kingdom.'

From Nathanial's face he could tell that his father didn't believe that any more than he did, which was just as well. The sooner he realised the threat that Darian posed to them, the better.

And now he had another problem to deal with: letting Melissa down. He went into school on Thursday morning, feeling apprehensive. It wasn't like he hadn't disappointed her before. How many strikes was he going to get before she finally gave up on him?

He broke the news to her at lunchtime. 'I'm really sorry. It's just . . . he's this guy my father works with sometimes. He lives overseas. It's really hard to see him and . . . we have to meet him.'

She *was* disappointed. 'Prison-dad strikes again,' she said, only half joking.

He smiled and kissed her but she was off with him. After a few minutes she said that she needed to get on with her work. Adam nodded and hugged her. 'I'm really sorry. I want to meet your friends. We'll do it another night.'

'Yeah,' she said but her face was saying something different – and Adam didn't like it.

Chapter 12

t was depressing coming home from school on Friday. As Adam ate dinner he tried not to think about what he *could* have been doing right then. There was still no sign of Darian, which was a relief for everyone but no one could completely relax. He could appear at any moment; the spectre at the feast.

The evening dragged by. Luc had disappeared out as soon as dinner was over. Aron was on duty handling the call-outs and Chloe and Elise had gone up to their rooms early. By eleven o'clock Adam was yawning and wishing he could go to bed and crash out with some music on. Instead he was changing into his good suit and trying to flatten his sandy hair into a semi-respectable state. He glared at his reflection in the mirror. Right now he should have been somewhere on Flip Street with his arms round Melissa, kissing her. They should have spent a whole evening kissing and talking and eating pizza, like normal people did. At the very least he should have been taking his clothes off (albeit on his own), not getting dressed and going to have breakfast in Japan in the middle of the night.

He stomped downstairs, seething with resentment, and sloped into the den. Auntie Jo was perched on the sofa, laptop on her knee. Instead of a slasher film there was a different kind of horror playing out on the TV: lots of people in Lycra leaping about in unison and screeching motivational slogans. Adam winced. 'I would so much rather have zombies.'

'A few of this lot are definitely from the zombie genus,' Auntie Jo said. She glanced up. 'All set for your big night out?'

'Not really,' he said sourly. It *could* have been a big night out but Nathanial and Hikaru had thwarted that particular plan. He nodded at the TV. 'Can we put something else on? I mean, sitting here watching it doesn't actually count as exercise.'

Auntie Jo sighed and passed him the remote. 'I know but I like to try and trick my body into thinking it's doing something.'

Adam flicked through the channels until he found something stupid and gory enough to satisfy both of them. They sat and watched in companionable silence (broken only by occasional bouts of mocking the stupidity of the average horror film hero) until Nathanial came in just before midnight. Like Adam he was smartly dressed, although unlike Adam this was nothing unusual.

'Ready to go?'

Adam nodded. He gave Auntie Jo a mock salute as she trilled, 'Have fun!'

Nathanial led the way out into the garden. It was a little cooler tonight and there was a fresh, green smell in the air. Adam looked around at the street lamps glowing beyond the trees. Sam and Morty barked in greeting but fell quiet at Nathanial's command. In a moment all this would be behind them and they would be blinking in the daylight of a new morning in Japan.

They stepped into the Hinterland and the world became even dimmer and quieter. Nathanial turned to Adam. 'Hikaru has placed our Keystone out in readiness so we'll have no problem finding our way. I know you haven't been there before so it might be best if you hold my arm. I have a clearer picture of where we're aiming for.'

Adam nodded, and clasped his father's wrist, feeling awkward. He closed his eyes and listened to Nathanial's voice. 'At the foot of the mountains there's a house in traditional Japanese style. The gardens are laid out in grass and trees. There's a pond with carp and a stone bench beside it . . .' He was talking softly, giving small details, trying to create the scene for Adam until – there, a hook, at the back of his throat. Adam could see it . . . feel it . . . he squeezed Nathanial's arm, feeling the pull of the Keystone where it lay in Hikaru's garden and a second later they swooped.

The sensation was never pleasant for Adam but when he opened his eyes he was blinking in daylight. He put his hand to his nose and when he examined his fingers a single drop of blood was smeared across the tips. Nathanial passed him a handkerchief wordlessly and he cleaned himself up, looking around, mesmerised by their surroundings.

The place Nathanial had tried to conjure up in words was all around them. The house was three storeys of white plaster, interspersed with dark beams, the roof curving on top. They were standing at the far end of a long, ornamental garden, dotted with trees and stone benches. There was a small shrine with bright flags hanging from a cord. Behind them was a vast pond, as still as glass, reflecting the sky above. The mountains rose up all around them, the house a small oasis in an otherwise wild and empty landscape.

They stepped out of the Hinterland and into a new morning in a new world. The air was cold and fresh and thin. Nathanial bent down and picked up the Mortson Keystone placed reverently in the open hands of a stone Buddha, a long, smooth oblong, just a portion of a full-sized Keystone. He slipped it into an inner pocket of his camel-hair coat and they started towards the house, Nathanial murmuring instructions to Adam as they walked. 'We'll remove our shoes when we step into the *genkan* – the entrance porch. Assume we'll bow, rather than shaking hands. Just follow my lead and you'll be fine.'

As they reached the house the door opened. A small, slim Japanese man emerged, smiling at Nathanial. He bowed in greeting and they did the same – but he followed up by clasping Nathanial's hand warmly between his own smaller hands. 'Welcome, Nathanial Mortson. Welcome to my home. It is an honour.' He turned and reached for Adam's hand. 'And welcome to you, Adam Mortson.'

Adam muttered something polite in return, feeling awkward. They followed Hikaru through the door into the *genkan*, the low hallway where shoes were removed. He gestured to a small step up into the main house. 'There are slippers for your comfort.' They followed his lead and kicked off their shoes, stepping into beautifully embroidered silk slippers. Adam's feet just about fitted in but Nathanial's heels hung over the back. Of course he made no mention of it, already moving forward to greet Hikaru's family. There were two sons, Daichi and Hayan, both older than Adam, and two daughters around Chloe's age called Hoshi and Megumi. Hikaru's wife Rita welcomed them warmly. She was small and dark-haired with a strong Spanish accent. She bowed but followed up by kissing Nathanial and Adam on both cheeks.

Adam followed everyone else into a low room with walls made of glass. It overlooked the gardens and the mountains beyond. The floor was covered in smooth, springy *tatami* matting, the edges bound together with pale cord. The walls were painted a soft grey, broken at intervals by exquisite paintings in subdued colours. Two vases stood side by side, each containing a mixture of bamboo and foliage, and the main wall was broken by a recess containing a floral arrangement in a plain vase and a paper plaque hanging above, painted with calligraphy. The whole scene conveyed a sense of calm and order, the same kind of feeling Adam got when he stepped into his father's study.

Rita waved them towards a long, low, lacquered table laid with small bowls and chopsticks. 'Please join us for breakfast.'

Adam tried to kneel the way Hikaru's family did but it was amazing how quickly it began to hurt. He decided to copy Nathanial and sat down cross-legged. Rita and her daughters served food, although it wasn't the kind of breakfast Adam was familiar with. There was rice, soup and pieces of fish. There were vegetables chopped finely and a thin, brown sauce to dip them in. He felt a twinge of relief when a final platter appeared covered in small pastries, along with some chopped-up fruit. Rita smiled at him. He had a feeling this was the kind of food she had grown up with.

They ate and drank, enjoying the morning sunshine. Nathanial admired the garden and Hikaru talked about the principles behind it; the way everything fitted together to create something in harmony with the landscape beyond. There was no sign of any other human life. It was beautiful but the remoteness of it all made Adam feel twitchy. At least in London he could leave the Luman world behind him; hop on a bus and go to school or Flip Street or anywhere normal. Here there would be no escape.

Their visit might have seemed like a social call but Hikaru was a busy man, overseeing a Kingdom teeming with souls. The women cleared the food as soon as it was finished and the two sons bowed deeply and left the room. Rita served tea to her husband and visitors, dark green in tiny, exquisite, handle-less cups. She smiled and padded across the *tatami*, sliding the screened doors closed behind her.

Hikaru's manner changed subtly although his words were still hospitable. 'I am delighted to see you, Nathanial, and most glad to see your son almost grown.'

'Thank you for having us. As you say, Adam is approaching manhood. I hope that in the near future he will be Marked and join us in our work.'

'I believe you still attend a school establishment, Adam?' At Adam's startled nod, Hikaru inclined his head. 'As you can imagine, it is most unusual for a Luman of your age and standing to have continued in education. Unorthodox – but it interests me. I share your love of learning.' He turned away and looked out over his domain. 'Had I been born into a different life, I believe I would have chosen to work in a university. Of course, for a Luman the road we follow is laid out from birth.' His face was placid.

'Adam is aware of this, Hikaru.' Was there just the faintest hint of an edge to Nathanial's voice? 'His time at school is drawing to a close and soon he will fully commit himself to our work. To ease this transition we have agreed that Adam should have one last opportunity to experience life beyond our world. He will soon be visiting Japan with his friends on a school trip.'

The last words sounded awkward coming from Nathanial's mouth. Hikaru raised his eyebrows. 'That is most understanding of you. Perhaps you have reason to believe this will help Adam's . . . adjustment.'

There was a silence, filled with the ghostly, unmentionable presence of another Mortson who had found the adjustment impossible. Looking at his father, Adam could trace some of the same features he had only seen in his uncle's photograph. The difference was that Lucian's eyes had held the haunted expression of someone adrift.

Nathanial cleared his throat. 'I see this as an opportunity to learn more about our own world too. With that in mind I would like to offer you his assistance while he is here.'

Hikaru nodded. He picked up the porcelain teapot and poured more of the green tea into Nathanial's cup. When he put it down Nathanial immediately poured tea into Hikaru's cup in return. The Luman murmured his thanks. His face was impassive but his eyes had narrowed a little. He looked like a man who was puzzling over something. Nathanial didn't seem surprised at this but sat drinking his tea. Adam tried to do the same but the tea had a rich, mulchy taste that made him grimace. He set the cup down.

At last Hikaru nodded. 'Thank you for your generous offer.

I have little knowledge of the kind of visit your son will make but I imagine he will be with his fellow pupils at most times?' At Adam's nod he frowned a little. 'It would seem important to be discreet about our Luman world and take no action that might reveal it for scrutiny. I believe there will be limited opportunity for Adam to accompany me without arousing suspicion – but if such an opportunity should arise,' and he turned to Adam, 'I invite you to visit us here.'

Adam glanced at Nathanial and at his father's slight frown he said, 'Thank you.'

Hikaru turned to Nathanial. 'And as much as it is in my power to do so, I will watch over Adam while he is in my Kingdom.'

'Thank you, Hikaru.' Nathanial looked satisfied. He picked up his tea and raised it in a toast to the other man. 'We are grateful for your kindness.'

Adam took his own cup and managed a swig of the cabbagey tea. He tried to channel Auntie Jo and not breathe through his nose. It helped a bit.

Their meeting was at an end. Hikaru stood and they followed him back to the *genkan*, sliding their feet back into their shoes. Outside in the ornamental garden they strolled across the grass and along the edge of the pond, admiring the reflection of the mountains, listening as Hikaru explained a little about the history of the house, which had been in his family for generations; a long, unbroken line of High Lumen. Adam stared up at the morning sky. In a few minutes they would be plunged back into the darkness of London at night.

At last they came to the stone Buddha. Nathanial reached into his pocket and gave the Keystone back to their host. Hikaru gestured at the Buddha's upturned palms. 'When you return to Japan your Keystone will be here, Adam. You may visit us whenever an opportunity presents itself. You will be most welcome.'

Adam bowed, finding it more natural now, especially when Hikaru did the same. His father was bowing too but once again he clasped Hikaru's hand as they murmured the traditional parting words between Lumen, 'Our Light is your Light, brother.'

At Nathanial's nod, Adam clasped the keystone round his neck and stepped forward into the Hinterland. When Nathanial joined him, they watched Hikaru raise his hand in a final salute, then turn and walk back towards the house. Adam opened his mouth to speak but Nathanial shook his head and said softly, 'Home first, please.' A gentle reminder that this wasn't their Kingdom and that the Hinterland wasn't as private as it seemed.

They swooped with ease, the Mortson Keystones beneath the London house acting as a homing beacon. Adam blinked and squinted as they returned to the physical world, stepping into the night air and the crunch of gravel beneath their feet. The dogs raised their heads in greeting, roused from sleep but too comfortable to stand. Adam followed his father into the kitchen and stared at the clock. It was almost two a.m. and the house was silent.

Elise had left them a flask of hot milk and honey. As Nathanial poured a cup, he finally spoke. 'That went well. Don't worry that Hikaru didn't seem keen to bring you on jobs. He gave you permission to be in his Kingdom and that's the main thing.'

Adam stared at his father. Stupid as it seemed, it hadn't occurred to him that Hikaru, as High Luman of Japan, could have kept him from being in the country. After all, Hikaru was responsible for everything the Lumen there did, just as Nathanial was responsible for managing the Kingdom of Britain. 'What would you have done if he hadn't?'

Nathanial stifled a yawn. 'I hoped the situation wouldn't arise. There's a long spirit of co-operation between our Kingdoms.' He smiled faintly. 'Besides, Rita loves London. If we returned their Keystone and withdrew their visiting rights, she would have made her displeasure clear. Like most of us, Hikaru is a practical man. He believes in keeping his wife happy.'

Adam grinned. 'I'm going to bed. Goodnight.'

'Goodnight.' As Adam reached the door, Nathanial called him back. 'Remember, Adam, you will be a guest in Hikaru's Kingdom. You MUST abide by our laws or risk ruining Hikaru's reputation.' Just as Adam's heartbeat quickened, wondering what his father knew, Nathanial continued. 'I haven't forgotten your over-zealous attempt to guide the suicide bomber on your own, back in the springtime. I was able to protect you but the Japanese are sticklers for rules. If you try to guide souls on your own, he *will* report you to the Concilium.'

Adam blinked at him, then nodded. As he climbed the stairs to bed, he almost laughed. If only his father knew all the things he'd done, he would realise one solo guiding job was the least of his worries. If he knew there should have been lots of other people stepping into their Lights that day he would have been apoplectic. It didn't matter though; with Darian snooping about, Adam was going to be the best-behaved junior Luman in history.

He promised himself there would be no trouble, lying on his bed, staring through the darkness at the ceiling. No trouble at all.

Chapter 13

n Saturday morning Adam woke up late. It was weird, blinking into the morning light all over again. He glanced at his alarm clock and added nine hours. It was early evening in Japan. Hikaru and his family would be eating dinner together while Adam was about to get up and have his second breakfast. Hopefully this one would come with normal tea, not the cabbagey green stuff.

As soon as he walked into the kitchen he knew something was wrong. Auntie Jo was sitting at the table, swirling a lurid purple smoothie round in a tall glass. Elise and Chloe were standing beside her, poring over a battered cookbook and exchanging rapid-fire bursts of French, the way they tended to when they were talking about food. They looked up when Adam came in but didn't speak, so it was left to Auntie Jo to break the bad news. 'We have a guest for dinner tonight. Friend of the Mortsons, Darian DuSnoop.'

Adam felt sick, the way he always did when Darian's name was mentioned. 'Great.' What else was there to say? He could hardly come clean, apologise and admit that it was all his fault that they had an unwelcome visitor to look forward to.

Elise frowned and looked at Adam. 'Your father said that your visit to Hikaru was a success. I am glad for you but make no mention of it to Darian tonight. It will only raise awkward questions about your insistence on attending school.'

'Let him enjoy it, Elise,' Auntie Jo said. 'The trip is Nathanial's parting gift.'

Adam scowled. 'It's Yoshimi Murai's gift. He's the one paying for it.' Auntie Jo raised an eyebrow but didn't say anything.

Chloe looked up, face curious. 'What are you going to do when you finish school?'

Adam shrugged, feeling his spirits slip down another notch. 'Whatever I'm told to do.' His voice sounded flat.

Elise pursed her lips. 'You will do what your brothers do and every other Luman your age. You will prepare for your Marking! Now, *concentre-toi un peu!*' She tapped her finger on the cookbook, drawing Chloe's reluctant eyes back to the yellowing pages. The big decision of the day was whether to serve veal or venison.

Adam grabbed a banana and left them to it.

Adam spent most of the day lurking in his bedroom. He tried to phone Melissa a couple of times. He knew she was working but he hoped she would take pity on him and ring back on her break. When she didn't his general gloom deepened – along with his hatred of Darian.

It was so tempting to blame Darian for all his woes. Without his sudden interest in the Mortsons, things could have continued as they were. Adam could have waited years before he ever had to be Marked because there would be no threat to Nathanial's position as High Luman. Heinrich might be stepping into his Light soon but without an enemy the Mortsons wouldn't *need* his protection. And if Adam could have stayed on at school, just maybe he could have gone to university. Somewhere far away from London; somewhere he could have a normal life, have friends and a girlfriend, totally removed from the Luman world.

Now everything was in jeopardy. Not just his own dreams but his family's position in their world. He hadn't forgotten Luc's words after Uncle Paddy and Ciaron and Caitlyn's visit. *Things are changing round here, in case you hadn't noticed . . . The Concilium are watching Father. Watching all of us. And if someone has screwed up in the Kingdom of Britain we won't be able to take our pick any longer . . . You know you have exactly no future with Melissa, don't you? You are never going to do better than Caitlyn . . . Whatever she's offering take it.*

Luc wasn't a saint but he wasn't stupid either. Sometimes he had a knack for seeing things more clearly than Adam would have liked. For now, his brother was assuming another Luman was the one making mistakes and drawing the Concilium's eyes to the High Luman. The thing that saved Adam from suspicion was, as always, his infamous uselessness at being a Luman. Still, he was getting better at it. He couldn't hide behind his nosebleeds and vomiting fits forever, especially now that they were less frequent.

And there was the problem. Blaming Darian was easier than facing up to his own share of the responsibility. Adam was the one who had broken Luman law over and over again. He was the one giving Darian the excuse he needed to strike. As he put on his dress suit and tie, Adam glared at himself in the mirror and promised himself: *No more. No more interfering. No more snooping. From here on in, I am the perfect Luman-in-training.*

His family was waiting in the hall looking tense, with the exception of Auntie Jo, who was nowhere to be seen. Elise was tight-lipped, straightening ties and re-pinning an errant strand of Chloe's hair. Nathanial was talking to her in a low voice, trying to reassure her. 'It's not a formal evening, my dear. I think it would be better to wait for him in the parlour. A simple family meal is all he is coming here for.'

'*Non.*' Elise shook her head, ripping out another hairpin, making Chloe wince. She bent the pin open between her teeth and slid it back into place. 'Everything must be *comme ça*. Just so. We will give him no reason to complain about our hospitality. He is our honoured guest and we will welcome him.' She spat out the last words, her cheeks flushing.

Nathanial nodded and rested his hand gently on the back of her neck. 'As you wish.' He turned to Adam and cleared his throat. 'Adam, would you mind calling your aunt? I'm not sure where she is.'

'No need,' a voice trilled from the top of the stairs. 'I'm on my way!'

Adam turned – and gawked. He would have liked to see the expression on everyone else's face but he couldn't tear his eyes away from the vision on the stairs. He suspected everyone else was looking pretty similar to him – their eyes and mouths gaping.

Auntie Jo glided down the stairs like a film star. She had ditched her kaftan and clumpy shoes, settling instead on a fuschia pink silk dress and silver heels. Her hair had not only been washed but brushed as well and for the first time in living memory she was wearing a full face of make-up. Adam stared at her, mesmerised. Sometimes you got so used to seeing a person one way that you forgot they could be someone else. This Auntie Jo wasn't the one from the den, watching her zombie films or exercise DVDs. This Auntie Jo was a throwback to the past; an older version of the Auntie Jo from her photo, the one where she stood laughing and sparkle-eyed between her two brothers.

Luc broke the silence by wolf-whistling, making everyone jump. Elise frowned and swatted his arm. 'Enough! Quickly, Josephine. Darian will be here momentarily.'

Auntie Jo shrugged and took her time. At the bottom of the stairs she paused and checked her reflection, licking lipstick off her teeth. Every time she moved she wafted jasmine perfume all around her. She met Adam's eyes in the hall mirror. 'What's wrong? Can't your aunt get glammed up once in a while?'

Adam grinned. 'You can if you want to.'

'You look very nice, Jo,' Nathanial said. He sounded tired.

'You look like you're on the pull,' Luc murmured, just loud enough for Adam and Auntie Jo to hear. Adam's eyes widened even further but Auntie Jo gave a small, secret smile and said nothing.

The door knocker crashed against the hard wood. Adam looked around his family – Nathanial impassive, Elise pale and tense, Auntie Jo and Luc smirking, Aron and Chloe looking worried – and from nowhere felt a sudden, fierce wave of love. There was no time to consider it or question it or even be embarrassed about it. This was his family. He would not let them down. Darian would not catch him out.

At Elise's nod, Aron opened the door so Darian could step inside. Adam bit his lip, trying to stifle the hatred he felt just being in the Frenchman's presence. No one else in this house knew how dangerous he really was or the lengths he would go to in order to destroy them, only Adam.

Nathanial extended his hand. 'You are welcome to our home.'

Darian smiled with his mouth but his eyes were dead as he shook Nathanial's hand. He turned to Elise and embraced her, kissing each cheek in turn. His face softened for a moment but Elise stood rigid and unyielding. 'Welcome, *Curator*. It is an *honour* to have you here.'

She might as well have slapped his face. Darian took a step back and his expression hardened. He nodded at the others without greeting them. 'The honour is mine.'

It was Auntie Jo who rescued the situation. 'This way, Darian, please. Let me get you a drink.' She bustled through to the parlour, one hand resting on Darian's arm. Adam noticed that her nails were painted the same hot pink as her dress. He exchanged glances with Luc. Auntie Jo hated Darian more than any of them. She wasn't being this nice out of affection.

The atmosphere in the parlour was thick enough to cut with a knife. Adam tugged at his collar, feeling like he might choke to death on the tension in the air. Conversation was stilted in the extreme but Nathanial and Auntie Jo persevered while Elise made herself scarce in the dining room. Adam had never seen her so nervous before. How could Darian bear it? And yet the Curator seemed relaxed. Of course, why wouldn't he be? He was the predator, not the prey.

And then, just as Adam had reached screaming point, there was another thunderous knock at the door. Adam's heart hammered madly in sympathy. Nathanial frowned, looking confused. Elise dashed out of the dining room. 'I shall answer. Please, enjoy your drinks.'

The parlour was silent. They listened to the front door opening, then Elise's voice sounding light and happy when a deeper male voice responded. The door closed and Elise returned to the parlour. Her cheeks were flushed and her eyes were brighter. 'We have another guest!' She gestured behind her as Heinrich came in.

He smiled around the parlour, nodding at Darian. 'I hope you will forgive my intrusion. I wanted an opportunity to speak with you and when Elise mentioned that you would be joining the Mortsons for dinner I requested an invitation. I was not certain I could attend, hence the surprise.'

Adam glanced at his father, expecting Nathanial to look relieved, but instead he looked angry. He tried to imagine himself into Nathanial's position, and realised, dismayed, that this looked exactly like it was – Heinrich rushing to the Mortsons' defence because they needed protecting. Making Nathanial look weak, like he had something to hide. Making Darian even more determined to get to the bottom of things.

Elise knew it too. She was talking too loudly and too quickly, chattering gaily as she poured Heinrich a drink and positioned him next to Darian, avoiding meeting her husband's eye. She announced that the dinner would be served shortly but instead of helping with the food, Auntie Jo lingered in the parlour, standing between Darian and Nathanial. Each time Darian spoke she nodded, smiled or laughed as though his every sentence was the most fascinating thing she had ever heard. From anyone else Darian might have been flattered but the way Auntie Jo kept clutching his arm and giggling was making him look distinctly unnerved.

'What the hell is she doing?' Luc hissed.

Adam shrugged. Auntie Jo's mind was unfathomable at the best of times. The only thing he was sure of was that she was up to something.

Her plan notched up a gear when they went into the dining room. The long table was beautifully laid as ever but Auntie Jo ignored her usual seat and sat down beside Darian. There was a long, awkward silence. Luman protocol was absolutely clear on who sat where – the host and guests of honour at the top of the table, followed by the hostess, followed by sons and unmarried females. Auntie Jo was literally bottom of the pile in the Luman world – but she was sitting beside Darian, ignoring his horrified glances. Adam squinted at her, frowning. There was only one time an unmarried woman could freely sit beside a male guest: when he was also unmarried and an understanding existed between them or was in the pipeline. A betrothal.

Elise walked into the dining room, holding a soup tureen – and promptly stopped as though she had run into a brick wall, glaring in disbelief at Auntie Jo. 'Josephine . . .' she began and tailed off, obviously wondering how to proceed without making a scene. She glanced from a tight-lipped Darian to Heinrich and Nathanial, who were both showing abnormal levels of interest in their napkins.

'I'm fine thank you, Elise,' Auntie Jo said easily. 'I'm just

145

enjoying what Darian has to say.' And when Darian reached for his napkin, shaking it tersely into his lap, she *winked* at Elise and picked up her own napkin.

Elise stared at her for a long moment, then nodded and placed the tureen on the table. She began serving soup with the stunned look of a wounded soldier, while Chloe passed fresh bread around.

Adam had endured many strange and painful formal meals but this one had to be right up there with the worst of them. It was like the women in his family had temporarily lost their minds. Elise sneakily inviting Heinrich along, Auntie Jo flirting with Darian . . . What was next? Was Chloe going to start tap-dancing up and down the table?

He counted off the courses, praying for the meal to end. Conversation was laboured, with Heinrich and Elise talking at admirable length about the weather. The venison was cleared and delicate fruit pastries followed. When the men finally stood up to go to the drawing room there was an almost audible gasp of relief.

Adam let the others lead the way out of the dining room and followed at a distance. Instead of climbing the stairs he waited for a clear moment and fled into the den, slumping down on the battered sofa, feeling his food churning uneasily in his stomach. How was he going to avoid Darian tonight? Usually they were in a much bigger party so it was easier to lie low. Tonight, though, he knew it would be better to go upstairs and answer any questions Darian had with a polite smile on his face, letting the lies drip off his tongue like syrup. Pretending the whole row in Ireland hadn't happened.

There were voices outside in the hall, female voices, and the sound of glasses clinking. His mother, aunt and sister were taking drinks upstairs. He knew he had to go up. He would be missed. It was so obvious he wasn't there. But somehow, as the soup and venison roiled and turned in his stomach, Adam couldn't make his feet move. He was going to betray them all. Some word or gesture would give him away and Darian would know once and for all that he was guilty.

Time was passing. Adam put his head in his hands, feeling shattered. He had to get it together but he couldn't do it. It was all very well deciding to lie but it was starting to wear him down. He was lying to everyone, everywhere. Lying to his friends, lying to Melissa, lying to his family. Now he was lying to the Concilium too. It was too much. How many lies could you tell before you began to lose sight of what was true?

There were footsteps on the stairs. Adam sat up, alert. It was a heavy male tread, pausing every few steps, as though the person was trying to be quiet and listen. Adam knew who it was straight away. Who else would be sneaking about the house other than Darian? He almost ran to the door but some instinct propelled him behind the sofa instead, pushing himself into the narrow gap against the wall.

He had barely settled when the door opened. He couldn't see but he could hear the long pause as the visitor surveyed the room; several footsteps and there was the sound of someone moving books and DVDs on the shelf. Another long pause. Adam imagined Darian staring around the room, searching for something and not finding it. The footsteps retreated through the door and into the hall.

Adam waited, counting to ten, to make sure it wasn't a trap to draw him out but as the footsteps continued along the hall he had a sudden flash of insight. He knew where Darian was going – Nathanial's study. He crawled out from his hidey-hole, brushing dust off his jacket sleeve and scuttled to the door, then hesitated. What was he going to do? Burst out and confront Darian? Surely there was no need. What could Nathanial have in his study that would be incriminating? He hadn't done anything wrong. Maybe it would be better to let Darian have his snoop and find out that Nathanial was innocent – assuming of course that the Frenchman wouldn't plant false evidence. Adam wouldn't put anything past him.

Still lurking by the door, he heard more footsteps on the stairs. The decision was out of his hands. He stayed where he was, wondering who was there now. A moment later a familiar voice called out, 'Darian! I was wondering where you'd gone.' There was the pock of high heels on the tile floor.

Adam took a deep breath and pressed his eye to the crack in the door. He had been wondering all night what Auntie Jo was up to but he had a feeling he was about to find out.

'I am here to investigate wrong-doing, as you know.' There was an edge to Darian's voice.

'Wrong-doing in Nathanial's study? What do you imagine is lurking in there?' Auntie Jo beamed up at him. 'Well, you know Nathanial would be only too happy to show you. There's no need to be so sleuth-like about it.' She took a step closer. 'But it is nice to finally get you all to myself.'

Darian stared at her, oozing dislike and distrust but too well-trained to be outright rude. 'Have you some confession to make?'

Auntie Jo tilted her head to one side. 'Of course I have but then you knew that, didn't you? It's OK, Darian. It's just you and me here. I know this isn't the usual way things are done but we're both a bit past the giddy teenage stage, aren't we? So here I am, just a woman standing in front of a man, waiting for the words that will set us free.'

Darian sneered. 'And what do you think I have to say?'

'There's no need to be shy, Darian. Tell me why you're really here. What you *really* want.'

'What I *want* is to bring the rogue in this King—'

'You want *me*, Darian. Don't think I haven't noticed. I still remember Aron's Marking ball.' Auntie Jo curled her fingers round his arm like a vine. 'How could I forget it? You whisked me round the dance floor as though I were a feather.'

Darian was gaping at her. Behind the den door, Adam was gaping too. He had the same feeling he'd had when the Beast had spiked his drink at Cryptique: that the world was tilting on its axis and playing tricks on him. He remembered the Marking ball too. He remembered Darian's unwilling waltz with his aunt and her less than gracious acceptance. As for whisking her round like a feather . . . Adam's memory of the scene was more like a tin soldier prodding an angry elephant around the ballroom.

Auntie Jo wasn't letting Darian's stunned silence deter her. 'That night, I saw a side of you I had never seen before. Far from the arrogant, cruel, *vindictive* man I thought you were . . .' and here she tailed off for a moment, seemingly overwhelmed with some kind of emotion. She managed to compose herself and gave him another beaming smile. 'I saw a *different* man. A

149

man who had spent all these years masking his feelings, hiding behind coldness and hostility, just as I had. A man who just needed to be loved in return. And now I tell you – I am *ready*, Darian. I am ready to love you, at last!'

She stood on tiptoe and made a sudden lunge towards Darian, her mouth opening and closing like a goldfish. Darian gave a squawk of something between disbelief and terror and flung himself sideways, backing away from her, wide-eyed. It was a scene Adam had witnessed a thousand times in Auntie Jo's favoured horror films, the hero backing away from the relentless, slobbering mouth of a zombie, and tonight Auntie Jo was that zombie. 'Don't be afraid, my love,' she whispered, moving towards him, her arms stretching out, her face hungry. 'There is nothing to fear but fear itself.'

There was the sound of more feet at the top of the stairs and then a long stunned silence as whoever was there took in the scene below. Adam shrank back into the den, torn between his horrible fascination and fear of getting caught. A moment later he heard Nathanial's hesitant voice. 'Jo . . . is everything . . . what's going on?'

'What is the meaning of this, Darian?' Heinrich's voice was sharp.

'It's OK, Heinrich,' Auntie Jo trilled. 'Everything is fine. Darian and I have been reaching an understanding. We're going to be seeing a lot more of him here.'

'*Non!*' There was an edge of hysteria in Darian's voice. 'I . . . you . . . this is not true! This is the madness of your mind. I am here to investigate, nothing more!' He lapsed into impassioned French, jabbering at Heinrich, pleading for rescue.

Nathanial cleared his throat, following more of the conversation than Adam could. 'I think there might have been some miscommunication.'

'There has been no miscommunication!' Auntie Jo said firmly. 'Only two hearts beating alone for too long, when they should have been beating as one!' Behind the door Adam had a moment of hysteria and clamped his hands over his face, trying to stop his laughter escaping out of his mouth and nose. Auntie Jo had obviously been watching the romance channels on the sly, in between all the zombies.

Heinrich had reached the hall. 'I think it is best if perhaps we leave, Darian. I need to speak with you before I return home tonight.'

'Of course, Chief Curator.' Darian had fallen back on formality, like a drowning man clinging to flotsam. 'Perhaps my thanks can be passed on to our hostess for the delicious meal –'

'I made the pastries, Darian!' Auntie Jo broke in. 'I poured my heart into every sliver of succulent fruit! How I envied those apples as they brushed your lips!'

'Thank you for coming tonight, Curator, Chief Curator,' Nathanial said. Adam imagined hands being shaken and heard the murmur of parting words. As the front door opened, Auntie Jo bellowed, 'Come and visit us any time, Darian! There is *always* a place for you at our table, as there is in my heart! We shall dance again soon, *mon chéri*!'

The front door thudded closed. Adam flattened himself to the wall, wondering how to escape, until Auntie Jo said, 'You can come out now, Adam. The coast is clear.'

He couldn't exactly hide any longer. Cursing silently, he slipped out into the hall to be confronted by his father and aunt. Nathanial was frowning. 'What were you doing down here?'

Adam swallowed. 'I just . . . I felt a bit sick after dinner.' It wasn't a lie.

He hardly dared to glance at his aunt, but when he did Auntie Jo was grinning. 'It's all right, Adam. A performance like that deserved an audience. I have a feeling you appreciated it.'

Adam stared at her. Nathanial was staring too. 'What on earth were you thinking, Jo?' He sounded more baffled than angry.

Auntie Jo sighed. 'I was just being hospitable, brother.' She raised an eyebrow. 'Extremely hospitable. In fact, I was *so* hospitable that I'll be amazed if Darian ever dares to set foot in this house again, without Heinrich there to protect him.'

Nathanial and Adam exchanged glances. Then, without a word, Nathanial turned and walked back up the stairs, almost – but not quite – managing to hide his smile.

Chapter 14

dam was still grinning at Auntie Jo's performance while he sat on the bus to school on Monday morning but any smile was soon wiped off his face when he got to registration. Mr Fenton looked like he'd had a big weekend, judging by the bags under his eyes and the vodka sweating out of his pores, which meant his Monday morning rant wasn't up there with his best. He *did* manage to give them all a miserable booklet outlining the hours of work they should be doing every evening. Whoever had drawn up the timetable hadn't revised their maths or science; each day would have needed at least four extra hours to fit in all that studying.

It was a problem for Adam. He liked his subjects and wanted to do well. He was still hoping for a miraculous change of heart but knowing that he would have to leave school in December made it harder to do his work every night. It didn't help that he was having to go on so many call-outs.

However successful Auntie Jo's scheme might yet prove to be, Nathanial wasn't taking any chances. On Monday evening when Adam got home from school he found his father and brothers waiting for him. Nathanial led them all into the study and closed the door behind him. Adam glanced at his brothers, relieved that they looked as mystified as he felt.

Nathanial came straight to the point. 'Aron, you've done extremely well since your Marking. Your mother and I are proud of you. And now we'd like to see your brothers come of age too. We're going to ask for your help with this.'

Aron nodded, looking pleased but wary. 'What do you want me to do?'

'We're going to split the fast-response call-outs between us. When you go on call-outs, I would like you to take Luc along on as many as possible. I will bring Adam with me. You both need the experience.'

'But what about the rota we have?' Luc protested. 'Aren't we going to get any time off?'

'Not during the day,' Nathanial said firmly. 'You will go with Aron or me on the daytime call-outs while Adam is at school. In the evenings, Adam, you will come with me.'

'But what about my homework?'

'You don't need to worry about that when you'll be leaving school in December,' Nathanial said. He sounded uncharacteristically sharp. 'This Kingdom is still being observed. I want everything done by the book and I want all of my sons Marked and ready to take up their responsibilities.'

True to Nathanial's word, Adam was dragged off on two call-outs that evening. He fell into bed after midnight and when the alarm went off on Tuesday morning it was tempting to just lie there under the covers and doze. He flung himself out of bed and into the shower, keeping the water colder than normal. It worked. He caught his bus in the nick of time.

Melissa hadn't been in the day before. She still hadn't returned his calls from Saturday, so it was a relief when he saw her in registration. Adam lingered in the corridor, waiting for her to come out. He felt nervous. It wasn't a nice feeling. Usually he felt more comfortable with Melissa than anyone but he knew that she would still be annoyed about Friday night. When she came out and saw him waiting, her face fell. Adam's heart fell too. 'Hi.'

'Hi.' She wasn't really looking at him.

'Are you OK?' She didn't *look* OK. She looked exhausted.

'Mum had to go into hospital over the weekend. She never really got rid of that cold. They think it's just a chest infection but they wanted to be sure.' She paused. 'My aunt and I took her home last night. She was coughing a bit but then she fell asleep. I kept checking on her though.'

Adam felt sick with guilt. 'I rang over the weekend. I really wanted to go out on Friday night with you but I couldn't. I wish I had known your mum wasn't well.'

Melissa raised an eyebrow. 'Right. So what would you have done? Called round?'

'Yes,' he said, lying. Lying again. He would have tried. Maybe he would have managed for a couple of hours. Only then he would have come home and had a million questions to answer AND had to sit through a dinner with their friendly neighbourhood psychopath and the Chief Curator.

He could see Melissa didn't believe him. He took her hand,

desperate to make it up to her. 'Can I see you at lunchtime?'

'If you can come up to the art room.'

'I can. I will!' At least she kissed him, briefly. He watched her disappear down the corridor, her bag perched on her shoulder, but her head was drooping.

Someone crashed into him from behind, knocking him into the wall. The side of his head thunked off the concrete and the pain flared out in a bright bloom. When he opened his eyes and turned round Michael Bulber was standing there, surrounded by his pack. He was smiling at Adam with fake sincerity. 'Sorry, mate. Didn't see you there. It was an accident.'

'Yeah, of course it was,' Adam said. His disappointment and pain were crystallising into fury. He clenched his fists, feeling his hatred flow down his arms. It would be so easy to hit the Beast right now. Just let go. Get all the bad feelings out. He imagined it: the impact of his knuckles into the Beast's face; seeing his head snap back and blood spilling from his nose. The satisfying violence of it. The shock on Weasel's scrawny face. Maybe Melissa would come back and see it too.

It was thinking about Melissa that helped him bring his rage under control. She would be disgusted with him. She would look at him like he was a stranger, not the person she fell in love with. She *had* loved him. He just wasn't sure if she still did. The sadness of it diluted his anger. He had worked so hard to go to Japan. Was he going to blow it all now by hitting the Beast? Getting suspended? Getting struck off the list?

He took a deep breath in and blew it out again. He walked past the Beast, blocking out the sound of laughter. 'See you in Tokyo, you little prick!' Bulber called after him.

He counted to ten all the way to class and when he ran out of numbers he started again.

By the time he got to the library at break, news of the run-in had reached his friends. They were at their usual table, looking gloomy. Dan started talking before Adam even sat down. 'We have to do something about him. He's going to ruin everything. I don't want to go all the way to Japan to be murdered when I can just stay here and save myself a flight.'

Adam didn't even have to ask who he meant. 'What *can* we do? It must be great for him. I mean, he's a nutter, but at least his dad's a psycho too. There's no way The Bulb's going to do anything to stop him going.'

Archie was drawing yet another version of his perfect Japanese girlfriend. He raised his head and looked at Spike. 'Can't you do *something*?'

'No.' Spike's voice was flat. 'I'm already pretending to be the Sensai *and* doing some more work in my mum's office in the evening. It's good money but I'm way behind. I'm never going to get into . . .' He tailed off. 'Never mind.'

Dan rolled his eyes. 'Is this the hacker group you were trying to get into? Who cares? There's no point getting in with the hackers if the Beast is going to kill you before you can do anything.'

'But he isn't going to kill *me*.' Spike glanced at Adam and his eyes flickered. '*I'm* not the one he's after. So I'm keeping my head down.'

Adam shrugged, feigning indifference, but it hurt. He'd always been friends with Spike but things had gone so wrong last year. He knew he'd brought it on himself. It wasn't just going out with Melissa (Adam still didn't know if Spike had fancied her, as Dan had claimed) but the way he'd deleted the photo from Spike's laptop. His 'friend' knew he was hiding something. He *knew* he was being lied to. No one liked that.

After break he tried to focus on his work, surreptitiously starting his maths homework while he was in English. By lunchtime he couldn't wait to see Melissa and when he turned up at the art room she seemed pleased to see him too. She was posing for Jack, a boy in her art class. While he snapped photos of her Adam bit his tongue, trying to swallow down his jealousy and frustration. He could still remember her taking photos of *him*, then kissing him. 'Passion', she had called the piece she created. She was laughing and joking with Jack, not flirting, but it was making Adam edgy. He wanted to sweep her into his arms and snog her in front of everyone.

He did get some time with her alone just before the bell went. They slipped into the art store and as soon as they closed the door Adam kissed her. He pulled her in against him, feeling her back through her thin school blouse, feeling her hair on his cheek and the heat and softness in her mouth. She was kissing him back and suddenly he knew that everything was going to be OK. Whatever the magic was that kept two people liking – loving – each other, they still had it.

Someone opened the door and he waved them away. There were titters and the door closed again. Melissa was smiling, her lips curving against his neck. It made him smile too. 'I love you,' he whispered into her hair. 'I'm sorry I've been so crap.'

'Yeah, you have been,' she said. There was no malice in her

words; she was just telling the truth. They both knew it. 'But I'm going to let you make it up to me. I have to work this weekend but the shop is closing the following week for a big renovation. If my mum is feeling better she's supposed to be going to stay with her friend on the Saturday and I don't have to go. I'm going to have the flat all to myself.' She hesitated, suddenly looking shy. 'I thought you could come over.'

'Definitely,' Adam said. He kissed her again, to show her that he meant it. 'Nothing will keep me away!' He didn't care if somebody somewhere created a black hole and sucked the earth out of existence. In less than two weeks he was going to be in Melissa's flat and they would be *alone*.

The door opened once more and he waved his hand again – *go away*. This time a sarky voice replied, 'Adam Mortson, if you ever wave your hand at me like that again, I will chop it off.'

They leapt apart, turning to see Ms Havens in the doorway. She was cooler than most teachers but she was looking annoyed as well as amused. This was their one bolthole in school; they couldn't afford to lose it. 'Sorry, miss,' they muttered in unison, sidling out past her and grabbing their bags.

In the corridor outside he gave Melissa one last kiss. The smile she gave him carried him through two periods of carnage in history and an evening of call-outs and physics homework. Long after midnight he was still at his desk, trying to make sense of light refraction, filled with surprising optimism. They could still make this work.

His optimism continued as the week went on. Nathanial was giving him more and more responsibility on the call-outs, even forcing him to take the lead. Adam didn't want to be a

Luman – but he didn't want to botch anyone's entrance to the afterlife either. He might not have been as calming as Aron or as charming as Luc but as each soul stepped safely through their Light he had a fleeting moment of satisfaction. He had done the best he could. He was never going to be brilliant at this but he would settle for adequate.

School was OK too. The Beast was leaving him alone for the time being, probably being careful not to get busted before the trip. After that, all bets were off. Still, there would be lots of teachers there. He would just try and stay close to one of them and survive. With Melissa not going, there wasn't any point in him sneaking off anyway.

He kissed Melissa goodbye on Friday, grinning when she said, 'One week . . .!' Her mum was getting better and she was bubbly with relief. It was all good. He would see her as much as he could the following week and then on Saturday – they would get a whole day on their own, for the first time in weeks.

The weekend was quieter than usual. There were only three sudden deaths in twenty-four hours which meant everyone was at home and in a good mood. Nathanial's presence always kept things calm. There was one nervous moment on Sunday when Uncle Paddy and Ciaron arrived. Adam immediately looked up, waiting to see Caitlyn appear, but there was no sign of her.

He felt more relieved than disappointed. Things had been going so well with Melissa. He didn't want to complicate things by hanging out with Caitlyn. He couldn't help liking her a bit – even Luc thought she was gorgeous – but she wasn't Melissa. Maybe they could be friends. Just hang out in a friendly way, without any stress or awkwardness.

And in the middle of all this, it was Uncle Paddy who dropped the bombshell, blowing Adam's happiness out of the water.

They were all sitting together at the kitchen table. Elise had roasted a huge beef joint and served it up with a flourish. Everyone was talking. Adam had finished his homework ahead of time and was heaping his plate with roasties and gravy when Uncle Paddy casually said, 'Next Saturday. It was fast work, I'll give him that.'

'When is Heinrich anything other than efficient?' Auntie Jo speared some broccoli on her fork and studied it. 'Broccoli is so much nicer like this. The banana broccoli soup was just wrong.'

'It's starting a bit earlier than usual. Leaves more time for the party afterwards!' Uncle Paddy grinned around the table. '*You'll* enjoy that, Luc.'

Adam cut through the laughter. His mind had been elsewhere. 'What are you talking about?'

It had come out wrong – way too abruptly. Everyone turned and stared at him, Nathanial frowning slightly. 'The Marking ball, Adam.'

'Whose Marking ball?'

'Heinrich's son Alexander is coming of age.' Uncle Paddy winked. 'Don't worry, Adam. I'd say you were too busy dreaming about girls to be listening to us. Whoever she is, you'll see her there.'

You have no idea, Adam thought. He was trying not to panic. 'Yeah, but when is it?'

'Saturday,' Elise said, looking irritated. 'Do listen please. You must all leave your suits out so I can take them to the cleaner.'

'But I can't go,' Adam said. He knew he should have kept

his mouth shut but somehow his lips had flapped in protest before his brain had the chance to hit the brakes.

The silence that followed this statement seemed to last forever. 'You can't go? Really?' Auntie Jo was laughing. 'What have you got planned instead? A space mission? A diamond robbery?'

Luc was smirking across the table with sardonic pleasure. 'Maybe he has a hot date!'

'Enough!' Elise said. She was frowning now. She adored her second son but some things were too serious to make jokes about. 'You go too far, Luc!'

'Sorry,' Luc murmured, doing an excellent impression of contrition.

'What *are* you doing though?' Chloe was studying him.

The pressure of their eyes was squeezing all the air out of his lungs. 'I have . . . I have a study group. At school.'

'On a Saturday?' Auntie Jo was looking sceptical and if she wasn't on board no one else would be.

'It's because it's exam year.'

Nathanial cleared his throat. 'Well, you won't have to worry about exams, Adam. Certainly not on Saturday.'

Adam heard the subtext loud and clear. *You won't be around for the exams, Adam. You're leaving school. Relax and look forward to the ball.* The conversation moved on. Adam stared at his roast potatoes, feeling like he might choke at the sight of them.

Why had he ever dared to believe that something might go right for a change?

School the following day had a nightmarish quality. Usually he couldn't wait to see Melissa in registration but this morning he found himself hoping that she wouldn't be in – so of course, she was. She smiled at him across the room and he tried to smile back but his face felt rigid.

He still saw his friends at break but all he could think about was telling her at lunchtime. She would be furious with him. He had let her down so many times, not because he wanted to but because sometimes these things were just beyond their control.

In fairness, it wasn't just him. Melissa's life was difficult too. She did a lot for her mum – more than most people. She worked as many hours as she could, not because she wanted pocket money but to help pay the bills. *Especially* since her mum had been ill. That was the funny thing, he suddenly realised. They were from different worlds but what they both had in common was a sense of duty to their families; working to help them, not because they had a choice but because they had to.

He went up to the art room at lunchtime with his heart somewhere round about his throat. Melissa smiled when he came in, kissed him and showed him the photos that Jack had taken. She was so happy. *Tell her*, he thought. *Get it over with.* But she was laughing and chatting and a minute later she was sitting on his lap in the store stroking his face and kissing him and the voice shouting *Tell her!* was drowned out by the voice saying *Kiss her!*

And then the bell was ringing and he was in physics, holding his head in his hands and staring blindly at his textbook. *I should have told her. Still, she doesn't know that I know. Maybe it's better if I leave it till tomorrow. Maybe even Wednesday. Then I can say it was an emergency. Someone got sick. And I'll make it up to her. I'll do anything to make it up.*

And then suddenly, in about ten seconds, it was Thursday and he *still* hadn't told her. They were in the art store and she was sitting on his lap, talking, and he was watching her face as she talked and wishing his whole life was different. Wishing he had been born into a different family. Wishing he could be the kind of boyfriend she wanted.

He'd be really good at it. He cared about her. He wasn't scared of sickness or death. He would have helped her look after her mum, without complaint. They could have studied together and hung out, as well as all the other stuff. They were so *right* for each other and it wasn't fair. None of it was fair.

And his face had betrayed him. She was talking about the pizza she was going to make them for lunch and he flinched and she looked at him with her laser eyes and said, 'You aren't coming round on Saturday, are you?'

'No.' Why had he said it like that? It was all wrong. It was too final. He just couldn't bear telling her another lie. 'I have to do something. With –'

'With your family.' She wouldn't look at him.

'I don't want to,' he said, pleading. 'But I can't miss it.'

'Can't or won't?'

'Can't!'

'Just tell them you don't want to go.'

'It's not like that!' he said and now he felt angry. Angry with her, angry with his parents. Angry with his life. 'I have to go. It's a big deal for my family. It's . . . important. I have to be there.'

'I don't get this.' Melissa was standing up now and her face was hard. 'You keep saying you love me but you can't see me.

You make it sound like you're *scared* of your family sometimes. You can tell one of the teachers if they're *doing* something to you. They're not allowed to keep you a prisoner! It's cruel!'

'They're not cruel!' Adam snapped. 'They're just . . . My life is just different from yours! It's complicated!'

Melissa went very still. 'OK.'

'I didn't mean it like that –'

'No, it's fine. I know there's something going on with you and I keep waiting for you to tell me what the big secret is but you never do. And maybe your life *is* complicated but mine isn't exactly easy. You know, with my mum ill and trying to pay the rent and trying not to fail all my exams and stuff.' She turned to walk away.

'Melissa, I didn't mean it!' Why had he said that?! He was following her to the door and they were back in the art room and people were staring at them. Ms Havens was standing beside an easel but she turned and frowned.

'See you, Adam.' Melissa still wouldn't look at him.

'But we'll do something next week? Just tell me what day.'

'No.' And now she *did* look at him. 'This isn't working out, Adam. I really like you but . . .' She shrugged. 'This isn't enough any more. Hanging out in school all the time. I just want a boyfriend who does normal stuff. Someone I can see outside of these corridors once in a while.'

'But I'll do –'

'No.' She was shaking her head and her eyes were shiny. 'You *always* say that and I always listen. And nothing ever changes. So you just do your thing and I'll do mine.'

She was walking away and he couldn't do anything. And

then she was standing beside Ms Havens, who was talking to her, low and concerned, and then the art teacher looked up at Adam and scowled and said, 'I think you should go, Adam.'

And he glared at her, helplessly – and then he realised she was right. So he went.

Chapter 15

dam was miserable; more miserable than anyone had ever been, in the history of the world. A chiding voice at the back of his head reminded him that this probably wasn't true. He had witnessed death, destruction and misery on a scale very few people ever saw, without ending up in the Hinterland for a one-way trip through their Lights.

And yet . . . It *felt* true. It was like all the happiness in his life had been sucked down some kind of drain, in the shape of Melissa's mouth as she uttered those words. They ran on a loop through his head, repeating endlessly. *This isn't working out, Adam. I really like you but . . . I just want a boyfriend who does normal stuff.* Inside his chest was a paler version of himself, wearing sackcloth and ashes, kneeling on broken glass and wailing in anguish. If his heart had hurt before, this time it was a mortal injury. It made it hard to breathe, never mind smile and pick himself up.

At least he didn't have to go into school the day after the dumping. Elise insisted that he stay off so he could go for a final suit fitting. For once he didn't argue. He couldn't have faced a 'normal' Friday when absolutely nothing about it was normal. Seeing Melissa avoiding his eyes in registration . . . Trying to pretend to his friends that everything was OK . . . Forcing himself to sit in his classes and listen to the meaningless words falling from his teachers' mouths.

He had texted Melissa at least ten times on Friday and had finally made himself stop, worried that he was going to look like some mad stalker. In bed that night he had tried to comfort himself. *Just give her time. She'll be less angry tomorrow. There'll probably be a text waiting in the morning.*

Only there wasn't. It was Saturday, the day they should have been spending together, eating pizza and kissing each other. His phone screen was blank and indifferent. He felt sick with misery. He wanted to hide under the covers all day and not say a word to anyone.

And there was the extra dark bit of it all; this particular cloud had absolutely no silver lining. He was not only going to have to drag his battered soul out of bed and force it to eat and breathe and survive another day. He was going to have to dress it in a stupid black ceremonial cloak and drag it to a Marking ball and talk to people he didn't know and dance with girls who weren't Melissa, *even though his heart was bleeding*!

As he stumbled towards the kitchen he caught a glimpse of himself in the hall mirror. Above the black, fur-trimmed cloak his bloodshot eyes and electrified hair looked even more savage than usual. His brothers' laughter from the kitchen sounded like something designed to torture him. He slouched in, seething inside, and the conversation died away. Adam paused, slightly unnerved. He wasn't used to making such an impact.

'Cheer up, it's a Marking, not a funeral.' Luc was crunching through a piece of French toast that was more heaped sugar than bread. Aron was standing beside him, proudly wearing a cloak trimmed with white fur, showing that unlike his brothers he was already Marked. In fact, the last Marking the Mortsons had attended had been Aron's. That day he had been the one getting tattooed but today he would be safely on the other side of the room.

'Whatever,' Adam muttered. He grabbed a banana from the bowl on the kitchen table and forced a couple of bites down his throat. Marking ceremonies could last for a long time and although there would be plenty of food in the evening there would be nothing but drinks before then.

Luc raised an eyebrow. 'What's made you such a little ray of sunshine today?'

Adam glared at him but before he had a chance to answer the kitchen door opened and Nathanial appeared. He nodded, satisfied. 'Good, you're all here. I'm sorry we're going so early but it's a rare opportunity to catch up with people. Do make the most of today, won't you?' He looked at Aron, who nodded and then stared intently at the floor, a blush of colour flaring from his neck up to his temples. Adam stared at him, momentarily distracted from his own suffering. What was going on?

The door opened again and this time it was Auntie Jo in the doorway. For Aron's Marking ball she hadn't made much effort beyond putting on a nice dress (having been frogmarched to Madame Gazor, Elise's personal dressmaker). Today, though, she was having another red carpet moment. She was wearing a long, sweeping dress in a deep wine colour, with panels of black lace set into the skirt. Her lips and fingernails were painted to match the blood-red dress. Her black hair had been swept off her forehead and adorned with some kind of headpiece, mostly red and black feathers and sequins.

'Well, how do I look? Will this little number catch me a Curator?'

Luc grinned. 'Dunno. Depends if he likes his ladies a bit scary. And since we haven't seen him for two weeks I'm guessing he doesn't.'

Adam snorted and turned away. Luc didn't know as much as he thought he did. Darian liked all sorts of scary ladies, including the kind who carried a big knife and cut people's threads, sending them into the afterlife. Still, Auntie Jo wasn't really on a par with Morta. Thankfully she was much less vicious than the Fate had been.

'You look very nice, Jo,' Nathanial said – and it was true. The dress wouldn't have suited everyone, never mind the feather thing on her head, but somehow Auntie Jo was able to carry it off, in a *Bride of Dracula* way.

The kitchen door opened one last time and the missing Mortsons entered. As usual Elise was the epitome of understated elegance, blonde hair swept up into a knot at the back of her neck, resting on the collar of her cream silk dress and matching lace shrug. Chloe looked beautiful too, in a long, blue dress sparkling all over with silver crystals. She didn't look as happy as Adam expected. Maybe it was because of the shiny heels she was wearing. Adam could still remember her complaints about sore feet from the last Marking ball – but he could

170

remember her other complaints too, the ones she hadn't voiced to anyone else, like how she didn't want to go to balls and wait to be betrothed; how she wanted to be a Luman. The novelty of dressing up like a doll was already wearing off. A twinge of sympathy for her cut through his self-pity.

Elise ran an expert eye over her brood, raising an eyebrow at Auntie Jo's splash of colour but wisely not saying anything. In fact, she smiled a little. If she'd been outraged by Auntie Jo's breaching of protocol at the meal with Darian, she had obviously forgiven her thanks to the success of her scheme: keeping Darian at bay.

'You've all been to Heinrich's before,' Nathanial said. 'Keep the image in your mind and you'll be fine. Our Keystone is there as usual, so if you concentrate on the castle you'll feel it.'

They trailed out into the garden. There was a hint of sunshine through the clouds but the air was colder. Autumn was coming. Chloe shivered in her sleeveless dress and huddled closer to Aron, who threw a protective arm around her. They heard a car drive past beyond the high iron fence surrounding the house. Not for the first time Adam was glad of the old trees and shrubs blocking the house from view. The Mortsons avoided their neighbours beyond basic politeness. What would they think, Adam wondered, if they saw his family standing in the garden in their floor-length black cloaks? And what would they think if they saw what came next: the bit where their neighbours appeared to vanish into thin air?

At Nathanial's nod they stepped into the Hinterland. 'Remember the castle,' he began. 'The forest comes all the way up to the end of the lawn. Beyond are the grey walls and the charcoal spires of the towers.' His voice became softer as he gave more detail but this time Adam didn't need it. Heinrich's home was the kind of place that stuck in your memory. It was magical.

He felt the 'hook' of recognition, feeling the Mortson Keystone calling to him across the land and sea in between. Distance meant nothing in the Hinterland because the Hinterland was everywhere and nowhere. He closed his eyes and swooped.

Adam opened his eyes and there was the castle. He was the first of his family to get there – and that was a first in itself. A few seconds later Nathanial appeared beside him, relief washing across his face. When his youngest son had vanished he had probably half expected Adam to end up in Timbuktu. 'You're getting very good at this, just as we knew you would.'

Adam forced a smile. It was true. He *was* getting the hang of all things Luman. It was just a shame he wasn't happy about that, the way he would have been before.

The rest of the Mortsons arrived within moments. They paused for a second in the Hinterland, checking for loose hems and stray hairs, then stepped as one into the physical world.

Luc spoke for all of them. 'This place is amazing but it's bloody freezing!'

As they scurried towards the huge wooden doors of the castle music and voices drifted through the air towards them. Inside they were greeted by a smiling German Luman who led them towards a long, window-lined room overlooking the forest. The castle was surrounded on all sides by dark evergreens, probably an attempt to keep over-eager tourists at bay. Adam knew that Heinrich's family rarely opened the gates at the end of the winding driveway, preferring to stay at home and swoop in and out when necessary to avoid attracting attention.

Adam followed his parents towards long tables laid out with wine glasses and coffee cups. The Mortsons were early but certainly not the first ones here. Marking balls were important occasions in the Luman world, a chance to exchange news, show status and arrange betrothals. To be at the Marking of a Chief Curator's son was to be surrounded by the most powerful Luman families in the world. It wasn't an opportunity to be wasted.

As they approached the table Adam saw two surprising groups of people. First was Heinrich's extended family, who were huddled together, talking in low, angry voices. Beside them stood an even more surprising group: the Concilium. Adam stopped, disconcerted to see Darian glaring at them. It wasn't just Darian looking furious; the rest of the Curators had expressions that would have curdled milk.

Luc sighed. 'Great. They must be running late. Which means we're stuck here even longer.' A red-headed Luman girl walked past, wearing a sparkling black dress. She glanced at him and smiled. Luc gave her the benefit of one of his thousand-watt smiles and muttered, 'Maybe that's not such a bad thing after all.'

Nathanial greeted the Curators, exchanging handshakes and embraces. 'How wonderful to see you all. Has the Marking been delayed?'

Adam couldn't help but notice the black glances being exchanged between the Curators. It was Rashid, one of the younger, nicer Curators who answered. 'Our Chief Curator made the decision that only he would be present at the Marking.'

'I see.' Nathanial seemed bemused. 'And none of the family?'

'Only Alberta and the children.'

Nathanial frowned and nodded. 'I'm sure he has his reasons.' He exchanged small talk while his family helped themselves to drinks.

Adam didn't hear what else he said; his attention had been caught by Auntie Jo, who was putting on an elaborate performance for Darian. The Frenchman was studying his drink as if it were the elixir of life while she smiled, waved and generally attempted to catch his attention. At last he turned his back and talked intently to the Curator beside him.

Nathanial excused himself and the Mortsons retreated from the drinks table. Auntie Jo gave one last beaming smile to her beau but as soon as she turned away she became businesslike. 'What on earth is going on?'

'I don't know.' Nathanial was frowning slightly. 'It seems that only Heinrich, Alberta and the children are in the Oath Chamber. No one else was permitted to be present.'

Elise was frowning too. 'But such a breach of protocol . . . What was he thinking?'

'Well, by law the only people who *have* to be present are the Chief Curator, the new Luman and his father. And the Crone of course. It just so happens that in Alexander's case his father and the Chief Curator are the same person.'

Auntie Jo shrugged. 'Well, as you said, Heinrich must have his reasons.'

Nathanial cleared his throat. 'Yes. I'm sure he has.' If he had his suspicions what those reasons might be they didn't seem to be bringing him any reassurance.

There was a flurry of noise at the entrance. They turned and saw nine McVeys walking towards them, led by Uncle Paddy. The room was filling up and it seemed natural to join them. The Curators stood stiffly along one wall, just as Heinrich's family did, no doubt aware that the same conversation was repeating over and over again. Why weren't they inside, watching the Marking? Why had Heinrich decided to exclude them?

Adam was distracted from the scandal by a more pressing issue, namely Caitlyn. He hadn't seen her since the day in the garden. He could still see her running away from him, the grass weaving around her bare feet and legs and the challenge in her eyes when she had stood pressed against the hedge, daring him to kiss her; the faint lemonade smell of her skin. From the way her eyes darted around, not meeting his, he knew she remembered it too.

He could have kissed her. He had *wanted* to kiss her but he hadn't because of Melissa. And now Melissa wasn't here – would never be here, ever, in a million years and he was stupid, stupid, *stupid* for not kissing Caitlyn when he had the chance. Because, like Luc had said, if Caitlyn was interested he was a lucky guy and he was never going to get luckier. She was smart and funny and gorgeous – although if he was honest she was a bit scary too. There was something sharp and quicksilver about her; something, Adam realised, that reminded him of Luc.

Luc was ready for her. 'Hey, cous. You look nice. That's a great dress. Did you leave your tights at home today?'

Caitlyn glared at him, then walked over to Chloe to say hello, somehow managing to ram one very spiky black heel onto Luc's foot as she passed. Luc gave an agonised whimper and she smirked without saying a word. She ignored Adam completely.

Great. If it hadn't already been the worst day ever, it was now. Melissa and Caitlyn both hated him. Adam stood still, holding a cup of weird-tasting tea as it grew colder and the room grew hotter, filling up with chattering, excited Lumen from every country and Kingdom. His stomach grumbled and he regretted his tiny breakfast. His feet were sore from standing still and his head began to thump. Everyone else seemed to be having a good time. He wished he could flee outside and swoop home but there was no escape. Etiquette was everything in the Luman world.

'Why so gloomy?' Auntie Jo interrupted his misery.

He shrugged. 'It just takes forever.'

'I'm sure it feels a lot longer to the person getting Marked.'

Adam winced but he was feeling too sorry for himself to spare any sympathy for Alexander. 'It's so boring, just standing around waiting.'

Auntie Jo raised an eyebrow. 'Well, you're not really supposed to be standing around, are you? You're supposed to be mingling and talking to people and laughing at their jokes and checking out the girls. You're supposed to be looking for a wife.' At Adam's horror-stricken look she shrugged. 'You seemed quite interested after Aron's Marking ball. I thought you had someone in mind. So did your father.'

Adam groaned inwardly. It had been a useful cover story back when he had needed to find out more about Darian's hatred of Nathanial and obsession with Elise. Auntie Jo had assumed that he was worried the past scandal would tarnish his chances and it had suited Adam to go along with it. He hadn't realised that it would come back to bite him – and that his family were waiting for him to make a move on someone. 'I'm not really in the mood.'

Auntie Jo frowned. 'Well, don't wait too long. Get in the mood. Because if I can tell you one thing about the Luman world it's this: being well-married will not only make you happy, it will make you trustworthy in the eyes of others. And if you hope to follow in your father's footsteps, trust is the most important quality of all.'

Adam stared at her mutely. How could you be trustworthy when your whole life was a lie? His life at home was a lie because he had hidden Melissa and hidden his plans to stay at school and never be a Luman. And at school his whole life was a lie because he couldn't tell his friends or Melissa *anything* about himself, or none of the stuff that mattered.

He glanced sideways and caught Caitlyn watching him. She looked away immediately, colour tinting her cheeks. Adam stared at her for a moment. What would it be like, being betrothed to someone like Caitlyn? Being able to spend time with her and have everyone approve of it? Being able to go on jobs and come home and talk about them, not cover them up. Being with someone who knew the Luman world inside out, with all its demands. Living in the Luman world with an ally; someone who was on your side.

She felt him looking and turned towards him, meeting his eyes with her own. For a long moment they just stared at one another and then Adam felt himself smile. Caitlyn smiled back. Auntie Jo spoke and he muttered something in reply but there was a warm space in his chest where a moment before there had just been misery and loneliness. Auntie Jo was right – and so was Luc. If he *had* to get betrothed, he could do a lot worse than spend his life with Caitlyn.

A ripple of excitement moved through the crowd and a second later a trumpet blew. Adam turned to the far wall, where a flight of steps led up from the room they were in to a plain, wooden doorway. Heinrich was standing on the steps, quite alone, looking down at the crowd below, who were staring up expectantly, waiting for Alexander to appear.

Adam remembered this bit from Aron's Marking. Alexander would appear, his chest a raw mess of fresh tattoo, and be presented as a Marked Luman. The crowd would go nuts. There would be toasts and gifts and general back-slapping and then they would all go and eat enough to feed a small country.

But Heinrich was still standing there and something about his posture was spreading unease through the crowd. The murmur of noise died away, leaving silence. Adam studied the Chief Curator's face and there was some expression he couldn't place, something between joy and terror, like a man on a high diving board poised to jump. Everyone could see it and beside him Elise put her hand to her mouth and whispered, 'Oh, Heinrich, *t'as fait quoi?*' *What have you done?*

Then Heinrich smiled at them and offered his hand to someone on the other side of the door and as the figure walked through he called out in a strong voice, 'I present to you my daughter Susanna, Marked Luman!'

Chapter 16

he silence that followed Heinrich's words was deafening. He stood at the top of the stairs, holding his eldest daughter's hand. Adam stared at her, tall and fair-skinned with her blonde hair pulled back. Her face was serene and now that she was standing there beside him, so was Heinrich's.

The crowd below could never be described as serene. The silence wasn't calm – it was a deep breath. There was a murmur – quiet, disbelieving – that rippled and rolled, gathering momentum until the wave broke and the room was full of voices, a rising chorus of shock, disgust, outrage – and something else. Something that might have been excitement.

'What has he done?' Auntie Jo, like Elise, had her hand pressed to her mouth in disbelief – but her eyes were gleaming.

Elise rounded on Nathanial, which was unusual in itself. 'Did you know? Did you know he would do this and keep it from me?' Her words were stumbling, her French accent amplified the way it always was when she was upset.

'Of course not.' Nathanial's voice had the flat calm of truth.

His face had leached all colour and he was staring up at his old friend with something between anger and pity. 'Of course not.'

'He is ruined!' Elise whispered. Her eyes were brimming with tears.

'He's the Chief Curator,' Auntie Jo said and to Adam's surprise she took his mother's hand and squeezed it. 'If anyone can pull this off it's Heinrich. Let's hear what he has to say.'

It took a long time before Heinrich could say anything. The noise was like water, rolling and crashing, endlessly circling round the room. Every time there was a lull, a fresh roar would rise up. No one was shouting *at* Heinrich. Courtesy was sacred in the Luman world, especially in a man's own house, and Heinrich wasn't just any man. He was the Chief Curator – and that was the only reason the rest of the Concilium hadn't seized him and dragged him off to face judgement.

Heinrich simply stood still and so did Susanna. Adam stared at her admiringly. Her face remained impassive although a blush had spread up her chest and neck, into her face. She was wearing the black and white cloak of a Marked Luman and a modified version of a man's Marking shirt which exposed her breastbone without revealing her breasts. Maybe because of the closer fit the V in her shirt was stained with blood and ink but her tattoo was visible, black and gory over her heart.

At last the talking died away and Heinrich held up his hand. The silence became expectant. Heinrich cleared his throat. 'I feel, my friends, that I must apologise. Not for the Marking of my daughter but for the necessary secrecy around this endeavour.

'For many long years I have served humanity and my fellow Lumen as best I can. I am not the oldest of our kind. I am not the most learned or the fastest. My family is honourable, as are your own, but we are not the most ancient family. I have nothing to distinguish me beyond the trust that you, my own people, have placed in me. I am forever humbled by your kindness, your dedication and your self-sacrifice. The fact that humanity at large is unaware of what you do every day is testament to the laws that govern our world; the secrecy that protects us from scrutiny.

'But there is one aspect of our world that has troubled my conscience for some time and that is the place of our womenfolk. The world beyond our own has moved on apace; in fortunate countries women can live a life of their own choosing. They may choose betrothal and family life or they may choose the world of work. Many women choose both. And yet here in our own world a girl's life is chosen for her, by dint of her gender, however unsuited she may be to the life thrust upon her. But it was not always the case.

'In my studies of *The Book of the Unknown Roads* I have delved far into the past. Why, I asked myself, did our daughters and wives share our abilities to swoop and feel the passing of souls if they cannot use these gifts? Why afflict them with such pointless suffering, to know a human life is ending, without the opportunity to point the way onto the Unknown Roads? And in the course of my research, my suspicions were confirmed. Our ancestors, the first Lumen, made no distinction between male and female. Lumen were judged on merit alone, regardless of their gender. It was only as time passed and the Luman world became more fractured that women began to fulfil a different purpose: peace. Healing division. Bringing factions and families together through betrothals. Their role as Lumen was expunged from our collective memory but the evidence is there in the early writings, should you wish to seek it.'

He paused and gestured to his daughter. 'Since childhood, Susanna has shown a unique sensitivity to the passing of souls. Her death sense, to use that crude term, is more acute than my own. She swoops with skill, speed and accuracy. As the time has come for her to think about betrothal I have watched her unhappiness grow. I have watched her railroaded onto a path that she may choose willingly in the future but not yet. And when I saw the happiness and confidence of my sons it occurred to me that what we do to our girls – the removal of their free choice – is wrong.

'And so, I decided to act.' Heinrich spread his hands, drawing them in; appealing to them. 'Our world is swift to act when a soul departs the physical world, but we are so very slow to act when we are asked to change. There is a phrase that is sometimes uttered by humanity which struck a chord with me. *Be the change you want to see in the world around you.* Susanna has chosen to be that change. I hope, in time, that you will forgive my deception and understand why we have acted in this way. Now, as my guests, please eat, drink and celebrate this historic day. Celebrate the Marking and coming of age of this new Luman.'

There was an awkward silence. Then, somewhere near the back of the room, someone began to clap. A moment later another person joined in. Then another. A woman's voice called out, shrill and triumphant, only to be shouted over by a deeper, male voice. Beside Adam, Auntie Jo stared straight ahead; then she too began to clap.

182

'Josephine,' Elise hissed and gripped her sister-in-law's arm, only to have it shaken off. Auntie Jo clapped harder.

There was a whoop behind them. It was Caitlyn. She was clapping. And so, Adam realised with a deepening sense of unreality, was Chloe. Her face was flushed and terrified and exhilarated and she wouldn't look at either of her parents until Nathanial put a hand on her shoulder and said quietly, 'Enough.' She clapped a few times more, then faltered.

In the room packed with hundreds of people, perhaps sixty or seventy had applauded, only a few of them men. Caitlyn had stopped when Ciaron had grabbed her arms and talked into her ear, low and urgent. The clapping had died away and the air was tense. Too late, Adam realised he should have joined in. His brain had taken too long to process what Heinrich was saying and now he wanted to jump up beside the Chief Curator and shout to them all that he agreed, that Heinrich was right – but the moment was lost.

The mood in the hall was darkening. Heinrich and Susanna were coming down the stairs, followed by Heinrich's wife and children, including Alexander. Adam couldn't help feeling sorry for him – and admiring him. As far as the Luman world was concerned it was his day. How long had he known that he wouldn't be the one coming of age today? His cheeks were very red but he looked proud and determined as he walked beside his father and sister.

As Heinrich reached them, he paused and looked from Nathanial to Elise. He tried to smile. 'I am so very sorry to have deceived you.'

Elise pursed her lips and looked at the ground. Heinrich's

face fell and Adam felt a flare of rage. How could his mother do this now, after everything Heinrich had done for them?

Perhaps Nathanial realised this. 'It was a shock, old friend.' He was struggling to find the words. 'I think . . . you must have your reasons, even if I can't see them.'

Heinrich smiled and leaned in closer. Adam was just able to catch his words. 'I told you I wanted to bring a great storm before I left this world. And now I have.' He squeezed Nathanial's shoulder and moved on towards the doorway.

Adam looked from face to face, taking in the different expressions: anger, bewilderment, anxiety, hope. What were they supposed to do now?

Auntie Jo cleared her throat. 'Well, I don't know about you lot but I'm starving. Shall we go and eat?'

Usually the feast after the Marking was one of the highlights of the day. The girls and women would scurry off to the serving tables, unveiling dishes they had prepared at home and offering them to the men with smiles. Everyone would eat their fill and then the dancing would begin. The ballroom would be a whirl of music and colour, coy smiles from the unattached while parents kept a close eye on their offspring.

Tonight things were different, because so many people had left as soon as the Marking had ended. Instead of bursting at the seams the room seemed half empty. Behind the serving tables there were fewer girls than there were dishes. It seemed that some families had simply abandoned their food and gone home.

'How could they leave?' Aron was staring round the room, looking uneasy.

Auntie Jo was the one who answered. 'They left because they didn't want their daughters associated with what happened, in case it damages their prospects. And in case they got any funny ideas about getting Marked.'

Luc was biting his lip and looking uncharacteristically nervous. 'But Heinrich's the Chief Curator! They must know it looks really bad walking out on him.'

'Maybe they don't think he'll be Chief Curator much longer,' Adam said, thinking aloud. He cringed when he realised they had all turned towards him.

'Can they do that?' Chloe was wide-eyed. 'Can they sack a Chief Curator?'

'None of us are indispensable.' Elise was terse. She turned to her husband. 'It is best if we leave too. Soon. We will have something to eat and then we will go home.'

'No.' Nathanial looked grim. 'Heinrich has been our friend for a long time. I won't abandon him tonight. Whatever he has done, we will stay as courtesy dictates.'

'He hasn't murdered anyone!' The words burst out of Adam's mouth before he could stop them. 'Seriously, you're all talking like he's done something terrible.' He took a deep breath. 'Maybe he hasn't done anything bad! At school the girls all do the same as the boys; they do their exams, they get jobs, they go to university. What's wrong with that?'

'Our ways are not their ways!' Elise hissed and to Adam's shock he saw she was actually shaking with emotion. 'We do not live as they do! And this is why you must leave this *school* if you cannot see that what Heinrich has done is *wrong*!'

'No one else is getting Marked tonight, Elise,' Auntie Jo said dryly. 'No one's going to wrestle you to the ground and tattoo you. You're perfectly safe.'

'Do you think this is a joke?' Elise rounded on her sister-in-law. Whatever uneasy truce had existed between them in the last few weeks was a distant memory now. 'Do you plan to become a Luman because you never became a wife?'

Adam stared at his mother in shock. Had she *actually* just said that?! She knew as well as anyone why Auntie Jo hadn't married: because after their brother's suicide, her betrothal had been broken off, just as Nathanial's had been. The difference was that Elise had ignored her family's wishes and eloped with Nathanial; a rebellious side to his uptight mother that Adam could barely imagine. It was Heinrich who had married his parents. He had always been their friend. No wonder Nathanial wouldn't abandon him now. All of this was supposed to be relegated to the past, but how could Auntie Jo resist blurting out the whole thing?

For a moment she seemed to be thinking about it. Then, as Adam watched, Auntie Jo took a deep breath in and out. 'Not everyone was as forgiving as you were, Elise. That's why I never became a wife.'

Elise pursed her lips and seized Chloe's arm. 'Come. The food must be served.'

Nathanial watched them walk away, apparently shell-shocked. 'I'm sorry, Jo. Elise had no right to say that.' He tailed off, realising that his sons were watching. 'Let's all just have something to eat.'

As they made their way to the serving tables, the three male McVeys and the younger girls joined them. Ciaron nodded at them and began talking to Aron. Adam hesitated, then slipped in closer to his father, hoping to overhear his conversation.

Uncle Paddy was grim-faced. 'Well, this has set the cat among the pigeons for sure. Did you know what he was up to?'

'I had no idea,' Nathanial said softly.

'They'll ruin him, the silly bugger.' Uncle Paddy shook his head, almost admiringly. 'I don't know what possessed him!'

'I think he knows they won't be able to do anything to him for much longer.'

'He's certainly going out with a bang, I'll give him that. But why the hell did he do it? It's hard enough managing Caitlyn as it is. She'll have my head wrecked after this.'

They were shuffling along the line in front of the table. Up ahead Adam could see his sister, standing stiffly beside Elise. Her face was pale and pinched but she was trying to smile as she ladled out some kind of casserole onto plates. Just before her, Auntie Orla was keeping a watchful eye on Caitlyn and her younger sisters. Aine and Sorcha looked cheerful but Caitlyn was glaring at every boy who came near her, as though daring them to ask for food. When a smiling Australian was foolish enough to do so she dropped a mound of champ onto his plate with a splat that flecked his ceremonial cloak with potato. He beat a hasty retreat while Auntie Orla leaned forward and hissed something into her eldest daughter's ear.

As Adam drew closer she turned to him, eyes glittering. 'Do you want some spuds?'

Adam grinned. 'Only if you don't make me wear them.'

She smirked and ladled a dollop onto his plate with a little more care. When she turned to Luc she smiled sweetly. 'Champ?'

Luc arched an eyebrow. 'I'll pass, thanks. I'm gorgeous enough without you decorating me.'

They had no trouble finding a seat this evening. Even when the girls and women finally sat down to eat there were still empty tables. Chloe was allowed to sit beside Ciaron but instead of their usual easy chatter the conversation seemed stilted.

As soon as they had finished Elise suggested that they leave, only to be told firmly by Nathanial that they would be staying until the dancing had begun. Adam's curiosity was piqued. The Curators were already moving towards the dance floor (Darian was steering well clear of Auntie Jo). It was traditional for the newly Marked Luman to help lead the dancing, having picked a partner first. Did that mean that Susanna would have to pick someone to dance? Judging by the anxious glances and murmurs as they moved back into the ballroom, he wasn't the only one wondering.

'Where's your chick? The one from your Marking?' Luc asked Aron. He was scanning the room, looking doleful at the reduced number of girls available.

'She was here but her parents must have taken her home.' Aron looked glum. He had chosen a pretty Indian girl as his dance partner. Adam could still remember her brilliantly coloured sari and the jewels in her hair. No wonder Aron was disappointed that she'd gone.

Music rang out from the front of the room. Susanna was standing there, still wearing the heavy ceremonial cloak. She looked very alone. Her father was beside her and he nodded encouragingly. She took a deep breath and walked towards a tall, blond boy, smiling in a way that suggested she knew him – but the boy's mother suddenly moved forward, took his arm and pulled him away into the crowd. Susanna faltered and stood still.

'That cowardly little toad,' Auntie Jo said, loud enough to make people turn and stare. 'She's a beautiful girl and the Chief Curator's daughter. Normally the boys in here would be killing each other to dance with her.'

That was probably true but there was nothing normal about this Marking ball. Susanna was glowing red, a deep blush staining her chest from her tattoo all the way up to her forehead. Behind her Heinrich's face had darkened and Adam could see that the Chief Curator was angry. More than angry – he was furious. Whatever he had done, he hadn't expected people to snub his daughter so publicly. Susanna was holding her head up high but her eyes were darting around like a hunted animal, looking for a way out. The band was becoming aware that something was wrong and the music was slowing down and the whole thing was awful . . .

So awful that suddenly, without planning it, Adam found himself moving forward. One foot stepped in front of the other and within seconds he was standing where the blond-haired boy had been. He looked at Susanna, who stared back at him in confusion, until he smiled. The relief in her face made Adam feel happy and sad at the same time. He had missed his chance to clap after Heinrich's speech. He wasn't going to mess up again.

Susanna cleared her throat. 'Would you do me the honour of this dance?' Her voice was small, like she was saying something unfamiliar – which she was. These were the words that Adam and his brothers had been trained to say.

Now *he* found himself struggling. What did Chloe say at this kind of moment? 'Uh . . . yeah. That would be great.'

She smiled at him. Adam stepped up to her and took her hand, putting his hand on her waist. This bit was easy – it was just dancing, like he'd danced before at so many balls. Susanna was older than him, taller and pretty gorgeous and normally she was so far out of his league that he wouldn't have *ever* found himself in this position, but now that he was here, he might as well make the best of it.

The dance floor was filling up around him. He tried not to look at too many people but he couldn't help noticing that as Heinrich and Alberta danced past him they were smiling. Susanna lowered her head and whispered in his ear, 'Thank you.'

'No problem,' he said, wishing it was true. His parents had just waltzed past and although he couldn't see his father's expression, his mother's face was pale and set.

When the dance ended he bowed at Susanna and she curtsied. He almost suggested that *he* should be the one curtsying, then decided it was too soon for jokes. Susanna seemed relieved the whole thing was over. She murmured her thanks once more and then disappeared into the crowd.

Adam stood still, wondering what to do next. People were staring at him and most of them weren't looking kindly. He felt a tap on his shoulder.

Caitlyn was grinning at him. 'Since you're doing charity dances, I thought *I'd* take pity on *you*. Want to dance?'

'Not really,' Adam said. When her face changed he realised how it had sounded. Quickly he stepped towards her and took her hand. 'I don't want to dance. I kind of want to get out of here.'

Caitlyn gave him a small, secret smile. 'Funny you should say that. I know just where to go.'

Chapter 17

t wasn't too difficult to slip away unnoticed. Outside the castle the air was cold and green with pine. Here, far from any big town or city, the sky was bright with moonlight. In the gardens Caitlyn kicked her shoes under an ornamental shrub and took his hand. 'It's this way.'

Adam allowed himself to be led across the lawn, jogging to keep up. As they reached the dark wall of trees at the end of the lawn he hesitated. He could remember looking out of an upstairs window at a never-ending forest. 'What if we get lost?'

Caitlyn glanced at him. 'Would it be so bad if we did?' When he didn't answer she sighed. 'It's OK. I know where I'm going. I've been here a few times before.'

They stepped into the shadows. Moonlight slanted into the spaces between the trees but he still couldn't see much. Caitlyn didn't seem to be having any problems and he kept hold of her hand, small and cool in his. It felt different from Melissa's. He tried to ignore the ache this sent through him.

Caitlyn turned back to him. 'There's a kind of path. It's hard to see but I can feel it with my feet.'

It felt like they were walking for a long time but it couldn't have been more than a couple of minutes. The trees were still dense around them but up ahead it seemed brighter. Sure enough, a moment later they emerged into a small clearing. There wasn't much there – a gazebo, a pond and a bench. Oil lanterns hung around the edges of the gazebo and Caitlyn dropped Adam's hand and reached up to the eaves, searching until she triumphantly produced a box of matches. Adam watched her flitting from lantern to lantern, leaving a trail of light behind her.

When she finished she returned the matches to their hiding place and paused. They looked at each other across the clearing. It was Caitlyn who moved first, padding over to the bench and sitting down. After a moment's hesitation, Adam sat beside her.

Neither of them spoke. Adam stared at the pond, silvery with reflected moonlight. Every so often the wind gusted, sending ripples through the water. *Melissa would love this*, he thought. *Only she doesn't want to be with me any more. And even if she did, I couldn't bring her here. I couldn't even bring her home.*

He turned his head and found Caitlyn watching him. He shifted along the bench towards her. She leaned forward until their noses were touching. He almost stopped but her hair tickled his face and a rush of emotions flooded through him; loneliness, desire, curiosity. She pressed her lips to his and he froze, breathing in slowly, wondering at the strangeness of it. Melissa was the only girl he had ever kissed. He had kissed her so often that he knew exactly how her mouth felt and tasted.

He kissed Caitlyn back. Her mouth was soft and she smelled lovely. When his fingers brushed across the lace on the back of her dress he could feel skin underneath, warm and alive. It made him feel like he couldn't breathe, especially when she kissed him harder. It should have been perfect. There was a full moon and lanterns and a deserted, magical place in the middle of a forest miles from anywhere, and it should have been the best moment of his life but it felt all wrong.

Caitlyn pulled away. He blinked at her. He was expecting her to look angry or upset but she bit her lip and studied him, considering. 'That didn't feel like I thought it would.'

Adam cleared his throat. 'Have you kissed someone before?'

Caitlyn grinned. 'Nah, my da keeps me locked up in a tower, waiting for a handsome prince to come and marry me. Of course I've kissed people, Adam. Have you?'

He nodded. 'Yeah.'

'Who?'

Adam sighed. 'Just a girl I know. From school.'

'Just once?'

'No. Loads of times. We were going out for ages.'

Caitlyn's eyes widened. 'Like a girlfriend?' At his nod she pulled her feet up onto the bench, tucking them under her dress, hugging her knees to her chest. 'How did you get away with that?'

'I lied.' Adam felt tired. 'I just told loads of lies. To my family and to my girlfriend. I lied at home about going out, to do work for school. And I lied to her all the time. I couldn't tell her about anything. Sometimes I had to go on jobs and then I couldn't see her and then I would have to lie some more.

That's why she dumped me. She got tired of me bailing on her. I would have dumped me too.' It was true. He couldn't blame Melissa.

Caitlyn was playing with the hem on her dress. 'It never works out.' She looked over at the pond. 'I met someone a couple of months ago. Ryan. People come on holiday where we live, because of the beaches and stuff. His parents had a caravan. I used to see him every morning and every evening when I was walking the dogs. And then the weather got bad and he went home. He gave me his email address and his mobile number but I chucked them away.' She stopped and chewed her lip. 'I couldn't tell him I wasn't allowed email. And what was the point in texting him? He would only want to meet up and I wouldn't be able to.'

Adam shrugged. 'You would be able to at first. But after a couple of months he would want more. He'd want to go out at the weekend and to come to your house to hang out. And then you'd have to start lying. And when you love someone you shouldn't lie to them.'

'Did you love her? The girl in school?'

'Yeah.' The ache in his chest was spreading all the way up to his throat, making it ache too.

'Sorry.' Her face was softer than he had ever seen it before. 'I liked Ryan a lot but . . . I don't know if I *loved* him. It must be crap. Loving someone and not being able to be with them.'

'I hate being a Luman.' He hadn't planned to say it. The words were just coming out, free at last. 'I hate it all so much. I just want to go to university and have a life. No Hinterland, no souls, no betrothals. Just normal stuff.'

'I would love to be a Luman.' Caitlyn sounded almost fierce. 'You saw what Heinrich did. Maybe everything will change. Maybe I'll be able to get Marked instead of getting betrothed.'

Adam didn't answer. What was there to say? She had seen what happened inside. People hadn't exactly jumped around celebrating. Even people like him who agreed with it hadn't cheered along. The thought made him pause. Was it possible that there were other Lumen who had silently applauded Heinrich, once they had got over the shock? Would they support him down the line? The Lumen who had left the ball early had made their feelings clear but plenty of others had stayed. Surely they hadn't all stayed out of fear or pity.

As if reading his mind Caitlyn took his arm. 'There were lots of people in there who'll be happy about Susanna, once they get used to the idea. *Especially* if they have lots of daughters instead of sons. And people love Heinrich. They'll help him if they can. Maybe your dad will let Chloe get Marked!'

Adam snorted. 'I wouldn't bank on it.'

'It only takes a few of us,' Caitlyn said softly. 'Just a few and then a few more, and then a few more. And suddenly it's normal, like women have always been Lumen. The way it was a long time ago.'

'I hope so,' Adam said – and he meant it.

Caitlyn hesitated. 'I thought . . . we could get betrothed, because we get on OK. Da says you have to get on with the person you'll be betrothed to and never mind about their Keystones or you'll be miserable. So I thought if we got on OK we could get betrothed. But I didn't know about the girl in your school. And if I can be a Luman, I'd rather do that first.

So . . . we're probably better just being friends.'

'That sounds good.' Adam smiled, relieved and just a tiny bit disappointed. Caitlyn was brave and fierce and gorgeous. Life would never have been dull with her. But there was plenty of time to think about betrothals. If she wasn't giving up hope on getting Marked, why was he giving up on school? Maybe there was still time to change his father's mind. It wasn't too late. And if he could stay at school . . . he could keep seeing Melissa.

He followed Caitlyn back to the castle, feeling less gloomy.

The fallout from the Marking ball was far-reaching. It started with Adam getting an earful from his mother as soon as they reached home, mainly for drawing attention to himself by dancing with Susanna. Nathanial stayed quiet but as usual Auntie Jo leapt to Adam's defence. 'You should be proud of him! Would you rather the poor girl had been left in the middle of the dance floor on her own? It's never nice to have unfriendly eyes on you in such a public manner, is it Elise? You of all people should know that!'

Elise had stormed off, furious and tearful. Instead of feeling upset, Adam felt a mixture of sympathy and frustration. He alone of his brothers and sister knew what Auntie Jo was getting at. Standing by Nathanial after his brother's suicide had probably been the bravest thing Elise had ever done. She had proved that she was capable of ignoring convention when it suited her – and facing condemnation for it. The trouble was she had spent every moment of her life since trying to be the perfect Luman wife, as if she could cast off the memory of what they had done.

But not everyone shared her feelings of dismay. Just the day after Susanna's historic Marking, the rumours were already coming in. Uncle Paddy called, alone and unannounced, just before dinner. Instead of stopping off in the kitchen for his usual banter he went straight into Nathanial's study and stayed there for quite some time.

If he'd hoped for a discreet visit and exit he was disappointed. When he and Nathanial returned to the kitchen they were greeted by Adam and the rest of the Mortsons, aware that something was up. Auntie Jo was sitting at the table, drinking one of her green smoothies. She chugged down a mouthful and waggled her glass at Uncle Paddy in mock threat. 'Now Patrick, don't make me do something that both of us will regret. We know this isn't a social visit. What's going on?'

Uncle Paddy looked at Nathanial, who nodded. 'I suppose there's no point making a secret of it. It seems that Heinrich has been busy today. Three more girls were Marked early this morning.'

There was a horrified gasp from Elise. She had been standing at the stove stirring a pan of sauce. Now she threw down the wooden spoon. 'What is this madness? Has he lost his mind entirely?'

'Who were they?' It was Chloe who had spoken. She looked petrified – and excited.

'*Va-t'en!*' His mother's voice was almost a shriek. 'Out! You have one hour of piano practice!'

'But I was going to do it after dinner –' Chloe protested.

'Get out! *Maintenant!*' Elise looked like a mad woman. Her eyes were savage.

For a moment, it seemed that Chloe was going to refuse to go. At last she turned and stormed out of the kitchen, slamming the door behind her.

'Are you going to throw me out too, Elise?' Auntie Jo's voice was hard.

Elise ignored her, turning her fury on Uncle Paddy. 'Do you see what you have done? Coming here with your stories of Heinrich's stupidity! I will not hear this in my house!'

Uncle Paddy was usually the most good-humoured man that Adam had ever met but something flinty came into his face. His voice was sharp. 'Do you think not talking about it will make it go away? And do you think your house is the only one to be affected by this? I have daughters myself, including Caitlyn, who's a force of nature at the best of times!'

'Chloe is to be betrothed to your son!' Elise had thrown her usual impeccable courtesy to the winds. 'Do you really wish to fill her head with stories of Markings and swooping? Do you wish to jeopardise everything? Your son is making a good match!'

'And your daughter is making an excellent match.' Uncle Paddy was bristling with quiet fury. 'Ciaron is a High Luman's son. You'd do well to remember that.'

Elise blinked, seeming to remember where she was. She breathed in slowly, then turned and walked out of the room, her heels stabbing across the stone floor.

Uncle Paddy turned to Auntie Jo. 'Are *you* going to go mad now? Every other woman I've spoken to today has gone bananas at me, so you might as well jump on the bandwagon.'

Auntie Jo smiled. 'Maybe I'll jump into the Hinterland instead and take off to Germany.'

'Enough, Jo!' Nathanial finally broke his silence. He looked like he'd been flattened by a truck.

Auntie Jo raised an eyebrow. 'Nathanial, I love you dearly, but you are my brother, not my father. I wasn't asking for your permission.' She turned back to Uncle Paddy. 'You never answered Chloe's question. Who were the girls who were Marked?'

'They were all from families with no sons. One from Italy, one from Australia, one from Canada.'

That made sense. Adam hardly dared to breathe. It hadn't been a one-off. Caitlyn was right – there were other people who supported what Heinrich had done. What was it she had said? *It only takes a few of us. Just a few more and then a few more, and then a few more. And suddenly it's normal.* The question was: would it become normal for Adam's family?

'Were any of them High Lumen?' Aron was frowning. He didn't seem thrilled about the whole thing. This didn't really come as a shock to Adam – his eldest brother was a traditionalist.

'No. All minor families.' Uncle Paddy hesitated. 'In fact, the High Lumen are having to decide what to do about them.'

'Heinrich is still the Chief Curator.' There was an edge to Auntie Jo's voice. 'Are you saying High Lumen should oppose him?'

'Of course he's not saying that, Jo.' Nathanial sounded impatient. 'But if the Concilium don't back Heinrich, they will simply declare no confidence in him and appoint a new Chief Curator.'

'But who would they pick instead?' Luc was sitting up straight in his chair, looking alert.

'Not Darian?' Adam blurted out, then hesitated when they all turned towards him. 'They wouldn't make him Chief Curator, would they?'

Auntie Jo snorted. 'I'd like to think the Concilium aren't that stupid. They're supposed to be our brightest and best. I'm sure they'll pick a more worthy candidate.'

She was trying to be comforting, Adam knew that. So why wasn't he feeling more reassured?

Chapter 18

ncle Paddy's visit left Adam deeply uneasy. Once he had said goodbye he retreated to his bedroom, away from all the frayed nerves and short tempers. Part of him was thrilled. If Heinrich kept Marking girls then maybe, eventually, his father would cave in and allow Chloe to be a Luman. It helped that Nathanial was so close to Uncle Paddy – and if anyone could wear a stubborn father down it was Caitlyn. He tried to imagine the scenes unfolding in the McVeys' household and shuddered.

But the second bit of news . . . the fact that the Concilium could turn on Heinrich. That bit wasn't so comforting. Auntie Jo's respect for the Curators was, in Adam's opinion, more generous than they deserved. After all, Darian had managed to weasel his way into the Concilium. They couldn't be *that* smart or they would see what a treacherous toad he really was.

He was relieved to be going to school the next morning – until he was sitting on the bus and remembered that he was going to have to face Melissa for the first time since their break-up. If there was any happy side effect of complete meltdown in the Luman world, it was the fact that he had been temporarily distracted from his misery. Now it returned with a vengeance, served up with a side order of nerves. How was he supposed to play this?

Breaking up was bad enough but he still had to see Melissa every day. Part of him was glad of that – maybe at least seeing her would give some comfort – but how was he supposed to react? He wished he could have asked Luc for advice but he knew his brother would only have smirked and made some crude comments about things you shouldn't do in your own nest.

Adam's fears were confirmed when he walked into registration. Melissa didn't even look at him, while Mr Fenton went into one of his patented rants, covering a wide range of topics from scruffy uniform to the perils of saliva exchange. The knife in his heart gave a sharp twist. So this was how it was going to be. He thought of all the things they used to talk about and laugh about and the knife twisted deeper. There was no one else he could have those kind of conversations with. He hadn't just lost his girlfriend; he'd lost his friend.

And that was how it was. Melissa avoided him as much as possible but when they occasionally ran into each other (once literally in the doorway of their form room) there was nothing but awkwardness, pained glances and strained smiles. He knew she still cared about him – sometimes he caught her watching him in registration or felt her eyes on him in biology – but she had backed off. He tried to talk to her a couple of times but she killed the conversation and moved on. Eventually Adam took the hint. She had taken the brutal but painful option of treating him like a splinter – pulling him out of her life in one swift move, rather than leaving him to fester.

He was back to spending most of his free time in the library with his friends. They were as sympathetic as they knew how to be – which meant they weren't very sympathetic at all. None of them had ever been dumped by the girl they loved. As far as he knew, none of them had ever been in love with any real, live girl. Still, at least they didn't torture him with talk of Melissa.

It helped that the Japan trip was looming on the horizon. The first week back after the break-up was torture but by the Friday morning Adam realised that in a week's time he would be heading to the airport. They were flying out at lunchtime on Friday, to arrive in Japan on Saturday morning local time. The plan was to spend five days in Tokyo, then travel north to a place called Hachimana for one night and day to visit one of Murai's many enterprises, then return to Tokyo on Thursday night. They would have three last days of sightseeing and travel home on Sunday night Japanese time, meaning they would be back in London on Sunday afternoon.

Adam was finding it hard to get excited. Too much had happened. His teachers were piling on ridiculous amounts of homework to make up for their week away, even though it would be during the half-term holiday. He spent his lunchtimes ploughing through chemistry and biology notes, writing revision cards for exams he would never sit. He told himself it was all part of his cover story, so no one would suspect he was leaving – but secretly he was happier thinking about oxidation and evolution. It helped him avoid thinking about Melissa.

The weekend was busy with call-outs and he did his share without complaint, albeit without any real enthusiasm. In between, he alternated between packing clothes and lying on his bed feeling numb. Why did he feel so bad? It wasn't like he had been able to spend every waking minute with Melissa – far from it. It was just that even when he wasn't with her, she had been with him, in some small, happy corner of his mind.

His one surprising source of sympathy was Luc. After dinner on Sunday evening, Adam climbed the stairs to his room, planning to listen to some angry music and try and drown out the wailing in his head. When he got there he found Luc had tipped his rucksack out on the bed and was picking through his clothes with complete disdain.

'How are we even related? You can't take this stuff. People will think you're a five-year-old.'

'Get out of here!' Adam exploded. He stormed across the room and grabbed his brother's arms, half pushing and half dragging him towards the door. For a few seconds he had the element of surprise – but Luc was taller and stronger in a lean, wiry sort of way. He pushed Adam away. Adam braced himself for a thump, almost relishing the prospect of a fight.

He was disappointed when Luc held up his hands in mock surrender. 'Easy, tiger! Don't shoot the messenger.'

Adam glared at him, full of hatred, knowing it wasn't fair. Luc made everything seem easy – girls, being a Luman; just being alive. 'What do you want?'

Luc leaned one shoulder against the door frame and folded his arms. 'To tell you that you'll be OK.' For once he wasn't smirking.

Adam blinked. 'What are you talking about? I'm fine!'

'No you're not. But you will be. It only hurts this badly once. And then you'll never fall like that again.'

Adam turned away. 'I don't know what you're talking about.'

'She dumped you, didn't she? Your girl from Cryptique. Lovely Melissa in the white dress.' When Adam rounded on him looking murderous he shrugged. 'What? She's pretty. And nice. But there are *lots* of nice, pretty girls out there. The secret is – have fun, then move on. Because one day you're going to get betrothed, to someone who knows what it's like to live the way we do. Anyone else until then is just for fun.'

'Well, if it's all just fun what do you know about it hurting?'

There was a brief flicker of something in Luc's eyes. 'Everyone makes one mistake. I did. But I learned from it. So now I keep it short and sweet. Sunshine and roses.'

Adam stared at him. Luc made it sound so attractive but what he had had with Melissa was special. 'You don't know what you're missing out on.'

'I know when something is doomed. I even told you to call time and get out of there but you wouldn't listen. But it had to end – so try and remember that she's done you a favour.' Luc raised an eyebrow. 'Trust me. Love is overrated. You'll realise that after a few weeks.'

He was almost gone when Adam called after him. 'Who was she? The girl you liked?'

Luc halted but didn't look back. 'Someone a bit like Melissa,' he said softly. He walked away and a moment later Adam heard his brother's door close.

* * *

And then it was Monday. Four days of school before the trip. He spent registration trying not to stare at Melissa and trying not to listen to Fenton, who was even more hung-over and irritable than normal. He reached the library at break, feeling a kind of weary relief to be there. Dan and Archie were talking in low voices. There was no sign of Spike. 'What's up?'

Dan was brushing his fingers through a stack of sunflower seeds, twitchy as a squirrel. 'We don't know yet. But there are rumours!'

'About what?' Adam yawned. Whatever the latest scandal was, he didn't care.

'You haven't heard?!'

'Heard what?' Adam was getting irritated now. He had a sudden feeling of dread. He hoped they weren't going to tell him Melissa had a new boyfriend. Even thinking about it made him feel slightly sick. Surely she hadn't forgotten him *that* quickly?

'It's the Beast. He's not going to Japan. Well, hopefully not.' Dan looked heavenwards with an expression of deepest longing.

Adam blinked at them stupidly. Archie grinned and kept his voice down. 'He did something at the weekend. He was out with his mates and they got in some kind of fight. Only it got a bit mad, the place got smashed up and he got arrested. Someone in my art class was in the same club and saw it. There were loads of police!'

'And the governors must have heard about it and they've called some big meeting,' Dan said, his voice wobbling with joy. 'Our form teacher is a governor and she was going on at us this morning, being all mysterious, saying that if we got into trouble this week we could still get pulled from the trip as *someone was about to find out!* We thought it was just the usual blah-blah-scary-scary but she must have known about him!'

Adam stared at them in disbelief. There was no time to ask questions; footsteps approached and a moment later a grinning Spike was sitting down. 'I can confirm that, Godzilla aside, Tokyo will be officially Beast-free!'

There was a moment of silence. '*Yessss!*' Archie hissed, while Dan beamed from ear to ear. 'Are you sure?'

Spike nodded. 'Positive. I helped Miss Feswick when her computer kept crashing. I knew they were having a meeting in The Bulb's office – so I dropped round to see if she needed anything doing. Turned out she did – and we had a little chat. Anyway, the governors came out and then The Bulb came out and bollocked me for nothing, so I scarpered. And then when I logged into his email, Murai's governor had scanned the final list in and signed it off. The Beast isn't on it.'

'What about Weasel?' Dan was biting his lip. 'Is he still going?'

Spike shrugged. 'His name's there but I doubt it. And even if he does go, what's he going to do? Without the Beast there to protect him, he's dead if he tries anything. He'll be sticking to the teachers like glue. Everyone else hates him.'

'The Beast has *really* bad taste in mates,' Archie said.

Adam snorted. They had no idea. He'd narrowly avoided a run-in with Baz and co. himself. Smashing up nightclubs was the least of their sins. He really hoped they had resisted arrest . . .

'This is going to be brilliant!' Dan was nodding and using his sunflower seeds to make a smiley face. 'I can't wait. I love going away. And I love planes. That bit when they close the doors and tell everyone to prepare for departure.'

Archie was sketching a plane. 'I like the fast bit at the start. When the plane kind of warms up and then goes mental along the runway and goes up in the air dead fast. And you feel like your stomach's still on the runway when the rest of you is in the sky!'

Adam stayed quiet. He didn't have anything to contribute; he'd never been on a plane before. But someone else was staying quiet too. When he glanced at Spike, he was staring at his laptop with ferocious concentration. He looked pale. 'Are you all right?'

'Of course I'm all right,' Spike snapped. 'Why wouldn't I be all right?'

'They had this programme on last week about plane crashes,' Dan chirruped, blissfully unaware that Spike was squirming in his seat. 'I was trying to see where you should sit so that if you crash you're all right.'

'Where *should* you sit?' Archie paused, his pen poised in mid-air.

Dan shrugged. 'They didn't really say. It depends on the kind of crash. There are loads of different types. There are the ones where the plane nosedives into the ground and the kind where it just falls out of the sky. And then there are the ones where it sort of breaks apart in the middle . . .'

There was a thump. Spike had slammed his laptop shut and was glaring at Dan. 'All right. We get the picture.' His face was now pale *and* shiny.

'You're not scared of flying, are you?' Archie leered and

moved his pen quickly, filling in a figure behind the plane window. It seemed to be all terrified eyes and a screaming mouth. He tilted his drawing so the plane was aiming for the ground. 'Look, here's you!'

Spike stood up, grabbed his laptop and swore at them before storming off. Adam stared after him and tried not to smile but he couldn't help it. It wasn't that he liked Spike being scared; it was just that it was nice to see that he was capable of something as human as mortal fear.

Dan grinned. 'He is totally bricking it. Who knew? Even robots have feelings!'

The Beast wasn't in school all week. Adam had heard various rumours – that he had broken bones, broken teeth or a broken nose. Privately Adam suspected that only his pride was hurt. At least he didn't have to be worried that the Beast would strike before the trip, now that he had nothing to lose.

The sun rose and fell and suddenly it was Thursday. He was in registration and Fenton was giving them last-minute instructions about what to bring and not to bring. They were to be at the airport no later than 11 a.m. on Friday morning. They were to *bring their passports!* They were to *behave themselves* or they would be *flayed alive!* They were to make sure they brought a *coat!* And their *passports!* He wasn't amused by the chorus of titters that followed this, nor the anonymous voice that hissed, '*Yes, Mum!*'

Throughout the lecture, Adam couldn't help watching Melissa. She was sitting very quietly and when everyone else stood up to go she slipped up to Fenton's desk. He heard her ask where she should go in school time and Fenton answered with uncharacteristic kindness. Adam fled into the corridor, not wanting to eavesdrop, but when he got there he hesitated, then waited for her.

She came out a few minutes later, head down, looking miserable. When she saw Adam she started and for a moment her face lit up. Then she took a step back and the shutters came down.

'Hi,' Adam said. He couldn't think of anything else.

She almost smiled. 'Hi yourself.'

'How are you?'

She shrugged. 'OK. And you?' Distant, polite, meaningless. The kind of thing you would say to a stranger.

His heart hurt. 'I've been better,' he said. Her face changed and he cursed himself. He had always done this – blurted out the truth. There were probably rules for this kind of thing but he didn't know them. That was the strange thing. However many lies he had told her about his life, he had always been honest about how he felt.

Her face softened. 'Yeah, me too.'

He thought she was going to walk away so he asked quickly, 'How's your mum?'

'She's OK. Not brilliant but OK. She's getting there.'

'That's great.' Silence. He studied her face. He missed it. This was the closest he had been to her for two weeks. He looked at her eyes and her nose and her mouth. Her lips were chapped, as though she'd been biting them. It didn't stop him wanting to kiss them.

'Well, have a good time in Japan,' she said, too brightly, and he could see tears sparkling in her eyes.

Adam took her hand. 'I miss you,' he blurted out. 'I really miss you. I . . . wish you were coming to Japan.'

She smiled, sadly and sweetly. 'What difference would it make, Adam? We'd only have to come home again, wouldn't we?'

She walked away, taking a sliver of his heart with her.

Chapter 19

nd then, at last, it was time. Adam had risen at dawn to do some last-minute packing. He knew that some people would have parents dropping them off at the airport but he had decided to travel alone. It was better for his family to keep a low profile. Luc *had* offered him a lift on his illicit motorbike, but having fought this hard to get to Japan Adam didn't want to perish on the way to the airport. He had declined the offer and decided to get the train.

His family gathered in the hallway to see him off. He had imagined tear-stained faces and declarations of affection but his send-off was mainly limited to mocking his special Bonehill hoodie and 'hilarious' advice about water-jet toilets and blowfish sushi. He did at least get hugs from Auntie Jo and Chloe – and to his surprise a fierce kiss and tight embrace from his mother. 'We will miss you. *Garde-toi bien,*' she whispered. *Take care.*

He patted the dogs one last time and dropped his rucksack into the boot of Nathanial's battered Volvo. It wasn't used very often and there was an anxious moment when the engine coughed and revved but it soon roared into life. Nathanial drove the way he did everything else – carefully and courteously.

'Are you excited?' he asked.

'Yeah.' And now that the time had come, Adam *was* excited. He would finally get away from his family and have one normal week in the normal world. It had only taken him nearly sixteen years.

'You will visit Hikaru, won't you? The sooner the better. He may not want your help but it would be polite to offer if you get the chance.'

Adam's excitement dipped a notch. He wasn't escaping the Luman world entirely but he would do his best to keep it to a minimum. 'Yeah, sure.'

Nathanial smiled. 'And enjoy yourself.' He hesitated. 'I know you'll be sorry to leave school but it's good to go out on a high note.'

At the train station he lifted the rucksack onto Adam's back and shook his hand. 'Have a good time and take care of yourself.' He smiled again and squeezed Adam's shoulder. 'We'll be glad to see you home safe and well.'

Adam nodded, cheeks flaming. This was practically an emotional outburst by his father's standards but all Adam could think about was getting away. He felt a pang of guilt.

It was easier once he was on the train. He held his rucksack beside him and a smaller bag for the flight. He was almost free. As the train rattled past houses and trees and roads he found himself smiling. OK, Melissa wasn't going but his friends were. It would be a laugh. He would take loads of photos. And then someday, when he was an experienced Luman, he could sift

214

back through the snapshots and remember the life he used to have, once upon a time. His smile faded.

Adam had wondered if it would be difficult to find his group but it turned out there weren't too many large parties, all dressed in royal blue hoodies, being terrorised by a stocky, bald man brandishing a tour guide's flag. He sighed as he lugged his rucksack across the terminal. Why did The Bulb have to go on the trip with them? He spotted his friends in the throng and slipped in beside them.

'Hannah Murphy forgot her passport,' Dan whispered, nodding at a sobbing girl being comforted by her friends. 'She's waiting to see if her dad will get it here in time. Think he's getting a taxi.'

It was agreed that one teacher would wait behind with the unfortunate Hannah while everyone else deposited their suitcases at check-in and streamed through security into the shopping hall beyond. Adam kept a careful eye on what everyone else was doing. He did set the bleeper off at security with a pocketful of change and had to endure a frisking from a surly airport security man and an apoplectic glare from The Bulb. Still, having made it this far they were let loose on the shops for an hour, with strict instructions to meet back at the departure board.

Spike immediately abandoned them and headed off to the nearest coffee shop, muttering something about last-minute Wi-Fi access. Adam trailed round with Dan and Archie, watching with disbelief as Archie bought a bottle of very pungent aftershave, enormous sunglasses, a gold baseball cap and some very baggy jeans.

'Japanese girls love English guys,' Archie said, looking happy. 'And they like rap too. So an English rapper is like, their god!'

'But you can't rap,' Dan protested.

Archie shrugged. 'It's just talking fast. How hard can it be?'

Adam was getting impatient. He wanted to get on the plane. He had never been on one before. He wanted to see if it looked the way they looked in films. He wanted to see the air stewards do their safety routine for real. He had even watched a video online, showing how you worked the seatbelt, just so he wouldn't get caught out.

Archie ran out of money before they ran out of time. They waited for their group to meet up and trooped off to the departure gate, a beaming Hannah Murphy clutching her passport like a trophy.

And then, all of a sudden it was time. They were actually getting on the plane and Adam's heart leapt with excitement. He urged his friends to the front of the line. They shuffled along in a queue, herded by a teacher. Dan was whistling between his teeth, something vaguely familiar. A grey-haired man in front turned and glared at him. Dan stopped and blinked at him.

'What's the tune?' Adam couldn't help asking.

'"Don't Fear the Reaper",' Spike muttered. His face was grey.

Their passports were checked and then they were inching along the covered walkway. Finally, Adam took his first ever steps onto a plane. He grinned at the air hostess, who smiled automatically but recoiled slightly in the face of such manic delight. He tried to tone down his excitement but *how could he*?! How could he not be excited at flying through the air in a *machine*?

The plane was filling up fast, people cramming bags into overhead lockers and settling into their seats. One lady at the front of the plane was already absorbed in her book while a cheerful-looking man beside her had pulled out some crochet. Each row had ten seats, two blocks of three with a block of four in the middle. Adam was seated in a row with his friends, while a delighted Archie was sitting across the aisle in the centre of the plane with three girls. They looked less thrilled than he did.

By a cruel twist of fate, Spike had ended up with the window seat, with Adam and Dan beside him. 'Do you want to sit here?'

Adam hesitated. Having the window seat would be cool but it also meant being stuck beside only Spike for the next thirteen hours, without Dan there to talk to if things got tense. 'Don't you want to see?'

'Not really,' Spike said through clenched teeth.

'He'd rather not look,' Dan said ever-helpfully. 'You know, if we crash.'

Adam shrugged and squeezed past Spike, strapping himself into his seat. He awarded himself points for getting it right first time.

There was a small screen on the back of the seat in front. It flickered into life and a safety video began to play in both Japanese and English. He watched it with interest – or at least he tried to. It was hard not getting distracted by Spike's low-level mutterings. 'We're six rows away from the nearest exit. It's too far. We're right on the outer limit of the safe zone.' He glared at Adam's blank incomprehension. 'Seven rows. The survival zone is within seven rows of the exit. That's where you want to be. How do you not know this stuff?'

Adam shrugged. 'It's probably better not thinking about it all too much.'

'Yeah,' Dan piped up. 'I mean, even if you're sitting right beside the door you can't exactly open it and step out in mid-air, can you?'

Spike gave a strangled whimper and rifled through his hand luggage. He pulled out two white tablets and swallowed them without water. 'Wake me up when we get to Japan.'

The engine had been there in the background, a dim, bass hum. Now it revved up a gear. The cabin stewards were scurrying about doing final checks, most of them smiling Japanese women. There was a brief, unsettling jolt and the plane began to roll backwards, away from the airport. Adam's heart quickened. The engine kicked up a notch and the plane paused, then trundled forward.

They seemed to taxi for a long time. It was like being in a really slow car. The wheels bumped at intervals, in a way that didn't exactly inspire confidence, sending Spike into fresh paroxysms. Dan was humming tunelessly, seemingly perfectly at ease.

And then the plane stopped. The engine noise rose up in a wild hum and Adam's seat trembled beneath him, like a dog on a leash, quivering – and then with a sudden high-pitched roar the plane surged forward, out of the starting block, gathering speed while Adam stared out of the window at the world blurring past and Spike gripped the armrest and moaned. And at last, they were up, the sudden weightlessness sending Adam's stomach into freefall, before it caught up with the rest of him, just like Archie had said it would. They were in the air.

Adam sat back in his chair with a contented sigh. He was on his way.

For Adam, the beginning of the flight had a magical quality. He was here, in a metal can, hurtling through the sky. Sitting by the window made it hard to talk to his friends (Spike was white, sweaty and silent) but gave him the perfect chance to look down on a world he had never seen before. Seeing everything so far below made him feel small inside but not in a bad way. Cars and houses and motorways looked like toys. It reminded him of seeing the Tapestry of Lights; billions of tiny specks of life endlessly moving.

As soon as the seatbelt signs went off, Dan scurried off to explore but Adam was happy enough to stay in his seat and keep watching the world below. The Bulb prowled past, snarling that no one was allowed more than one fizzy drink and if they misbehaved he would keep them on the plane and send them straight back to England.

'Pretty smooth so far,' Spike said. The colour was returning to his face and his voice had a lazy, drawling quality. Adam wondered what the white tablets were but decided not to ask. 'Take-offs and landings are what you have to worry about. That's when there's maximum chance of human error.'

'I think we should be safe enough for the next twelve hours or so. Anyway, the odds are pretty much in our favour,' Adam said.

Spike smirked. 'Somebody has to be the one in a million. Everybody thinks they're going to win the lottery so why don't they think it'll be *their* plane that falls out of the sky?'

He shuddered. When he looked at Adam he seemed almost accusing. 'You don't seem very afraid.'

'Sometimes things happen that we can't control.' Adam felt a twinge of sympathy. Right now he wished he could just tell Spike, *It's going to be OK. When you die, there's nothing to worry about.* What was the point though? They wouldn't believe him anyway. He cleared his throat. 'I mean, it's not like we can do anything about it if the plane is going to crash. We just have to sit back and try and enjoy the ride.' As if on cue a smiling steward handed him a tray, with a mixture of recognisable food and some less identifiable Japanese food.

Spike shook his head, refusing the food. 'Don't want to dilute the tablets,' he muttered. 'Want to sleep.'

But he didn't. Instead he seemed to hover somewhere between sleep and wakefulness. Adam ate his food with relish, loving the plasticky strangeness of it, only to look sideways and find Spike smirking at him in a sleepy, knowing, unnerving way. 'You all right?'

'I did some snooping on you.' Spike was smiling in a carefree way so at odds with his normal uptight self-control that Adam found himself at a loss. 'Over the summer. You said your dad was a businessman so I did some digging.'

Adam's pulse quickened with anger and fear. 'What do you mean snooping?'

'I know you think I forgot about the photo you deleted but I didn't. I couldn't get it back so I thought I'd see what else I could dig up.' He waggled his finger, the contrast between his words and his slack, happy face somehow making his words more sinister. 'And I couldn't find anything on your dad. I mean, I found his name – Nathanial Mortson. Weird spelling. But not anything else.'

'Why would you?' Adam protested. 'He has the most boring job ever. He's not a celebrity. Why would he be on the internet?'

'Because *everyone* is on the internet. Unless they've something to hide and even then it's nearly impossible.'

Adam felt his temper rising but he kept it in check. He had a feeling he would never get more out of Spike than he was getting right now. 'Well, you *found* his name. So obviously he doesn't have anything to hide.'

'No.' Spike shook his head. 'It means that whatever he's hiding, he has really good people working on it. The *best* people. Big-money people.'

'You're completely mental.' Adam's voice was flat but his heart was pogoing madly in his chest. 'My father goes to work each day. I go to school. My mother makes us dinner. We are the most boring family ever.'

'I don't think so,' Spike said, almost cheerfully. His head was lolling to one side now and he had a stupid grin plastered across his face. 'I'm going to find out what you're hiding. I always find what I'm looking for. Apart from the photo. But I'll find that too, eventually. There's always a way.'

Adam said nothing. He watched Spike's head slide sideways along the back of his seat, until gentle snores could be heard. Dan returned soon afterwards but Adam pointedly put his headphones on and tried to watch an idiotic film on the little screen in front of him.

Eventually, as darkness fell outside, he must have fallen asleep.

The flight passed surprisingly quickly, in a blur of dozing and eating. There was one exciting interlude when Archie tried to impress the girls beside him by eating his entire portion of wasabi and almost died in the process. Miss Lumpton was summoned to stand over his red-faced, eye-streaming, wheezing form, whereupon she pronounced him an idiot and left him to make a gasping recovery. His gloom was only compounded by the fact that the girls beside him remained singularly unimpressed.

Through the plane window Adam could see land beneath them. A video appeared on the mini-screens and the air stewards led the Japanese passengers through some gentle stretches, getting their muscles ready to get off the plane. Adam could have done with some stretches himself. He felt cramped and desperate for the loo. He had spent the entire flight huddled beside a sleeping Spike, not wanting to wake him and get subjected to any further interrogation.

Still, they were nearly there. He pushed past his drooling 'friend' and joined the queue for the toilet. Inside the tiny cubicle he breathed through his mouth and stared at his reflection in the mirror. In the ghastly light he looked pale and gaunt and exhausted. It turned out that as well as being an engineering miracle, flying got boring pretty quickly. He would never slag off swooping again.

When he got back to his seat, Spike was rubbing bleary eyes and wiping the side of his mouth. 'Just landing to get through,' he said, voice a harsh croak. 'As long as I get to see the supercomputers I can die happy.' He gave no sign at all of remembering what he'd said earlier.

Adam didn't answer. He felt the plane fall and watched the ground move gently towards them, looked forward to the moment when he could get off and never have to sit beside a drugged-up Spike again.

The next few hours passed in a blur of security, passports, bag collection and herding from one place to another. The mysterious Murai had sent one of his assistants to help them, a quietly spoken man called Kenai. There was a fraught train ride with various teachers flapping and Kenai guiding them off one packed train and onto two coaches. The boys were put on one coach and the girls on another. It turned out they would be staying at separate guest houses, much to Archie's horror. Dan was more prosaic. 'So even if Melissa *had* been here, you wouldn't have been able to hook up with her.' It was cold comfort for Adam.

Still, just being in Japan was amazing. They passed from busy streets to narrow ones, fat electrical cables dangling overhead as they headed further out into the suburbs. Tokyo was huge, the scale of it hard to fathom. There were people everywhere and the shop fronts were plastered with bright signs in unintelligible kanji. It was impossible to know what they were, apart from the cafes and bars. They at least had windows full of bright pictures of sushi and bowls of soup.

At last they pulled up outside a flat-fronted building, larger than most of the others. 'Out,' barked Mr Fenton, too tired to rant at them beyond one mouth-frothing exhortation to bring their passports and all their bags.

'What is this place?' Dan was eyeing the door with consternation.

'It's just a hostel. Hope it's got Western toilets and showers.' Spike looked grumpy and hung-over.

Inside the corridors were bland and clean. Adam and his friends were on the second floor close to the stairs. The four of them were directed into a tiny room with four bunk beds and a cubbyhole apiece for their belongings. There was a brief but frenzied scramble for the top bunks and to his delight Adam won. It helped having bigger, stronger brothers at home. His friends were no competition. Aron could have taken them all down with one hand tied behind his back.

They were summoned back to the communal lounge downstairs, where The Bulb was waiting. His eyes were bulging out of his bald head with a potent mixture of exhaustion and nervous energy. He made a series of toe-curling threats and advised them to spend a few hours resting and contemplating what they wanted to get out of the trip. Then he outlined their itinerary for the next few days and reminded them that they would be leaving Tokyo to visit a fish-processing factory along the eastern seaboard.

As soon as The Bulb mentioned the factory, something strange happened. Adam's head went light. There was an intense roar of sound, like water crashing on rock, and the sound of screaming. But then, a split second later, it was gone.

Adam frowned. He was tired, that was all. He pushed it from his mind and followed his friends back to the room, trying to get ready for the best holiday of his life.

Chapter 20

he next few days passed in a blur of jet lag, excitement and non-stop visiting. The mighty Murai himself came to meet them on their third day. They were visiting an electronics factory he owned and he had cleared an hour in his packed schedule.

He was a tiny, dapper man with an expansive smile and endless patience for their questions. His fluent English and cut-glass accent made the British royal family sound like cockneys in comparison.

Murai spoke fondly of his time in England, at Bonehill and Cambridge. He had special regard for his former head teacher (they couldn't help but notice the rather unguarded and sceptical glance he threw at The Bulb, who was too busy glaring at his pupils to notice). It transpired that Murai's funding of the trip wasn't purely altruistic. He had created a scholarship fund for British students to do intensive Japanese courses and study at Japanese universities, specifically in science and engineering. When he mentioned that he co-sponsored the Tokyo Supercomputer Convention even Spike stood up straighter, looking eager.

Dan snorted derisively. 'Who would go and look at computers when the world RPG Exhibition is on?!'

His answer was lost in the sudden stampede towards the exit. They were going on a sightseeing tour that afternoon – a sushi bar for lunch, followed by a visit to a famous Buddhist temple. No one was really that interested in temples but it had to be more interesting than the electronics factory, or at least the limited bits of it they had been allowed to see.

Adam picked at his lunchtime sushi. He hadn't been feeling well and that was always a cause for alarm, because Lumen rarely got ill, thanks to their keystones. Adam only ever felt really unwell when he was having a serious premonition – when lots of people were about to die.

He tried to rationalise it away at first, hoping it was just his first brush with jet lag, but all the signs were there. He knew them now: the queasy feeling in his stomach, light-headedness and bizarrely vivid dreams. What he didn't know yet was exactly what was going to happen. Tokyo was a huge city, bursting at the seams with millions of people. It would be so easy for a train to derail or for dozens of cars to pile into one another.

There was one thing he did know though. He wasn't going to do anything about it, even if he did figure it out. Darian might have backed off, distracted by his fear of Auntie Jo and Heinrich's unexpected move – but he wouldn't take his eye off the ball for long. It would be hard not to intervene but this time Adam knew it would be a suicide mission. Plus, getting involved in an accident in Japan would start an international incident.

He thought his mind was made up until they got back to the hostel that evening. They had an hour of free time before they had to go out for dinner and on to a theatre to see a traditional Japanese dance and music performance. His friends and most of the others settled into the communal lounge, gathering round the TV and watching, fascinated, as a Japanese game show played. The host was a shrieking man with blond tips in his hair, who was chasing some very pretty Japanese girls round a studio. The girls were dressed like porcelain dolls, with ringlet curls, ivory faces and eyelashes like spider legs. They were squealing and trying to hobble to safety on platform shoes.

Archie's eyes were like saucers. 'You see! I told you they dressed up like that!'

Dan was frowning. 'They're a bit weird looking.'

Archie scowled. 'They're no weirder than your elf people.'

The host had caught up with them and now appeared to be trying to bite one of the girl's pants off with his teeth. The room full of boys had fallen completely silent. Even Mr Fenton and The Bulb were slack-jawed. It took The Bulb a few seconds to realise that this probably wasn't wholesome family entertainment. He seized the remote control and changed the channel, landing on a sumo match. There was a subdued chorus of disapproval, swiftly stifled by The Bulb's murderous glare.

Adam took advantage of the moment to slip away. In the room, he turned on the ceiling fan and crawled up into his bunk, lying on the cover with his hands behind his head, watching the fan circle. His stomach was churning. He had spent all day trying to convince himself that he'd eaten something unusual – but he knew that his doom sense was waiting to show him something. Blocking the premonition would only make him feel worse. The sooner he saw whatever vision was lying in

227

wait, the sooner he would feel better. He would feel guilty too, knowing he was going to ignore it, but he would worry about that when it happened.

The room was quiet as the ceiling fan whirred around and around and around. He closed his eyes and felt the weight of his body pulling him into the mattress. He let his mind go wandering, listening to the fan hum over and over again . . .

He was standing at the top of a sloping drive. The wind blew in his face, cold and heavy with an unpleasant fishy, diesel tinge. Ahead of him were long, low buildings where men and women were moving about, dressed in identical grey overalls with matching grey caps. Forklift trucks were zipping across the yard, moving crates of fish and seafood, gleaming grey and silver against their beds of ice.

From his vantage point Adam could peer past the fish-processing plant and see the roofs of more buildings on a street below. The land sloped sharply and in the gaps between the buildings Adam could see something glinting blue. Water, reflecting the sunshine. He couldn't see far. He needed to get higher.

Behind him a truck roared. He swung round and watched it turn up a steep lane, leading to a tall white building. It was elegant and futuristic, a landmark four storeys high looking down on the buildings below. Curious now, he followed the truck up the sharp slope as fast as he could. He knew that he wasn't really there; if he had been his breath would have been coming and going in fast gasps.

It took a minute to climb to the top of the lane and stand in front of the white building. Adam stared through glass doors into a light and airy reception area. Two metal staircases rose up far above. He could see an attractive receptionist talking into a headset. Two men in suits were hurrying down one of the stairwells holding briefcases. The whole building conveyed a sense of calm purpose.

Then, without warning, time jolted. Adam found himself standing some distance away, at the edge of a cliff. He fell to his knees with shock, clutching his hands over his ears. A siren was blaring, rising and falling. He was looking down on the processing plant below and the men and women inside were flooding out, running across the yard, towards the steep track he had just climbed. What had happened? It was like time had slipped, moving him forward by seconds or minutes or hours. When he looked over his shoulder at the white building, all the windows had shattered. He could see the glass lying on the ground below. The people inside were screaming. What the hell was going on?

It was the other sound that made him turn back; that fired up nerves in some primitive, animal part of his brain. The people below didn't seem to notice; they were too busy running up the hill. More people were pouring out of houses and appearing from side streets. The sound was a low roar, still far away, but Adam's eyes were drawn irresistibly to the sea beyond the factory. He was looking straight out onto the Pacific Ocean, stretching away as far as the eye could see. If he climbed into a boat right now and set off across the water, he would eventually find himself thousands of miles away, landing on the western coast of America.

At first the sea seemed calm but as he looked his eye was

caught by a movement; the movement of water, faster than the waves rolling towards the shore. He squinted against the breeze and frowned. What was it about the water that looked different? It was just a slightly bigger wave. Wasn't there some nursery rhyme about every seventh wave being bigger than the others? He couldn't see them as they crested and broke, the shore hidden by the buildings.

Adam felt cold. Something was wrong. The sirens were still wailing and the last of the grey-clad workers were leaving the factory when the building behind them exploded. Not with fire but with water – a black, filthy wall of water, surging over the men and women running up the slope, the roar devouring them as they screamed and Adam screamed and . . .

Adam jolted awake when the bedroom door burst open. He sat up fast, struggling to breathe, hitting his head on the low ceiling. 'Ouch!'

Dan was standing in the doorway staring at him. 'What are you doing?'

'What does it look like I'm doing?' His voice came out strangled. His chest was still tight and he bent over double, trying to breathe. The vision was all in his head – at least for now – but it had felt so real that his body had fallen for it hook, line and sinker.

Spike pushed past Dan and grabbed his coat. 'You came for a *nap*?'

Archie's leering face peered round the door. 'He wasn't napping, were you, mate? Just having a little bit of . . . happy time.' He sniggered.

Adam stared at him stupidly. What were they all doing here? What was *he* doing here? He didn't even know which bit of what he was seeing was real. He sat up, almost hitting his head all over again. 'What do you want?'

'We have to go,' Dan said. 'That dance thing. And the screechy singing.' He launched into a demonstration, sounding like a cat being disembowelled and strangled with its own intestines.

Adam rolled onto his side and swung down from the bunk, still dazed. He staggered, feeling groggy and sick but trying to hide it. 'I'm ready.' He shoved his feet into his boots and grabbed a hoodie, following them downstairs and out into the cool night air. Light drizzle was falling and moisture hazed his face as they stepped onto the waiting coach. He licked his lips, dreading the taste of salt water.

He sat quietly, watching the buildings roll by as they made their way to the theatre. Seeing the same architecture made his stomach clench with the familiarity of the vision, even though there was no ocean here. He knew already that his premonition hadn't been about Tokyo and there was only one place they would be visiting outside Tokyo. He turned to Archie. 'What's the name of that place we're going to again? The place with the fish factory?'

'Hachimana.' Archie yawned.

'How far away is it?'

'Couple of hours on the train. We get the really fast one.' Archie rolled his eyes and looked longingly out of the bus window. 'See over there? That's Shibuya. We could be hanging out there with cute cos girls and instead we're going to go and watch Japanese opera.'

Adam stayed silent. He wasn't going to be watching anything. He had places to be.

His opportunity came when the performance was just about to start. He had deliberately held back until everyone else was seated and made sure he sat beside the aisle, away from his friends, pleading a dodgy stomach. The teachers were sitting several rows in front, although he knew Fenton was out in the foyer, keeping watch. Hopefully no one would notice his absence. He waited for the lights to go down, then eased out of his seat and scurried up the few rows of steps.

It was simple enough to get past Fenton; he was sitting on the stairs, his head against the wall, dozing. Adam moved silently across the carpeted floor, searching until he recognised the symbol for the men's toilet. The last few stragglers were leaving and heading into the performance. Within moments he was in an empty cubicle ready to go.

He closed his eyes and reached for his keystone, then stepped forward into the Hinterland. Once he was there it was easier to feel the particular vibration and resonance of the Mortson Keystone, especially when he visualised it, cradled in the stone Buddha's hands, the mountains rising all around them. He knew he could do this. He felt the snag at the back of his throat and swooped.

Last time he had been here it had been early morning. Tonight it was amazingly dark and frost glinted on the ground, even here near the foot of the mountains. The only visible lights were the lamps glowing in the house beyond the garden and the thousands of stars pinpointed above. Adam couldn't help staring up for a minute, just enjoying the sight. They were the only human beings for miles around. His breath billowed out in front of him as he walked towards the house, using the light on his phone to help him.

As he got closer the glass window slid open and a man's silhouette stood framed in what had become a doorway. Hikaru greeted him. Adam mirrored the man's bow, holding it a fraction longer than Hikaru, then shook his hand. He eased his boots off before stepping inside onto the tatami matting. They were in the same room as last time.

Hikaru knelt before the low table. 'Rita will bring us tea.'

Now that he was here, without his father's guidance, Adam felt uncomfortably aware of all the things he could say and do wrong. 'Thank you.' That was probably a safe-enough start.

Maybe Hikaru realised this. He smiled suddenly, his face softening and becoming less implacable. 'You are welcome here, Adam. Please be at ease. I am happy you have come.'

'I would have come sooner but . . . I couldn't get away. Without people noticing.'

'I understand.' The screen door slid open and Rita came in, beaming a welcome. She set a tray on the table and embraced Adam warmly. There were a few obligatory questions about health, family and his visit so far and then, with one last smile, she murmured goodbye and padded across the floor, sliding the door behind her.

Hikaru poured the tea and Adam cringed, expecting the same cabbagey variety as last time. To his relief this one was different, a clear, pale green with a sweet fragrance. Maybe he hadn't hidden his dislike as well as he'd thought. As if reading his mind Hikaru said, 'Japanese tea is very fine but it is an acquired taste for some.'

Adam nodded. He took a scalding sip, feeling his tongue go numb and swallowing with an effort. What was he supposed to say now? He cleared his throat. 'I . . . Thank you for allowing me to come here. I'm enjoying your country very much. If I can do anything to help you, please tell me. I could help you on a job?' He cringed as soon as the words were out of his mouth. Help him? *Help* the High Luman of a whole country?

Far from seeming offended, Hikaru bowed gravely. 'Thank you, Adam. Your offer is most kind. But, as our guest, you should enjoy your stay in peace.' He paused. 'In truth, our culture is somewhat different. There is a preference here for an older Luman to guide people into their Lights. It gives people a sense of security. In addition, there is still a distrust of outside cultures, particularly for some of our older citizens.'

Adam bobbed his head awkwardly, feeling nothing but relief. He was off the hook. More importantly, he'd also seen how to steer the conversation around to the direction he needed it. 'Do other Lumen help when there are big jobs though? Like, when something really major happens?'

Hikaru nodded. 'Of course, if necessary. However, we have many fast-response Lumen. Our country is very beautiful but compared to your Kingdom, our natural placement is more . . . volatile.'

Adam pressed him. 'You mean you get earthquakes and things?'

'*Hai.*' Hikaru poured more tea into Adam's cup, then nodded his thanks as Adam refilled his cup in return. 'We have many earthquakes. Most are small but larger earthquakes do occur and in the past they caused great numbers of deaths. Happily today building methods have improved and casualties are fewer both in number and frequency.'

Adam hesitated. If he asked the next question, Hikaru would be sure to remember it in a few days when the worst happened. Still, if Adam wasn't going to intervene, it wouldn't matter. It would just be a curious foreigner asking about a very real risk of Japanese life. 'And what about earthquakes at sea? The ones that cause tidal waves?'

'*Tsunami*. This is what you are speaking of, *hai*?' Hikaru fell silent for a moment, holding the porcelain cup delicately between his fingertips and sipping his tea. 'Our country has been devastated by these waves in the past. You have seen the famous *Ukiyo-e* prints?' He stood and moved to the bookcase on the wall, pulling out a heavy hardback book with an ornate fan on the cover. He knelt at the table once again and turned the pages until he found what he was looking for, then slid the book across to Adam. '*Dozo*. Please look.'

Adam stared at the drawings, recognition flaring. He had seen these kinds of pictures on clothes and posters in some of the indie shops round Flip Street. He knew they were famous, the simple, graceful woodblock prints of fishermen, their tiny boats rising up on the curling tips of vast waves.

Hikaru was pointing at one picture. 'This picture is called "The Great Wave". It is by a very famous Japanese artist called Hokusai. Many people think it shows a tsunami when in fact it is simply a large wave in the open sea. *Tsunami* means *harbour wave*. It is not a tidal wave because it is not caused by the ebb and flow of tides. It is, as you rightly say, the result of an earthquake beneath the sea floor. As the great plates push together, one slips and rises up, displacing the water on the surface. As the water rushes towards land, the speed and force creates not just one wave but many waves, much more powerful than any normal wave. In the open sea the wave will not be felt but when it reaches land, it can be . . . disastrous.'

'Do they happen often?'

Hikaru shook his head. 'I am thankful that large tsunamis are rare.'

Adam knew he had to ask one more thing, even though he quailed at the thought. 'And is there any way of knowing when they will happen?'

Hikaru studied him in silence for what felt like a long time. 'I am not sure what you are asking me, Adam Mortson.' His voice was subtly different; cautious and harder-edged. 'We have no Seers in this Kingdom and even if we had, they would of course not intervene in these events.'

Adam blinked, thinking fast. So Hikaru knew the rumours from the Kingdom of Britain. He knew there was an investigation. And now Adam had made himself a suspect. He breathed in slowly, trying to keep his voice even. 'Of course not. But I mean, is there some science stuff that can help? Can it predict these earthquakes?'

Hikaru watched him carefully, then put down his tea cup soundlessly. 'Nothing can predict an earthquake, Adam. But there is a monitoring system at sea, to warn coastal areas. When a large earthquake occurs in these areas the alarm system activates and tells people they must move to higher ground, away from the shore. I do not understand the workings of this system but it has undoubtedly saved many lives. As for those who are not saved . . . they are the only ones we need be concerned with. For it is the dead we help, not the living.'

When he finished speaking Hikaru stood up smoothly. Adam understood that their meeting was at an end and struggled to his feet without any of Hikaru's grace. They walked to the sliding glass door and Adam slipped his feet back into his boots. He turned back to Hikaru and bowed. 'Thank you for having me.'

'Enjoy your remaining time in our country, Adam. Make the most of your vacation from Luman life. All too soon your time here will be over and you will return to your own Kingdom, ready for work.'

Adam nodded and turned back into the darkness. As he walked away from the house he grimaced. He'd heard Hikaru's message loud and clear behind the politeness.

Don't interfere in things, Adam. Save your troublemaking for your own Kingdom.

Chapter 21

dam swooped back to the theatre without incident. There was a hairy moment when he emerged from the toilet cubicle and found himself face to face with The Bulb. He looked even more bull-necked than usual this close. 'What are you doing here, Mortson?'

Adam stared at him. Was he really supposed to answer that? A tickle in his nose gave him a bolt of inspiration. He raised his fingers and pulled them away smeared with blood. 'Nosebleed, sir. I thought it had stopped but it hasn't.'

The Bulb stared at him with the kind of look normally reserved for squashed dog mess on the underside of a favourite shoe. 'Well, get a tissue, you idiot!'

'Yes, sir,' Adam muttered. He grabbed a few squares, thankful that this toilet actually provided some toilet roll. He reached the door into the auditorium just as everyone else began streaming out. It was easy enough to lurk at one side and slip into the crowd as though he had never left his seat. He waited with the rest of his classmates until his friends appeared.

Archie was scowling while Spike and Dan were sniggering. It turned out that Archie had been drooling over one of the dancers, unaware that he was watching *kabuki* and that the 'hot babe' he was admiring was actually a man dressed as a woman. He had apparently given a fairly detailed account of what he would like to do with 'her' after the performance. Judging by the grin on Dan's face this was the highlight of his trip to date.

Adam tried to pretend that he was just as entertained by the whole thing but his head wasn't really there. He went straight to bed when they got back to the hostel, ignoring the chorus of derision. Lying on his bunk he felt torn. He wanted to go and hang out with everyone else in the lounge. He was supposed to be enjoying himself, not having freakish premonitions. He had a whole lifetime of Luman crap to look forward to. Couldn't he just *enjoy* his last few weeks of freedom?

He couldn't intervene in the tsunami. He *knew* he couldn't. So why was he even thinking about it? Hadn't he caused enough harm last time he'd messed about? All right, most of that was down to Morta and her psychopathic need to kill as many random people as possible – but he should have learned his lesson. Intervening to save people seemed like a good idea but you had no way of predicting the consequences down the line. Not to mention the more immediate consequences for himself and his family, especially his father. Darian would do whatever he could to take everything from Nathanial, not excepting his life and his wife. Why did Adam keep giving him opportunities on a plate? *Not this time.*

And yet, even though it was crazy, Adam found himself calling the vision to mind as he drifted off to sleep. It was a time when his mind would be most relaxed and open; the perfect time to get more information. The perfect time to go a little deeper into what was going to happen.

And then he was there again, on the slope overlooking the processing plant. The sirens were already blaring and workers were flooding past without seeing him. They were running for high ground as if they knew what was going to happen but there wasn't enough warning. Some of them were going to make it to safety but the last group wouldn't. He'd already seen *what* happened to them. Now he needed to know *when* it was going to happen.

He ran out of the yard, ignoring the safety of the steep slope up to the white building. Instead he turned left out of the gate and ran until he found a street that pointed downhill towards the sea. He stuck to the pavement, weaving and bobbing between people and cars, even though he wasn't there. The street was long and winding but after thirty seconds of flat-out sprinting he reached the main road. He looked frantically to the left and right, eyes searching – until there it was, a flat black sign bearing bright red digital numbers, hanging outside some kind of electronics store. He stared at the sign, willing the display to change from temperature to time.

Everyone else was running in the opposite direction, trying to get to higher ground, but there wasn't enough time; he knew it. People were fighting their way into the tallest buildings or trying in vain to get up the street away from the water, hidden behind the buildings on the other side of the road. It was all happening too fast. 'Come on,' Adam muttered, not looking at the street, not looking at the shore, watching the clock, watching the clock, waiting, waiting for the numbers to change.

And then the water erupted into the street. He turned; he couldn't help it. The speed and the force were astonishing down here. The water seemed alive, pouring towards him from all directions. Cars were picked up, still with their passengers inside, moving towards him, converging. *I'm not here, I'm not here, I'm not here*, he told himself again and again, trying to overcome his gut instinct to bolt for safety. He turned back to the sign and it flashed in his face: 11:08.

He woke, sweating, a second before the debris hit.

Adam barely slept that night, although he pretended to when the other three returned to the room. Once the light was out, he lay in the darkness, listening to his friends breathing and snoring peacefully around him. His body was rigid with the horror of what he'd seen.

He had seen pictures of tsunamis before, on TV programmes about disasters. Somehow though, they hadn't captured the full horror of seeing the water hurtling towards you. How did it move so fast? And worse, it didn't even look like water any more; just a terrible black wall of filth and cars and debris, all of it huge and inanimate and lethal. Even as he stood there in the vision, he had seen how many people weren't going to make it – and that was just within his view. Hachimana was only one small coastal city. A tsunami could stretch for hundreds of miles along a coastline, affecting dozens of towns and villages.

It was obvious that the sirens only sounded a few minutes before the water hit. How could people get away in time? They might even mistake it for a drill at first, or think it was just a precaution – although in a country accustomed to tsunamis, most people would probably take it seriously. But even so, there just wasn't enough *time*. They needed more warning.

And now, here he was, lying safely in his bed and knowing this was going to happen and not knowing what he was going to do about it. He felt sick. It wasn't fair. No one should have the burden of this kind of knowledge if you weren't allowed to do anything about it. This wasn't like the bomb – there was nothing he could do to prevent it. All he wanted was a way to give people a fair chance to get out.

As dawn crept round, Adam struggled to think up a plan. He imagined, for a moment, presenting himself to the Japanese authorities and telling them what was going to happen. How would they react? Lock him up? Tell him he was wasting police time and hand him over to The Bulb? Hikaru would hear about it (he had no doubt the Japanese Luman was keeping a discreet eye on him) and then when the tsunami struck he would realise he was dealing with a Seer. He wouldn't be the only Luman interested in a British Seer. Adam might as well hand himself over to Darian and the Concilium right now.

Going public was another way. He could find a TV station, turn up there, tell them some story about being a boy prophet. Only, would they believe him? If they didn't Hikaru would know and the same scenario would unfold. If they *did* believe him he would probably be locked up in a laboratory somewhere and studied like a rat. He would be exchanging one prison cell for another. And even if Darian would find it harder to come for him, he wouldn't hold back from trying to destroy Nathanial.

When Fenton came round and banged their bedroom door,

Adam lay in his bunk, pretending to be asleep. He couldn't face another day, pretending to be normal. He waited till his friends went down for breakfast. For a moment, he was tempted to just go. He could take his stuff, swoop home and tell his father everything. He wouldn't save anyone from the tsunami and he would cause all kinds of trouble for his teachers but at least he wouldn't have to stand and watch hundreds of people die right in front of him when he could have saved them.

Adam sighed and climbed down from his bunk. *One day at a time*, he thought. *Don't do anything crazy. Just take one day at a time.*

He didn't eat much at breakfast; the thought of filling his stomach with rice and miso soup only intensified his nausea. After the meal they walked to the nearest JR station. The girls in their year and the female teachers were already at the station, waiting. So was Kenai, accompanied by three more of Murai's smiling minions. Today they were splitting into four groups going to different places: an art gallery, a cookery demonstration, the RPG Exhibition and the Supercomputer Convention.

The Supercomputer Convention was in Shibuya, a convenient Metro ride away. Their group split into several parties, with only Mr Fenton willing to accompany the role players to the RPG Exhibition. Dan had a newfound adoration of Fenton. It probably helped that he had a different form tutor. Archie had gone with him, in the hope of seeing Japanese girls dressed up like manga characters.

Kenai was accompanying the elect band of computer geeks to the convention. On the way, he explained Murai's involvement in the whole thing. Spike was hanging on Kenai's every word but Adam barely listened. He stood in the packed train, holding on tight to the loop hanging down from the ceiling, feeling dizzy and detached.

He staggered along behind the rest of his group, not really noticing his surroundings. He didn't care about computers, or not in the way that Spike did. The only reason he had picked the convention was because the art gallery would make him think sad thoughts about Melissa, the food would make him feel even more sick and he couldn't face stepping into the alternate universes of the RPG Exhibition. Things were weird enough in his head without frolicking through all the costumes.

Still, it *was* impressive here. They paused outside the station and Kenai gave them a moment to take photos. As the traffic lights changed hundreds of people swarmed across the pedestrian crossing. Adam watched through filmy eyes. That was the thing about Japan – there were so many people. If an earthquake struck, or a tsunami, or a typhoon, so many people were crammed on top of each other. If the earthquake was going to be big enough to cause a tsunami further up the coast, would it bring down buildings in Tokyo? Would people die here too? He wasn't getting any premonitions but then maybe the scale of the tsunami was blocking out all the other people who would be affected. At least Tokyo had strict building controls to avoid buildings collapsing.

The Bulb was in excellent form but he seemed nervous too. He bombarded Kenai with questions, most of them about the male toilets at the convention. Kenai was looking increasingly baffled by the interrogation. Spike smirked. 'The Bulb thinks he's meeting the Sensai here, in one of the toilets. He's going to be spending a long afternoon checking out the facilities.'

The convention was happening in one of the skyscrapers near the station, spread across one vast floor. Kenai signed their group in, got them passes to put round their necks and led them into the main exhibition hall. Every inch of space was dotted with people or computer equipment. White partition walls were covered in screens, displaying the latest computers and software from all over the world. The whole room was buzzing with animated conversation in dozens of different languages.

Spike looked like he was about to pass out. He elbowed Adam in the ribs hard enough to hurt. 'Do you know who that *is*?!' He was nodding and hissing in the direction of a thin man with thick glasses. He looked a bit like one of the science technicians in school. His name meant nothing to Adam, much to Spike's disgust. He launched into a long list of the man's achievements but cut it off when Kenai told them their meeting point and time and offered to give them a tour.

Most of the diehards followed him eagerly. Adam was left with the other stragglers who hadn't known what else to do with their day. He knew a few of them but he didn't want to get into conversation with them, especially the girl with the blonde hair who kept shooting him evil looks. He knew she was one of Melissa's friends and decided now was a good time to make himself scarce.

At first, he tried to get out into the street but a stern-faced security guard told him that his pass would be revoked if he left the building. Frustrated, he went back into the exhibition space. The noise, the glossy partitions, the bright lines of code and geometric patterns on the monitors . . . It was all like some horrible conspiracy to make him feel even worse than he already did.

In the past, his premonitions had made him feel sick up until the point when he knew what was going to happen – and what he should do about it. He had thought if he allowed the vision to unfold he would have received the message and been left to get on with his life in relative peace. But something about this disaster was making him feel worse, not better. Maybe it was the scale of it. There could be so *many* casualties, maybe even people he knew.

The thought gave him pause. Up until now he'd been so busy thinking about all the Japanese people who would die that it hadn't occurred to him who else might get caught up in the wave. In the vision he had been standing up high, out of the way, at the processing plant. But how far would the water come up the hill? Maybe it would reach them too. Or what if some of their group were down at the waterside when the wave struck?

It doesn't matter because I can't do anything about it! Adam's nails were digging into his palms and he tried to take a deep breath, pushing the sick feeling down inside. He started walking, hoping the movement would give him something to focus on other than the guilt. He was going to let hundreds, maybe thousands of people die, just to save his own skin. *And my family. I'm saving my family too.* He felt a fresh wave of hatred for Darian. If he had left them alone in peace maybe Adam could have done something but not while they were being investigated.

He had almost reached the far end of the exhibition space when the announcement caught his attention. It was in Japanese but one word jumped out at him: *tsunami*. A moment later the message was repeated, this time in English. 'Delegates attending the seminar on tsunami warning systems should please make their way to lecture room B.'

Adam stopped dead. There was no getting away from it, was there? But why were they talking about tsunamis at a computer convention? For a moment a pang of curiosity cut through the fog in his head. He looked around, hoping to see people moving towards lecture room B but there wasn't exactly a mob stampeding in that direction. Then, as he passed two men, he heard them talking in French and gathered that they shared his niche interest. They were consulting some kind of floor plan and he followed them back towards the entrance and down a short corridor.

There were an optimistic number of seats set out and Adam slipped into the back row, feeling conspicuous. A wiry woman with grey hair was up on a low stage, standing behind a laptop. More people were filtering in and the lights in the room dimmed, just as a large projector screen flared into life. It was cooler here and the darkness was soothing. Adam closed his eyes. He wasn't sure what he was hoping to achieve from this but at least he had found somewhere to sit in peace.

The woman introduced herself in English as Dr Someone from the University of Somewhere and immediately launched into a horribly complicated explanation of the computer equipment she would be using. Adam wished that Spike was there to decode. In his absence he did the next best thing and turned on the voice recorder on his mobile. He wasn't sure what he was hoping to achieve.

Luckily when it came to the tsunamis Adam was no less informed than a lot of the people around him and Dr Expert explained it in layman's terms. 'The tsunami warning system is a state-of-the-art system being deployed in earthquake regions around the globe. It is impossible to calculate how many lives have been saved. Just a few minutes' warning can be the difference between life and death for those living in coastal areas.'

Adam sat up rigid as she explained how the system worked, holding his mobile steady, desperate not to miss a word. For the first time in days, something like hope kindled inside him. As Auntie Jo liked to say, there was more than one way to skin a cat. Up until now he had convinced himself that only he could warn people about the tsunami.

Just maybe there was another way.

Chapter 22

dam stayed until the bitter end of the talk, even though Dr Expert descended back into computer gibberish. He didn't care if he didn't understand it – he knew someone who would. All he had to do now was figure out how to make Spike listen to it.

As it transpired, this was easier than Adam had dared to imagine. He was back at the meeting point with a few minutes to spare, whereas a scowling Spike was dragged to the door by a harried-looking technician. 'I only needed another minute,' he protested.

When he saw Adam he grinned. 'How *amazing* is this place? Seriously, I would swap all of Tokyo for a few more hours here. I was just trying to find out how they had created the cluster and they got this goon to take me away.'

Adam raised an eyebrow. 'How exactly were you finding stuff out?'

Spike smirked. 'Magic.' He refused to be drawn.

Kenai appeared beside them. 'Your principal is missing. Bulber-San. Have you seen him?'

They shook their heads. He pursed his lips but was too polite to say anything. Adam considered him for a moment. 'Have you worked for Mr Murai for a long time?'

'*Hai*. Since I left university. I am his communications assistant.'

'Do you know the place we're travelling to? Hachimana?'

'Of course. I visit it frequently.'

'To see the fish?' There was a mocking edge to Spike's voice that made Adam want to slap him. Why didn't he just keep his mouth shut?

Either Kenai didn't notice or chose not to notice. 'The fish-processing plant is not the only business Murai-San has in Hachimana. He also owns a large research and development plant there. Microprocessors are the main product, not unlike the ones in our exhibition stand.'

Spike's eyes widened. 'Are we going there?'

Kenai smiled. 'Unfortunately we will not have time. You will however see the many innovative machines developed by Murai-San for the processing of fish.' Now there was a mocking edge to *his* voice that almost made Adam smile.

He cleared his throat. He knew he was taking a chance but he had to find out more. 'Hachimana is on the coast, isn't it?' At Kenai's nod he hesitated. 'Will we be safe there?'

'Safe from what?'

'I was in one of the talks. It was about tsunamis.' Adam tried to sound nervous and found it came quite naturally under the circumstances. 'The lecturer said that there are loads of earthquakes every year and some of them cause tsunamis. Are we in danger?'

'I am sure the lecturer also told you that Japan has the most sophisticated earthquake detection and tsunami-warning system in the world. In fact, Murai-San himself has manufactured some of the cutting-edge equipment used, especially that used for undersea monitoring.'

'But what if a tsunami comes?' Adam didn't want to push his luck but surely there had to be some kind of back-up plan. He was getting genuinely nervous, for his friends as well as the people living in Hachimana. From what Dr Expert had said, a big tsunami could travel hundreds of metres inland. Adam hadn't seen the full scale of the wave, only what it looked like at shore level. What if the water travelled uphill and swamped the processing plant with all the Bonehill visitors inside? What if his doom sense was shrieking madly because he was sensing his *own* death?

'If an earthquake should happen, all our facilities have been built to withstand even a powerful quake. And in the event of a tsunami warning, we will evacuate the plant and move to higher ground. In fact, we will withdraw to the research building that I spoke of. It is a four-storey building at the highest point in Hachimana, just a short walk away.'

Adam nodded. The white building. He knew where Kenai was talking about from his premonition, not that he was going to tell Kenai that. He murmured his thanks, still pretending to be scared. Inside he was jumping up and down with joy. He risked a sidelong glance at Spike, who was staring thoughtfully after a retreating Kenai. Adam knew what he would be thinking about: how to get into that research plant. What he *didn't* know was that Adam was going to give him the way.

A dejected-looking Bulb returned, escorted by a security guard, blustering about having needed the facilities. There was a pungent smell around him that Adam recognised as *sake*. Kenai led them onto the Metro and two hours later they were back at the hostel, eating *yakitori* and rice balls. Dan and Archie were already there, gabbling and interrupting each other in their excitement to talk about the RPG Exhibition. Judging by Archie's phone, he had spent most of the afternoon taking photos of smiling Japanese girls making peace signs, dressed in a variety of weird and wonderful outfits. Spike meanwhile was emailing The Bulb, explaining the Sensai's unfortunate absence, which gave Adam time to plan his next move.

The entertainment for the evening was a large karaoke bar for a couple of hours and then a return to the hostel to pack. They would take their bags with them the following day on a coach tour, then catch an afternoon train to Hachimana. After one overnight stay they would return to Tokyo for a final few days of sightseeing, before catching their flight back to London. Privately, Adam was pretty sure they wouldn't be travelling anywhere unless the tsunami really was confined only to the Hachimana area.

Before they left, he grabbed his headphones and stuck them in his pocket. He made sure that he fell into step beside Spike as they walked the few blocks to the karaoke shack. It felt awkward. He'd avoided having any kind of real conversation with Spike since the weirdness on the plane. Adam still felt a cold shock of fear and anger, thinking about his so-called friend snooping into his life. He was taking a big risk. There was no way Spike would ever believe the warning was just a coincidence but he would worry about that when it happened.

Once again, luck was on his side. It was Spike who brought Hachimana up. 'I can't believe we have to go to a fish factory. Why the hell can't we just stay in Tokyo? Or better yet, why can't we go to the research lab? I mean, seriously, what can they actually do with fish? Machines to chop them into pieces? Big deal.'

'Yeah.' Adam hesitated. If he took the plunge, there was no going back. 'The only way they'll let us near the research place is if there's a tsunami.'

'Some chance,' Spike muttered, looking gloomy.

Not for the first time, Adam found himself wondering if Spike cared about anyone. Sometimes he seemed more like a machine than a person. Who else would think a tsunami was a price worth paying for a trip to a computer factory? Not that Adam was in any position to judge. He had been putting his own safety and his family's before all the people who would be caught up in the wave. Now he was going to lie to his friend and use him. Still, it was for the right reasons. Wasn't that enough?

He took a deep breath. Crunch time. 'There might be a way.'

Spike didn't even look round. 'What, you can make an earthquake happen, can you?'

Adam shook his head. 'Of course not. But we don't actually have to make anything happen. We just have to make it *look like* something's going to happen.'

'And how are we going to do that?' Spike seemed sceptical but interested. This was exactly what Adam was banking on.

'I'll tell you later,' he whispered. They had arrived at the Karaoke Kingdom, which turned out to be a multi-storey building with an array of karaoke rooms, each complete with a screen, microphones and a telephone for ordering drinks. Mr Fenton and The Bulb were explaining very slowly and loudly to the manager that under no circumstances were alcoholic drinks to be provided to any of the rooms with Bonehill students inside. There didn't seem to be a similar ban on the teachers' personal karaoke chamber . . .

The karaoke was more of a laugh than anyone had really expected, mainly because the teachers left them in peace. It was one of the few nights when they got to spend any proper time with the girls and in spite of everything else on his mind, Adam was missing Melissa. Seeing her friends dressed up beneath the colourful lights and hearing the music reminded Adam of the night in Cryptique. After their disastrous evening there he would never have believed that she would give him another chance. They had come so far and then it had all gone so wrong.

He didn't feel like singing, even in a mob. Archie proved definitively that there was more to rap than wearing baggy clothes and talking very fast. Dan stood up and sang some kind of rock ballad in a high, pure voice, which led to startled silence followed swiftly by a chorus of derision. Being Dan, he didn't take it personally but grinned as he sat down. 'They're just jealous. In a few years I'll be in a boy band and loaded.'

Archie scoffed at him. 'I thought you were going to be a dentist?'

Dan shrugged. 'Maybe I'll buy a chain of dentists with my band money. That'll keep my dad off my back.'

Adam left them to their bickering, muttering that he was going to find the toilets. Instead, he waited in the corridor, and within a minute Spike had slipped outside too. Adam suppressed a grin. Usually it was Spike baiting traps but tonight he was the prey and Adam was the fisherman.

There was a niche in the wall with a vase full of dried flowers. They perched there, separated by the vase. Adam didn't know how long they had before Dan and Archie came to find them so he got straight to the point. 'I went to the tsunami talk earlier, about how the warning system works. Listen to this.' He passed Spike one of the headphones and slipped the other bud into his own ear.

They sat in silence until the recording ended, interrupted occasionally by the crash of doors opening and closing as groups of people ran up and down the corridors laughing. No one bothered them and no teachers shooed them back inside. As it finished, Spike turned to Adam. 'Is that it?'

'Yeah.'

'And?' Spike looked irritated rather than pleased.

Adam stared at him. 'I thought it would help.'

'How?' Spike stood up, as though he was going to walk away.

Adam stood up too. 'Did you understand how it works?'

Spike rolled his eyes. 'It's not exactly complicated. There are sensors on land and beneath the seabed to pick up any seismic activity. When there's an earthquake they detect the vertical P waves and beam the information to Tokyo by satellite. It sounds the alarm system so people have a few seconds to get ready before the S waves get everything shaking. And if the earthquake is beneath the seabed it monitors the sea level and triggers the tsunami warning system if there are going to be any big waves hitting the shore.'

'So there you go then.' Spike was still looking bemused. Adam sighed. 'I told you, there doesn't have to *be* an earthquake or a tsunami. It just has to look like there's *going* to be one, to trigger the warning system. And then they'll evacuate us to higher ground. And in our case that means Murai's research facility.'

Understanding dawned in Spike's face – but the look he gave Adam was more incredulous than pleased. 'So you want me to trigger a fake earthquake in the system, get a tsunami warning declared and thousands of people evacuated for nothing?'

But it's not for nothing! Why couldn't he just tell him the truth? Just blurt it out and accept that he would look crazy? *Because it's Spike and he won't just let it alone. I can always pretend it was a coincidence and there won't be anything he can do about it – but if I tell him the truth, he'll never let it go.* Adam tried to look casual. 'I thought this was the kind of thing you'd do for a laugh. After all, you'd get to see the research plant. You could get all sorts of stuff there for your hackers' group. Plus pulling off a stunt like that would definitely get you in.' He hesitated, hating himself. 'Although they did say the warning system was totally unhackable.'

'They would never say that,' Spike said flatly. 'Nothing is unhackable. They probably meant that no one would want to hack into it.' He chewed his lip, staring into space. 'I might give it a go at home sometime.'

'Nah.' Adam breathed in slowly, keeping his voice level. 'What would be the point in that? At least if you do it here we'll get to see the research plant. Plus, you'll get to see the evacuation. All the sirens and stuff . . . it would be pretty cool.'

'Yeah, I guess.' Spike fell silent.

Adam stayed quiet, holding his breath. This was it. This was the moment when it could all work out or it could all fall apart. The power was in Spike's hands . . . and he had no idea. Of all the people in the world, why did it have to rest with someone like him?

Spike looked at him. 'I know *how* I'd do it,' he said slowly. 'But tell me one thing. Why *should* I? I know you want me to do it. But just tell me *why*.'

Adam shrugged. 'I don't like fish guts any more than you do.'

Spike smirked. 'I'm not buying it.' He started walking away.

Adam stared after him in desperation. What was he going to do now? 'OK, OK, I'll tell you why.' He looked at Spike's expectant face and somehow words started pouring out of his mouth. 'Because this trip . . . I thought it was going to be brilliant. But then I split up with Melissa and she didn't come on the trip anyway. And I've felt sick the whole time I'm here. And Murai and Kenai are smug twats and I want to see The Bulb crapping himself when the sirens go. And I don't want to spend a day in a fish factory. I . . . I don't know. I just want to see it play out. To see it all happen and know that *we* did it.'

Spike studied him for a long moment. Then at last he nodded and grinned. 'Fair enough. Maybe we should send The Bulb down on to the beach for something before the alarm goes. Then he'll *really* shit himself.'

Adam grinned back. He felt like laughing or crying or jumping up and down screaming. He felt like he'd just sold his soul to the devil – but he didn't care. He *couldn't* care. *If this works out, it will all have been worth it.*

He followed Spike back to the karaoke room, hovering somewhere between triumph and terror.

For the first time in days, Adam was happy again. Maybe it was the knowledge that he was finally doing something, without doing it at all. The weight of responsibility had been heavy on his shoulders from the moment he had realised what was going to happen. Now that he was sharing the load he felt lighter than air.

They left the karaoke bar within the hour and headed back to the hostel to pack. There was an hour in front of weird Japanese TV (short skirts, pervy hosts and shrieking seemed to be a key feature of evening entertainment) but most people were tired and headed to bed before it got stupidly late. Their itinerary had been packed with visits. Adam wished he had been able to enjoy it all more. He wasn't going to enjoy the tsunami – but the relief of thinking about the people who would be saved was better than the guilt of thinking about all the people who were supposed to die.

Assuming of course that Spike was able to get into the system. He had vanished upstairs as soon as they got back, presumably to start investigating the warning system. For the first time a pang of doubt crept into Adam's mind. Surely Spike would be able to do it? The stuff he could do with a laptop was scary, mainly because he didn't seem to have any respect for laws or ethics or privacy. Although once again, Adam reflected, on this occasion he wasn't in any position to judge.

When he went up to their room, he hardly dared to look at Spike. What if he said it was impossible? There was so little time to act. But although Spike was frowning, his brow was furrowed with concentration, not defeat. He opened his mouth to speak but Adam shook his head, nodding towards Dan and Archie, who were still bickering while they stuffed socks and souvenirs into their rucksacks. Spike shrugged but stayed quiet.

That night, for the first time all week, Adam fell into a deep and dreamless sleep. When he woke the next morning he ate a good breakfast and cheerfully sat on the warm, steamy-windowed coach for four hours as they crawled through the Tokyo traffic, ostensibly staring at landmarks. They could have walked through sewage for all he cared. And at last, just after lunchtime, they boarded the train for Hachimana.

The train journey itself was different from any train journey in England. Everything still looked exotic and alien. Apartment blocks and billboards blurred past, interspersed with trees and small parks. Glossy skyscrapers gave way to more modest office buildings as they left Tokyo behind. There were scraps of green but flat land was so precious that it was a long time before they saw any real break in the buildings.

Spike didn't notice anything about the surroundings. He was totally absorbed in his laptop, making the most of the Wi-Fi on board. Archie and Dan barely noticed his silence; they were used to him disappearing into one of his projects. Adam tried to act normal, conscious that tomorrow when this was all over he didn't want anyone to think that he had been behaving oddly. Some of the buoyant feeling had deserted him. Now that he was almost there, the enormity of what was going to happen was making him shiver. He realised, with a shudder, that it was Halloween.

He wondered how his parents would feel, once they heard what had happened. Their first thoughts would be for his safety. But tonight they would all be blissfully unaware of what was to come, heading off to Ireland to see the McVeys. Uncle Paddy always threw a Halloween party – he said he liked the irony. Of course the real irony would be the following day – All Souls' Day. *Please let all the souls be saved*, Adam thought fervently.

By Japanese standards, Hachimana was a small city. They stepped off the train several stops before the main Hachimana station. The boys and girls were separated once again and frogmarched off in different directions. Their accommodation was in the suburbs in an apartment block owned by Murai, normally used to house seasonal workers. For now the apartments lay empty. An unsmiling supervisor put them into rooms. They were bleak and bland, empty apart from six futon mats lying on each floor, covered by a thin sheet and blanket. The teachers got a room between two. Adam and his friends had Mr Fenton and Mr Donnelly as their teachers in residence. It wasn't brilliant but it was better than having The Bulb. He probably would have made them wrestle for their food.

Nobody felt like going too far, after dragging their luggage from the station. The joyless supervisor wheeled a trolley along the corridor, laden down with vast bowls of rice, soup, noodles, fish and pickles. There were small bean-paste buns for after and coffee for the teachers. Everyone else drank water. Adam ate a bit, then spent a lot of time watching the clock on his mobile phone. Every minute brought them closer to zero hour. He let his eyes wander round the room, taking in all the familiar faces. How could he keep his mouth shut when all he wanted to do was blurt out that everyone should just stay up here tomorrow, safely out of the way?

He stacked his bowl with all the others and slipped into the corridor outside. To his surprise Spike was out there, his laptop perched on his knee, typing frantically. He glared up at Adam. 'You have no idea how much security there is on this stuff. The sensors are a no-go – you're talking satellites there and it's way too risky. So I'm going for the control centre.'

Adam nodded, trying to look wise. 'Can you do it?' His rice and fish suddenly seemed to be creeping back up his throat.

'Yeah, as long as I keep getting Wi-Fi. I'm picking up better signals out here than I was inside. Just keep Fenton in there.' Spike's attention was already back on the screen, his fingers tapping out a tattoo.

It was another hour before Spike came back into the apartment and to Adam's relief he grinned and nodded. Some of the tight, coiled feeling eased out of Adam's chest.

It was happening. They could do this.

It was going to work out.

Chapter 23

hen Adam woke up the next morning, it was from a deep and dreamless sleep. The room was warm and humid from the breath and heat of six bodies, squeezed in too close for comfort. He lay for a moment, getting his bearings, then felt his stomach curl and roll as he realised where he was and what day it was. Hachimana. All Souls' Day. Ground zero.

He was the first one awake. He glanced over towards the door, where Spike was still sleeping, one protective hand resting on his laptop. Adam crept past, sliding the wooden screen door aside and stepping into the small kitchen area beyond. In the bathroom he had time to shower, crouching on the tiled floor, ignoring the low stool. He definitely preferred a standing, Western-style shower.

He had just finished getting dressed when the front door opened and the surly supervisor came in. She ignored his *Ohayou gozaimasu* and wheeled a trolley of rice, fish and miso inside, complete with a stack of bowls and a large urn of green tea. A bleary-eyed Fenton emerged from his room, throwing baleful glances back at Donnelly, whose snores had filled the whole apartment the night before. He slid the other bedroom doors aside and growled at them all to get up and dressed.

Adam took a bowl and piled it high with rice. It wasn't what he would have chosen to eat for possibly his last meal but once the tsunami struck it could be hours or even days before they got to sit down and eat again. He looked around the others, wishing he could tell them to stop turning up their noses and eat something, while they still could. An eerie sense of unreality was gripping him. This wasn't a secret he would have chosen to know but without it they might all die. If something went wrong with his plan, there was nothing to say that his classmates and teachers wouldn't become victims like everyone else. *He* might become a victim. Then he would meet Hikaru and his family again, one last time, as they took his keystone and guided him on to the Unknown Roads.

He pushed these dark thoughts away and copied everyone else; finishing food, scraping bowls, packing up their rucksacks. For the billionth time of the trip Fenton exhorted them to *Check their passports!* Adam slipped his into his pocket and checked that his keystone was safely round his neck. His rucksack felt heavier today. He wondered if he would still have it at the end of the day. Absurdly, he realised that he would probably never see his favourite hoodie or his phone charger again.

They climbed down four flights of stairs and gathered in the courtyard outside. Until now Adam had been avoiding Spike's eye. Spike hadn't missed this. 'Don't tell me you're chickening out?'

Adam shook his head. Chickening out wasn't an option. He

just still didn't know how he would explain it when an actual tsunami struck. 'No.'

'Good.' Spike pulled out his mobile phone and frowned. 'We're going to miss the train.'

Adam pulled out his own phone to check the time. Sure enough, they only had ten minutes to get to the station. That way they would be at the fish-processing plant with an hour to spare, a safe margin in case Spike hit any last-minute snags. His stomach clenched hard enough to hurt.

Fenton didn't seem to be in any hurry to leave. He was taking a desultory headcount. 'Put your bags down. We're still waiting for Mr Bulber's group.'

Adam stared at him in dismay. The Bulb probably had them wrestling each other on the tatami mats or something equally stupid. He turned to Spike, trying to keep the urgency out of his voice. 'Have you much to do when we get there?'

Spike shrugged. 'I've done as much as I can. I just need to run the program I coded. It should only take a couple of minutes if I get a good connection.'

Adam nodded, not daring to say any more. There was a high-pitched shrieking coming from the hallway and The Bulb burst out into the daylight, his group streaming beside him. The supervisor was waving her hands and jabbering in short angry bursts of Japanese, interspersed with a few English words. Adam was sure he caught something about *rice ball* and *toilet*. The Bulb was trying to sound placatory but gave up and nodded to Mr Fenton, indicating that it was time to make their escape. Adam didn't need to be asked twice. He seized his rucksack, dizzy with relief. They were moving.

They might still get there on time.

Only they didn't. At the bottom of the street, none other than Mr Fenton thought that he had lost his passport. After a thorough search of all his baggage the passport was discovered in the concealed pocket inside his jacket. Someone else's rucksack strap snapped and The Bulb insisted on trying an amateur repair job in the middle of the pavement, while irate Japanese workers stepped into the road to get past. When they eventually reached the train station, it was to the sight of their train disappearing into the distance. Kenai had mysteriously reappeared and tersely told them that the girls had gone on ahead and that they would have to wait twenty minutes for the next train.

For a moment, Adam felt like screaming. He fought back the urge to chase the train along the tracks and leap on board. What was the use? Without Spike he couldn't do anything anyway. No one else seemed to mind. It was fair to say that a tour of a fish-processing plant wasn't on anyone's highlights list. Dan and Archie joined everyone else at the vending machines, buying boxes of Pocky and bottles of Pocari Sweat, mostly because they liked the names.

Spike was the only other person looking irritated at the delay. 'Idiots. I knew we were going to miss it. At this rate it will hardly be worth hacking into the system. We're only going to get a couple of hours at the research plant.'

'Of course it'll be worth it!' Adam's temper was stretched to breaking point and he was in danger of losing it with exactly the wrong person. He forced himself to breathe in. 'Two hours of computers are better than two hours of fish guts!'

'Easy for you to say,' Spike muttered. 'You're not the one

breaching their security. I don't know much about the Japanese prison system but I hope it's better than Thailand's. I saw that film about the backpackers with the heroin . . . They must have been mentalists!' He tailed off, his face dark.

Adam might have started to panic but for Kenai's timely return. He informed them that there was another train they could catch, which would require three stops instead of one but they would still arrive in the centre of Hachimana before the next express train. A few minutes later they were on board, listening to the cheerful *bing-bong* of the announcement system, standing awkwardly in the aisle under the curious stares of local people.

Adam counted off the stops, bouncing up and down on the soles of his feet. His whole body felt curiously alive, one big wave of adrenalin waiting to break. He swayed with the movement of the train, clinging to the ceiling strap, eyes closed. People swarmed on and off the train. Two stops to go . . . His hearing was almost superhuman. A baby further down the carriage was crying and her mother shushed her in a singsong voice. The Bulb said something in a low voice and the other teachers laughed, just loudly enough to seem insincere. One stop to go . . . There was a humming sound in Adam's ears. After a moment he realised *he* was the one humming, low and droning, blocking everything else out. Getting ready.

And at last the train pulled into Hachimana's main station. Adam stared around the carriage, mesmerised, as everyone else fustled about gathering bags and coats. They were here at last. The unreality of it . . . To be here, in a place he had never seen before, knowing that in less than an hour everything would be different. He watched the Japanese people on the train step off, holding their packages, helping their children and the elderly, moving quietly, self-contained. His throat clenched tight and he suddenly felt close to tears. He wished for one frantic moment that he could stop this; that he could make the earthquake never happen.

There was no point thinking about it. He stood up and grabbed his rucksack, swallowing down the ache in his chest. As they walked the short distance from the station to the factory his eyes darted from landmark to landmark. They turned on to the main street, running parallel to the shoreline, and Adam stopped dead, earning curses and protests from the people behind him. He couldn't help it. He had just seen the electronics store and the digital clock. He stared at it, fascinated. The time blinked and then steadied – 10:29. At exactly 11:08 it would be engulfed and the store behind it smashed to pieces. He imagined the red numbers blinking, then flashing out of existence along with the rest of the street. As they walked past a shudder ran through his body.

Kenai led them up the street he recognised from his dream. It took a lot longer climbing up the hill than it had taken Adam to run down it, especially carrying their gear. Kenai explained apologetically that Hachimana station was too small for luggage lockers. Adam felt nothing but relief. Faffing about would have slowed them down even further and if they kept their bags with them there was a chance people might have something to eat and drink in the hours after the tsunami, even if it was just sweets.

And finally, they had arrived. They turned right from the road into the yard. Ahead of them, down the sloping entrance lane, were the long, low buildings. The girls and female teachers were already there. They raised a mocking jeer that made The Bulb scowl and Kenai's lips press together so tightly that they almost vanished. The group straggled down towards the buildings.

Adam felt someone nudge his ribs. He turned and saw Spike jerking his head towards a small equipment shed on their right. 'Over here,' Spike whispered. 'There's no point going inside or we'll just lose even more time.'

Adam nodded. They fell to the side of the group and Spike crouched on one knee, pretending to tie his shoelace. As soon as the group passed them, they slipped in behind the shed. Spike dropped straight to the ground and pulled out his laptop. He typed very fast, then stopped and waited, a slight frown between his eyebrows.

The wait stretched, along with Adam's nerves. 'What's wrong?'

'Not picking up any Wi-Fi signals.' Spike shrugged and pointed back towards the road. 'Some of the houses there looked like they were about to fall down. Whoever's living in them . . . let's just say Wi-Fi probably isn't top of their priority list.'

Adam stared at him in horror. 'What, so that's it?'

'No, not necessarily. It's just trickier. Luckily I came prepared.' Spike reached into his shoulder bag and pulled out several cables, two small, flat boxes and his mobile phone. 'I'm going to have to improvise. It'll take a bit longer. Make sure no one is looking for us.'

Adam swallowed down a scream of frustration. When he'd

heard the tsunami talk, he'd thought somebody somewhere was on his side. Now it seemed like everything that *could* go wrong *was* going wrong. He peeked his head round the side of the shed. None of the teachers were watching and Archie was talking to one of the girls from the plane with a huge grin on his face. Only Dan was standing on the edge of the group, looking around with a bemused expression. *Don't worry about us, Dan!* Maybe somebody somewhere *was* on their side because a second later Kenai began to speak to the group, gesturing to the building behind him.

'Got it!' Spike said. He grinned and held his hands up in the air, like a footballer who'd just scored a goal. He waggled his fingers. 'Now just wait for the magic.'

He began typing again, very fast. Adam closed his eyes and leaned back against the shed, feeling as if every nerve in his body was tingling. Either this was going to work or it wasn't. It was out of his hands now. He pulled out his mobile and checked the time. It was 10:48. In exactly twenty minutes the tsunami was going to hit the shoreline.

Seconds stretched into hours. Spike was still typing. The sound of his fingers pattering on the keyboard was shredding Adam's last remaining nerve. He wanted to scream. Instead he breathed in and then out, slowly, then forced himself to do it again. *In . . . and out . . . and in . . . and out.* His head began to feel pleasantly light. *There's nothing else to do*, a voice sang at the back of his mind. *Nothing more to do.*

'Done!' Spike hissed, slamming the laptop shut. At the same moment a loud voice called from beside them. 'You, boys! What you do?'

Adam almost lashed out. He was beyond thought now; his

body was charged for fight or flight. Spike scrambled up beside him as they stared in silence at a very angry security guard. 'You no be here!' He walked over to the edge of the shed and shouted something in Japanese. Twenty seconds later Kenai appeared, followed by The Bulb.

Adam had a dim sense of muttered imprecations and dire threats as they were hustled back towards the rest of their group. He didn't care. He couldn't breathe. He looked at Spike for reassurance and saw his friend smirking in the way he always did when he had pulled something big off. The Bulb deposited him beside Fenton, who snarled in his ear and told him not to move an inch from his side.

Adam stared blindly ahead of him. Nothing was happening. Kenai had resumed his speech, giving them nothing more than a hostile glance. He was telling them where they should put their bags once they were inside and people were wearily grabbing their rucksacks again and . . . *nothing was happening*! Adam swivelled his head towards Spike and made a sharp, questioning movement with his hand. Spike glared at him and mouthed a single word: *Wait*.

The girls at the front of the group were stepping through the steel doors, into the processing plant. There was a chorus of squeals as the fish and diesel stench intensified around them. Adam's stomach lurched. He was going to throw up. It hadn't worked. All of it had been wasted and in eighteen minutes hundreds or thousands of people would be dead.

And then there was a sound. A low crackle and groan brought the speakers in the yard to life. People stopped and turned. The groan became louder, wailing, a high siren calling out a warning, rising and falling, then looping over again. Everyone stopped.

Kenai was staring at the speaker with his mouth slightly open. From inside, two men in boiler suits and hard hats stepped through the doors and spoke to him in rapid Japanese. Adam heard the word before anyone else even registered.

Kenai turned to them with an odd expression. 'A tsunami warning has been issued. We must move to higher ground. There is no need for panic but we must move swiftly.'

'A what warning?' The Bulb was blinking stupidly.

Kenai gave him a cool glance. 'There has been an earthquake, perhaps out beneath the sea. It may cause a tsunami. There is a plan that we must all follow. At once.'

'Do you mean a tidal wave?' The Bulb bellowed.

He might as well have shouted 'Alien invasion'. There was a moment of horrified silence, quickly followed by a crescendo of screams and swearing. At the same time the steel doors opened again and the workers inside flooded out of the building and began walking swiftly through the yard. Some of them paused and talked to Kenai, gesturing to the rucksacks. Kenai hesitated, then nodded and some of the men seized the Bonehill bags from the girls.

Kenai raised his voice over the chaos. 'The workers will help you with your belongings.'

And then they were moving. Adam hardly dared to look around him. His head was swirling with relief and when he looked at Spike he found him grinning back. As they reached the gate they turned right instead of left and crossed the road, following the track winding up towards the tall white building behind the processing plant. They weren't alone. Dozens of Hachimana's inhabitants were appearing, filling the streets, their faces anxious and questioning. As they walked the convoy

271

behind them grew. On this part of Japan's coast, the city centre was simply a narrow strip perched on a flat ledge before the ground rose up steeply behind.

Within minutes they were standing outside the glossy, white research building. Kenai gestured them to one side. For the first time he looked stressed. Adam almost felt sorry for him. He had a feeling the Japanese man was more used to dealing with Murai's whims, rather than a group of teenagers. It must be bad enough getting foisted with a group of foreign school kids at the best of times, never mind when you thought you might have to get them through a natural disaster unscathed.

Dan and Archie drew up alongside Adam. Dan was wheezing for breath and threw his rucksack on the ground, reaching for his inhaler. Adam felt a moment of guilt – until he remembered that he had at least given Dan a chance to get to high ground. All the other people who might have struggled to get there had been given a head start. It was all he could do for them.

Some of the research centre reception staff had come out of the building and were directing local people inside. There was the large entrance foyer with the metal staircases on either side. It was weird seeing it here in real life, not that he had ever doubted his premonition. The stream of residents seemed never ending. Archie was staring round with his mouth open. 'How are we all going to fit in?'

Spike's grin had disappeared. He was scowling now. He stood beside Adam and muttered, 'What are they all doing here? I thought it would just be us and the people from the fish-guts plant. They're never going to let us all inside.'

Adam shrugged. 'This must be an evacuation point for

everyone.' He pointed along the road to the right, where another tall building could be seen. 'Probably people are going there too.'

'Well you could have at least found out that everyone would come here before I did the hack,' Spike snarled.

Adam didn't answer. For a second he hated Spike – until he reminded himself that his friend didn't *know* there was going to be a tsunami. He looked around at the constant stream of people being directed into the building. No one was running. No one was panicking. If anything, people were looking confused.

Adam moved closer to Kenai who was talking rapidly in Japanese, frowning. Mr Fenton, who had been uncharacteristically quiet, stepped up beside their guide and waited for him to turn, looking irate. 'Is this a real alert or a false alarm? Because I thought an earthquake big enough to cause a tsunami would be felt here on land or be so far out at sea that we could be waiting here for hours.'

Kenai's frown deepened. 'Obviously there can sometimes be false alarms but it is better to be safe I think. We have contacted the Japan Meterological Association for more information. They are the body with responsibility for tsunami warnings. Please keep your students together.'

Adam chewed his lip. He'd forgotten that in between rants Fenton was a physics teacher and probably did actually know something about tsunamis. He glanced at his phone screen, feeling sick. 11:01. Seven minutes till the tsunami hit. He glanced sideways at Spike. He was crouching on the ground, typing ferociously. Something about his expression made Adam uneasy. 'What are you doing?'

'Cancelling the alert. This whole thing was a waste of time.

We're not getting any tour of the research lab.'

'Don't cancel the alert.' There was a ringing sound in Adam's ears.

Spike glared at him, then nodded towards some of the elderly people who were being helped up the hill by friends and family members. 'Look, it was a good idea but it didn't work out. And people are being evacuated for nothing. Little grannies will be dropping dead all over Japan if we make them run up big hills for a tsunami that doesn't exist.'

'DON'T CANCEL THE ALERT.' It was too loud and people were looking round but Adam didn't care. They had come this far. It was nearly OK.

Spike ignored him. He was typing very fast again. He wasn't listening and Adam didn't have time to make him listen. Instead, he made him stop typing. He bent down, grabbed Spike's laptop and wrenched it from his friend's grip.

Spike was staring at him. 'What are you doing? Give me my laptop.' He scrambled to his feet and grabbed the casing. He pulled it away from Adam, cursed at him and turned away, ready to resume typing – until Adam took hold of it, pulled it away and this time threw it. There was a moment in slow motion where they both watched it arcing away through the air, the sunlight glinting on the metal casing, before it crashed to the ground.

Spike's mouth had fallen open. 'What the fuck are you doing? *What did you do to my laptop?!*'

Adam didn't answer. He didn't have to.

The ground began to shake.

Chapter 24

hen the earthquake struck, Adam felt something bizarrely close to relief. It was happening. The whole thing was finally happening. His bit was over. Now it was up to every person to survive as best they could.

The shaking started small, just a tremble beneath their feet. Then it intensified, fast, and then again. The people who were still walking up the hill stopped and staggered, a few falling to the ground. There were screams all around Adam. He grabbed Spike's arm and dragged him to the ground even as Kenai bellowed, 'Get down!'

The screaming wasn't the only thing they could hear. The buildings all around them were juddering and dozens of alarms were blaring from homes and businesses along the main street. They could hear the rattle of thousands of objects vibrating in unison – cars bouncing on their wheels, windows shaking in frames, and from inside the building the sound of furniture juddering across the tiled floor. Through the glass doors Adam could see people cowering in the doorways and sheltering beneath the metal staircases. The ground shook harder and a second later the doors and windows shattered, glass shards exploding out of frames and scattering along the ground. Part of the plasterboard ceiling collapsed and there were more screams. Now the people inside the building were trying to get back outside.

'Move away from the walls,' Kenai shouted. He scuttled along the ground like a crab and Adam did the same. Dozens, then hundreds of people were scrambling out into the open lane where there was no danger of falling objects. Adam looked left and his eyes hooked on a crack where the asphalt road met plain dirt. The road was moving away from the raw earth and then back again, with a weird, whispering groan, barely audible. Adam imagined it yawning open, swallowing people whole and then snapping closed again forever.

It didn't happen. The earthquake continued, not subsiding but not getting stronger. People had fallen silent. A few had managed to pull out mobile phones and started recording footage. There was one sharp jolt that sent a fresh wave of screams through the crowd, then the shaking began to diminish. After another minute it tailed off. Adam looked around with the same stunned eyes he could see on everyone else's faces. They were all still alive. He didn't know if anyone inside had been injured but as the shaking subsided more Japanese workers and locals were running out through the empty frame that had housed the doors.

'Is everyone OK?' It was Fenton to the rescue again. The Bulb staggered to his feet beside him, looking like a man who had just witnessed the end of the world.

You haven't even seen the half of it, Adam thought.

The alarms were still blaring all around them, including the tsunami sirens. Fenton was staring at the loudspeakers and frowning. 'There must have been another earthquake at sea, before the one here. That must have been what set the first alarms off.'

Kenai was holding a walkie-talkie and speaking very fast. 'No one must leave this area. The earthquakes were powerful enough to cause a large tsunami. Everyone must stay here on high ground.'

Now that the shaking had mostly stopped, more people were arriving with every minute that passed. Adam checked the screen on his mobile. It was 11:03. In five minutes the tsunami would strike the shore. He turned around, searching for his friends. He found Dan and Archie in the middle of an animated group, all of them talking at once, a few trying unsuccessfully to make phone calls and a couple still wiping shocked tears from their cheeks.

There was only one person he couldn't see. At last he spotted him, standing on the edge of the group, looking blankly back out to sea. Spike was cradling his fractured laptop under one arm, holding it close to his body. He didn't look upset or frightened the way other people did. Instead he was very calm, but his eyes were far away. Adam recognised the look immediately and felt his chest contract. This was the bit where Spike started trying to figure out what the hell had just happened.

He had to speak to him now, alone, before he came over and started asking questions or making accusations that everyone would hear. As Adam approached him, Spike turned and saw him. His face tightened and he stepped away.

'Spike, wait.'

'Don't come any closer to me.' He didn't even sound like Spike, his voice was so flattened.

Adam stopped and held up his hands, placating. 'Look, I know it seems really weird, but I swear it was just a coincidence.'

Spike laughed, one sharp bark. 'You are so full of shit.'

Adam paused. The thing with Spike was . . . you never knew what he would do next. How should he play this? Deny everything? Admit to half the truth? Pretend he was some kind of wonder boy who could see the future? 'Look, I know you're pissed off. But what you did today . . . you probably saved loads of people's lives.' He pointed at some of the most recent arrivals: women with babies in their arms, a man on crutches, another man pushing a wheelchair. 'If the tsunami alarm had only just sounded, none of these people would have made it in time.'

'How do you know?' Spike was glaring at him but there was a thin, malicious smile on his lips. 'There might not *be* a tsunami. And if there is it might not happen for hours. But I think you *do* know. So how long would they have had, Adam? How long would they have had to escape?'

Adam met his stare. 'About five minutes,' he said quietly. He checked his phone one more time. 'They would have one minute left from now. That's all anyone would have had.'

Spike looked like he was going to throw up. 'Stay away from me,' he hissed. He backed away from Adam, returning to the safety of the group.

There was a noise in the distance, like a train miles away but rattling closer. From here, they could see over the roofs of the houses and the low buildings of the fish-processing plant. The main street was hidden, bar small glimpses in the gaps between the buildings behind. But out beyond they could see the waters of the Pacific Ocean. The breeze was fresh and off shore some of the long waves rolling in had white caps, but even from here they could see out beyond what looked like a dark line on the surface of the water. It was moving slowly towards the land. As it got closer it began to crest like the other waves. There were shouts from up above and when they turned to look they could see some of the research and admin staff up on the roof, pointing out and shouting. Adam didn't need to understand Japanese to know what they were talking about. One of the women had produced a small pair of binoculars while others were filming with their mobile phones.

Adam turned back to the sea, watching the big waves break white, seeming to run over the rest of the waves. And then, as they got closer to the shore, they disappeared from view. It didn't matter. Adam had seen what happened when they hit the street in his premonition. He had watched the waters burst through between the buildings and swirl up the street, gathering cars and signs and parts of buildings and sweeping through in a great, black, boiling mass, obliterating everything. The people on the roof must have been able to see some of what was happening because they were shrieking and calling out in Japanese, exclamations and little cries of horror.

Were there any people left down there? Adam hoped not. He knew that Japanese people were cautious and had a healthy respect for earthquakes and their aftermath. He was sure that anyone who could get to higher ground had done so. There were more calls from the roof and when he looked back at the sea he could see more of the long white waves crashing towards the shore. The noise was louder too, even from this distance away: a roar, like a speeding train or a plane taking off, almost loud enough to drown out the car alarms and the crash of wood and masonry giving way before the water.

And then, without warning, the water rose up and smashed through the fish-processing plant where they should have been standing. The buildings were light and prefabricated, a mixture of wood and metal sheeting, and the black torrent tore through them like paper. More screams rose up all around them as the building below lifted up from the ground, beginning to move with the current. The roar of water was indescribable. It was everywhere. Around him, people were turning and running, instinctively heading back towards higher ground, but Adam couldn't tear his eyes away as the water poured up the driveway, obliterating the yard and the sheds where he had stood with Spike.

'Get into the building and up the stairs,' Kenai shrieked somewhere close by.

It was Fenton who grabbed Adam, bellowing 'Come on!' while the water raced and churned along the road at the bottom of the steep lane to the research centre. It should have been filled with cars driving and people walking, not trees and houses. The sheer force of the torrent was beginning to drive the sea water up the lane, a lapping, encroaching tide of smashed-up cars and bits of boats and a million heavy, lethal pieces of debris moving towards them, each piece acting like a domino, pushing the water and rubbish ever higher.

'*Come on!*' Fenton roared again and Adam finally came to his senses and ran. The entrance had turned into a free for all and the Bonehill rucksacks were causing chaos, people falling over them in their haste to get inside. They reached the shattered door frame and one of the receptionists grabbed Adam's hand and pulled him left in the direction of one of the two staircases. He suddenly seemed to be surrounded by Japanese workers, with none of his friends in sight.

He ran up the metal stairs as fast as he could, stumbling over abandoned coats and handbags and a hard hat which one of the processing plant workers must have dropped. Up one flight of stairs, then another. How far should he go? Up another flight, carried along in a human tide. His breath was sobbing in his chest but there was one more flight. There wasn't much room now; the top floors were already crowded with people. He stopped, not sure where to go, and someone crashed into him from behind, sending him sprawling into the crowd.

Adam staggered back to his feet, looking around wildly. Where should he go? He didn't recognise anyone. From the edge of the landing he could see across the atrium and his school friends seemed to be over on the far side. The relief at seeing them was quickly followed by a question: how the hell was he going to get over to them?

There were more screams and shouts and suddenly water was surging into the foyer below. Wood and steel and bits of unidentifiable stuff stacked up against the entrance, casting a dark shadow inside. Even from here it was clear that the water had lost its force. This was the maximum extent of its reach. Unless there were more waves to come or more big aftershocks, they were probably safe.

Someone tapped his arm timidly. When he turned around one of the receptionists was smiling shyly at him. She pointed across the atrium. 'Your friends are there.'

'Yes. Thank you. *Aregatou*,' Adam mumbled, wishing he had bothered to learn more than a few words of Japanese. 'Is there a way for me to get across?'

She shook her head. 'Very far.' She bit her lip and bowed. 'My English is not good. I apologise.'

'No problem,' Adam stammered. 'Your English is very good. Much better than my Japanese.'

She smiled and bowed again. 'I take you to . . . American. Visitor here.' She looked around, frustrated, presumably trying to find someone who spoke English, but most of the people around them were men from the fish-processing plant. 'This way.'

Adam was reluctant to let his friends out of his sight but there was no point standing there on his own for hours. At least he could find some people to talk to and maybe find out how long they were likely to be stranded. He waved across, hoping someone would see him, but none of his group seemed to notice. The lady was disappearing through the crowd and he didn't want to lose her so he followed swiftly.

Every inch of the stairwell and corridors was packed with people, as were the offices. His new guardian moved nimbly through the gaps while he blundered along behind, muttering '*Sumi masen*' every time he stood on someone. Eventually they reached a small boardroom and inside were the other overseas visitors. Judging by the accents in the room they weren't just from America but lots of different countries.

'You stay here,' the woman said and Adam thanked her again, feeling bereft when she disappeared. He stepped into the room, feeling nervous. No one noticed him at first. Most of the people were gathered around the window, pointing out and exclaiming at things. A few of them had their mobile phones pressed against the glass. For a moment Adam lurked by the door. Then a man with tanned skin and very white teeth spotted him and gave him a welcoming grin. 'Hey, kid. Come on in. We won't eat you.'

What else was he going to do? Adam slipped in and was greeted with questions: was he all right? What was he doing here? Did he want a cup of coffee? (Never, not even after a tsunami.) Did he want to see outside? He was careful to say as little as possible and eventually even the friendly American gave up on him, after telling him to sit down and get comfy and pointing out a 'washroom' behind a screen in the corner.

Adam sat close to the door. The corridor was still packed. People were still trying to make mobile phone calls, with little success. Everyone left him alone. He rested his head back against the wall and closed his eyes. All the fear and tension of the last few days had left him, along with the adrenalin that had kept him going this long. Now there was nothing to do but sit back and wait. It could be a long time before he got anywhere. He felt the kind of bone-deep exhaustion he sometimes felt in the middle of the night, when he had been woken from sleep to go on a call-out.

He couldn't help thinking about his family. It was 02:25 in London and without Spike's warning there might have been hundreds or thousands of people dead all along the Japanese coast. Of course, there still would be casualties. Thinking about this roused him from his stupor. There were probably Lumen here, right now, standing in the Hinterland amidst the debris. And the obvious thing to do for someone like him, even if he hadn't known about the tsunami, was to go into the Hinterland and volunteer to help.

He didn't want to. Finding any casualties at all would feel like a personal failure – they were people he should have found a way to save and hadn't managed. But he *could* just have a look, and what was more, he could turn it to his advantage. Once he was in the Hinterland the water and debris downstairs would be no problem. He could simply stroll across the foyer and up the other stairs, then find a quiet spot to emerge back into the physical world.

The quiet spot bit was going to be the problem. Adam peered out into the corridor and found lots of curious eyes looking back. Hachimana definitely wasn't on the tourist trail and groups of foreigners were probably a bit of a novelty. Normally he could just find an empty room and vanish without anyone noticing but that wasn't going to be an option here.

Unless . . . His eyes roamed round the boardroom, settling on the door in the corner. The bathroom. There was a screen across the door, shielding it from view of the people at the window. They were still looking out and judging by their conversation the water was beginning to recede. Adam didn't go over to see. He took advantage of their distraction and stood up, slipping across the room, behind the screen and through the door. There was a Western-style toilet and hand basin there and very little else. Adam didn't care; he wasn't planning on hanging about. He reached beneath the neckline of his top and grasped his keystone, then stepped forward into the Hinterland.

Usually he hated being there but today Adam felt some of the tension leave him. Being stuck in one place with so many people wasn't fun. Here he felt weightless and free. It was weird walking through the crowded corridors; he had never had to walk 'through' so many people before but once he reached the lower levels it got easier. He almost went straight across to the opposite side to find his friends but when he thought about it, he knew it would be more 'normal' for a Luman to go and see if there were any souls needing guidance. He couldn't work alone – he hadn't been Marked yet – but he would be expected to go and offer his help to any adult Luman on the scene. He might even run into a Luman he knew.

But as he walked through the mounds of cars and buildings there were no souls in sight. No one seemed to have died here. He kept going, instinctively searching for roads and footpaths, but the landscape had been completely altered. What had once been a bustling city had become a giant landfill, teeming with rubble, wood and twisted metal. The sea was already receding although Adam knew that waves could keep coming for hours after an earthquake. The people who lived here knew that and for now they were wisely staying on high ground.

It was a ghost town – but thankfully there were no ghosts waiting for him. He felt a thrill of triumph. He had done it! No one had died. There was nothing more for him to do, other than go back to the research building and carry on with his life.

At least he thought so, until a familiar voice said, 'Adam Mortson. I thought I might see you here.'

Chapter 25

dam turned around, feeling strangely calm. Maybe it was because he had always known this moment would come. 'What are you doing here?'

Darian smiled. 'What else would I be doing, Adam? Only seeking the dead. And the soon-to-be dead.'

'There are no dead here. I've looked.'

'Not a soul to be seen. A little strange, don't you think?'

Adam shrugged. 'They have a good warning system here.'

'An *excellent* warning system. A warning system so *effective* that the earthquake monitors sounded a full thirteen minutes before the earthquake!'

Adam stared at him stolidly. Inside his chest his heart was beating against his ribs, a bird in a cage, desperate to get out. He was trying to sound confident but his voice betrayed him. 'Is my father here?'

'He will be soon.' Darian's smile widened. He looked like a wolf. 'Did you know, Adam, that by law every Curator and High Luman must have a prison cell in their home?'

Adam didn't give him the satisfaction of answering. 'I want to see my father.'

'Your father is *working*. There are still dead to care for. But of course, we both know that there should have been very many more.' Darian was studying him. 'Come, Adam. Talk to me. They say confession is good for the soul. Perhaps I can help you.'

'I don't have anything to confess.'

'But you do. You have been breaking our laws for some time now, have you not? Like, for example, your intervention in the park a few weeks ago. I saw you that day. You just cannot leave the souls alone.'

It was getting hard to breathe. Adam's thoughts were racing backwards, back to the park and the fair and the ice-cream van . . . and the man. The man in the shadows, watching, his face concealed by his hood in spite of the sunshine. *He was there! The whole time he was watching and waiting. But did he see Melissa too?* Adam felt sick but he forced his mouth to move. 'I don't know what you're talking about.'

Darian sighed. 'I had hoped to avoid any unpleasantness. I see that you will leave me with no choice. As stupid and intractable as your parents!'

The mask had slipped. Behind the handsome face and the perfect manners he could see it for just a moment: rage, hate and a great swirling vortex of pain. A pain that had lingered so long it had transformed into something black and twisted, eating the man alive, leaving only a brittle, perfect veneer. There was still a part of Adam that pitied him. He knew what it was like, losing someone you cared about. Everyone had lost someone. The difference was that some people were able to move on without turning that pain back onto everyone around them. 'You won't get her back. My mother. No matter what you do to me or my father, you'll never get her back. If you hurt us she'll only hate you more.'

Darian's whole face was rigid. He was fighting for self-control. 'No more talking. We have a journey to make.' He began walking.

Adam backed away. It was crazy. Here in the Hinterland there was nothing to hide behind. But in the physical world . . . 'Stop. You need me to be alive.'

Darian held his hands up. 'I have no intention of killing you. You are not Marked. There are others who will answer for you. But you will stand before the Concilium and confess your crimes.'

'Not if I go back to the physical world, I won't. Right here.' Adam pointed to a vast pile of twisted metal and wood beside him. 'What do you think I'll look like if I step right into the middle of this? They'll have to get me out in pieces.'

'There is no need for this drama,' Darian said. 'Accept your fate.'

'You don't get it, do you?' His voice was trembling. *If I kicked you hard, your whole shell would crack and fall apart. You're just dust and ashes.* 'I will do anything to protect my family. *Anything.* This is on me, not them. So if I have to get crushed to pieces to do that, then that's what I'll do.' Darian's expression almost made Adam laugh. 'You're so full of it. You think you love my mother but you don't. But I do. And that's why I'll do this if you take one more step towards me.'

'What will this achieve?' That weird detachment had come over Darian again, the same detachment that let him stand back and watch Morta kill people to get at Nathanial. He was studying Adam as though he was some kind of specimen he could dissect and make sense of. He didn't even seem angry any more. 'You must face the consequences of your actions.'

'*You* haven't.' Adam shook his head, feeling weary. 'But it doesn't matter. You're not High Luman here. You don't get to decide what happens to me.'

'You think Hikaru will help you?' Darian laughed. He started to speak again. 'When he knows what you have done, here, in *his* Kingdom, he will –'

Adam didn't hear the rest. His mind wasn't there any more. He wasn't seeing the shattered landscape all around them; he was seeing the mountains rising up around a cool, green garden, smelling cold, clean air away from the stench of mud and sea water and diesel and sewage. As soon as he could feel the place he gripped his keystone and swooped.

He knew Darian would only be seconds behind him. When the stone Buddha appeared Adam threw himself forward into the physical world. He ran towards the house shouting for Hikaru. Would the High Luman even be here? He could be anywhere along the eastern seaboard, sending souls into their Lights. He shouted for Rita too. He reached the glass doors overlooking the garden and slammed his hands against the glass, over and over, still calling for Hikaru.

When he turned back towards the Buddha, Darian was walking towards him. There was no sense of urgency, just a terrible, cold purpose. Adam turned back to the house, about to hit the glass again – then fell back in shock as Rita appeared on the other side of the door, her mouth hanging open. She slid the door open and Adam threw himself inside, without taking his boots off. 'Hikaru, I need to speak to Hikaru, please help me, he's going to kill me,' he babbled, the words pouring out in a torrent.

Rita's daughters ran into the room, alarmed. Rita looked from Adam to the Curator moving smoothly towards the door and gave the older girl a sharp command in Japanese. She stood frozen, staring in confusion, until Rita spoke again, this time in Spanish. 'Hoshi! *Vamos!*' It seemed to bring her back to her senses and she disappeared.

'Say nothing,' Rita said quietly and stepped in front of Adam, moving to the door. 'Curator. It is a pleasure to see you. I thought you would be busy at the earthquake sites, along with the rest of the Concilium.'

'I had other business to attend to. Unavoidable business. I'm sorry you have been disturbed. This boy must come with me now.'

'My husband will be home soon. Please, come in.'

'This is not a social visit. You do not wish to obstruct a Curator in his work, I trust?'

'Of course not.'

'Give me the boy.'

'Where do you intend to take him?'

'I will take him where I choose! I am a member of the Concilium.' Darian stepped towards her, his face set with cold rage.

Rita was frightened but she was hiding it as well as she could. 'He is not Marked. He is not of age. I cannot give him to you without a guardian present.'

291

Adam wasn't sure what might have happened next. Darian had lost all reason. His face was ugly with rage. But looking beyond the Frenchman he saw a sight more glorious than he could have dreamed of: Hikaru striding through the garden. And better yet, his sons were with him, Hoshi hurrying behind.

Darian wasn't happy to see him. 'Hikaru.'

Hikaru took his time, removing his shoes pointedly before he stepped into the house. He looked from Darian to Adam and nodded at the floor. 'If you would be so kind.'

Adam started fumbling with his laces, shamed into action even at this most ridiculous of times but Darian moved to take his arm, until Rita stepped in front of him again. 'I apologise for the intrusion but we will not be staying. I will be removing this boy from your Kingdom. There will be no further trouble from him.'

'And what trouble has he caused?'

'I must bring him before the Concilium immediately.' Darian tried to smile. 'You need not concern yourself with this matter.'

He made to step around Rita but she blocked him again. Adam froze, wondering what was going to happen next. Hikaru was watching his wife and his eyes flicked to Adam's for a moment. It was impossible to read his expression. 'My wife seems to have some concerns about you removing Adam Mortson from our home.'

'She has nothing to be concerned about. Unless you believe a Curator incapable of following the law?'

'You are taking this boy into custody, are you not?' Hikaru waited for Darian's reluctant nod. 'For what crime?'

Darian laughed. 'For a series of crimes that you will struggle to comprehend. Crimes only a handful of our kind could even detect.'

Hikaru nodded. 'And if you are one of these, might I assume that a Seer would be required? You believe this boy to be a Seer?'

'These are matters for the Concilium.'

'But did his crimes take place here? Today, for example?'

'Only one of a long list of crimes.' Darian had waited until Rita was distracted and now he stepped smoothly to the side and gripped Adam by his arm. 'And that is why I will take him away from here, before any more harm is done.'

Hikaru's eyes widened. 'But Curator, if he is a criminal then what you need is a cell. And we have such a cell right here.'

As cells went, it probably wasn't the worst in the world. There was a squat toilet in the corner, behind a lacquer screen. There was a futon on a small wooden base, currently folded up into a seat. There was a carved table and a wooden chair, all of it illuminated by a single recessed light. That was the one thing missing: natural light. Adam had no idea if it was day or night. The battery on his mobile phone had finally packed in. He sat on the futon, leaning his head back against the wall.

He had been here for a long time and no one had come to see him. There had been an hour when he had felt frightened, then another hour when he had paced up and down the cell in anger. Now he just felt tired. Eventually he summoned the energy to unroll the futon mat and lay down, pulling the hood on his top over his eyes. He spent a few minutes enjoying the warm, red glow behind his eyelids before he fell asleep.

He woke later to the sound of the heavy wood and metal door opening. Blinking up he saw Rita standing in the doorway with a tray. She gave him a wan smile and placed the tray carefully on the table. The room filled with the smell of miso, sesame oil and meat pasties. There was a plastic bottle of water too and lying on the tray, a single sheaf of foliage from the garden. Seeing the green stalk in this bare room was oddly touching.

'Come and eat,' Rita said softly.

Adam stood a little unsteadily and sat down at the table. She handed him a plastic spoon and he ate the soup obediently, then drank the water. He felt dreamy and unreal, like he was waking from an anaesthetic and finding himself trapped in a nightmare. 'How long have I been here?'

'It is evening.' Rita was frowning but not like she was angry at him – more that she was worried. 'The Concilium are here. And your parents are here too.'

Adam's heart quickened. He wasn't sure what the emotion behind it was – something between relief and anxiety. 'Can I see them?'

'Soon, I hope.' She hesitated. 'The things that Darian has said . . . It is difficult to believe.' When Adam opened his mouth she held up her hand quickly, silencing him. 'Don't tell me anything, Adam. It is better not to speak to anyone without your father here.'

Adam nodded and picked up one of the meat pasties. It was full of peppers and tomato and was very definitely not from a Japanese recipe book. 'Do you like living here?'

'It's very beautiful. *Muy bonito.* My home is a happy one. My husband is a good man and my children are healthy. I am a lucky woman.'

Adam almost pointed out that she hadn't actually answered the question, then decided not to. What would be the point? If she hadn't been here she would have been somewhere else far from home. He bit his lip. 'What's going to happen to my father?'

'That is not for me to decide, Adam.' Rita gathered up the tray, leaving him the rest of the water. He thought she was angry at him but then she bent her head and kissed him gently on the cheek. She kept her mouth close to his ear and whispered urgently, 'I don't know what you did today, Adam. And if you did intervene as Darian says . . . then you broke our laws. But in my heart, I am happy that you did it. I pray that your own life will not be forfeited for the lives you saved today.' She squeezed his shoulder and carried the tray from the room without another word. The thud of the lock turning was horribly loud.

Adam walked around a bit, then refolded the futon into a seat. He sat, staring at the walls, wondering what was going on back in Hachimana. Would the waters have receded yet? If so, people would be going outside. They would be starting to gather together again and someone would notice that he was missing. He wondered who it would be. If it was Spike . . . what would he tell them? It wasn't like anyone would believe his story, plus he could hardly confess to hacking into the warning system.

Footsteps rang on the stone floor outside and the lock rattled. When the door opened he saw Rashid, the young, Indian Curator, standing in the doorway. He looked at Adam with something between sternness and pity then turned to the people still in the corridor. 'A few minutes.'

When he stepped back his place was filled by his mother – and his father. Elise rushed into the room and he wondered for a moment what she was going to do. Slap his face? Launch into a tirade?

Instead she flung her arms around him and squeezed him tightly, crushing him against her. 'Oh, my darling,' she whispered and stepped back, taking his face in both hands and studying him. 'He did not hurt you?'

Adam didn't have to ask who she meant. He shook his head mutely.

She was still holding his face, her eyes bright with tears. 'What have you done, Adam? *T'as fait quoi?*'

'He's safe, Elise,' Nathanial said. He stood in front of Adam, looking at him with a curious expression on his face. It took Adam a moment to realise that it was the look you gave someone when you thought you knew them, then realised that you didn't really know them at all. He led his wife gently to the chair and waited for her to sit. There was a silence.

'I'm sorry.' Adam knew he had to say something but as soon as he said the words he knew they weren't the whole truth. 'I'm sorry that you're here like this. I didn't want that to happen.'

Nathanial was waiting, wary and expectant. When Adam didn't say any more he frowned. 'What Darian is saying . . . The man is insane.' He was lying and Adam knew it. His father hated Darian but he *knew* that there was truth in his accusations. He was waiting for Adam to deny it, *hoping* he would deny it – but he *knew*. He knew it was all true.

Somehow that made it easier. All it would take now was for Adam to confess. But if he did . . . It was so *final*. There was no going back from it. Everything was changed forever and he wasn't quite ready. 'Is Auntie Jo here?'

'No.' Elise was very still but two tears had overflowed and were running down her cheeks. Her voice was steady. 'She wanted to be here but she had to look after your sister.'

Adam nodded. He hadn't thought about Chloe in all of this. Would she be this generation's Auntie Jo? Would Ciaron abandon her now that the Mortsons were tainted by scandal? He hadn't wanted that at all but what was the alternative? A wedding but thousands of funerals. *It was worth it*, he told himself, pushing away the sick feeling inside.

'We need to know what happened.' It was Nathanial speaking this time. He took a deep breath. 'If we are going to help you, we need to know exactly what you did.'

'You *know* what I did,' Adam said. He felt tired again. It was quite sudden. He sat down on the futon and stared at the floor.

'But it's not possible,' Nathanial said, his voice barely above a whisper. 'You . . . We thought you had lost the ability . . . You never told us.'

'Why would I tell you?' Adam felt flat inside. 'You would only have made me go on more jobs. And I would have had to stand there and *wait* for people to die and not do anything. Who could do that? Who could do that without going completely mad?'

'But you must have felt them!' Elise said suddenly. Her face was pale and ghastly. 'You were so sick as a child when they were going to die! How could you hide such a thing?'

Adam shrugged. 'I sort of blocked the premonitions out for a while. And then I thought if I saved people you wouldn't need me to be a Luman and I could stay at school. But then it all got out of control.' He thought of Morta and her revenge; the light, lethal flick of the Mortal Knife, severing threads. He would never forget the way they had fluttered to the ground, the Light ebbing out of them. It still made him feel like crying.

'You have *lied* to us,' Nathanial said. He looked more bewildered than angry.

'You didn't give me any choice!' Adam's temper ignited, out of nowhere. 'I told you before, I hate this! All of it. I don't want to be a Luman. I *never* wanted to be a Luman.'

'Do you think this is the life I wanted?' Nathanial shouted. 'We don't choose to be what we are, Adam!'

Adam blinked at him. It gave him a strange satisfaction when his father lost control. 'Uncle Lucian chose.'

Elise made a choking, gasping sound. 'What . . . What are you talking about?'

Nathanial was deadly calm again. 'That was not a *choice*. It was an act of desperation that had consequences for us all!'

It was true. In a way, they were all here because of Lucian. Darian had probably thought Elise was his again when the Mortsons had been plunged into scandal. For her to elope rather than marry him must have been the final, crushing blow to his pride. It was a pain he had never recovered from; a pain warped into a new purpose.

There were more sounds in the corridor outside. Elise and Nathanial exchanged alarmed glances and Elise rushed back to Adam's side, taking his arm and pulling him in close to her. He almost smiled. He was taller than her now but she was still ready to go into battle for him. All these years he had felt like nothing but a disappointment to her. Maybe he had been wrong. Maybe her disappointment had come from her love; knowing how difficult the road ahead would be unless he could become the man they wanted him to be.

The door opened again. This time it was Heinrich who came into the room. Adam stared at him, appalled. He hadn't seen the Chief Curator for several weeks and the change in him was terrible. There had always been a lightness and joy around Heinrich, in spite of the job he had. Now he looked old and exhausted, very much like a man who would soon be stepping through his Light – and would be happy to do so.

Elise spoke first. 'They cannot have him. I will go in his place. There is a rule in our law for that. There must be such a rule.'

Heinrich smiled tiredly. 'There is no need for such a gesture, my dear.' He was looking at Adam, really studying him, as though it was their first meeting. 'The charges against you are very serious.'

Adam said nothing. What was there to say? He liked Heinrich. He didn't want to insult him by lying to him. They all knew he was guilty.

'There is no evidence against him. No direct evidence.' Nathanial was talking quietly but fervently. 'I made some provisional enquiries into the boy Sebastian. It's clear that he has a history of this kind of interference. I don't pretend to understand the technology he uses but he has some experience of this kind of thing.'

Adam glared at him. 'It's not Spike's fault. You can't do anything to him. He's not a Luman!'

Heinrich held up a hand. 'I have no intention of pursuing your friend. Whatever laws he has broken, they are not *our*

299

laws. And as your father has said there is no direct evidence against you. It is therefore better that you say nothing of what you might have done when you address the Concilium.'

Here it comes, Adam thought. Until now, it had all felt unreal but hearing those words brought it home to him. He would have to stand before them all and listen to Darian's accusations and then he had two choices: to lie or to tell the truth.

'What saves you, Adam, is that you are not yet of age. You have not been Marked. You have taken no oath and therefore broken no oath. Thus in our eyes and the eyes of the law you are a child. Because of this you are not truly accountable.'

'Who is, then?' The sharpness in his voice was an echo of the anxiety he was feeling.

Heinrich wouldn't meet his eye. 'Your father is still your guardian and in that sense is responsible. However, because you were in another Kingdom during this time, technically the High Luman here is accountable for your actions. It is a rather unusual point of law and is still under discussion. However, if you protest your innocence and insist that this is all just a coincidence . . .' Heinrich tailed off and shrugged. 'No one Luman is responsible. It is just one of those things.'

Elise took his arm in her hand and squeezed it, beaming at him. Adam tried to smile back but none of it was making any sense. They knew he was guilty and they were letting him off. They were letting everyone off. Luman Law was civilised but ruthless when it had to be. 'So what will happen?'

'What will happen is that you will come of age. You will be Marked and take the oath. You will be an adult in our eyes and responsible for your actions. And then . . .' Heinrich paused and looked him in the eye. There was a steeliness there and in his voice when he spoke again. 'Then you will become a full Luman. You will be observed by the Concilium. You will work alongside your father and you will prove every day that we have not made a mistake. You will be the best man and the best Luman that you can be. You will, in time, prove yourself enough to marry and to have children who will become Lumen in their turn. You will do all of this and the past will be the past. How you live your future will wipe the slate clean. You will step through your Light with peace in your heart, knowing that you have devoted your life to our ways.'

'So nothing will happen to Father? Or Spike or Hikaru?' As Heinrich shook his head, Adam slumped down onto the futon. He watched his father smiling and shaking the Chief Curator's hand; watched his mother embracing Heinrich and thanking him. None of it was making any sense. He listened to them talking. '*A quiet ceremony, no ball . . . We will see how soon the Crone is available, perhaps tomorrow . . . Luc will understand . . . Shouldn't harm the betrothal, Patrick is a friend . . . Marianne, his cousin twice removed, a very suitable match . . . No need for anyone beyond these walls to hear of what has happened.*' His head was spinning. They were writing his life like a script from now until the moment he died and he was supposed to be grateful.

'Adam.'

He looked up and realised they were all waiting for him. Nathanial was smiling but he looked impatient. 'Did you hear what Heinrich said?'

'Erm . . . no. Sorry. What was it?'

Heinrich was frowning slightly. 'When you stand before the

Concilium you explain that you are innocent of all charges, that your friend Sebastian has a history of this behaviour and that you will be leaving school and dissociating entirely from him. You will thank the Curators and Hikaru for their understanding and remain here until your Marking can be completed. You will then return home and work with your father, through a period of house arrest, until the Curators are satisfied that you can be trusted to obey our laws.'

Bizarrely Adam thought of Dan and Archie and Spike. He wondered what they were doing right now. They would think he was dead. It was an odd thought. As far as they were concerned, he might as well be dead. He would never see them again. He would never set foot in his school again. Even if he was eventually pardoned, he would spend the rest of his life living down the shame of his actions. He would be forced to spend every hour guiding souls and pretending to be someone else; pretending to be the Luman he'd been born to be. He thought about the photo he had discovered and the uncle he had never known but who had shared his hatred of the Luman world. Now, staring into the future, he could feel the same sensation that Lucian must have had – a sense of being trapped into a life you didn't want, barely able to breathe.

For the first time since Darian had found him, Adam felt a pang of misery for himself. He had saved so many people today. They would have a period of adjustment, while they tried to make sense of what had happened and what they had lost. But after this, they would be free to carry on with their lives, making choices for themselves, striving to be who they *wanted* to be. Why didn't he get the same chance?

His mother kissed both his cheeks. She was walking towards the door and Nathanial was smiling cautiously and they were almost out of the room when Adam spoke. They turned, all three of them, and looked at him questioningly. 'What did you say, son?' It was Nathanial speaking.

And Adam, looking from one face to the other, cleared his throat.

'I said no.'

Chapter 26

nder other circumstances, the silence that followed this pronouncement would have been comical. Today, in this cell, seeing their confusion, it was anything but. Adam bit his lip and stared between them, at the door behind. 'No. I won't take the deal. I don't want it.'

'What do you mean, Adam?' Elise had a half-smile, as if she was waiting for some kind of punchline.

'I don't want it. What you're offering. It's not what I want.'

Nathanial was staring at him, incredulous and angry. 'Heinrich is offering you your life!'

'No he's not.' Adam laughed, surprising everyone, himself included. He looked at Heinrich, wishing he could just say thank you but he couldn't. 'You're offering me someone else's life, not mine.'

Heinrich seemed puzzled. 'I am afraid I do not understand.'

'I don't want to be a Luman. I don't want to come of age and be Marked. I don't want to guide souls. I hate it. All of it. Have you any idea what it's like, knowing what I know?

Knowing people are going to die and that I'm not allowed to do anything about it? I hate our laws and I hate being a Luman. I won't do it.'

'This isn't a multiple choice test, Adam.' Nathanial was wrestling to keep himself under control. 'If anyone can prove what you did you could be executed. Do you understand that? Even though you aren't of age!'

'I want my own life.' He was speaking quietly but forcefully, trying to make them understand. 'All those people today who could have died, will get to live their own lives. So will my friends and my teachers and . . . the people who sit on the bus with me every morning. All the people we guide. Until they die they get to choose what to do and who to be. And that's what I want.'

'You are being ridiculous,' Nathanial said. He was angry now; more angry than Adam had ever seen him. 'How can you say this? You know better than anyone that most people have very little freedom. Their lives are dictated by their race and nationality and their poverty or wealth. Their *choices* are taken from them by war and famine and hardship. By an earthquake. There is no freedom.'

'Yes there is!' Adam shouted. He was on his feet now, clenching his fists, his anger flowing through him like electricity. 'People can't control where they're born or everything that happens to them but they can choose what to do with the cards they get dealt! What's the point of having a life if you can't use it? There's a reason why people don't know about us and what we do. Life is for the living! I want my own life. If I can't have that then I may as well not be here!'

They were staring at him like he was mad. Heinrich was looking helplessly from Nathanial to Elise and back to Adam. 'But what is it that you want to do, Adam? If not be a Luman?'

What *didn't* he want to do? Even thinking about it was like firecrackers going off in his head. It turned his brain into tentacles. 'I want to go to school. Go to university. Travel all over the world. Live wherever I choose. Be a doctor or whatever *I* want. Not what you want me to be.'

'This is not your path, Adam.' His mother was looking at him, pleading.

'I want to choose my own path. I'll walk the Unknown Roads when the time comes but until then, the path I choose should be mine.'

'But you have a good life! *Non?*' Elise was close to tears.

'But it's not *my* life!' How could he make them understand? 'And if it's not my life it's no life at all. I may as well go up there and tell them what I did and let them kill me. Because I can't be who you want me to be and sooner or later I'm going to mess up again. School helped me block the premonitions. Being *happy* helps me block them. Sooner or later I'm going to do something major and destroy you all. Maybe it's better getting it over with now, while I'm here. At least this way no one can blame Father.'

Adam looked at Elise. She was pale and trembling. He was hurting her. He was always hurting them and disappointing them, just by being who he was. 'I'm sorry I'm not what you want me to be. I've really tried. But I can't do it any more.'

'You would rather die and leave your family? To go to a *school?*' She was crying now. Her hands were covering her mouth and her shoulders were heaving.

'No. I don't *want* to die.' The anger was gone. It was futile trying to make them understand but some stubborn part of him wouldn't let him quit trying. 'But if I do . . . then it's done. I won't have to worry any more that I'm letting you all down or shaming you or ruining Chloe's life. And I can walk the Unknown Roads freely. I can follow the directions or I can ignore them. I'll be free to choose. Like Lucian did.'

The silence that followed this stretched on for a long time. Adam hung his head in his hands. He was exhausted. It was finished. He was under no illusions about what would happen next. He would confess and he would have to do it in such a way that his father and Hikaru didn't suffer the consequences. He would make the Concilium angry. Give them no choice but to make an example of him. And then, someone would send a message to the Fates. The Mortal Knife would flash and his life would be over. It wouldn't hurt. There were worse ways to go.

And then . . . There would be Light. There would be the Hinterland, one last time. He would have to give his keystone to someone. There would be no goodbyes. They wouldn't let his father guide him under those kind of circumstances. He wondered what would be on the other side. Directions only got you so far. Would he be alone? Or would Lucian and all those other Mortsons who had gone before him be there, waiting? Waiting to show him a whole new path.

His mother's sobbing brought him back to the present. He raised his head, afraid to look at her. He had never wanted to hurt her or let her down. Nathanial's face was ashen. 'You can't do this. You don't understand the consequences. Don't you think Lucian tried? Don't you think he wanted to find another way? But even if you could walk away . . . You wouldn't just lose the Luman world. You would lose us. Your family.'

'It doesn't have to be like that.'

'There are laws, Adam!'

'And laws change!' Adam looked at Heinrich. 'You said it yourself. Maybe we're too slow to change. We're so far behind the rest of the world we're dinosaurs. But *you* changed things. You Marked Susanna. And if women can be Lumen too, maybe you don't *need* every single man to be one. Maybe I can go and do something else useful. Help people in a different way.'

Heinrich was studying him again. 'You're like him,' he said abruptly. He turned to Nathanial and smiled sadly. 'There is something of Lucian in him.'

'Yes.' Nathanial nodded. His voice was flat, the emotion deliberately squashed out of it. 'Jo says the same. She always has.'

'There will be a scandal. You are a High Luman and this will be seen as a failure on your part, if Adam does not follow in your footsteps. There will be questions. There are no rules for this situation.'

'Then we will make rules.' They all turned. Elise, the most puritanical conventionalist in the history of Luman-kind, was going rogue. She wiped her eyes and shrugged. 'So there will be a scandal. There was a scandal before *et voilà* . . . here we are! We survived.' She stopped and for a moment a terrible anger passed across her face. 'I have lived in the shadow of Darian's obsession for too many years. No more. Let the past be the past.'

She paused and walked over to Heinrich, kissing his cheeks in turn. '*Je suis désolée.* I am sorry I did not support you. You have been a friend to us for so long. The world is changing and there are no rules. So, we will make new rules. After all, what purpose is there in being a High Luman or a Chief Curator if you cannot rewrite the law?'

Heinrich was smiling at her sadly. 'The Concilium will not accept this.' He fell silent, studying Adam, but his thoughts were somewhere else. It was a long time before he spoke. 'It must *look* as though Adam will obey. There must be no talk of school or travelling the world. You realise this, Adam, yes? You must promise the Concilium that you accept our laws, that you intend to be a Luman. Your true thoughts must remain a secret.'

Adam stared at Heinrich stupidly. He wasn't sure he was following. 'But . . . You'll let me stay at school?'

'Being a Seer is a burden, Adam. In time you may learn to carry this gift with more grace. But if your school helps you with this transition . . . helps you to survive, to live . . . then yes, you may stay at school.' Heinrich shook his head. 'It must be a remarkable place to inspire such devotion.'

Adam thought about it for a moment. 'It is.' It was true. Not every day. Some days it was rubbish and boring and it had people like Michael Bulber. But it also had his friends and Melissa and the chance to learn things and the chance to be the kind of person he had always wanted to be. And he wouldn't be there forever. Because he had a life waiting for him. A whole life. And school was going to help him make that life happen.

Another thought occurred to him. He knew he was pushing his luck but he had a feeling that this was his one chance to negotiate and then the doors were going to slam closed hard.

What was that saying? Shoot for the moon and you'll reach the stars. 'There's something else.' He looked at their raised eyebrows and pushed on. 'I want to be able to meet up with people. Outside school. Normal people. I want to be able to see my friends. Not every night. Just some nights.' He wasn't mentioning any names. There was only so much 'change' they could handle in one go.

Nathanial frowned. 'You will still have to help us, Adam. On call-outs. I won't let you walk away from our world entirely. Not until you're older. Until you're sure.' He hesitated. 'But as long as you do your share . . . I don't see why you shouldn't have a few nights out. Being a Luman has certainly never held Luc back.' He gave a wry smile.

Heinrich held out his hand. 'Adam. We are agreed?'

Hardly daring to believe it, Adam took the older man's hand and shook it. 'Yes.'

He didn't know how it was going to work. None of them did.

But at least they were going to try.

The next twelve hours passed in a blur for Adam. There was a long stretch of quiet disbelief in his cell, wondering if this was all just a cruel joke, while his parents and Heinrich were above ground, negotiating terms and soothing ruffled feathers. In time Rashid returned and escorted him along a corridor beneath the house, into the Oath room. The Concilium were waiting for him, all thirteen of them. Their chairs were angled towards him while Adam had to kneel on a cushion before them. His parents were sitting over at one side. It was hard not to keep looking for them. Hikaru was sitting on the other side of the room. It was much easier to avoid his eyes – Adam wasn't sure how he would ever face the Japanese Luman again.

The charges against him were read out. He had to defend himself. It was horrible. Heinrich had briefed him on what to say but he was so tired and dazed that it was hard to choose the right words. In the end, this probably helped him. Afterwards, he realised how young and shattered he must have looked; how completely inept. He certainly didn't *look* like a master conspirator.

That role was reserved for Darian. The Frenchman did his very best to prove that Adam was a Seer; that he had interfered with the Fates; that he was a liar. It got easier to lie then. Adam just channelled every ounce of his hatred into pleading his innocence. No, he wasn't a Seer – he might have been when he was a baby but he had lost the art, which was a shame as he would have been a better Luman. No, he would never dare to intervene in the fates of men. He knew better than that. It was against Luman law. His friend Spike liked hacking into things and although Adam himself didn't understand how he had done it, for once it had helped save people. He wouldn't know; he hadn't had anything to do with it all.

Darian was getting more and more angry. He was trying and failing to keep his composure but his mask was slipping. His vendetta was becoming clearer and clearer. As he realised he was losing, he kept looking over at Elise, helpless and furious. It was Heinrich who finally intervened, perhaps trying to save Darian from shaming himself even more.

Adam wasn't sure how he felt about Heinrich. He knew the older man cared about the Mortsons but he also knew that Heinrich was supposed to be impartial. Why was the Chief Curator so determined to save him? Any punishment he would have faced was no more than he deserved. And yet, as he remembered Heinrich's face when his daughter was rejected at the Marking ball, Adam realised that *no one* was truly impartial, no matter how much they liked to think they were. If ever a good deed had been repaid ten times over, it was today.

And then the trial was over. Only now the real test began. As the Crone entered the room, Adam felt a shudder run through him. Luc had tormented him that he would never get Marked and right now that was an attractive idea. He had always imagined it happening at some distant time in the future, preferably when he was a medical student and had researched local anaesthetics . . . Elise pressed a white cloth to his brow and gave him slivers of fruit from a silver dish. Nathanial stood beside him, a hand on his shoulder, while the Crone mixed Mortson Keystone into her ink and pulled his shirt to one side. Adam looked down at his breastbone, the skin pale and unbroken. It would never look like this again.

The Crone began. It was agony, not least because it was a Mark Adam had never wanted to bear. But with every movement of the Crone's hand and the fresh wave of pain the tattoo pen brought, Adam thought about what he was gaining. School. His friends. Melissa. His life. His freedom. He repeated the list on a loop, breathing in and out, squeezing his eyes closed to keep tears from spilling onto his cheeks and shaming him.

And then, hours or days or weeks later, it was done. He felt weak and sick and shaky. His mother left the room so he could make his Oath. It was hard to listen to the words but he managed to repeat them after Heinrich, barely audible. A cloak was brought in and placed around his shoulders; black with the white fur trim of an adult Luman. He had come of age.

It was a strange moment. Usually there was a celebration to follow but not this time. His mother returned to the chamber and slipped her hand through his arm. Her face was sad. This wasn't the Marking ceremony she would have wanted for one of her sons. If anything, the atmosphere was sombre. It was obvious that not everyone in the Concilium agreed with their Chief Curator's decision. Some of them avoided Heinrich's eye and looked at Adam with nothing but contempt. But now that they were leaving it was time for the worst moment of all – facing Hikaru.

Adam stayed close to his parents and Heinrich as the High Luman approached. The rest of the Curators had already left, Darian barely waiting for the door to close behind him before he began ranting at the madness of the situation. If he hadn't been so evil himself, Adam would have felt more sympathy for him. His scheme had backfired. Win for Mortson. But Hikaru was a different matter. He had been shamed by what had happened and it was a shame that would probably never fade, however innocent he was.

Hikaru was as inscrutable as ever. He bowed to Heinrich and nodded at Nathanial and Elise. Nathanial bowed and Adam followed. He held the pose for a long time; as close as he could come to an apology – but it didn't feel enough. 'I'm sorry,' he blurted out.

'Why are you sorry, Adam? You have done nothing wrong in the eyes of the law. Our Concilium has absolved you.' There was no trace of sarcasm in Hikaru's tone but somehow he managed to convey very clearly that he knew Adam was guilty. 'And now we must decide how to proceed.'

Heinrich stepped in. 'We have decided that it would only raise questions if Adam fails to return to Hachimana. He tells us that he was in the same building with his friends and many other witnesses. Because of this it would be difficult to explain his disappearance in the tsunami.'

'I have made enquiries. His group are still in Hachimana. They will be taken by coach back to Tokyo as soon as the roads are passable. It would be best if Adam returned to the city immediately. While they are still in the city Adam can say that he simply became separated from them and was found by one of the city residents.'

It was agreed. Adam had a moment with his parents and Heinrich before he left. His mother kissed both his cheeks and held his face in her hands for a long moment. 'Take care, my darling.' He nodded and turned to his father. Nathanial hesitated, then put his arms round him and hugged him. Adam stood rigid, pleased and embarrassed. His father was usually more of a hand-shaker.

Heinrich held out his hand and Adam shook it. 'Thank you, sir.' The words sounded odd but felt right.

Heinrich's expression was stern. 'You are an adult now. You understand what this means?'

Adam nodded. He did know. From here on in, he was responsible for his actions in the eyes of Luman Law. There would never be another second chance like this. He understood that. But *they* had made promises too. 'So I'll be able to stay . . .?'

Nathanial cleared his throat. 'We made you a promise, Adam. Keep your oath and we will keep ours.'

It was time. They climbed stone stairs and re-entered the house. Adam had hoped to say goodbye to Rita but there was no sign of anyone else. In the garden, Adam reached for his keystone – then realised he didn't need it any more. It was part of him, just as the Luman world was part of him, whether he liked it or not. They stepped into the Hinterland and with one final bow, Hikaru took his arm.

It was time to go back.

Chapter 27

t was surprisingly easy to rejoin his group. Adam had worried about cover stories and yet more lies, but in the event it wasn't really necessary. Maybe it was because of the chaos after the tsunami. Adam had experienced natural disasters and their aftermath from the safety of the Hinterland but experiencing them in the physical world was a whole different story.

Much of Hachimana's seafront strip was completely destroyed, along with low-lying villages and towns for two hundred miles along the eastern coast of Japan. The devastation was difficult to comprehend. It was only afterwards, watching the footage on the news, that Adam really began to grasp the scale of what had happened – and what could have happened without the early warning. The sea had smashed the main street to pieces, pushing the debris inland towards the research centre, then retreated, scouring what was left off the face of the earth.

Adam and Hikaru stood in the Hinterland, surveying the destruction. From here, just outside the research centre, they could watch the comings and goings as the local people began to try and clear access routes and get supplies to the people who needed them. The weather had taken a milder turn but the work looked arduous. Family groups huddled together, sharing whatever food and shelter they had cobbled together. And there, at the side of the research centre, were his group. The teachers looked exhausted but they were herding people together and passing out some kind of emergency rations from inside the building. They mostly seemed to be crackers and slices of pickle.

They wandered through the reception foyer, still unseen. Inside, people were trying to sweep up glass and splintered wood. They were calm, waiting their turn politely for cleaning supplies and blankets. Adam was struck by their quiet patience and dignity. Would people in London have behaved like this? He wasn't sure. He hoped so.

At last they spotted Kenai. This would be Adam's last chance to talk to Hikaru. 'Thank you.'

Hikaru didn't answer. He seemed distracted, watching the clear-up go on around them. At last he turned back to Adam. 'This is a volatile landscape. There have been tsunamis before and there will be tsunamis again. Many souls have been lost in the past. Perhaps in the future we will be able to rely on science to predict when these events will occur. Perhaps there will never again be a tsunami where lives are lost.'

Adam nodded. 'I hope so.'

'You will never return to this country, Adam Mortson.'

Adam looked at him, startled. From anyone else he might have expected it to be a wind-up but it was clear that Hikaru wasn't joking. 'OK.'

Hikaru bowed. 'And now we shall return to the physical world.'

Within moments Adam was standing before Kenai, whose face was one of stunned relief. He was actually smiling, beaming in fact. There was an animated conversation in Japanese accompanied by lots of bowing. Adam had simply wandered off, that was all, and been found by Hikaru. He had been fed and given a bed for the night because it was too dangerous to bring him back during the dark hours, with the electricity supply down. And now he was here, safe and well – and Kenai gave him a long, appraising glance to check that this was so. There was more bowing and Hikaru gave Adam one last piercing look. 'Bye,' Adam whispered to his receding back.

And a minute later there was a roar of happy disbelief when Kenai escorted him triumphantly through the building and back to his friends and teachers.

It was four days before they finally landed back in London. They had spent two more cold, uncomfortable, hungry evenings in Hachimana, waiting for the main roads to Tokyo to reopen. Adam had expected more tears and complaints but sitting on the coach, crawling along the highways, they could look towards the distant sea at patches of lunar landscape. Where they passed towns and cities whole streets and districts were just gone, scoured off the face of the earth. People had improvised makeshift shelters, too scared to return to their buildings until the aftershocks subsided.

The airport was like a refugee camp, with thousands of tourists and travellers desperately trying to get flights home. The great Murai met them at the airport, led them into a private

318

lounge and presented them each with a small sack containing clean clothes, toiletries and snacks. He was taking the tsunami almost personally. He bowed deeply and apologised for the disruption to their visit, offering to fly them all out to Japan again in the springtime. Judging by the looks on their teachers' faces that was never going to happen . . .

Murai had managed to commandeer one of his own planes and informed them that they would be flying home the following morning. Strangely, this was the point when the tears came. It was like no one had dared to believe they would ever see their families again and now that it seemed like they might, some of the shock finally wore off. There was lots of hugging. Fenton was spotted soon afterwards, wiping his eyes and toasting Murai with *sake*. The Bulb was unusually quiet but he sat beside Miss Lumpton, holding her hand and smiling.

Archie nodded in their direction. 'Do you think he was disappointed that he never met the Sensai?'

Adam shrugged. 'I think he's probably just happy to be alive.'

'Did Spike send him another Sensai email?' Dan was rooting through the emergency sack Murai had given them and triumphantly produced a packet of cashew nuts. He poured them into his mouth and gave a deep sigh of contentment.

'Don't know,' Archie said, scowling across the lounge. 'It's not like he's telling us anything.'

Adam's stomach clenched. Most of his group were queuing up for the shower rooms or standing by tables full of tea and noodles. Spike was sitting with the other computer geeks, pointing at something on a laptop screen, talking animatedly. He was still clutching his broken laptop. Almost as if he felt

Adam's eyes, he turned and stared for a long moment, his face a mask, then looked away.

So that was how it was going to be now. Maybe it was inevitable. Maybe it was even for the best. There was no easy answer he could give his 'friend' and he knew that Spike wouldn't give up until he got one. Maybe they were over there right now, trying to unearth more secrets about the Mortsons. Adam didn't think so. Spike didn't like sharing the glory with anyone else.

Adam sighed and joined the queue for dinner.

And then, twenty-four hours later, they were stepping off the plane and into the airport building. Passport control was a nightmare – so many of their group had lost their passports and were travelling on emergency documents – but Fenton escorted Adam and a few others through the barriers and into the arrivals area. There was no luggage to collect; what little they had they were wearing.

Most of his group rushed straight through the glass doors and into the waiting arms of sobbing parents and siblings. Adam felt a pang of loneliness. He knew it was better if his parents avoided the airport – there were too many cameras and too much security. It was the same reason he was going to get the train home instead of just swooping.

Fenton was looking around. 'Have you someone collecting you?'

'Yes, sir,' Adam lied. 'They'll be out the front.'

'Maybe I should go with you . . .' Fenton began, then tailed off as a small, brown-haired woman ran towards him. He made a choking sound and ran to embrace her. 'I'm sorry, I was such a fool,' he sobbed into her hair.

Adam grinned. There was nothing like a near-death experience to make people realise what was important to them. He had a feeling he had just solved the mystery of Fenton's recent vile temper and heavy weekends. He'd also solved the problem of how to get away without a guardian there to collect him. He waved at his form tutor's back and followed the signs to the train station.

Within an hour he was walking off the train into grey cloud and fine drizzle. Nathanial was waiting by the car, the rain misting his camel-hair coat. He smiled. 'You seem to be travelling a bit lighter this time.'

Adam nodded. He flung the emergency kitbag in the back and climbed into the passenger seat. As they eased through the traffic he stared out of the window, marvelling at how it looked so familiar and so *different* at the same time.

Nathanial left him to his thoughts but cleared his throat as they approached the house. 'We've kept the details of what happened to a minimum. Obviously they all know about the tsunami and that you . . . ran afoul of the law. And your Marking of course.'

Adam turned to him. 'What did they say?'

'They were just glad to hear you were safe, Adam.' Nathanial hesitated. 'Be tactful with Luc, won't you? It's rather unusual for a younger brother to be Marked before the elder. Aron was teasing him about it.'

Adam bit his lip, suppressing a grin. He knew he shouldn't be taking any pleasure in it but it was so rarely that he *ever* got one over on Luc that he had to make the most of it when the chance came. He was only human!

He jumped out of the car to press his palm to the electronic control. Nathanial drove on and Adam followed on foot. There were some throaty, joyous barks and Sam and Morty tore across the grass and leapt on him, almost knocking him back into the street. He grinned and blinked back tears. 'Hello, you two.' He spent a few minutes basking in their affection, bracing himself for returning to the house. He felt nervous. Why?

But he couldn't put it off forever. Nathanial was standing by the back door, waiting patiently. Adam jogged across the grass and joined him. The rain had stopped and the sun was trying to come out. His father gave him a questioning look: *Ready?* Adam nodded and Nathanial opened the back door.

They were all in the kitchen, sitting round the table. The kitchen smelled like fresh-baked bread and soup. There were flowers on the table in a vase and hanging from the ceiling was a banner in Chloe's loopy writing, saying: *Welcome home Adam Mortson, Marked Luman*. His mother turned from the stove, smiling. She was holding a cake, decorated with the Mortson seal.

There were kisses and hugs and a spine-shattering back-thump from Aron. The last one to greet him was Luc. There was an awkward silence.

Luc sighed. 'Trust you to get *everything* arse over tits. You couldn't even wait and get *Marked* when you were supposed to.' He smirked. 'Good to see you're alive. And nice tracksuit by the way.'

'Yeah, thanks.' Adam finally smiled, feeling some of the tight, sick feeling go out of his stomach.

'Come and have lunch,' Auntie Jo said, putting her arm around his back and leading him to the table. 'I'm going to have a slice of bread in honour of the prodigal's return. I may even have cake!'

Adam sat down in his usual place. He was lightheaded with exhaustion. Elise smoothed his hair back from his forehead and kissed his cheek, placing a bowl of soup in front of him. 'Eat, a little. Then bed!'

Adam nodded and obediently took a spoonful of soup. He ate quietly, letting the noise wash over him, wondering how much they really knew. Did they know that Adam wasn't going to be a Luman, even though he was Marked? Did they realise he had a whole different life planned, one that would take him away from this table and this house and the whole Luman world?

Someday soon, he wouldn't be here. It was a strange thought. He looked around the table, at his family; Auntie Jo teasing Chloe; Luc and Aron fighting good-naturedly over the last slice of bread; Nathanial talking quietly to Elise. She was smiling and she looked happier than she had for a long time, like she had thrown a heavy weight off her shoulders. Everything was changing. It was always changing. You couldn't stay in the present any more than you could live in the past.

And some day he *really* wouldn't be here any more. He wouldn't be in the physical realm at all. His life here would be over and he would be . . . somewhere else. That was a *really* strange thought. The time you had here was so precious. There were so many things Adam wanted to do and be. And now, because of everything that had happened, he might get the chance to make them happen.

It was all too much to think about just now. The spoon slipped out of his hand and clattered into the bowl. His head was spinning. A moment later he felt Nathanial's hand on his arm, helping him to his feet. 'I've got you, Adam. I think you need some rest.'

He allowed his father to help him from the kitchen. In the background, dimly, he heard Luc call, 'I'll eat your cake for you!' There was laughter.

At the top of the stairs Nathanial opened his bedroom door and nodded towards the bed. 'Sleep for as long as you need to.'

Adam nodded. He reached into his pocket and felt for the small, hard booklet he had kept safe for so long. He pulled out his passport and handed it to his father.

Nathanial hesitated. 'I'll look after it for now, Adam. Keep it safe for you. Apparently they last for years.' He stared at it for a moment. 'I have a feeling you'll be using it a lot.' He smiled, half sadly. 'Rest now.'

Adam kicked off his boots, collapsed on his bed and fell into a deep and dreamless sleep.

Chapter 28

t was two days before Adam returned to school (The Bulb's one concession after their ordeal) but when he did it felt like he had never been away. He woke up that morning and felt a smile so big that it almost broke his face. He couldn't get his uniform on fast enough and hopped impatiently from foot to foot until the bus arrived. Today was the first day of the rest of his life.

Judging by the buzz in the corridors a lot of people were feeling that way. It was strange, how being so close to something awful made you grateful for what you had. Lots of people who normally ignored him smiled and greeted him and he grinned back. It was nice. It probably wasn't going to last but he would enjoy it while it did.

Mr Fenton was whistling as he unlocked their form room door. He'd had a haircut and shaved. He looked . . . shinier. He frowned when he saw Adam. 'Where did you bugger off to at the airport? I thought you'd got lost.'

'Sorry, sir. My father came and picked me up.'

'Hmph. Well, you're here in one piece anyway.' Fenton gave him what might have been a smile and strolled inside, whistling again. Adam grinned. Whatever had happened after the airport reunion had put his form tutor in an excellent mood.

He was just about to step inside when someone called his name. 'Adam.'

He turned, feeling his heart jump. Melissa was standing a few doors down, staring at him transfixed, as though she was seeing a ghost.

He wanted to run over to her and slide his fingers into her hair and kiss her, hard. Unfortunately she wasn't alone; three of her friends were beside her. He lifted his hand and gave what was supposed to be a jaunty wave. Judging by her mates' expressions, he hadn't pulled it off. 'Hi.'

The bell rang and hordes of people appeared from nowhere, laughing and jostling their way past, barging into their form rooms. He waited for a moment, hoping she was going to talk to him but her friends seemed to be hugging her and laughing at something (possibly him) and suddenly he felt stupid. He slipped into the form room and studiously avoided her eyes as Fenton gave them a rambling welcome back and reminded them that natural disasters aside, they had exams just after Christmas that they needed to begin revising for.

Adam made sure he was the first one out of the door – but Melissa was faster than he had given her credit for. 'Adam.'

He turned and this time she was much closer. He studied her face; her pale skin; the slight shadows under her eyes; her mouth. The pain of losing her swept back all over again, startling him with its ferocity. He swallowed hard. 'Hi.'

'You're OK.' When he nodded she bit her lip and looked at the ground. 'I was really scared something had happened to you. Ellen said you were missing for a whole night.'

Adam nodded, glad he had his cover story well practised by now. 'I just got lost. It was stupid. Some people found me and brought me back.'

'That's great.' She was watching him. Her eyes had that laser look they sometimes got, when she was trying to *tell* him something. For a while he'd been really good at reading her. They had been so close he just *knew* what she wanted. Now, it was like the last six months had never happened. There was a wall between them and he didn't know how to cross it.

Maybe she felt it too, the wall that was there. She looked sad. 'Well, I'm glad you're OK.'

'I miss you,' he blurted out, just as she was walking away. Everything he felt, all the words that he felt were in his mouth, ready to fall out in a torrent and wash her away but they all seemed to get stuck.

She bit her lip again. 'Yeah. Me too.'

It gave him hope but he needed time to think. 'Can I see you at lunchtime?'

'I have stuff to do in art.'

'I know. I can come up there.'

'What's the point, Adam?' She looked angry now, as well as sad. 'It just . . . It wasn't working any more.'

The corridor was emptying. Fenton's class were charging towards them, fresh from assembly, and he came out to bellow them into a line. When he saw Adam and Melissa there he looked puzzled, then irritated. 'What are you two still doing here? Get to class!'

They were going in opposite directions. Adam felt desperate. He had a feeling that if he didn't get through to her now she would disappear. She would get sucked back into her art and her friends and, down the line, someone else who loved her the way he did. 'Please?' he said. 'Just quickly.'

'*Get to class*, you two!' Fenton's good temper was disappearing fast.

Melissa sighed. 'OK,' she said, already turning and walking away. 'But just for a minute.'

Adam grinned at Fenton and ran to maths. He had planned to work hard and make the most of every second in school now that he was allowed to be here but that was before he'd had the chance to put things right. He kicked himself for not meeting her at break time but it would give him more time to choose the right words.

When the bell rang he went to the library as usual but for a few minutes he was the only one there. First Dan and then Archie appeared and sat down. Dan pulled out a packet of almonds and tipped them onto the table with a contented sigh. 'I never thought I would get to do this again.'

Archie snorted. 'Yeah, it would be kind of ironic if you survived an earthquake and a tsunami but then died of some germ you picked up off a table.'

Dan shrugged and offered Adam an almond. 'Was everyone really happy to see you?'

Adam nodded. 'Yeah. But I mostly just slept when I got home.'

'Yeah, me too. But we went out for dinner last night and my dad let us get ice cream afterwards. He's normally really anti-sugar.'

'Putting himself out of business a bit, isn't he?' Archie said, sketching a picture of Dan's dad armed with a drill and a sign above him reading *Dark Lord Dentistry.*

'Oh, and my mum says that if you start to get flashbacks and stuff that's normal and you have to talk to someone about it.' Dan rattled this off with the air of a man who had repeated it many times already that morning.

Adam waited but no one was mentioning the obvious. 'Where's Spike?'

Archie shrugged. 'Probably hanging out with his new mates. The computer ones.'

Dan nodded. 'He got into the hacking thing. Remember the group he was trying to get in with? He pulled off something really big and they let him in. He wouldn't tell me what it was but he said he has to do loads of other stuff now just to *stay* in.' Dan looked gloomy. 'We need a new Spike. How are we going to keep The Bulb off our backs now?'

'We won't need to. We've been to Japan,' Archie said.

Adam half listened to their banter, feeling relieved. He wasn't stupid enough to think that he was off the hook completely but maybe having a break from Spike would buy him some time. Plus, Spike wasn't good at sharing the limelight. If his 'big hack' had been the tsunami stuff, he wouldn't be keen to admit to his hacker friends that he'd been tricked into doing it.

'He'll be sorry when he finds out I could have got him sorted out with the girls.' Archie was talking in an overly casual way.

'You know, because I'm going out with Hannah Murphy now.'

'They hooked up on the plane in the toilet,' Dan piped up. 'We're all going out on Friday night. She's bringing some of her mates. I'm going!'

Archie gave Adam a benevolent look. 'Do you want me to fix you up?'

Adam hid a smile. 'Thanks but I'm OK.'

'You're back with Melissa, aren't you?' Dan grinned. 'Reeled her in again, have you?'

'Dunno. Maybe. I'm going to see her at lunchtime.'

The bell rang. Archie winked. 'Well, if it doesn't work out, you know where to find me!'

As Adam climbed the stairs to the art room, his heart was thudding. All the times he had been up there and taken it for granted. Now that he was here it felt like he was being admitted into some kind of amazing palace of delights. He was a bit nervous that Ms Havens would be there. She hadn't exactly looked happy with him on his last visit. Still, maybe nearly dying would buy him some sympathy.

He paused in the corridor, loosening his tie and opening his top button. He felt like he was suffocating. *Just tell her how you feel. Just tell her it's going to be OK.* The calm voice in his head saying this stuff wasn't the same as the guy jumping up and down in his chest, telling him to run away before he made a tit of himself. *That* guy sounded like Luc.

He took a deep breath and slipped into the art room. The radio was playing but Melissa was there, alone. She glanced up from her work and froze. 'Hi.'

'Hi,' Adam said. He felt dizzy with nerves. It was crazy. He felt like he was asking her out all over again, which in a way he was. But back then he hadn't let her down or given her any reason to say no. Could she really forgive him? His heart sank.

Melissa gave him a wry smile. 'It's OK. I'm not going to bite you.'

He tried to relax. He went and stood beside her. 'Is this what you're doing for the show?'

'Yeah.' She stepped aside so he could see it. 'Do you recognise it?' Her voice was very quiet.

'Of course I do.' Adam stared at the picture, wishing he could step into the canvas. She had used paints and fabric and sparkling threads to create a park. The plants and trees had created a cocoon around a faded beach towel where two figures were shaped in blocks of charcoal, sitting facing each other, looking into one another's eyes. The only thing touching was the girl's hand on the boy's face while the sun shone down on them. It was the most joyful, most secretive thing Adam had ever seen.

He looked at it for a long time, feeling an ache in his chest. 'It's . . . brilliant. Really great.'

Melissa shrugged. 'It was a really good day.' She sighed. 'At least it was until the bit where you ran off and I thought you'd gone home. And then when you came back, I had to go anyway. One of us always has to be somewhere else.'

He took her hand and turned her gently, until she was facing him. 'I'm sorry I was so crap. I didn't want to be. But things are going to be different now.'

She pulled her hand away. 'You always say that.'

'But I'm allowed to go out more now. I talked to my parents. I can meet up with you outside school.'

'It's not just that, Adam.' Melissa walked away, towards the window. She stared out, avoiding his eyes. 'It's everything. The secrets and the lying to me. I know there's stuff you're not telling me.'

For a wild moment, Adam wondered if she was talking about Caitlyn . . . but that was crazy. There was no way she could know that. 'I don't have secrets.'

'You're lying again,' she said. She sounded resigned rather than angry. 'You said it took a long time to get to know you. You told me to trust you. And I did, for ages. And I kept waiting for *you* to trust *me* but . . .' She shrugged. 'It never happened.'

Adam stared at her. He wanted to tell her everything. Just blurt it all out and slump to the ground and hope that she would pick him back up. He knew that he couldn't. 'What if they're not my secrets to tell?'

'But some of them *are*.' She turned and faced him then. 'Do you think I'm stupid? Do you think I don't know what you can do?'

Adam's heart was beating faster. She had never seen him swoop, he was sure of it. And he had never mentioned Lumen or Lights or *The Book of the Unknown Roads*. 'What do you think I can do?'

'You can see when bad things are going to happen. And you try to stop them.'

Adam stared at her, suddenly feeling like all the air had been sucked out of the room. It was the way she had said it; so simply, like it was nothing to be afraid of. Like it didn't freak her

332

out. He needed to laugh and tell her she was crazy. He could do it too but she was looking at him and her face was so calm and serious that he knew, somewhere deep in his heart, that if he lied to her now this would be the last conversation they would ever have. But if he told her too much, he was signing both their death warrants. He settled for saying nothing at all.

Melissa sighed. 'Look, you knew my mum was sick without even meeting her. And that night when we went to Petrograd? And you took off somewhere? Michael Bulber told me that he had gone looking for some guy but you were there instead, like you'd warned the guy off. And then today your friend Spike cornered me. He started asking me all these questions about your family and then he told me you were able to see the future and know things like when earthquakes were going to happen. He told me to stay away from you.'

Adam's mouth was dry. He knew he should deny it all but something wouldn't let him do that. *You will lose her.* He swallowed and licked his lips. 'And what did you say?'

Melissa met his eyes. Her voice was very quiet. 'I told him that the only thing keeping me away from you was you.'

Adam cleared his throat and looked at the ground. 'You said you wanted a boyfriend who did normal things.' His voice sounded flat.

'You *are* normal and you do lots of normal things.' She smiled. 'You just do some not-normal things too. But don't lie to me. That's the thing I hate, more than anything.'

'I can't see the future. But sometimes I know when something bad is going to happen or people are sick or they're going to have an accident.' His mouth was moving and words were falling out and it felt so good that he wanted to sink to his knees and wrap his arms around her waist and just close his eyes. 'But I can't control it. I can't see lottery numbers or anything.'

She laughed. 'That's a shame. I thought that might be why you always seem to have money.' Her face became serious. 'But it's more useful knowing when an earthquake is going to happen. Or knowing that my mum is sick. That's amazing.'

'Why are you not freaking out?' Adam was watching her hard, waiting for her to turn and run, but she was just standing there, like everything was fine.

Melissa shrugged. 'You're not the only one who can do weird stuff. My friend in work can suss guys out as soon as she meets them. Like, she knows if they're nice or horrible and she's never wrong. She says she just *knows*. And my gran used to be able to find things people had lost, like their purse or their wedding ring or even someone in their family. They would go to her flat and she would tell them what she saw. She said she would just daydream and she would see water or a street sign or whether it was a dark place. She said it was like seeing a photo.'

'Did it work?' The scientist in Adam was sceptical – but then who was he to judge? He wouldn't believe in *himself* if he'd heard someone on the street talking about Lumen.

'Most of the time the people would come back to her and tell her they had found what they were searching for.' Melissa stepped closer to him. 'I'm not saying it's the same thing as what you do. I'm just saying . . . some people are different. They can do things that other people can't do but it doesn't make them bad. Especially if they help people.'

'I can't talk about this stuff,' Adam said, suddenly frightened. He couldn't bear the thought of people staring at him in the corridors, whispering and pointing. 'It doesn't happen very often. And it's not who I am. It's not what I want to do with my life.'

'I won't tell anyone,' Melissa said. She looked at her painting; the little cocoon they were sitting in. 'I just thought it could be *our* secret, instead of yours. And then you wouldn't have to lie to me all the time.'

Our secret. There was something about those words that made Adam feel happy and nervous at the same time. 'Does that mean we can go out again?'

'Are you *allowed* to go out with me? Are your parents letting you out of the prison house?'

'Yes!' Now that he had started he tried to keep telling her as much of the truth as he could. 'It's just . . . the work my father does. It's kind of a family business. And they thought I was going to go into it too but I've told them I won't because I want to do other things. So now they know and it's OK. I don't have to do as much any more. Sometimes, if it's really busy, I might have to help out. But I can go out now. We can hang out.'

She was looking at him. 'Is this for real?'

'Yes.' Adam put his arms around her and pulled her in against him. Some kind of elastic band inside him snapped and released the tension out of his body. It was the way she felt; the way she fitted in against him, warm and familiar. He kissed her hair, not quite daring to kiss her mouth yet. 'I really want this to be right again. Things are going to be different, I promise.'

He didn't know how things were going to work out. Whatever Spike thought, he couldn't tell the future. He just knew that there was no one he liked spending time with more than Melissa – and they were going to be getting a *lot* more time together. He would make sure of it.

He just hoped she never wanted to go to Japan.

The sun was sinking low when Adam got off his bus home. The clocks had gone back. Summer was behind him and winter was approaching but for once he didn't feel miserable about it. As he got close to the house he was overtaken by a luridly dressed runner, although this time she was wearing a hoodie rather than a singlet. 'You snooze, you lose, Adam!' she chortled and Adam grinned and ran after her.

Auntie Jo beat him easily and held her arms up in the air, dancing triumphantly for an imaginary crowd. 'So, you lived to face another half-term.'

'Yeah.' Adam placed his palm on the scanner pad and they walked inside together.

Auntie Jo was quiet for a moment. 'All that time, Adam.' She stopped and waited for him to stop and face her. 'You kept your secrets for all that time.' When Adam shrugged, not sure what to say, she shook her head. 'They could have killed you, you know. The Concilium. Don't you ever put us through that again.'

'I won't.' And he wouldn't – just as long as he was able to leave the Luman world behind. Maybe he could learn to block his death sense as well as he could block his doom sense.

Auntie Jo was studying him. 'Your father told me that you know about our brother. Lucian.'

336

It was the first time Auntie Jo had ever mentioned his name or even his existence. For months he had felt like he was lying to her, pretending not to know about his uncle. Now it seemed that *everything* was coming out into the open. 'Yes.'

'He was a good man.' Her voice was low and fierce. 'He was a good Luman too but he hated it, all of it. The deaths when he felt them . . . They hurt him, badly. Not just in his body but in his soul too.'

Adam nodded. He understood. That was how he felt every time he ignored his doom sense. Somehow he had learned to block it out and saved himself from going mad in the process. For Lucian, the pain of it had been too much. 'I wish I could have met him.'

'You are so like him, you know.' Auntie Jo's eyes were bright with unshed tears but her voice was steady. 'He could be stubborn but he was kind too, just as you are. I will never forget how you danced with Susanna at her Marking ball. You made me very proud that night. Proud of the man you're becoming. Whatever happens and whatever people say over the months and years ahead, always remember that. You are a good man.'

Adam looked at the ground, feeling his cheeks burn at all this praise. It was strange hearing her call him a man when at school he was still a child – but he was Marked now. He *was* a man in the eyes of the Luman world and he would be treated as such. 'Susanna would never have danced with me any other time.' He grinned. 'I got lucky.'

'Luckier than you know,' she said wryly. 'Her father was the man who spared your life.'

'Will Heinrich be OK?' He hesitated. There was so much he

wasn't supposed to know. 'I mean, I know he's getting old and he won't be around forever but will he still be Chief Curator?'

'For now.' Auntie Jo sighed. 'He has his loyal supporters on the Concilium still, just as he has his opponents. Your Marking was rather divisive but in the end most of them didn't really want to execute an unmarked teenager, even if a few felt that it would send a clear message.'

Adam didn't have to ask who *did* want him executed. 'And what about Susanna? Will they keep letting him Mark girls?'

'That's not as clear-cut. He did produce the texts from *The Book of the Unknown Roads*, so no one doubts that women were once Lumen. Sometimes people prefer to rewrite history for their own ends. They've been very successful over the last few thousand years. The wise girls are training now, as fast as they can, trying to get Marked while Heinrich is still Chief Curator. It's surprising how many fathers were taking their daughters on call-outs on the sly. And more of them will get brave.'

'Is Chloe going to be a Luman?'

'I don't think she knows what she wants yet. Certainly your parents would take some convincing but where others lead they may still follow. We had some visitors from Ireland today, while you were at school. One of them asked me to pass on her greetings.'

'Caitlyn?'

'Yes. Don't ask me how but she's persuaded Patrick to take her on some call-outs with him. Personally I think she's nicer to the wolfhounds than she is to most people but . . .' Auntie Jo shrugged. 'She seems quite keen on you.'

Adam shook his head. 'We're just friends.'

'Hmmmm. I thought there might be another betrothal on the cards.'

They started walking again. Adam was desperate to change the subject. 'Do you think you'll get Marked?'

Auntie Jo smiled. 'I might do. I think I'd be a rather glamorous final vision for any soul, wouldn't I?' She waggled her eyebrows and Adam grinned. Her face changed and she looked more serious. 'But I have a choice now, that's the main thing. Being free to choose. It's important. You know that better than anyone.'

Adam nodded, feeling his throat constrict. He still remembered Heinrich's face as he stood above them all, about to present his daughter to the room; the terror and joy mingling together. He understood that feeling now. How powerful it was to be free. The privilege of it. The privilege of living a life you were choosing for yourself.

They had reached the back door. 'So what will you do?' Auntie Jo interrupted his thoughts. 'Will you try to be a Luman, at least some of the time?'

'I don't know yet. I don't think so.' His voice was quiet. He thought about his family and the bonds that tied them together. And he thought too about school; about his friends and his classes and himself in a sixth form blazer. And of course Melissa. He couldn't stop thinking about her. He didn't know how things would work out but at least he was free to give it his best shot.

He thought about the Tapestry of Lights, the souls moving in an endless, bewitching dance. Some were getting brighter; others were fading. Nothing stayed the same. But that was

OK; that was how the future was made, a thread at a time; a decision at a time.

Auntie Jo opened the door into the kitchen and Adam heard familiar voices inside. Happiness washed over him, filling his chest with warmth. The world was changing, every day. Sometimes you could tear up the old rules and make new ones; better ones. Rules that made the *whole world* better.

He could be whoever he wanted to be. Anything was possible, if he wanted it enough; if he worked for it. Anything could happen.

Anything at all.

Acknowledgements

This bit never gets old. My thanks as ever to my lovely agent Gillie Russell and equally lovely editor Emily Thomas. Huge gratitude also to the wonderful team at Hot Key. It is a total pleasure and a privilege working with you all.

My thanks to Sperrin Integrated College, Magherafelt for continued support; the Flowerfield Writers for moving me and making me laugh in turn; the many wonderful teachers, librarians and pupils who have welcomed me into their schools across the UK; the booksellers who have generously given up their time to arrange events; the lovely staff in Portstewart and Coleraine Libraries who allowed me to set up camp for part of the first draft; and as ever the mighty PWA – Julie Agnew, Mandy Taggart and the inestimable Bernie McGill for wit, wine and enduring the crazy eye on more than one occasion.

Thanks to Dr Malachy Ó Néill and Dr David Barr (both University of Ulster) for the translations. Special thanks to Dr Shane Murphy (INGV) who talked me through the intricacies of tsunami warning systems. Thank you also to Kerry McLean, Maurice McAleese and all at BBC Radio Ulster, for easing me into the world of live radio. On a personal note, sincere thanks to Tom Delap, assisted by Linda Mairs, for expertise and kindness in equal measure.

Finally, thanks to my family, especially my parents Derek and Patricia McCune and my parents-in-law Michael and Gretta Murphy, my sister Claire, my brother Gareth and my aunt Joanie. Thank you also to my friends – we may be scattered all over the place but you're often in my thoughts.

And the biggest thanks of all to my husband Colm and daughter Ellen. You're the people who make me smile every day.

D.J. McCune

D.J. McCune was born in Belfast and grew up in a seaside town just north of the city. As a child she liked making up stories and even wrote some down, including a thriller about a stolen wallaby.

D.J. McCune read Theology at Trinity College, Cambridge, but mostly just read lots of books. She lives in Northern Ireland with her husband and daughter – and two cats with seven legs between them.

FAULT LINES is the third book in the DEATH & CO. series.

If you'd like to know more you can find her at:

www.facebook.com/djmccuneauthor

http://debbiemccune.tumblr.com

Twitter @debbiemccune

Thank you for choosing a Hot Key book.

If you want to know more about our authors
and what we publish, you can find us online.

You can start at our website

www.hotkeybooks.com

And you can also find us on:

We hope to see you soon!